THE BEST OF
BOVA
VOLUME III

BAEN BOOKS
by Ben Bova

✳ ✳ ✳

The Best of Bova: Volume I
The Best of Bova: Volume II
The Best of Bova: Volume III
Mars, Inc.
Laugh Lines
The Watchmen
The Exiles Trilogy

With Les Johnson
Rescue Mode

THE BEST OF BOVA
VOLUME III

BEN BOVA

BAEN

THE BEST OF BOVA: VOLUME III

This is a work of fiction. All the characters and events portrayed in this book are fictional, and any resemblance to real people or incidents is purely coincidental.

Introduction © 2017 by Ben Bova; "Sepulcher" first published in *Asimov's Science Fiction* © November 1992; "The Man Who …" first published in *Maxwell's Demons* © September 1978; "Conspiracy Theory" first published in *Analog Science Fiction and Fact* © April 1993; "The Great Moon Hoax" first published in *The Magazine of Fantasy & Science Fiction* © September 1996; "Build Me a Mountain" first published in *2020 Vision* © February 1974; "Crisis of the Month" first published in *The Magazine of Fantasy & Science Fiction* © March 1988; "Free Enterprise" first published in *Analog Science Fiction/Science Fact* © February 1984; "Vision" first published in *Analog Science Fiction/Science Fact* © January 1980; "Moon Race" first published in *Jim Baen's Universe* © December 2008; "Scheherazade and the Storytellers" first published in *Gateways* © July 2010; "Nuclear Autumn" first published in *Far Frontiers* © April 1985; "Lower the River" first published in *Analog Science Fiction and Fact* © June 1997; "The Café Coup" first published in *The Magazine of Fantasy & Science Fiction* © September 1997; "Remember, Caesar" first published in *The Magazine of Fantasy & Science Fiction* © March 1998; "Life as We Know It" first published in *The Magazine of Fantasy & Science Fiction* © September 1995; "Delta Vee" first published in *Twice Seven* © August 1998; "We'll Always Have Paris" first published in *New Frontiers* © July 2014; "The Babe, the Iron Horse, and Mr. McGillicuddy" by Ben Bova and Rick Wilber, first published in *Asimov's Science Fiction* © March 1997; "Greenhouse Chill" first published in *Analog Science Fiction and Fact* © January 2000; "Brothers" first published in *In the Field of Fire* © February 1987; "Interdepartmental Memorandum" first published in *Challenges* © July 1993; "World War 4.5" first published in *Challenges* © July 1993; "Sam Below Par" first published in *Analog Science Fiction and Fact* © July 2012; "High Jump" first published in *Amazing Stories* © Summer 2000; "The Question" first published in *Analog Science Fiction and Fact* © January 1998; "Waterbot" first published in *Analog Science Fiction and Fact* © June 2008; "Duel in the Somme" first published in *Apex Science Fiction & Horror Digest* © June 2006; "Bloodless Victory" first published in *New Frontiers: A Collection of Tales About the Past, the Present, and the Future* © July 2014; "Mars Farts" first published in *Free Stories* © March 2013; "A Pale Blue Dot" first published in *New Frontiers: A Collection of Tales About the Past, the Present, and the Future* © July 2014; "Stars, Won't You Hide Me?" first published in *Worlds of Tomorrow* © January 1966; "Monster Slayer" first published in *Absolute Magnitude & Aboriginal Science Fiction* © June 2003.

A Baen Books Original

Baen Publishing Enterprises
P.O. Box 1403
Riverdale, NY 10471
www.baen.com

ISBN: 978-1-4814-8259-2

Cover art by Adam Burn

First Baen printing August 2017

Distributed by Simon & Schuster
1230 Avenue of the Americas
New York, NY 10020

Printed in the United States of America

10 9 8 7 6 5 4 3 2 1

To Toni and Tony and the radiant,
resplendent, romantic Rashida.

And to Lloyd McDaniel,
without whose unstinting help this book
would never have seen the light of day.

CONTENTS

The reasonable man adapts himself to the world; the unreasonable one persists in trying to adapt the world to himself. Therefore all progress depends on the unreasonable man.

—George Bernard Shaw

THE BEST OF BOVA

VOLUME III

INTRODUCTION

Here it is, a lifetime's work in three volumes containing eighty stories published over fifty-four years, from 1960 to 2014. They range from the Baghdad of *The Thousand Nights and a Night* to the eventual end of the entire universe, from the green hills of Earth to the fiery surface of a dying star, from corporate board rooms to a baseball field in heaven. With plenty of stops in between.

Re-reading these stories—some of them for the first time in decades—I am struck with a bitter-sweet sadness, recalling friends who have died along the way, passions and problems that drove the invention of the various tales. It's as if I'm a ghost visiting departed scenes, people whom I have loved, all gone now.

Yet they live on, in these stories, and perhaps that is the real reason why human beings create works of fiction: they are monuments to days gone by, memories of men and women who have been dear to us—or visions of what tomorrow may bring.

Every human society has had its storytellers. There is a fundamental need in the human psyche to produce tales that try to show who we truly are, and why we do the things we do.

Most of the stories in this collection are science fiction: that is, the stories involve some aspect of future science or technology that is so basic to the tale that if that element were removed, the story would collapse.

To me, science fiction is the literature of our modern society.

Humankind depends on science and technology for its survival, and has been doing so since our earliest ancestors faced saber-toothed cats. We do not grow fangs or wings, we create tools. Tool-making—technology—is the way we deal with the often-hostile world in which we live.

Over the past few centuries, scientific studies of our world have led to vastly improved technologies, better tools with which to make ourselves healthier, richer and more free. Science fiction is the literature that speaks to this.

Every organism on Earth is struggling to stay alive, to have offspring, to enlarge its ecological niche as widely as possible. We humans have succeeded so well at that quest that there are more than seven billion of us on this planet, and we are driving many, many of our fellow creatures into extinction.

The stories in this collection examine various aspects of humankind's current and future predicaments. Some of the tales are somewhat dated: written half a century ago, they deal with problems that we have already solved, or bypassed. Many of the stories tell of the human race's drive to expand its habitat—its ecological niche—beyond the limits of planet Earth. Many deal with our interactions with our machines, which are becoming more intelligent with every generation.

The people in these stories include heroes and heels, lovers and loners, visionaries and the smugly blind.

I hope you enjoy their struggles.

—**Ben Bova**
Naples, Florida
November 2014

SEPULCHER

One of the great attractions of science fiction is its breadth of scope.

John W. Campbell, Jr. was the most powerful editor in the history of the science-fiction field. John was a big man, and he was not above using his size and the force of his personality to drive home the points he wanted to make. He often compared science fiction to other forms of literature by spreading his long arms wide and declaiming, "This is science fiction! All the universe, past, present, and future." Then he would hold up a thumb and forefinger about half an inch apart and say, "This is all other kinds of fiction."

By that he meant that all the other kinds of fiction restrict themselves to the here and now, or to the known past. All other forms of fiction are set here on Earth, under a sky that is blue and ground that is solid beneath your feet. Science fiction deals with all of creation, of which our Earth and our time is merely a small part. Science fiction can vault far into the future or deep into the past.

Indeed, science fiction has often been called "the literature of ideas." This has been both its strength and its curse. All too often the idea takes center stage and all the other considerations of good fiction, such as characterization, plot, mood, color, etc., become weak and pale. In its worst manifestation, the supremacy of the idea generates the "gimmick" story, in which a brilliant protagonist meets a problem that has stumped everybody else and solves the problem without raising a sweat. Gimmick stories are predictable, their characters usually wooden. Such stories are essentially vehicles for the author to show off how bright he or she is.

Yet the idea content of science fiction gives the field enormous power and drive, when the ideas are properly matched by characterizations and all the other facets of good fiction. That is the underlying challenge of science fiction: to combine dazzling ideas with superb characters.

"Sepulcher" began as an idea story. For years I had a tiny scrap of paper tucked in my "Ideas" file. It read "Perfect artwork. Everyone sees themselves in it."

The idea intrigued me, but the reason that scrap of paper stayed in my file was that I knew the idea by itself was not sufficient for a good story. A good story needs believable characters in conflict.

As I mulled over the basic idea, I reasoned that the story would need several characters, so that the reader can see how this work of art affects different people. I began to see that the artwork would have to be an alien artifact. If a human being could create a work of art so powerful that everyone who sees it experiences a soul-shattering self-revelation, then the story would have to be about the artist and the power he or she gains over the rest of humankind.

That might make a terrific novel someday. But I was more interested in a short story about the work of art itself—and several people who are deeply, fundamentally changed by it.

I settled on three characters: a former soldier who has become a kind of holy man; a hard-driving man of vast wealth; and an artist who is near the end of her life. Each of them undergoes a transformation when he or she sees the alien artwork.

Notice, as you read the story, that much of the action takes place offstage. The soldier has already been transformed when the story begins. The billionaire's experience is offstage. We see only the artist and her moment of truth as she sees the artwork and is transformed by it.

The artist, incidentally, is a character I originally wrote about in an earlier story. When I began seriously to develop "Sepulcher," she presented herself to me as the perfect character to serve as the focal point of this tale.

In the final analysis, "Sepulcher" is a story that deals with the purpose of art. Why do we create works of art? Why do painters paint their pictures and writers write their stories? Beneath all the other facets of "Sepulcher," that is the fundamental idea that we examine.

"I WAS A SOLDIER," he said. "Now I am a priest. You may call me Dorn."

Elverda Apacheta could not help staring at him. She had seen cyborgs before, but this . . . person seemed more machine than man. She felt a chill ripple of contempt along her veins. How could a human being allow his body to be disfigured so?

He was not tall; Elverda herself stood several centimeters taller than he. His shoulders were quite broad, though; his torso thick and solid. The left side of his face was engraved metal, as was the entire top of his head: like a skullcap made of finest etched steel.

Dorn's left hand was prosthetic. He made no attempt to disguise it. Beneath the rough fabric of his shabby tunic and threadbare trousers, how much more of him was metal and electrical machinery? Tattered though his clothing was, his calf-length boots were polished to a high gloss.

"A priest?" asked Miles Sterling. "Of what church? What order?"

The half of Dorn's lips that could move made a slight curl. A smile or a sneer, Elverda could not tell.

"I will show you to your quarters," said Dorn. His voice was a low rumble, as if it came from the belly of a beast. It echoed faintly off the walls of rough-hewn rock.

Sterling looked briefly surprised. He was not accustomed to having his questions ignored. Elverda watched his face. Sterling was as handsome as cosmetic surgery could make a person appear: chiseled features, earnest sky-blue eyes, straight of spine, long of limb, athletically flat midsection. Yet there was a faint smell of corruption about him, Elverda thought. As if he were dead inside and already beginning to rot.

The tension between the two men seemed to drain the energy from Elverda's aged body. "It has been a long journey," she said. "I am very tired. I would welcome a hot shower and a long nap."

"Before you see it?" Sterling snapped.

"It has taken us months to get here. We can wait a few hours more." Inwardly she marveled at her own words. Once she would have been all fiery excitement. *Have the years taught you patience?* No, she realized. Only weariness.

"Not me!" Sterling said. Turning to Dorn, "Take me to it now. I've waited long enough. I want to see it now."

Dorn's eyes, one as brown as Elverda's own, the other a red electronic glow, regarded Sterling for a lengthening moment.

"Well?" Sterling demanded.

"I am afraid, sir, that the chamber is sealed for the next twelve hours. It will be imposs—"

"Sealed? By whom? On whose authority?"

"The chamber is self-controlled. Whoever made the artifact installed the controls, as well."

"No one told me about that," said Sterling.

Dorn replied, "Your quarters are down this corridor." He turned almost like a solid block of metal, shoulders and hips together, head unmoving on those wide shoulders, and started down the central corridor. Elverda fell in step alongside his metal half, still angered at his self-desecration. Yet despite herself, she thought of what a challenge it would be to sculpt him. *If I were younger*, she told herself. *If I were not so close to death. Human and inhuman, all in one strangely fierce figure.*

Sterling came up on Dorn's other side, his face red with barely suppressed anger.

They walked down the corridor in silence, Sterling's weighted shoes clicking against the uneven rock floor. Dorn's boots made hardly any noise at all. *Half machine he may be*, Elverda thought, *but once in motion he moves like a panther.*

The asteroid's inherent gravity was so slight that Sterling needed the weighted footgear to keep himself from stumbling ridiculously. Elverda, who had spent most of her long life in low-gravity environments, felt completely at home. The corridor they were walking through was actually a tunnel, shadowy and mysterious, or perhaps a natural chimney vented through the rocky body by escaping gases eons ago when the asteroid was still molten. Now it was cold, chill enough to make Elverda shudder. The rough ceiling was so low she wanted to stoop, even though the rational side of her mind knew it was not necessary.

Soon, though, the walls smoothed out and the ceiling grew higher.

Humans had extended the tunnel, squaring it with laser precision. Doors lined both walls now and the ceiling glowed with glareless, shadowless light. Still she hugged herself against the chill that the others did not seem to notice.

They stopped at a wide double door. Dorn tapped out the entrance code on the panel set into the wall and the doors slid open.

"Your quarters, sir," he said to Sterling. "You may, of course, change the privacy code to suit yourself."

Sterling gave a curt nod and strode through the open doorway. Elverda got a glimpse of a spacious suite, carpeting on the floor and hologram windows on the walls.

Sterling turned in the doorway to face them. "I expect you to call for me in twelve hours," he said to Dorn, his voice hard.

"Eleven hours and fifty-seven minutes," Dorn replied. Sterling's nostrils flared and he slid the double doors shut.

"This way." Dorn gestured with his human hand. "I'm afraid your quarters are not as sumptuous as Mr. Sterling's."

Elverda said, "I am his guest. He is paying all the bills."

"You are a great artist. I have heard of you."

"Thank you."

"For the truth? That is not necessary."

I was a great artist, Elverda said to herself. *Once. Long ago. Now I am an old woman waiting for death.*

Aloud, she asked, "Have you seen my work?"

Dorn's voice grew heavier. "Only holograms. Once I set out to see *The Rememberer* for myself, but—other matters intervened."

"You were a soldier then?"

"Yes. I have only been a priest since coming to this place."

Elverda wanted to ask him more, but Dorn stopped before a blank door and opened it for her. For an instant she thought he was going to reach for her with his prosthetic hand. She shrank away from him.

"I will call for you in eleven hours and fifty-six minutes," he said, as if he had not noticed her revulsion.

"Thank you."

He turned away, like a machine pivoting.

"Wait," Elverda called. "Please—how many others are here? Everything seems so quiet."

"There are no others. Only the three of us."

"But—"

"I am in charge of the security brigade. I ordered the others of my command to go back to our spacecraft and wait there."

"And the scientists? The prospector family that found this asteroid?"

"They are in Mr. Sterling's spacecraft, the one you arrived in," said Dorn. "Under the protection of my brigade."

Elverda looked into his eyes. Whatever burned in them, she could not fathom.

"Then we are alone here?"

Dorn nodded solemnly. "You and me—and Mr. Sterling, who pays all the bills." The human half of his face remained as immobile as the metal. Elverda could not tell if he was trying to be humorous or bitter.

"Thank you," she said. He turned away and she closed the door.

Her quarters consisted of a single room, comfortably warm but hardly larger than the compartment on the ship they had come in. Elverda saw that her meager travel bag was already sitting on the bed, her worn old drawing computer resting in its travel-smudged case on the desk. Elverda stared at the computer case as if it were accusing her. *I should have left it home*, she thought. *I will never use it again.*

A small utility robot, hardly more than a glistening drum of metal and six gleaming arms folded like a praying mantis's, stood mutely in the farthest corner. Elverda stared at it. At least it was entirely a machine; not a self-mutilated human being. To take the most beautiful form in the universe and turn it into a hybrid mechanism, a travesty of humanity. Why did he do it? So he could be a better soldier? A more efficient killing machine?

And why did he send all the others away? she asked herself while she opened the travel bag. As she carried her toiletries to the narrow alcove of the bathroom, a new thought struck her. *Did he send them away before he saw the artifact, or afterward? Has he even seen it? Perhaps.*

Then she saw her reflection in the mirror above the washbasin. Her heart sank. Once she had been called regal, stately, a goddess made of copper. Now she looked withered, dried up, bone thin, her face a geological map of too many years of living, her flight coveralls hanging limply on her emaciated frame.

You are old, she said to her image. *Old and aching and tired.*

It is the long trip, she told herself. *You need to rest*. But the other voice in her mind laughed scornfully. *You've done nothing but rest for the entire time it's taken to reach this piece of rock. You are ready for the permanent rest; why deny it?*

She had been teaching at the university on Luna, the closest she could get to Earth after a long lifetime of living in low-gravity environments. Close enough to see the world of her birth, the only world of life and warmth in the solar system, the only place where a person could walk out in the sunshine and feel its warmth soaking your bones, smell the fertile earth nurturing its bounty, feel a cool breeze plucking at your hair.

But she had separated herself from Earth permanently. She had stood at the shore of Titan's methane sea; from an orbiting spacecraft she had watched the surging clouds of Jupiter swirl their overpowering colors; she had carved the kilometer-long rock of *The Rememberer*. But she could no longer stand in the village of her birth, at the edge of the Pacific's booming surf, and watch the soft white clouds form shapes of imaginary animals.

Her creative life was long finished. She had lived too long; there were no friends left, and she had never had a family. There was no purpose to her life, no reason to do anything except go through the motions and wait. At the university she was no longer truly working at her art but helping students who had the fires of inspiration burning fresh and hot inside them. Her life was one of vain regrets for all the things she had not accomplished, for all the failures she could recall. Failures at love; those were the bitterest. She was praised as the solar system's greatest artist: the sculptress of *The Rememberer*, the creator of the first great ionospheric painting, *The Virgin of the Andes*. She was respected, but not loved. She felt empty, alone, barren. She had nothing to look forward to, absolutely nothing.

Then Miles Sterling swept into her existence. A lifetime younger, bold, vital, even ruthless, he stormed her academic tower with the news that an alien artifact had been discovered deep in the asteroid belt.

"It's some kind of art form," he said, desperate with excitement. "You've got to come with me and see it."

Trying to control the long-forgotten longing that stirred within her, Elverda had asked quietly, "Why do I have to go with you, Mr. Sterling? Why me? I'm an old wo—"

"You are the greatest artist of our time," he had snapped. "You've *got* to see this! Don't bullshit me with false modesty. You're the only other person in the whole whirling solar system who *deserves* to see it!"

"The only other person besides whom?" she had asked.

He had blinked with surprise. "Why, besides me, of course."

So now we are on this nameless asteroid, waiting to see the alien artwork. Just the three of us. The richest man in the solar system. An elderly artist who has outlived her usefulness. And a cyborg soldier who has cleared everyone else away.

He claims to be a priest, Elverda remembered. *A priest who is half machine.* She shivered as if a cold wind surged through her.

A harsh buzzing noise interrupted her thoughts. Looking into the main part of the room, Elverda saw that the phone screen was blinking red in rhythm to the buzzing.

"Phone," she called out.

Sterling's face appeared on the screen instantly. "Come to my quarters," he said. "We have to talk."

"Give me an hour. I need—"

"Now."

Elverda felt her brows rise haughtily. Then the strength sagged out of her. *He has bought the right to command you*, she told herself. *He is quite capable of refusing to allow you to see the artifact.*

"Now," she agreed.

Sterling was pacing across the plush carpeting when she arrived at his quarters. He had changed from his flight coveralls to a comfortably loose royal blue pullover and expensive genuine twill slacks. As the doors slid shut behind her, he stopped in front of a low couch and faced her squarely.

"Do you know who this Dorn creature is?"

Elverda answered, "Only what he has told us."

"I've checked him out. My staff in the ship has a complete dossier on him. He's the butcher who led the *Chrysalis* massacre, fourteen years ago."

"He—"

"Eleven hundred men, women, and children. Slaughtered. He was the man who commanded the attack."

"He said he had been a soldier."

"A mercenary. A cold-blooded murderer. He was working for Toyama then. The *Chrysalis* was their habitat. When its population voted for independence, Toyama put him in charge of a squad to bring them back into line. He killed them all; turned off their air and let them all die."

Elverda felt shakily for the nearest chair and sank into it. Her legs seemed to have lost all their strength.

"His name was Harbin then. Dorik Harbin."

"Wasn't he brought to trial?"

"No. He ran away. Disappeared. I always thought Toyama helped to hide him. They take care of their own, they do. He must have changed his name afterward. Nobody would hire the butcher, not even Toyama."

"His face . . . half his body . . ." Elverda felt terribly weak, almost faint. "When . . . ?"

"Must have been after he ran away. Maybe it was an attempt to disguise himself."

"And now he is working for you." She wanted to laugh at the irony of it, but did not have the strength.

"He's got us trapped on this chunk of rock! There's nobody else here except the three of us."

"You have your staff in your ship. Surely they would come if you summoned them."

"His security squad's been ordered to keep everybody except you and me off the asteroid. He gave those orders."

"You can countermand them, can't you?"

For the first time since she had met Miles Sterling, he looked unsure of himself. "I wonder," he said.

"Why?" Elverda asked. "Why is he doing this?"

"That's what I intend to find out." Sterling strode to the phone console. "Harbin!" he called. "Dorik Harbin. Come to my quarters at once."

Without even an eyeblink's delay the phone's computer-synthesized voice replied, "Dorik Harbin no longer exists. Transferring your call to Dorn."

Sterling's blue eyes snapped at the phone's blank screen.

"Dorn is not available at present," the phone's voice said. "He will call for you in eleven hours and thirty-two minutes."

"God *damn* it!" Sterling smacked a fist into the open palm of his other hand. "Get me the officer on watch aboard the *Sterling Eagle*."

"All exterior communications are inoperable at the present time," replied the phone.

"That's impossible!"

"All exterior communications are inoperable at the present time," the phone repeated, unperturbed.

Sterling stared at the empty screen, then turned slowly toward Elverda. "He's cut us off. We're really trapped here."

Elverda felt the chill of cold metal clutching at her. Perhaps Dorn is a madman, she thought. *Perhaps he is my death, personified.*

"We've got to do something!" Sterling nearly shouted.

Elverda rose shakily to her feet. "There is nothing that we can do, for the moment. I am going to my quarters to take a nap. I believe that Dorn, or Harbin, or whatever his identity is, will call on us when he is ready to."

"And do what?"

"Show us the artifact," she replied, silently adding, *I hope.*

Legally, the artifact and the entire asteroid belonged to Sterling Enterprises, Ltd. It had been discovered by a family—husband, wife, and two sons, ages five and three—that made a living from searching out iron-nickel asteroids and selling the mining rights to the big corporations. They filed their claim to this unnamed asteroid, together with a preliminary description of its ten-kilometer-wide shape, its orbit within the asteroid belt, and a sample analysis of its surface composition.

Six hours after their original transmission reached the commodities-market computer network on Earth—while a fairly spirited bidding war was going on among four major corporations for the asteroid's mineral rights—a new message arrived at the headquarters of the International Astronautical Authority, in London. The message was garbled, fragmentary, obviously made in great haste and at fever excitement. There was an artifact of some sort in a cavern deep inside the asteroid.

One of the faceless bureaucrats buried deep within the IAA's multilayered organization sent an immediate message to an employee of Sterling Enterprises, Ltd. The bureaucrat retired hours later, richer than he had any right to expect, while Miles Sterling personally contacted the prospectors and bought the asteroid outright for enough money to end their prospecting days forever. By the time the decision-makers in the IAA realized that an alien artifact had been discovered they were faced with a *fait accompli*: the artifact, and the asteroid in which it resided, were the personal property of the richest man in the solar system.

Miles Sterling was no egomaniac. Nor was he a fool. Graciously, he allowed the IAA to organize a team of scientists who would inspect this first specimen of alien existence. Even more graciously, Sterling offered to ferry the scientific investigators all the long way to the asteroid at his own expense. He made only one demand, and the IAA could hardly refuse him. He insisted that he see this artifact himself before the scientists were allowed to view it.

And he brought along the solar system's most honored and famous artist. To appraise the artifact's worth as an art object, he claimed. To determine how much he could deduct from his corporate taxes by donating the thing to the IAA, said his enemies.

But over the months of their voyage to the asteroid, Elverda came to the conclusion that buried deep beneath his ruthless business persona was an eager little boy who was tremendously excited at having found a new toy. A toy he intended to possess for himself. An art object, created by alien hands.

For an art object was what the artifact seemed to be. The family of prospectors continued to send back vague, almost irrational reports of what the artifact looked like. The reports were worthless. No two descriptions matched. If the man and woman were to be believed, the artifact did nothing but sit in the middle of a rough-hewn cavern. But they described it differently with every report they sent. It glowed with light. It was darker than deep space. It was a statue of some sort. It was formless. It overwhelmed the senses. It was small enough almost to pick up in one hand. It made the children laugh happily. It frightened their parents. When they tried to photograph it, their transmissions showed nothing but blank screens. Totally blank.

As Sterling listened to their maddening reports and waited impatiently for the IAA to organize its handpicked team of scientists, he ordered his security manager to get a squad of hired personnel to the asteroid as quickly as possible. From corporate facilities on Titan and the moons of Mars, from three separate outposts among the asteroid belt itself, Sterling Enterprises efficiently brought together a brigade of experienced mercenary security troops. They reached the asteroid long before anyone else could, and were under orders to make certain that no one was allowed onto the asteroid before Miles Sterling himself reached it.

"The time has come."

Elverda woke slowly, painfully, like a swimmer struggling for the air and light of the surface. She had been dreaming of her childhood, of the village where she had grown up, the distant snow-capped Andes, the warm night breezes that spoke of love.

"The time has come."

It was Dorn's deep voice, whisper soft. Startled, she flashed her eyes open. She was alone in the room, but Dorn's image filled the phone screen by her bed. The numbers glowing beneath the screen showed that it was indeed time.

"I am awake now," she said to the screen.

"I will be at your door in fifteen minutes," Dorn said. "Will that be enough time for you to prepare yourself?"

"Yes, plenty." The days when she needed time for selecting her clothing and arranging her appearance were long gone.

"In fifteen minutes, then."

"Wait," she blurted. "Can you see me?"

"No. Visual transmission must be keyed manually."

"I see."

"I do not."

A joke? Elverda sat up on the bed as Dorn's image winked out. *Is he capable of humor?*

She shrugged out of the shapeless coveralls she had worn to bed, took a quick shower, and pulled her best caftan from the travel bag. It was a deep midnight blue, scattered with glittering silver stars. Elverda had made the floor-length gown herself, from fabric woven by her mother long ago. She had painted the stars from her memory of what they had looked like from her native village.

As she slid back her front door she saw Dorn marching down the corridor with Sterling beside him. Despite his longer legs, Sterling seemed to be scampering like a child to keep up with Dorn's steady, stolid steps.

"I *demand* that you reinstate communications with my ship," Sterling was saying, his voice echoing off the corridor walls. "I'll dock your pay for every minute this insubordination continues!"

"It is a security measure," Dorn said calmly, without turning to look at the man. "It is for your own good."

"My own good? Who in hell are you to determine what my own good might be?"

Dorn stopped three paces short of Elverda, made a stiff little bow to her, and only then turned to face his employer.

"Sir: I have seen the artifact. You have not."

"And that makes you better than me?" Sterling almost snarled the words. "Holier, maybe?"

"No," said Dorn. "Not holier. Wiser."

Sterling started to reply, then thought better of it.

"Which way do we go?" Elverda asked in the sudden silence.

Dorn pointed with his prosthetic hand. "Down," he replied. "This way."

The corridor abruptly became a rugged tunnel again, with lights fastened at precisely spaced intervals along the low ceiling. Elverda watched Dorn's half-human face as the pools of shadow chased the highlights glinting off the etched metal, like the Moon racing through its phases every half-minute, over and again.

Sterling had fallen silent as they followed the slanting tunnel downward into the heart of the rock. Elverda heard only the clicking of his shoes, at first, but by concentrating she was able to make out the softer footfalls of Dorn's padded boots and even the whisper of her own slippers.

The air seemed to grow warmer, closer. *Or is it my own anticipation?* She glanced at Sterling; perspiration beaded his upper lip. The man radiated tense expectation. Dorn glided a few steps ahead of them. He did not seem to be hurrying, yet he was now leading them down the tunnel, like an ancient priest leading two new acolytes—or sacrificial victims.

The tunnel ended in a smooth wall of dull metal.

"We are here."

"Open it up," Sterling demanded.

"It will open itself," replied Dorn. He waited a heartbeat, then added, "Now."

And the metal slid up into the rock above them as silently as if it were a curtain made of silk.

None of them moved. Then Dorn slowly turned toward the two of them and gestured with his human hand.

"The artifact lies twenty-two point nine meters beyond this point. The tunnel narrows and turns to the right. The chamber is large enough to accommodate only one person at a time, comfortably."

"Me first!" Sterling took a step forward.

Dorn stopped him with an upraised hand: The prosthetic hand. "I feel it my duty to caution you—"

Sterling tried to push the hand away; he could not budge it.

"When I first crossed this line, I was a soldier. After I saw the artifact I gave up my life."

"And became a self-styled priest. So what?"

"The artifact can change you. I thought it best that there be no witnesses to your first viewing of it, except for this gifted woman whom you have brought with you. When you first see it, it can be— traumatic."

Sterling's face twisted with a mixture of anger and disgust. "I'm not a mercenary killer. I don't have anything to be afraid of."

Dorn let his hand drop to his side with a faint whine of miniaturized servomotors.

"Perhaps not," he murmured, so low that Elverda barely heard it.

Sterling shouldered his way past the cyborg. "Stay here," he told Elverda. "You can see it when I come back."

He hurried down the tunnel, footsteps staccato. Then silence.

Elverda looked at Dorn. The human side of his face seemed utterly weary.

"You have seen the artifact more than once, haven't you?"

"Fourteen times," he answered.

"It has not harmed you in any way, has it?"

He hesitated, then replied, "It has changed me. Each time I see it, it changes me more."

"You . . . you really are Dorik Harbin?"

"I was."

"Those people of the *Chrysalis* . . ."

"Dorik Harbin killed them all. Yes. There is no excuse for it, no pardon. It was the act of a monster."

"But why?"

"Monsters do monstrous things. Dorik Harbin ingested psychotropic drugs to increase his battle prowess. Afterward, when the battle drugs cleared from his bloodstream and he understood what he had done, Dorik Harbin held a grenade against his chest and set it *off*."

"Oh my god," Elverda whimpered.

"He was not allowed to die, however. The medical specialists rebuilt his body and he was given a false identity. For many years he lived a sham of life, hiding from the authorities, hiding from his own guilt. He no longer had the courage to kill himself, the pain of his first attempt was far stronger than his own self-loathing. Then he was hired to come to this place. Dorik Harbin looked upon the artifact for the first time, and his true identity emerged at last."

Elverda heard a scuffling sound, like feet dragging, staggering. Miles Sterling came into view, tottering, leaning heavily against the wall of the tunnel, slumping as if his legs could no longer hold him.

"No man . . . no one . . ." He pushed himself forward and collapsed into Dorn's arms.

"Destroy it!" he whispered harshly, spittle dribbling down his chin. "Destroy this whole damned piece of rock! Wipe it out of existence!"

"What is it?" Elverda asked. "What did you see?"

Dorn lowered him to the ground gently. Sterling's feet scrabbled against the rock as if he were trying to run away. Sweat covered his face, soaked his shirt.

"It's . . . beyond . . ." he babbled. "More . . . than anyone can . . . nobody could stand it . . ."

Elverda sank to her knees beside him. "What has happened to him?" She looked up at Dorn, who knelt on Sterling's other side.

"The artifact."

Sterling suddenly ranted, "They'll find out about me! Everyone will know! It's got to be destroyed! Nuke it! Blast it to bits!" His fists windmilled in the air, his eyes were wild.

"I tried to warn him," Dorn said as he held Sterling's shoulders down, the man's head in his lap. "I tried to prepare him for it."

"What did he see?" Elverda's heart was pounding; she could hear it thundering in her ears. "What is it? What did *you* see?"

Dorn shook his head slowly. "I cannot describe it. I doubt that anyone could describe it—except, perhaps, an artist: a person who has trained herself to see the truth."

"The prospectors—they saw it. Even their children saw it."

"Yes. When I arrived here they had spent eighteen days in the chamber. They left it only when the chamber closed itself. They ate and slept and returned here, as if hypnotized."

"It did not hurt them, did it?"

"They were emaciated, dehydrated. It took a dozen of my strongest men to remove them to my ship. Even the children fought us."

"But—how could . . ." Elverda's voice faded into silence. She looked at the brightly lit tunnel. Her breath caught in her throat.

"Destroy it," Sterling mumbled. "Destroy it before it destroys us! Don't let them find out. They'll know, they'll know, they'll all know." He began to sob uncontrollably.

"You do not have to see it," Dorn said to Elverda. "You can return to your ship and leave this place."

Leave, urged a voice inside her head. *Run away. Live out what's left of your life and let it go.*

Then she heard her own voice say, as if from a far distance, "I've come such a long way."

"It will change you," he warned.

"Will it release me from life?"

Dorn glanced down at Sterling, still muttering darkly, then returned his gaze to Elverda.

"It will change you," he repeated.

Elverda forced herself to her feet. Leaning one hand against the warm rock wall to steady herself, she said, "I will see it. I must."

"Yes," said Dorn. "I understand."

She looked down at him, still kneeling with Sterling's head resting in his lap. Dorn's electronic eye glowed red in the shadows. His human eye was hidden in darkness.

He said, "I believe your people say, *Vaya con Dios.*"

Elverda smiled at him. She had not heard that phrase in forty years. "Yes. You too. *Vaya con Dios.*" She turned and stepped across the faint groove where the metal door had met the floor.

The tunnel sloped downward only slightly. It turned sharply to the right, Elverda saw, just as Dorn had told them. The light seemed brighter beyond the turn, pulsating almost, like a living heart.

She hesitated a moment before making that final turn. What lay beyond? *What difference*, she answered herself. *You have lived so long that you have emptied life of all its purpose.* But she knew she was lying to herself. Her life was devoid of purpose because she herself had made it that way. She had spurned love; she had even rejected friendship when it had been offered. Still, she realized that she wanted to live. Desperately, she wanted to continue living no matter what.

Yet she could not resist the lure. Straightening her spine, she stepped boldly around the bend in the tunnel.

The light was so bright it hurt her eyes. She raised a hand to her brow to shield them and the intensity seemed to decrease slightly, enough to make out the faint outline of a form, a shape, a person.

Elverda gasped with recognition. A few meters before her, close enough to reach and touch, her mother sat on the sweet grass beneath the warm summer sun, gently rocking her baby and crooning softly to it.

Mama! she cried silently. *Mama.* The baby—Elverda herself— looked up into her mother's face and smiled.

And the mother was Elverda, a young and radiant Elverda, smiling down at the baby she had never had, tender and loving as she had never been.

Something gave way inside her. There was no pain: rather, it was as if a pain that had throbbed sullenly within her for too many years to count suddenly faded away. As if a wall of implacable ice finally melted and let the warm waters of life flow through her.

Elverda sank to the floor, crying, gushing tears of understanding and relief and gratitude. Her mother smiled at her.

"I love you, Mama," she whispered. "I love you." Her mother nodded and became Elverda herself once more. Her baby made a gurgling laugh of pure happiness, fat little feet waving in the air.

The image wavered, dimmed, and slowly faded into emptiness. Elverda sat on the bare rock floor in utter darkness, feeling a strange serenity and understanding warming her soul.

"Are you all right?"

Dorn's voice did not startle her. She had been expecting him to come to her.

"The chamber will close itself in another few minutes," he said. "We will have to leave."

Elverda took his offered hand and rose to her feet. She felt strong, fully in control of herself.

The tunnel outside the chamber was empty.

"Where is Sterling?"

"I sedated him and then called in a medical team to take him back to his ship."

"He wants to destroy the artifact," Elverda said.

"That will not be possible," said Dorn. "I will bring the IAA scientists here from the ship before Sterling awakes and recovers. Once they see the artifact they will not allow it to be destroyed. Sterling may own the asteroid, but the IAA will exert control over the artifact."

"The artifact will affect them—strangely."

"No two of them will be affected in the same manner," said Dorn. "And none of them will permit it to be damaged in any way."

"Sterling will not be pleased with you."

He gestured up the tunnel, and they began to walk back toward their quarters.

"Nor with you," Dorn said. "We both saw him babbling and blubbering like a baby."

"What could he have seen?"

"What he most feared. His whole life had been driven by fear, poor man."

"What secrets he must be hiding!"

"He hid them from himself. The artifact showed him his own true nature."

"No wonder he wants it destroyed."

"He cannot destroy the artifact, but he will certainly want to destroy us. Once he recovers his composure he will want to wipe out the witnesses who saw his reaction to it."

Elverda knew that Dorn was right. She watched his face as they passed beneath the lights, watched the glint of the etched metal, the warmth of the human flesh.

"You knew that he would react this way, didn't you?" she asked.

"No one could be as rich as he is without having demons driving him. He looked into his own soul and recognized himself for the first time in his life."

"You planned it this way!"

"Perhaps I did," he said. "Perhaps the artifact did it for me."

"How could—"

"It is a powerful experience. After I had seen it a few times I felt it was offering me . . ." he hesitated, then spoke the word, "salvation."

Elverda saw something in his face that Dorn had not let show before. She stopped in the shadows between overhead lights. Dorn turned to face her, half machine, standing in the rough tunnel of bare rock.

"You have had your own encounter with it," he said. "You understand now how it can transform you."

"Yes," said Elverda. "I understand."

"After a few times, I came to the realization that there must be thousands of my fellow mercenaries, killed in engagements all through the asteroid belt, still lying where they fell. Or worse yet, floating forever in space, alone, unattended, ungrieved for."

"Thousands of mercenaries?"

"The corporations do not always settle their differences in Earthly courts of law," said Dorn. "There have been many battles out here. Wars that we paid for with our blood."

"Thousands?" Elverda repeated. "I knew that there had been occasional fights out here—but wars? I don't think anyone on Earth knows it's been so brutal."

"Men like Sterling know. They start the wars, and people like me fight them. Exiles, never allowed to return to Earth again once we take the mercenary's pay."

"All those men—killed."

Dorn nodded. "And women. The artifact made me see that it was my duty to find each of those forgotten bodies and give each one a decent final rite. The artifact seemed to be telling me that this was the path of my atonement."

"Your salvation," she murmured.

"I see now, however, that I underestimated the situation."

"How?"

"Sterling. While I am out there searching for the bodies of the slain, he will have me killed."

"No! That's wrong!"

Dorn's deep voice was empty of regret. "It will be simple for him to send a team after me. In the depths of dark space, they will murder me. What I failed to do for myself, Sterling will do for me. He will be my final atonement."

"Never!" Elverda blazed with anger. "I will not permit it to happen."

"Your own life is in danger from him," Dorn said.

"What of it? I am an old woman, ready for death."

"Are you?"

"I was, until I saw the artifact."

"Now life is more precious to you, isn't it?"

"I don't want you to die," Elverda said. "You have atoned for your sins. You have borne enough pain."

He looked away, then started up the tunnel again.

"You are forgetting one important factor," Elverda called after him.

Dorn stopped, his back to her. She realized now that the clothes he wore had been his military uniform. He had torn all the insignias and pockets from it.

"The artifact. Who created it? And why?"

Turning back toward her, Dorn answered, "Alien visitors to our solar system created it, unknown ages ago. As to why—you tell me: Why does someone create a work of art?"

"Why would aliens create a work of art that affects human minds?"

Dorn's human eye blinked. He rocked a step backward.

"How could they create an artifact that is a mirror to our souls?" Elverda asked, stepping toward him. "They must have known something about us. They must have been here when there were human beings existing on Earth."

Dorn regarded her silently.

"They may have been here much more recently than you think," Elverda went on, coming closer to him. "They may have placed this artifact here to *communicate* with us."

"Communicate?"

"Perhaps it is a very subtle, very powerful communications device."

"Not an artwork at all."

"Oh yes, of course it's an artwork. All works of art are communications devices, for those who possess the soul to understand."

Dorn seemed to ponder this for long moments. Elverda watched his solemn face, searching for some human expression.

Finally he said, "That does not change my mission, even if it is true."

"Yes it does," Elverda said, eager to save him. "Your mission is to preserve and protect this artifact against Sterling and anyone else who would try to destroy it—or pervert it to his own use."

"The dead call to me," Dorn said solemnly. "I hear them in my dreams now."

"But why be alone in your mission? Let others help you. There must be other mercenaries who feel as you do."

"Perhaps," he said softly.

"Your true mission is much greater than you think," Elverda said, trembling with new understanding. "You have the power to end the wars that have destroyed your comrades, that have almost destroyed your soul."

"End the corporate wars?"

"You will be the priest of this shrine, this sepulcher. I will return to Earth and tell everyone about these wars."

"Sterling and others will have you killed."

"I am a famous artist, they dare not touch me." Then she laughed. "And I am too old to care if they do."

"The scientists—do you think they may actually learn how to communicate with the aliens?"

"Someday," Elverda said. "When our souls are pure enough to stand the shock of their presence."

The human side of Dorn's face smiled at her. He extended his arm and she took it in her own, realizing that she had found her own salvation. Like two kindred souls, like comrades who had shared the sight of death, like mother and son, they walked up the tunnel toward the waiting race of humanity.

THE MAN WHO . . .

Political campaigning in America has become a combination of the Olympics, the World Series and the Super Bowl. Too often, the man who is the better campaigner turns out to be mediocre or worse at governing after he is elected. But in American politics nowadays, the campaign's the important part. A politician's first priority is to get elected. Governing is an afterthought.

"HE DOESN'T HAVE CANCER!"

Les Trotter was a grubby little man. He combed his hair forward to hide his baldness, but now as I drove breakneck through the early Minnesota morning, the wind had blown his thinning hair every which way, leaving him looking bald and moon-faced and aging.

And upset as hell.

"Marie, I'm telling you, he doesn't have cancer." He tried to make it sound sincere. His voice was somewhere between the nasality of an upper-register clarinet and its Moog synthesis.

"Sure," I said sweetly. "That's why he's rushed off to a secret laboratory in the dead of night."

Les' voice went up still another notch. "It's not a secret lab! It's the Wellington Memorial Laboratory. It's world famous. And . . . god damm it, Marie, you're *enjoying* this!"

25

"I'm a reporter, Les." Great line. Very impressive. It hadn't kept him from making a grab for my ass, when we had first met. "It's my job."

He said nothing.

"And if your candidate has cancer—"

"He doesn't!"

"It's news."

We whipped past the dead bare trees with the windows open to keep me from dozing. It had been a long night, waiting for Halliday at the Twin Cities Airport. A dark horse candidate, sure, but the boss wanted *all* the presidential candidates covered. So we drew lots and I lost. I got James J. Halliday, the obscure. When his private jet finally arrived, he was whisked right out to this laboratory in the upstate woods.

I love to drive fast. And the hours around dawn are the best time of the day. The world's clean. And all yours. A new day is coming. This day was starting with a murky gray as the sun tried to break through a heavy late winter overcast.

"There's ice on the road, you know," Les sulked.

I ignored him. Up ahead I could see lighted buildings.

The laboratory was surrounded by a riot-wire fence. The guard at the gate refused to open up and let us through. It took fifteen minutes of arguing and a phone call from the guard shack by Les before the word came back to allow us in.

"What'd you tell them?" I asked Les as I drove down the crunchy gravel driveway to the main laboratory building.

He was still shivering from the cold. "That it was either see you or see some nasty scare headlines."

The lab building was old and drab, in the dawning light. There were a few other buildings farther down the driveway. I pulled up behind a trio of parked limousines, right in front of the main entrance.

We hurried through the chilly morning into the lobby. It was paneled with light mahogany, thickly carpeted, and *warm*. They had paintings spotted here and there—abstracts that might have been amateurish or priceless. I could never figure them out.

A smart-looking young woman in a green pantsuit came through the only other door in the lobby. She gave me a quick, thorough inspection. I had to smile at how well she kept her face straight. My jeans and jacket were for warmth, not looks.

"Governor Halliday would like to know what this is all about," she said tightly. Pure efficiency: all nerves and smooth makeup. Probably screws to a metronome beat. "He is here on a personal matter; there's no news material in this visit."

"That depends on his X-rays, doesn't it?" I said.

Her eyes widened. "Oh." That's all she said. Nothing more. She turned and made a quick exit.

"Bright," I said to Les, "she picks up right away."

"His whole staff's bright."

"Including his advance publicity man?" *With the overactive paws,* I added silently.

"Yes, including my advance publicity man."

I turned back toward the door. Walking toward me was James J. Halliday, Governor of Montana, would-be President of these United States: tall, cowboy-lean, tanned, good-looking. He was smiling at me, as if he knew my suspicions and was secretly amused by them. The smile was dazzling. He was a magnetic man.

"Hello, Les," Halliday said as he strode across the lobby toward us. "Sorry to cause you so much lost sleep." His voice was strong, rich.

And Les, who had always come on like a lizard, was blooming in the sunshine of that smile. He straightened up and *his* voice deepened. "Perfectly okay, Governor. I'll sleep after your inauguration."

Halliday laughed outright.

He reached out for my hand as Les introduced, "This is Marie Kludjian of—"

"I know," Halliday said. His grip was firm. "Is *Now's* circulation falling off so badly that you have to invent a cancer case for me?" But he still smiled as he said it.

"Our circulation's fine," I said, trying to sound unimpressed. "How's yours?"

He stayed warm and friendly. "You're afraid I'm here for a secret examination or treatment, is that it?"

I wasn't accustomed to frankness from politicians. And he was just radiating warmth. Like the sun. Like a flame.

"You . . . well . . ." I stammered. "You come straight to the point, at least."

"Saves a lot of time," he said. "But I'm afraid you're wasting yours. I'm here to visit Dr. Corio, the new director of the lab. We went to school together back East. And Les has such a busy schedule arranged for me over the next week that this was the only chance I had to see him."

I nodded, feeling as dumb as a high school groupie.

"Besides," he went on, "I'm interested in science. I think it's one of our most important national resources. Too bad the current administration can't seem to recognize a chromosome from a clavicle."

"Uh-huh." My mind seemed to be stuck in neutral. *Come on!* I scolded myself. *Nobody can have that powerful an effect on you! This isn't a gothic novel.*

He waited a polite moment for me to say something else, then cracked, "The preceding was an unpaid political announcement."

We laughed, all three of us together.

Halliday ushered Les and me inside the lab, and we stayed with him every minute he was there. He introduced me to Dr. Corio—a compactly built intense man of Halliday's age, with a short, dark beard and worried gray eyes. I spent a yawn-provoking two hours with them, going through a grand tour of the lab's facilities. There were only five of us: Halliday, Corio, the kid in the green pantsuit, Les and me. All the lab's offices and workrooms were dark and unoccupied. Corio spent half the time feeling along the walls for light switches.

Through it all something buzzed in my head. Something was out of place. Then it hit me. *No staff. No flunkies. Just the appointments secretary and Les. And I dragged Les here.*

It was a small thing. But it was different. *A politician without pomp?* I wondered.

By seven in the morning, while Corio lectured to us about the search for carcinoma antitoxins or some such, I decided I had been dead wrong about James J. Halliday. By seven-thirty I was practically in love with him. He was intelligent. And concerned. He had a way of looking right at you and turning on that dazzling smile. Not phony. Knee-watering. *And unattached,* I remembered. *The most available bachelor in the presidential sweepstakes.*

By eight-thirty I began to realize that he was also as tough as a grizzled mountain man. I was out on my feet, but he was still alert and interested in everything Corio was showing me.

He caught me in mid-yawn, on our way back to the lobby. "Perhaps you'd better ride with us, Marie," he said. "I'll have one of Corio's guards drive your car back to the airport."

I protested, but feebly. I *was* tired. And, after all, it's not every day that a woman gets a lift from a potential President.

Halliday stayed in the lobby for a couple of minutes while Les, the appointments girl and I piled into one of the limousines. Then he came out, jogged to the limo, and slid in beside me.

"All set. They'll get your car back to the airport." I nodded. I was too damned sleepy to wonder what had happened to the people who had filled the other two limousines. And all the way back to Minneapolis, Halliday didn't smile at me once.

Sheila Songard, the managing editor at *Now,* was given to making flat statements, such as: "You'll be back in the office in two weeks, Marie. He won't get past the New Hampshire primary."

You don't argue with the boss. I don't anyway. Especially not on the phone. But after Halliday grabbed off an impressive forty-three percent of the fractured New Hampshire vote, I sent her a get well card.

All through those dark, cold days of winter and early spring I stayed with Jim Halliday, got to know him and his staff, watched him grow. The news and media people started to flock in after New Hampshire.

The vitality of the man! Not only did he have sheer animal magnetism in generous globs, he had more energy than a half-dozen flamenco dancers. He was up and active with the sunrise every day and still going strong long after midnight. It wore out most of the older newsmen trying to keep up with him.

When he scored a clear victory in Wisconsin, the Halliday staff had to bring out extra busses and even arrange a separate plane for the media people to travel in, along with The Man's private 707 jet.

I was privileged to see the inside of his private jetliner. I was the only news reporter allowed aboard during the whole campaign, in fact. He never let news or media people fly with him. Superstition, I thought. Or just a desire to have a place that can be really private— even if he has to go thirty-five thousand feet above the ground to get the privacy. Then I'd start daydreaming about what it would be like to be up that high with him.

The day I saw the plane, it was having an engine overhauled at JFK in New York. It was still cold out, early April, and the hangar was even colder inside than the weakly sunlit out-of-doors.

The plane was a flying command post. The Air Force didn't have more elaborate electronics gear. Bunks for fifteen people. *There goes the romantic dream,* I thought. No fancy upholstery or decorations. Strictly, utilitarian. But row after row of communication stuff: even picturephones, a whole dozen of them.

I had known that Jim was in constant communication with his people all over the country. But picturephones—it was typical of him. He wanted to be *there,* as close to the action as possible. Ordinary telephones or radios just weren't good enough for him.

"Are you covering an election campaign or writing love letters?" Sheila's voice, over the phone, had that bitchy edge to it.

"What's wrong with the copy I'm sending in?" I yelled back at her.

"It's too damned laudatory, and you know it," she shrilled. "You make it sound as if he's going through West Virginia converting the sinners and curing the lepers."

"He's doing better than that," I said. "And I'm not the only one praising him."

"I've watched his press conferences on TV," Sheila said. "He's a cutie, all right. Never at a loss for an answer."

"And he never contradicts himself. He's saying the same things here that he did in New York . . . and Denver . . . and Los Angeles."

"That doesn't make him a saint."

"Sheila, believe it. He's *good.* I've been with him nearly four months now. He's got it. He's our next President."

She was unimpressed. "You sound more like you're on his payroll than *Now's.*"

Les Trotter had hinted a few days earlier that Jim wanted me to join his staff for the California primary campaign. I held my tongue.

"Marie, listen to Momma," Sheila said, softer, calmer. "No politician is as good as you're painting him. Don't let your hormones get in the way of your judgment."

"That's ridiculous!" I snapped.

"Sure . . . sure. But I've seen enough of Halliday's halo. I want you to find his clay feet. He's got them, honey. They all do. It might hurt when you discover them, but I want to see what The Man's standing on. That's your job."

She meant it. And I knew she was right. But if Jim had feet of clay, nobody had been able to discover it yet. Not even the nastiest bastards Hearst had sent out.

And I knew that I didn't want to be the one who did it.

So I joined Jim's staff for the California campaign. Sheila was just as glad to let me go. Officially I took a leave of absence from *Now*. I told her I'd get a better look inside The Man's organization this way. She sent out a lank-haired slouch of a kid who couldn't even work a dial telephone, she was that young.

But instead of finding clay feet on The Man, as we went through the California campaign, I kept coming up with gold.

He was beautiful. He was honest. Every one of the staff loved him and the voters were turning his rallies into victory celebrations.

And he was driving me insane. Some days he'd be warm and friendly and . . . well, it was just difficult to be near him without getting giddy. But then there were other times—sometimes the same day, even—when he'd just turn off. He'd be as cold and out-of-reach as an Antarctic iceberg. I couldn't understand it. The smile was there, his voice and manners and style were unchanged, but the vibrations would be gone. Turned off.

There were a couple of nights when we found ourselves sitting with only one or two other people in a hotel room, planning the next day's moves over unending vats of black coffee. We made contact then. The vibes were good. He wanted me, I know he did, and I certainly wanted him. Yet somehow we never touched each other. The mood would suddenly change. He'd go to the phone and come back . . . different. His mind was on a thousand other things.

He's running for President, I raged at myself. *There's more on his mind than shacking up with an oversexed ex-reporter.*

But while all this was going on, while I was helping to make it happen, I was also quietly digging into the Wellington Memorial Laboratory, back in Minnesota. And its director, Dr. Corio. If Jim did have feet of clay, the evidence was there. And I had to know.

I got a friend of a friend to send me a copy of Corio's doctoral thesis from the Harvard library, and while I waited for it to arrive in the mail, I wanted more than anything to be proved wrong.

Jim was beautiful. He was so much more than the usual politician. His speech in Denver on uniting the rich and poor into a coalition that will solve the problems of the nation brought him as much attention for its style as its content. His position papers on R&D, the economy, tax reform, foreign trade, were all called "brilliant" and "pace setting." A crusty old economist from Yale, no less, told the press, "That man has the mind of an economist." A compliment, from him. A half-dozen of Nader's Raiders joined the Halliday staff because they felt, "He's the only candidate who gives a damn about the average guy."

A political campaign is really a means for the candidate to show himself to the people. And *vice versa*. He must get to know the people, all the people, their fears, their prides, their voices and touch and smell. If he can't feel for them, can't reach their pulse and match it with his own heartbeat, all the fancy legwork and lovely ghostwriting in the universe can't help him.

Jim had it. He grew stronger every minute. He kept a backbreaking pace with such ease and charm that we would have wondered how he could do it, if we had had time enough to catch our own breaths. He was everywhere, smiling, confident, energetic, *concerned*. He identified with people and they identified with him. It was uncanny. He could be completely at ease with a Missouri farmer and a New York corporation chairman. And it wasn't phony; he could *feel* for people.

And they felt for him.

And I fell for him; thoroughly, completely, hopelessly. He realized it. I was sure he did. There were times when the electric current flowed between us so strongly that I could barely stand it. He'd catch my eye and grin at me, and even though there were ninety other people in the room, for that instant everything else went blank.

But then an hour later, or the next day, he'd be completely cold. As if I didn't exist . . . or worse yet, as if I was just another cog in his machine. He'd still smile, he'd say the same things and look exactly the same. But the spark between us just wasn't there.

It was driving me crazy. I put it down to the pressures of the campaign. He couldn't have any kind of private life in this uproar. I scolded myself, *Stop acting like a dumb broad!*

Corio's thesis arrived three days before the California primary. I didn't even get a chance to unwrap it. Jim took California by such a huge margin that the TV commentators were worriedly looking for something significant to say by ten that evening. It was no contest at all.

As we packed up for the last eastern swing before the National

Convention, I hefted Corio's bulky thesis. Still unopened. I was going to need a translator, I realized; his doctoral prose would be too technical for me to understand. We were heading for Washington, and there was a science reporter there that I knew would help me. Besides, I needed to get away from Jim Halliday for a while, a day or so at least. I was on an emotional rollercoaster, and I needed some time to straighten out my nerves.

The phone was ringing as the bellman put my bags down in my room at the Park Sheraton. It was Sheila.

"How are you?" she asked.

She never calls for social chatter. "What do you want, Sheila?" I asked wearily. It had been a long, tiring flight from the coast, and I knew my time zones were going to be mixed up thoroughly.

"Have you found anything . . . clay feet, I mean?"

The bellman stood waiting expectantly beside me. I started fumbling with my purse while I wedged the phone against my shoulder.

"Listen, Marie," Sheila was saying. "He's too good to be true. *Nobody* can be a masterful politician *and* a brilliant economist *and* a hero to both the ghetto and the suburbs. It's physically impossible."

I popped a handful of change from my wallet and gave it over to the bellman. He glanced at the coins without smiling and left.

"He's doing it," I said into the phone. "He's putting it all together."

"Marie," she said with great patience, as I flopped on the bed, "he's a puppet. A robot that gets wound up every morning and goes out spouting whatever they tell him to say. Find out who's running him, who's making all those brilliant plans, who's making his decisions for him."

"He makes his own decisions," I said, starting to feel a little desperate. If someone as intelligent as Sheila couldn't believe in him, if politics had sunk so low in the minds of the people that they couldn't recognize a knight in brilliant armor when he paraded across their view . . . then what would happen to this nation?

"Marie," she said again, with her *Momma knows best* tone, "listen to me. Find out who's running him. Break the story in *Now*, and you'll come back on the staff as a full editor. With a raise. Promise."

I hung up on her.

She was right in a way. Jim was superman. More than human. *If only he weren't running for President! If only we could . . . .* I shut off that line of thought. Fantasizing wasn't going to help either one of us. Lying there on the hotel bed, I felt a shiver go through me. It wasn't from the air conditioning.

Even with translation into language I could understand, Corio's thesis didn't shed any light on anything. It was all about genetics and molecular manipulation. I didn't get a chance to talk with the guy who had digested it for me. We met at National Airport, him sprinting for one plane and me for another.

My flight took me to San Francisco, where the National Convention was due to open in less than a week.

The few days before a National Convention opens are crazy in a way nothing else on Earth can match. It's like knowing you're going to have a nervous breakdown and doing everything you can to make sure it comes off on schedule. You go into a sort of masochistic training, staying up all night, collaring people for meetings and caucuses, yelling into phones, generally behaving like the world is going to come to an end within the week—and you've got to help make it happen.

Jim's staff was scattered in a half-dozen hotels around San Francisco. I got placed in the St. Francis, my favorite. But there wasn't any time for enjoying the view.

Jim had a picturephone network set up for the staff. For two solid days before the Convention officially convened, I stayed in my hotel room and yet was in immediate face-to-face contact with everyone I had to work with. It *was* fantastic, and it sure beat trying to drive through those jammed, hilly streets.

Late on the eve of the Convention's opening gavel—it was morning, actually, about two-thirty—I was restless and wide awake. The idea wouldn't have struck me, I suppose, if Sheila hadn't needled me in Washington. But it *did* hit me, and I was foolish enough to act on the impulse.

None of Jim's brain trusters are here, I told myself. *They're all safe in their homes, far from this madhouse. But what happens if we need to pick at one of their mighty intellects at some godawful hour? Can we reach them?*

If I hadn't been alone and nervous and feeling sorry for myself, sitting in that hotel room with nothing but the picturephone to talk to, I wouldn't have done it. I knew I was kidding myself as I punched out the number for Professor Marvin Carlton, down in La Jolla. I could hear Sheila's *listen to Momma* inside my head.

To my surprise, Carlton's image shaped up on the phone's picture screen.

"Yes?" he asked pleasantly. He was sitting in what looked like a den or study—lots of books and wood. There was a drink in his hand and a book in his lap.

"Professor . . ." I left distinctly foolish. "I'm with Governor Halliday's staff . . ."

"Obviously. No one else has the number for this TV phone he gave me."

"Oh."

"What can I do for you . . . or the Governor? I was just about to retire for the night."

Thinking with the speed of a dinosaur, I mumbled, "Oh well, we were just . . . um, checking the phone connection. To make certain we can reach you when we have to."

He pursed his lips. "I'm a bit surprised. The Governor had no trouble reaching me this afternoon."

"This afternoon?"

"Yes. We went over the details of my urban restructuring program."

"Oh—of course." I tried to cover up my confusion. I had been with Jim most of the afternoon, while he charmed incoming delegates at various caucuses. We had driven together all across town, sitting side by side in the limousine. He had been warm and outgoing and . . . and then he had changed, as abruptly as putting on a new necktie. *Was it something I said? Am I being too obvious with him?*

"Well?" the professor asked, getting a bit testy. "Are you satisfied that I'm at my post and ready for instant service?"

"Oh, yes . . . yes sir. Sorry to have disturbed you."

"Very well."

"Um—professor? One question? How long did you and the Governor talk this afternoon? For our accounting records you know. The phone bill, things like that."

His expression stayed sour. "Lord, it must have been at least two hours. He dragged every last detail out of me. The man must have an eidetic memory."

"Yes," I said. "Thank you."

"Good night."

I reached out and clicked the phone's off switch. If Jim had spent two hours talking with Professor Carlton, it couldn't have been that afternoon. He hadn't been out of my sight for more than fifteen minutes between lunch and dinner.

I found myself biting my tongue and punching another number. This time it was Rollie O'Malley, the guy who ran our polling services. He was still in New York.

And sore as hell. "Callin' on five o'clock in the motherin' morning and you wanna ask me what?"

"When's the last time you talked with The Man?"

Rollie's face was puffy from sleep, red-eyed. His skin started turning red, too. "You dizzy broad . . . why in the hell . . ."

"It's important!" I snapped. "I wouldn't call if it wasn't."

He stopped in mid-flight. "Whassamatter? What's wrong?"

"Nothing major . . . I hope. But I need to know when you talked to him last. And for how long."

"Christ." He was puzzled, but more concerned than angry now. "Lessee . . . I was just about to sit down to dinner here at the apartment . . . musta been eight, eight-thirty. 'Round then."

"New York time?" That would put it around five or so our time. *Right when Jim was greeting the Texas delegation.*

"No! Bangkok time! What the hell is this all about, Marie?"

"Tell you later," and I cut him off.

I got a lot of people riled. I called the heads of every one of Jim's think-tank teams: science, economics, social welfare, foreign policy, taxation, even some of his Montana staff back in Helena. By dawn I had a crazy story: eleven different people had each talked *personally* with The Man that afternoon for an average of an hour and a half apiece, they claimed. Several of them were delighted that Jim would spend so much time with them just before the Convention opened.

That was more than sixteen hours of face-to-face conversation on the picturephones. All between noon and seven p.m., Pacific Daylight Time.

And for most of that impossible time, Jim was in my presence, close enough to touch me. And never on the phone once.

I watched the sun come up over the city's mushrooming skyline. My hands were shaking. I was sticky damp with a cold sweat.

Phony. I wanted to feel anger, but all I felt was sorrow. And the beginnings of self-pity. *He's a phony. He's using his fancy electronics equipment to con a lot of people into thinking he's giving them his personal attention. And all the while he's just another damned public relations robot.*

And his smiles, his magnetism, the good vibes that he could turn on or off whenever it suited him. *I hate him!*

And then I asked myself the jackpot question: *Who's pulling his strings?* I had to find out.

But I couldn't.

I tried to tell myself that it wasn't just my emotions. I told myself that, puppet or not, he was the best candidate running. And God knows we needed a good President, a man who could handle the job and get the nation back on the right track again. But, at that bottom line, was the inescapable fact that I loved him. As wildly as any schoolgirl loved a movie star. But this was real. I wanted Jim Halliday . . . I wanted to be *his* First Lady.

I fussed around for two days, while the Convention got started and those thousands of delegates from all over this sprawling nation settled preliminary matters like credentials and platform and voting procedures. There were almost as many TV cameras and newspeople as there were delegates. The convention hall, the hotels, the streets were crawling with people asking each other questions.

It was a streamroller. That became clear right at the outset when all the credentials questions got ironed out so easily. Halliday's people were seated with hardly a murmur in every case where an argument came up.

Seeing Jim privately, where I could ask him about the phony picturephone conversations, was impossible. He was surrounded in his hotel suite by everybody from former party chief fans to movie stars.

So I boiled in my own juices for two days, watching helplessly while the Convention worked its way toward the inevitable moment when The Man would be nominated. There was betting down on the streets that there wouldn't even be a first ballot: he'd be nominated by acclamation.

I couldn't take it. I bugged out. I packed my bag and headed for the airport.

I arrived at Twin Cities Airport at ten p.m., local time. I rented a car and started out the road toward the Wellington Lab.

It was summer now, and the trees that had been bare that icy morning, geologic ages ago, were now full-leafed and rustling softly in a warm breeze. The moon was high and full, bathing everything in cool beauty.

I had the car radio on as I pushed the rental Dart up Route 10 toward the laboratory. Pouring from the speaker came a live interview with James J. Halliday, from his hotel suite in San Francisco.

". . . and we're hoping for a first-ballot victory," he was saying smoothly, with that hint of earnestness and boyish enthusiasm in his voice. *I will not let myself get carried away,* I told myself. *Definitely not.*

"On the question of unemployment . . ." the interviewer began.

"I'd rather think of it as a mismatch between . . ."

I snapped it off. I had written part of that material for him. But dammit, he had dictated most of it, and he never said it the same way twice. He always added something or shaded it a little differently to make it easier to understand. If he was a robot, he was a damnably clever one.

The laboratory gate was coming up, and the guard was already eyeing my car as I slowed down under the big floodlights that lined the outer fence.

I fished in my purse for my Halliday staff ID card. The guard puzzled over it for a second or two, then nodded.

"Right, Ms. Kiudjian. Right straight ahead to the reception lobby."

No fuss. No questions. As if they were expecting me. The parking area was deserted as I pulled up. The lobby was lit up, and there was a receptionist sitting at the desk, reading a magazine.

She put the magazine down on the kidney-shaped desk as I pushed the glass door open. I showed her my ID and asked if Dr. Corio was in.

"Yes he is," she said, touching a button on her phone console. Nothing more. Just the touch of a button.

I asked, "Does he always work this late at night?"

She smiled very professionally. "Sometimes."

"And you too?"

"Sometimes."

The speaker on her phone console came to life. "Nora, would you please show Ms. Kiudjian to Room A-14?"

She touched the button again, then gestured toward the door that led into the main part of the building. "Straight down the corridor," she said sweetly, "the last door on your right."

I nodded and followed instructions. She went back to her magazine.

Jim Halliday was waiting for me inside Room A-14. My knees actually went weak. He was sitting on the corner of the desk that was the only furniture in the little, tile-paneled room. There was a mini-TV on the desk. The Convention was roaring and huffing through the tiny speaker.

"Hello, Marie." He reached out and took my hand. I pulled it away, angrily. "So that 'live' interview from your hotel was a fake, too. Like all your taped phone conversations with your think-tank leaders."

He smiled at me. Gravely. "No, Marie. I haven't faked a thing. Not even the way I feel about you."

"Don't try that . . ." But my voice was as shaky as my insides.

"That was James J. Halliday being interviewed in San Francisco, live, just a few minutes ago. I watched it on the set here. It went pretty well, I think."

"Then . . . who the hell are you?"

"James J. Halliday," he answered. And the back of my neck started to tingle.

"But . . ."

He held up a silencing hand. From the TV set, a florid speaker was bellowing, "This party *must* nominate the man who has swept all the primary elections across this great land. The man who can bring together all the elements of our people back into a great, harmonious whole. The man who will lead us to victory in November . . ."

The roar of applause swelled to fill the tiny bare room we were in. ". . . The man who will be our next President!" The cheers and applause were a tide of human emotion. The speaker's apple-round face filled the little screen: "James J. Halliday, of Montana!"

I watched as the TV camera swept across the thronged convention hall. Everybody was on their feet, waving Halliday signs, jumping up and down. Balloons by the thousands fell from the ceiling. The sound was overpowering. Suddenly the picture cut to a view of James J.

Halliday sitting in his hotel room in San Francisco, watching *his* TV set and smiling.

James J. Halliday clicked off the TV in the laboratory room and we faced each other in sudden silence.

"Marie," he said softly, kindly, "I'm sorry. If we had met another time, under another star . . ."

I was feeling dizzy. "How can you be there . . . and here?"

"If you had understood Corio's work, you'd have realized that it laid the basis for a practical system of cloning human beings."

"Cloning."

"Making exact replications of a person from a few body cells. I don't know how Corio does it—but it worked. He took a few patches of skin from me, years ago, when we were in school together. Now there are seven of us, all together."

"Seven?" My voice sounded like a choked squeak.

He nodded gravely. "I'm the one that fell in love with you. The others . . . we're not *exactly* alike, emotionally."

I was glancing around for a chair. There weren't any. He put his arms around me.

"It's too much for one man to handle," he said, urgently, demandingly. "Running a presidential campaign takes an inhuman effort. You've got to be able to do everything—either that or be a complete fraud and run on slogans and gimmicks. I didn't want that. I want to be the best President this nation can elect."

"So . . . you . . ."

"Corio helped replicate six more of me. Seven exactly similar James J. Hallidays. Each an expert in one aspect of the presidency such as no presidential candidate could ever hope to be, by himself."

"Then that's how you could talk on the picturephones to everybody at the same time."

"And that's how I could know so much about so many different fields. Each of us could concentrate on a few separate problem areas. It's been tricky shuffling us back and forth—especially with all the news people around. That's why we keep the 707 strictly off-limits. Wouldn't want to let the public see seven of us in conference together. Not yet, anyway."

My stomach started crawling up toward my throat.

"And me . . . us . . ."

His arms dropped away from me. "I hadn't planned on something like this happening. I really hadn't. It's been tough keeping you at arm's length."

"What can we do?" I felt like a little child—helpless, scared.

He wouldn't look at me. Not straight-on. "We'll have to keep you here for a while, Marie. Not for long. Just 'til after the Inauguration. 'Til I . . . we . . . are safely in office. Corio and his people will make you comfortable here."

I stood there, stunned. Without another word Jim suddenly got up and strode out of the room, leaving me there alone.

He kept his promises. Corio and his staff have made life very comfortable for me here. Maybe they're putting things in my food or something, who can tell? Most likely it's for my own good. I do get bored. And so lonely. And frightened.

I watched his Inauguration on television. They let me see TV. I watch him every chance I get. I try to spot the tiny difference that I might catch among the seven of them. So far, I haven't been able to find any flaw at all.

He said they'd let me go to him after the Inauguration. I hope they remember. His second Inauguration is coming up soon, I know.

Or is it his third?

CONSPIRACY THEORY

I've been involved in the exploration of space for two years longer than NASA.

I became a space enthusiast when I was in junior high school and made my first visit to the Fels Planetarium, in Philadelphia. I got hooked on the grandeur and mystery of the vast starry universe. So much so that I began to read everything I could about exploring space. This got me interested in the fields of astronomy and astronautics.

I also found that there were fictional stories about going to the Moon and Mars and other worlds in space. That's how I discovered science fiction.

When the United States announced that it would attempt to place an artificial satellite in orbit, I jumped from newspaper reporting to the company that was building the launching rocket. I became a technical editor on Project Vanguard in 1956. Then came Sputnik, the Space Race, and the creation of NASA in 1958.

Most of the fiction I've written about space exploration and development has been based as solidly as possible on the known facts. When I write about factories on the Moon, you can depend on the accuracy of the physical facts. When I wrote my novel Mars, *I made it as realistic as humanly possible.*

A couple of years ago, however, while I was writing an essay about the history of our exploration of Mars, I was struck by a wave of nostalgia.

Back when I was sitting in the darkened dome of the Fels

Planetarium, there were still arguments raging about whether or not Mars actually was crisscrossed with canals. Most professional astronomers said no, but there were enough dissenters to allow dreamers (like me) to hope that perhaps there truly were intelligent engineers on Mars, desperately struggling to bring water from the polar ice caps to the desert cities of the planet.

Well, the pitiless advance of knowledge squelched those dreams. No canals on Mars. No cities. No intelligent Martians.

But as I sat thinking about my youthful dreams, it occurred to me that the solar system was much more interesting back before NASA started exploring it. Not only could we imagine intelligent, canal-building Martians, but there was the possibility that Venus was a steaming Mesozoic jungle beneath its perpetual cover of clouds.

Just for fun, I started tinkering with a story in which my teenaged view of the solar system was right, and NASA's data was all wrong.

Again, the bare idea was not enough to make a story. I had to figure out why NASA and the scientific establishment were feeding us wrong information. And who might be hurt by this conspiracy.

Or helped.

"I'M NOT EXACTLY SURE WHY," said Roy Huggins. "When I asked for another eye checkup, they sent me here."

"To see me," said Professor Schmidt, chuckling a bit.

"Yessir," Huggins replied. He was totally serious; he did not even notice the professor's little pun.

A silence fell over them. The athletically slim Huggins, sandy-haired and boyish-looking in his sweatshirt and jeans, seemed quite honestly puzzled. Herb Schmidt, chairman of the astronomy department, was a chunky, white-bearded Santa even down to the twinkle in his baby blue eyes. A Santa in a dark three-piece suit, sitting behind a desk covered with thick reports and scattered memos heaped high like snowdrifts.

The professor eased back in his creaking old swivel chair and studied his student thoughtfully.

How many times had they met in this stuffy little office? Ever since Huggins had taken his first class in astronomy, back when he'd been an undergraduate. Now the boy had turned into a man: a youthful, vigorous man with a fine intelligent mind that had been sharply honed.

Was he enough of a man to accept the truth? And to keep the secret? The next few minutes would decide.

"Why were you having your eyes checked?" the professor asked innocently.

Huggins had to clear his throat before he could answer, "I seem to be . . . well, seeing things that aren't there."

"Ghosts?" asked the professor smiling to show he did not mean it. "Elvis Presley, perhaps?"

The younger man shook his head. "At the telescope," he said in a low, unhappy voice.

"Let me see now." Schmidt made a pretense of searching through the papers scattered across his desk. "Your time at the facility is on . . ." He let the sentence hang.

"Mars," Huggins whispered. "I've been observing Mars."

Schmidt had known that all along. He stopped leafing through the papers and leaned back in his chair again, lacing his fingers together over his ample belly.

"Mars, eh?"

"I see—" Huggins swallowed again, "—canals."

"Canals?" the professor echoed.

"Well . . . markings. I—I checked with some of the maps that Lowell drew—just as a lark, you know."

"Percival Lowell? Way back then?"

Huggins' answer came out as a tortured moan. "They match. My drawings match Lowell's almost perfectly. A whole network of canals, all across the face of Mars."

"But the photos you've taken don't show any canals. I've seen your photographic work."

"There aren't any canals on Mars!" Huggins blurted. "You know that! I know that! We've sent spacecraft probes to Mars, and they proved there are no canals there! Lowell was crazy!"

"He was—enthusiastic. That's a kinder word."

Huggins nodded unhappily and chewed on a fingernail.

Schmidt heaved a big sigh. "I can see why you're upset. But it's not so bad. So you've got a problem with your eyesight. That doesn't matter so much nowadays, what with all the electronics—"

"There's nothing wrong with my eyes! I can see perfectly well. I had an eye test back home during the Thanksgiving break and I checked out twenty-twenty."

"Yet you see nonexistent canals."

Huggins' brief flare of anger withered. "It's not my eyes. I think maybe it's my mind. Maybe I'm having hallucinations."

The professor realized the game had gone far enough. No sense tormenting the poor fellow any further.

"There's nothing wrong with your mind, my boy. Just as there is nothing wrong with your eyes."

"But I see canals! On Mars!"

Stroking his snow-white beard, Schmidt replied, "I think it was Sherlock Holmes who pointed out that when you have eliminated all the possible answers, then the impossible answer is the correct one. Or was it Arthur Clarke?"

Huggins blinked at him. "What do you mean?"

"Did you ever stop to think that perhaps there really are canals on Mars?"

"Wha—what are you saying?"

"I am saying that Mars is crisscrossed by an elaborate system of canals built by the solar system's finest engineers to bring precious water to the Martian cities and farmlands."

Half-rising from his chair, Huggins pointed an accusing finger at his professor. "You're humoring me. You think I'm crazy, and you're humoring me."

"Not at all, my boy. Sit down and relax. I am about to entrust you with a great and wonderful secret."

Huggins plopped back into the chair, his eyes wide, his mouth half-open, the expression on his face somewhere between despair and expectation.

"You understand that what I am about to tell you must be kept totally secret from everyone you know. Not even that young woman you intend to marry may know it."

The young man nodded dumbly.

Schmidt leaned his heavy forearms on his littered desk top. "In 1946," he began, "an experimental spacecraft crash-landed in the

Sonoran Desert of New Mexico. Contrary to the rumors that have arisen every now and again, the crew was not killed, and their bodies have not been kept frozen in a secret facility at some Air Force base."

"No . . . it can't be . . ."

Smiling broadly, the professor said, "But it is true. We have been in contact with our Martian brethren for more than half a century now—"

"We?"

"A very small, very elite group. A few university dons such as myself. The tiniest handful of military officers. Four industrial leaders, at present. The group changes slightly as people die, of course. Three of our members are living on Mars at the present moment."

"You're crazy!"

"Am I?" Schmidt opened his top desk drawer and drew out a slim folder. From it he pulled a single photograph and handed it wordlessly to the goggle-eyed Huggins.

Who saw three figures standing in a dripping dank jungle. Only the one in the bush hat and moustache was human. They were standing in front of the enormous dead carcass of something that looked very much like a dinosaur. Each of them was holding a rifle of some unearthly design.

"Do you recognize that man?"

Huggins shook his head as he stared hard at the photograph. The man looked vaguely familiar.

"Howard Hughes, of course. Taken in 1957. On Venus."

"Venus?" Huggins' voice was a mouse's squeak.

"Venus," repeated the professor. "Underneath those clouds it's a world of Mesozoic jungles, almost from pole to pole."

"But Venus is a barren desert! Runaway greenhouse! Surface temperature hot enough to melt lead!"

"That's all a bit of a subterfuge, I'm afraid," said Schmidt. "Just as our erasure of the Martian canal network. A necessary deception."

"What . . . why?"

Schmidt's expression grew serious. "When the first Martians landed, back in '46, it quickly became clear to those of us privileged to meet them that Mars was ahead of the Earth technologically—not very far ahead. A century, perhaps. Perhaps only a few decades."

"How can that be?"

Ignoring his question, the professor went on, "They needed our help. Their own natural resources were dwindling at an alarming rate, despite their heroic efforts of engineering. And conservation, too, I might add."

"They came to take over the Earth?"

"Nonsense! Pulp-magazine twaddle! Their ethical beliefs would not allow them to step on a beetle. They came to beg for our help."

Huggins felt a tiny stab of guilt at his fear-filled gut reaction.

"It was obvious," Schmidt went on, "that the Martians were in desperate straits. It was even more obvious to the tiny group who had been brought together to meet our visitors that the people of Earth were not prepared to face the fact that their planetary neighbor was the home of a high and noble civilization."

"The emotional shock would be too much for our people?" Huggins asked.

"No," said the professor in a sad and heavy voice. "Just the opposite. The shock would be too much for the Martians. We humans are driven by fear and greed and lust, my boy. We would have ground the Martians into the dust, just as we did with the Native Americans and the Polynesians."

Huggins looked confused. "But you said the Martians were ahead of us."

"Technologically, yes. But by no more than a century. And ethically they are lightyears ahead of us. Most of us, that is. It is the ethical part that would have been their downfall."

"I don't understand."

"Can you imagine a delicate, ethically bound Martian standing in the way of a real-estate developer? Or a packager of tourist trips? The average human politician? Or evangelist? To say nothing of most of the military. They would have been off to nuke Mars in a flash!

"The fragile Martian civilization would have been pulverized. No, we had to keep their existence a secret. It was the only decent thing to do. We had to cover up the truth, even to the point of faking data from space probes and astronomical observatories."

"All this time . . ."

"We've had some close calls. The *National Enquirer* and those other scandal sheets keep snooping around. Every time a Martian tried to make contact with an 'ordinary' human being, as their ethical code insisted they should, the affair was totally misunderstood. Sensationalized by the tabloids and all that."

"What ordinary human beings?" Huggins asked.

"You see, the Martians are not elitists. Far from it! From time to time they have tried to establish contact with farmers and sheriff's deputies and people driving down country roads at night. You know the results. Scare headlines and ridiculous stories about abductions."

"This is getting weird."

But Schmidt was not listening. "We even had one writer stumble onto the truth, back in the late forties. Someone named Burberry or Bradbury or something like that. We had to wipe his memory."

"My god!"

"It wasn't entirely effective. We've learned how to do it better since then."

"Is that what you're going to do to me? Wipe out my memory?"

Leaning back in his chair again, Schmidt resumed his beneficent Santa expression. "I don't think we'll have to. We recruit only a very, very few young men and women. I have believed for some time that you have what it takes to be one of us."

"What does that mean—being one of you?"

Positively beaming at his student, Schmidt answered, "It means helping the Martians to use the abundant resources of Venus to maintain their own civilization. It means helping the people of Earth to gradually grow in their ethical maturity until they can meet the Martians without destroying them."

"That may take generations!" said Huggins.

"Centuries, more likely. It is one of the motivations behind our starting the environmental movement. If we can only get the great masses of people to treat our own planet properly we'll be halfway to the goal of treating other worlds properly. And other people."

"And in the meantime?"

Schmidt heaved a great sigh. "In the meantime we maintain the pretense that Mars is a barren desert, Venus is a greenhouse oven, and there's nothing out there in space to be terribly interested in—unless you're an egghead of a scientist."

Huggins began to understand. "That's why the space program was stopped after the landings on the Moon."

"Yes," the professor said. "A sad necessity. We've had to work very hard to keep the uninformed parts of the government—which is most of them—from moving our space program into high gear."

"Can—" Huggins hesitated, then seemed to straighten his spine and asked, "May I meet the Martians?"

"Of course! Of course you can, my boy. Their representative is waiting to meet you now."

Schmidt pulled himself up from his chair and came around the desk. "Right this way." He gestured toward the side door of the office.

His heart hammering beneath his ribs, Huggins got up and followed his professor's burly form.

Schmidt grasped the doorknob, then stopped and turned slightly back toward his student. "I must warn you of two things," the professor said. "First, our Martian visitor obviously cannot run around the campus in his native form. So he has disguised himself as a human. Even so, he has to be very circumspect about allowing himself to be seen."

A tingle of doubt shivered in the back of Huggins' mind. "He'll look human?"

"Completely. Of course, if you wish, he will remove his human disguise. We want you to be absolutely certain of what I've told you, after all."

"I see."

With a satisfied nod, Schmidt turned the knob and pushed the door open.

Huggins was asking, "What else did you want to warn me . . ."

Before he could finish the sentence he saw the disguised Martian sitting in the darkened little side room. Huggins' jaw fell.

"That's the other thing I meant to warn you about," said Professor Schmidt. "The Martians also have a rather odd sense of humor."

Huggins just stared. At Elvis Presley.

(With apologies to Ray Bradbury.)

THE GREAT MOON HOAX, OR, A PRINCESS OF MARS

This one you can blame on Norman Spinrad. Norm is one of the best writers in the science-fiction field, and a man who combines deep intelligence with a droll sense of humor.

In 1992, Norm invited me to contribute to an anthology he was putting together, Down in Flames. *In his own words, the basic idea of the anthology was to "satirize, destroy, take the piss out of, overturn the basic premises of . . . your own universe." In other words, Norm wanted a story that would be the antithesis of my usual carefully researched, scientifically accurate fiction.*

Well, I have a sense of humor, too. I immediately recalled "Conspiracy Theory" and decided to do another story in the same vein. Only this one would explain just about everything from UFOs to—well, read it and see.

I LEANED BACK in my desk chair and just plain stared at the triangular screen.

"What do you call this thing?" I asked the Martian.

"It is an interociter," he said. He was half in the tank, as usual.

"Looks like a television set," I said.

"Its principles are akin to your television, but you will note that its picture is in full color, and you can scan events that were recorded in the past."

"We should be watching the president's speech," said Professor Schmidt.

"Why? We know what he's going to say. He's going to tell Congress that he wants to send a man to the Moon before 1970."

The Martian shuddered. His name was a collection of hisses and sputters that came out to something pretty close to Jazzbow. Anyhow that's what I called him. He didn't seem to mind. Like me, he was a baseball fan.

We were sitting in my Culver City office, watching Ted Williams' last ball game from last year. Now there was a baseball player. Best damned hitter since Ruth. And as independent as Harry Truman. Told the rest of the world to go to hell whenever he felt like it. I admired him for that. I had missed almost the whole season last year; the Martians had taken me on safari with them. They were always doing little favors like that for me; this interociter device was just the latest one.

"I still think we should be watching President Kennedy," Schmidt insisted.

"We can view it afterward, if you like," said Jazzbow, diplomatically. As I said, he had turned into quite a baseball fan, and we both wanted to see the Splendid Splinter's final home run.

Jazzbow was a typical Martian. Some of the scientists still can't tell one from another, they look so much alike, but I guess that's because they're all cloned rather than conceived sexually. Mars is pretty damned dull that way, you know. Of course, most of the scientists aren't all that smart outside of their own fields of specialization. Take Einstein, for example. Terrific thinker. He believes if we all scrapped our atomic bombs, the world would be at peace. Yah. Sure.

Anyway, Jazzbow is about four-foot-nine with dark leathery skin, kind of like a football that's been left out in the sun too long. The water from the tank made him look even darker, of course. Powerful barrel chest, but otherwise a real spidery build, arms and legs like pipe stems. Webbed feet, evolved for walking on loose sand. Their hands have five fingers with opposable thumbs, just like ours, but the fingers have so many little bones in them that they're as flexible as an octopus's tentacles.

Martians would look really scary, I guess, if it weren't for their goofy faces. They've got big sorrowful limpid eyes with long feminine eyelashes like a camel; their noses are splayed from one cheek to the other; and they've got these wide lipless mouths stretched into a permanent silly-looking grin, like a dolphin. No teeth at all. They eat nothing but liquids. Got long tongues, like some insects, which might be great for sex if they had any, but they don't, and, anyway they usually keep their tongues rolled up inside a special pouch in their cheeks so they don't startle any of us earthlings. How they talk with their tongues rolled up is beyond me.

Anyway, Jazzbow was half in the tank, as I said. He needed the water's buoyancy to make himself comfortable in earthly gravity. Otherwise, he'd have to wear his exoskeleton suit, and I couldn't see putting him through that just so we could have a face-to-face with Professor Schmidt.

The professor was fidgeting unhappily in his chair. He didn't give a rat's ass about baseball, but at least he could tell Jazzbow from the other Martians. I guess it's because he was one of the special few who'd known the Martians ever since they had first crash-landed in New Mexico back in '46.

Well, Williams socked his home run and the Fenway Park fans stood up and cheered for what seemed like an hour and he never did come out of the dugout to tip his cap for them. Good for him! I thought. His own man to the very end. That was his last time on a ball field as a player. I found I had tears in my eyes.

"Now can we see the president?" Schmidt asked, exasperated. Normally he looked like a young Santa Claus, round and red-cheeked, with a pale blond beard. He usually was a pretty jolly guy, but just now his responsibilities were starting to get the better of him.

Jazzbow snaked one long, limber arm out of the water and fiddled with the controls beneath the inverted triangle of the interociter's screen. JFK came on the screen in full color, in the middle of his speech to the joint session of Congress:

"I believe that this nation should commit itself to achieving the goal, before this decade is out, of landing a man on the Moon and returning him safely to the Earth. I believe we should go to the Moon."

Jazzbow sank down in his water tank until only his big eyes

showed, and he started noisily blowing bubbles, his way of showing that he was upset.

Schmidt turned to me. "You're going to have to talk him out of it," he said flatly.

I had not voted for John Kennedy. I had instructed all of my employees to vote against him, although I imagine some of them disobeyed me out of some twisted sense of independence. Now that he was president, though, I felt sorry for the kid. Eisenhower had let things slide pretty badly. The Commies were infiltrating the Middle East and of course they had put up the first artificial satellite and just a couple weeks ago had put the first man into space: Yuri something-or-other. Meanwhile young Jack Kennedy had let that wacky plan for the reconquest of Cuba go through. I had told the CIA guys that they'd need strong air cover, but they went right ahead and hit the Bay of Pigs without even a Piper Cub over them. Fiasco.

So the new president was trying to get everybody's mind off all this crap by shooting for the Moon. Which would absolutely destroy everything we'd worked so hard to achieve since that first desperate Martian flight here some fifteen years earlier.

I knew that somebody had to talk the president out of this Moon business. And of all the handful of people who were in on the Martian secret, I guess that the only one who could really deal with the White House on an eye-to-eye level was me.

"Okay," I said to Schmidt. "But he's going to have to come out here. I'm not going to Washington."

It wasn't that easy. The president of the United States doesn't come traipsing across the country to see an industrial magnate no matter how many services the magnate has performed for his country. And my biggest service, of course, he didn't know anything about.

To make matters worse, while my people were talking to his people, I found out that the girl I was grooming for stardom turned out to be a snoop from the goddamned Internal Revenue Service. I had had my share of run-ins with the Feds, but using a beautiful starlet like Jean was a low blow even for them. A real crotch shot.

It was Jazzbow who found her out, of course. Jean and I had been getting along very nicely indeed. She was tall and dark-haired and really lovely, with a sweet disposition and the kind of wide-eyed innocence that makes life worthwhile for a nasty old S.O.B. like me.

And she loved it, couldn't get enough of whatever I wanted to give her. One of my hobbies was making movies; it was a great way to meet girls. Believe it or not, I'm really very shy. I'm more at home alone in a plane at twenty thousand feet than at some Hollywood cocktail party. But if you own a studio, the girls come flocking.

Okay, so Jean and I are getting along swell. Except that during the period when my staff was dickering with the White House staff, one morning I wake up and she's sitting at the writing desk in my bedroom, going through my drawers. The desk drawers, that is.

I cracked one eye open. There she is, naked as a Greek goddess and just as gorgeous, rummaging through the papers in my drawers. There's nothing in there, of course. I keep all my business papers in a germtight fireproof safe back at the office.

But she had found something that fascinated her. She was holding it in front of her, where I couldn't see what was in her hand, her head bent over it for what seemed like ten minutes, her dark hair cascading to her bare shoulders like a river of polished onyx.

Then she glanced up at the mirror and spotted me watching her.

"Do you always search your boyfriends' desks?" I asked. I was pretty pissed off, you know.

"What is this?" She turned and I saw she was holding one of my safari photos between her forefinger and thumb, like she didn't want to get fingerprints on it.

Damn! I thought. I should've stashed those away with my stag movies.

Jean got up and walked over to the bed. Nice as pie she sat on the edge and stuck the photo in front of my bleary eyes.

"What is this?" she asked again.

It was a photo of a Martian named Crunchy, the physicist George Gamow, James Dean, and me in the dripping dark jungle in front of a brontosaurus I had shot. The Venusian version of a brontosaurus, that is. It looked like a small mountain of mottled leather. I was holding the stun rifle Crunchy had lent me for the safari.

I thought fast. "Oh, this. It's a still from a sci-fi film we started a few years ago. Never finished it, though. The special effects cost too much."

"That's James Dean, isn't it?"

I peered at the photo as if I was trying to remember something that wasn't terribly important. "Yeah, I think so. The kid wanted more money than I wanted to spend on the project. That's what killed it."

"He's been dead for five or six years."

"Has it been that long?" James Dean was alive and having the time of his life working with the Martians on Venus. He had left his acting career and his life on Earth far behind him to do better work than the president's Peace Corps could even dream about.

"I didn't know he did a picture for you," she said, her voice dreamy, ethereal. Like every other woman her age she had a crush on James Dean. That's what drove the poor kid to Venus.

"He didn't," I snapped. "We couldn't agree on terms. Come on back to bed."

She did, but in the middle of it my damned private phone rang. Only five people on earth knew that number, and one of them wasn't human.

I groped for the phone. "This better be important," I said.

"The female you are with," said Jazzbow's hissing voice, "is a government agent."

Oh yeah, the Martians are long-distance telepaths, too.

So I took Jean for a drive out to the desert in my Bentley convertible. She loved the scenery, thought it was romantic. Or so she said. Me, I looked at that miserable dry Mohave scrubland and thought of what it could become: blossoming farms, spacious tracts of housing where people cooped up in the cities could raise their kids, glamorous shopping malls. But about all it was good for now was an Air Force base where guys like Chuck Yeager and Scott Crossfield flew the X-planes and the Martians landed their saucers every now and then. After dark, of course.

"Just look at that sunset," Jean said, almost breathless with excitement, maybe real, maybe pretended. She was an actress, after all.

I had to admit the sunset was pretty. Red and purple glowing brighter than Technicolor.

"Where are we going?" she kept on asking, a little more nervous each time.

"It's a surprise." I had to keep on going until it was good and dark. We had enough UFO sightings as it was, no sense taking a chance on somebody getting a really good look. Or even worse, a photograph.

The stars came out, big and bright and looking close enough to touch. I kept looking for one in particular to detach itself from the sky and land on the road beside us. All that stuff about saucers shining green rays on cars or planes and sucking them up inside themselves is sheer hooey. The Martians don't have anything like that. Wish they did.

Pretty soon I saw it.

"Look!" says Jean. "A falling star!"

I didn't say anything, but a couple of minutes later the headlights picked up the saucer sitting there by the side of the road, still glowing a little from the heat of its reentry from orbit.

"Don't tell me you've driven me all the way out here to see another movie set," Jean said, sounding disappointed. "This isn't your big surprise is it?"

"Not quite," I said, pulling up beside the saucer's spindly little ladder.

She was pretty pissed off. Even when two of the Martians came slithering down the ladder, she still thought it was some kind of a movie stunt. They had to move pretty slowly and awkwardly because of the gravity; made me think of the monster movies we made. Jean was definitely not impressed.

"Honestly, Howard, I don't see why—" Then one of the Martians put its snake-fingered hands on her and she gave a yelp and did what any well-trained movie starlet would do. She fainted.

Jazzbow wasn't in the ship, of course. The Martians wouldn't risk a landing in Culver City to pick him up, not even at night. Nobody but Professor Schmidt and I knew he was in my office suite there. And the other Martians, of course.

So I got Jazzbow on the ship's interociter while his fellow Martians draped the unconscious Jean on one of their couches. Her skirt rucked up nicely, showing off her legs to good advantage.

"They're not going to hurt her any, are they?" I asked Jazzbow.

"Of course not," his image answered from the inverted triangular screen. "I thought you knew us better than that."

"Yeah, I know. You can't hurt a fly. But still, she's just a kid . . ."

"They're merely probing her mind to see how much she actually knows. It will only take a few minutes."

I won't go into all the details. The Martians are extremely sensitive about their dealings with other living creatures. Not hurt a fly? Hell, they'd make the Dalai Lama look like a blood-thirsty maniac.

Very gently, like a mother caressing her sleeping baby, three of them touched her face and forehead with those tentacle-like fingers. Probing her mind. Some writer got wind of the technique second- or third-hand and used it on television a few years later. Called it a Velcro mind-melt or something like that.

"We have for you," the ship's science officer told me, "good news and bad news."

His name sounded kind of like Snitch. Properly speaking, every Martian is an "it," not a "him" or a "her." But I always thought of them as males.

"The good news," Snitch said to me, "is that this female knew nothing of our existence. She hadn't the faintest suspicion that Martians exist or that you are dealing with them."

"Well, she does now," I grumbled.

"The bad news," he went on, with that silly grin spread across his puss, "is that she is acting as an undercover agent for your Internal Revenue Service—while she's between acting jobs."

Aw hell.

I talked it over with Jazzbow. Then he talked in Martian with Snitch. Then all three of us talked together. We had evolved a Standard Operating Procedure for situations like this, when somebody stumbled onto our secret. I didn't much like the idea of using it on Jean, but there wasn't much else we could do.

So, reluctantly, I agreed. "Just be damned careful with her," I insisted. "She's not some hick cop who's been startled out of his snooze by one of your cockamamie malfunctioning saucers."

Their saucers were actually pretty reliable, but every once in a while the atmospheric turbulence at low altitude would get them into trouble. Most of the sightings happened when the damned things wobbled too close to the ground.

Jazzbow and Snitch promised they'd be extraspecial careful.

Very gently, the Martians selectively erased Jean's memory so that all she remembered the next morning, when she woke up a half a mile from a Mohave gas station, was that she had been abducted by aliens from another world and taken aboard a flying saucer.

The authorities wanted to put her in a nuthouse, of course. But I sent a squad of lawyers to spring her, since she was under contract to my movie studio. The studio assumed responsibility for her, and my lawyers assured the authorities that she was about to star in a major motion picture. The yokels figured it had all been a publicity stunt and turned her loose. I actually did put her into a couple of starring roles, which ended her career with the IRS, although I figured that not even the Feds would have had anything to do with Jean after the tabloids headlined her story about being abducted by flying-saucer aliens. I took good care of her, though. I even married her, eventually. That's what comes from hanging around with Martians.

See, the Martians have a very high ethical standard of conduct. They cannot willingly hurt anybody or anything. Wouldn't step on an ant. It's led to some pretty near scrapes for us, though. Every now and then somebody stumbles onto them and the whole secret's in jeopardy. They could wipe the person's brain clean, but that would turn the poor sucker into a zombie. So they selectively erase only the smallest possible part of the sucker's memory. And they always leave the memory of being taken into a flying saucer. They tell me they have to. That's part of their moral code, too. They're constantly testing us—the whole human race, that is—to see if we're ready to receive alien visitors from another world. And to date, the human race as a whole has consistently flunked every test.

Sure, a handful of very special people know about them. I'm pretty damned proud to be among that handful, let me tell you. But the rest of the human race, the man in the street, the news reporters and preachers and even the average university professor—they either ridicule the very idea that there could be any kind of life at all on another world or they get scared to death of the possibility. Take a look at the movies we make!

"Your people are sadly xenophobic," Jazzbow told me more than once, his big liquid eyes looking melancholy despite that dumbbell clown's grin splitting his face.

I remembered Orson Welles' broadcast of *The War of the Worlds* back in '38. People got hysterical when they thought Martians had landed in New Jersey, although why anybody would want to invade New Jersey is beyond me. Here I had real Martians zipping all over the place, and they were gentle as butterflies. But no one would believe that; the average guy would blast away with his twelve-gauge first and ask where they came from afterward.

So I had to convince the president that if he sent astronauts to the moon, it would have catastrophic results.

Well, my people and Kennedy's people finally got the details ironed out and we agreed to meet at Edwards Air Force Base, out in the Mohave. Totally secret meeting. JFK was giving a speech in LA that evening at the Beverly Wilshire. I sent a company helicopter to pick him up there and fly him over to Edwards. Just him and two of his aides. Not even his Secret Service bodyguards; he didn't care much for having those guys lurking around him, anyway. Cut down on his love life too much.

We met in Hangar Nine, the place where the first Martian crew was stashed back in '46, pretty battered from their crash landing. That's when I first found out about them. I was asked by Professor Schmidt, who looked like a very agitated young Santa Claus back then, to truck in as many refrigeration units as my company could lay its hands on. Schmidt wanted to keep the Martians comfortable, and since their planet is so cold, he figured they needed mucho refrigeration. That was before he found out that the Martians spend about half their energy budget at home just trying to stay reasonably warm. They loved Southern California! Especially the swimming pools.

Anyway, there I am waiting for the president in good old Hangar Nine, which had been so Top Secret since '46 that not even the base commander'd been allowed inside. We'd partitioned it and decked it out with nice furniture and all the modern conveniences.

I noticed that Jazzbow had recently had an interociter installed. Inside the main living area we had put up a big water tank for Jazzbow and his fellow Martians, of course. The place kind of resembled a movie set: nice modern furnishings, but if you looked past the ten-foot-high partitions that served as walls you saw the bare metal support beams crisscrossing up in the shadows of the ceiling.

Jazzbow came in from Culver City in the same limo that brought Professor Schmidt. As soon as he got into the hangar he unhooked his exoskeleton and dived into the water tank. Schmidt started pacing nervously back and forth on the Persian carpeting I had put in. He was really wound up tight: letting the president in on this secret was an enormous risk. Not for us, so much as for the Martians.

It was just about midnight when we heard the throbbing-motor sound of a helicopter in the distance. I walked out into the open and saw the stars glittering like diamonds all across the desert sky. How many of them are inhabited? I wondered. How many critters out there are looking at our Sun and wondering if there's any intelligent life there?

Is there any intelligent life in the White House? That was the big question far as I was concerned.

Jack Kennedy looked tired. No, worse than that, he looked troubled. Beaten down. Like a man who had the weight of the world on his shoulders. Which he did. Elected by a paper-thin majority, he was having hell's own time getting Congress to vote for his programs. Tax relief, increased defense spending, civil rights—they were all dead in the water, stymied by a Congress that wouldn't do spit for him. And now I was going to pile another ton and a half on top of all that.

"Mr. President," I said as he walked through the chilly desert night from the helicopter toward the hangar door. I sort of stood at attention: for the office, not the man, you understand. Remember, I voted for Nixon.

He nodded at me and made a weary smile and stuck out his hand the way every politician does. I let him shake my hand, making a mental note to excuse myself and go to the washroom as soon as decently possible.

As we had agreed, he left his two aides at the hangar door and accompanied me inside all by himself. He kind of shuddered.

"It's cold out there, isn't it?" he said.

He was wearing a summer-weight suit. I had an old windbreaker over my shirt and slacks.

"We've got the heat going inside," I said, gesturing him through the door in the first partition. I led him into the living area and to the big carpeted central room where the water tank was. Schmidt followed behind us so close I could almost feel his breath on my neck. It gave me that crawly feeling I get when I realize how many millions of germs are floating through the air all the time.

"Odd place for a swimming tank," the president said as soon as we entered the central room.

"It's not as odd as you think," I said. Jazzbow had ducked low, out of sight for the time being.

My people had arranged two big sofas and a scattering of comfortable armchairs around a coffee table on which they had set up a fair-sized bar. Bottles of every description, even champagne in its own ice bucket.

"What'll you have?" I asked. We had decided that, with just the three of us humans present, I would be the bartender.

Both the president and Schmidt asked for scotch. I made the drinks big, knowing they would both need them.

"Now what's this all about?" Kennedy asked after his first sip of the booze. "Why all this secrecy and urgency?"

I turned to Schmidt, but he seemed to be petrified. So absolutely frozen that he couldn't even open his mouth or pick up his drink. He just stared at the president, overwhelmed by the enormity of what we had to do.

So I said, "Mr. President, you have to stop this Moon program."

He blinked his baggy eyes. Then he grinned. "Do I?"

"Yessir."

"Why?"

"Because it will hurt the Martians."

"The Martians, you said?"

"That's right. The Martians," I repeated.

Kennedy took another sip of scotch, then put his glass down on the coffee table. "Mr. Hughes, I had heard that you'd gone off the deep end, that you've become a recluse and something of a mental case—"

Schmidt snapped out of his funk. "Mr. President, he's telling you the truth. There are Martians."

Kennedy gave him a "who are you trying to kid" look. "Professor Schmidt, I know you're a highly respected astronomer, but if you expect me to believe there are living creatures on Mars you're going to have to show me some evidence."

On that cue, Jazzbow came slithering out of the water tank. The president's eyes goggled as old Jazzie made his painful way, dripping on the rug, to one of the armchairs and half collapsed into it.

"Mr. President," I said, "may I introduce Jazzbow of Mars. Jazzbow, President Kennedy."

The president just kept on staring. Jazzbow extended his right hand, that perpetual clown's grin smeared across his face. With his jaw hanging open, Kennedy took it in his hand. And flinched.

"I assure you," Jazzbow said, not letting go of the president's hand, "that I am truly from Mars."

Kennedy nodded. He believed it. He had to. Martians can make you see the truth of things. Goes with their telepathic abilities, I guess.

Schmidt explained the situation. How the Martians had built their canals once they realized that their world was dying. How they tried to bring water from the polar ice caps to their cities and farmlands. It worked, for a few centuries, but eventually even that wasn't enough to save the Martians from slow but certain extinction.

They were great engineers, great thinkers. Their technology was roughly a century or so ahead of ours. They had invented the electric lightbulb, for example, during the time of our French and Indian War.

By the time they realized that Mars was going to dry up and wither away despite all their efforts, they had developed a rudimentary form of spaceflight. Desperate, they thought that maybe they could bring natural resources from other worlds in the solar system to revive their dying planet. They knew that Venus was, beneath its clouds, a teeming Mesozoic jungle. Plenty of water there, if they could cart it back to Mars.

They couldn't. Their first attempts at spaceflight ended in disasters. Of the first five saucers they sent toward Venus, three of them blew up on takeoff, one veered off course and was never heard from again, and the fifth crash-landed in New Mexico—which is a helluva long way from Venus.

Fortunately, their saucer crash-landed near a small astronomical station in the desert. A young graduate student—who eventually became Professor Schmidt—was the first to find them. The Martians inside the saucer were pretty banged up, but three of them were still alive. Even more fortunately, we had something that the Martians desperately needed: the raw materials and manufacturing capabilities to mass-produce flying saucers for them. That's where I had come in, as a tycoon of the aviation industry.

President Kennedy found his voice. "Do you mean to tell me that the existence of Martians—living, breathing, intelligent Martians—has been kept a secret since 1946? More than fifteen years?"

"It's been touch-and-go on several occasions," said Schmidt. "But, yes, we've managed to keep the secret pretty well."

"Pretty well?" Kennedy seemed disturbed, agitated. "The Central Intelligence Agency doesn't know anything about this, for Christ's sake!" Then he caught himself, and added, "Or, if they do, they haven't told me about it."

"We have tried very hard to keep this a secret from all the politicians of every stripe," Schmidt said.

"I can see not telling Eisenhower," said the president. "Probably would've given Ike a fatal heart attack." He grinned. "I wonder what Harry Truman would've done with the information."

"We were tempted to tell President Truman, but—"

"That's all water over the dam," I said, trying to get them back onto the subject. "We're here to get you to call off this Project Apollo business."

"But why?" asked the president. "We could use Martian spacecraft and plant the American flag on the Moon tomorrow morning!"

"No," whispered Jazzbow. Schmidt and I knew that when a Martian whispers, it's a sign that he's scared shitless.

"Why not?" Kennedy snapped.

"Because you'll destroy the Martians," said Schmidt, with real iron in his voice.

"I don't understand."

Jazzbow turned those big luminous eyes on the president. "May I explain it to you . . . the Martian way?"

I'll say this for Jack Kennedy. The boy had guts. It was obvious that the basic human xenophobia was strong inside him. When Jazzbow had first touched his hand Kennedy had almost jumped out of his skin. But he met the Martian's gaze and, not knowing what would come next, solemnly nodded his acceptance.

Jazzbow reached out his snaky arm toward Kennedy's face. I saw beads of sweat break out on the president's brow, but he sat still and let the Martian's tentacle-like fingers touch his forehead and temple.

It was like jumping a car battery. Thoughts flowed from Jazzbow's brain into Kennedy's. I knew what those thoughts were.

It had to do with the Martians' moral sense. The average Martian has an ethical quotient about equal to St. Francis of Assisi. That's the average Martian. While they're only a century or so ahead of us technologically, they're lightyears ahead of us morally, socially, ethically. There hasn't been a war on Mars in more than a thousand years. There hasn't even been a case of petty theft in centuries. You can walk the avenues of their beautiful, gleaming cities at any time of the day or night in complete safety. And since their planet is so desperately near absolute depletion, they just about worship the smallest blade of grass.

If our brawling, battling human nations discovered the fragile, gentle Martian culture, there would be a catastrophe. The Martians would be swarmed under, shattered, dissolved by a tide of politicians, industrialists, real-estate developers, evangelists wanting to save their souls, drifters, grifters, conmen, thieves petty and grand. To say nothing of military officers driven by xenophobia. It would make the Spanish Conquest of the Americas look like a Boy Scout Jamboree.

I could see from the look in Kennedy's eyes that he was getting the message. "We would destroy your culture?" he asked.

Jazzbow had learned the human way of nodding. "You would not merely destroy our culture, Mr. President. You would kill us. We would die, all of us, very quickly."

"But you have the superior technology . . ."

"We could never use it against you," said Jazzbow. "We would lie down and die rather than deliberately take the life of a paramecium."

Schmidt spoke up. "So you see, Mr. President, why this Moon project has got to be called off. We can't allow the human race en masse to learn of the Martians' existence."

"I understand," he murmured.

Schmidt breathed out a heavy sigh of relief. Too soon.

"But I can't stop the Apollo project."

"Can't?" Schmidt gasped.

"Why not?" I asked.

Looking utterly miserable, Kennedy told us, "It would mean the end of my administration. For all practical purposes at least."

"I don't see—"

"I haven't been able to get a thing through Congress except the Moon project. They're stiffing me on everything else: my economics package, my defense buildup, civil rights, everything except the Moon program has been stopped dead in Congress. If I give up on the Moon I might as well resign the presidency."

"You are not happy in your work," said Jazzbow.

"No, I'm not," Kennedy admitted, in a low voice. "I never wanted to go into politics. It was my father's idea. Especially after my older brother got killed in the war."

A dismal, gloomy silence descended on us.

"It's all been a sham," the president muttered. "My marriage is a mess, my presidency is a farce, I'm in love with a woman who's married to another man—I wish I could just disappear from the face of the earth."

Which, of course, is exactly what we arranged for him.

It was tricky, believe me. We had to get his blonde inamorata to disappear, which wasn't easy, since she was in the public eye just about as much as the president. Then we had to fake his own assassination, so we could get him safely out of the way. At first he was pretty reluctant about it all, but then the Berlin Wall went up and the media blamed him for it and he agreed that he wanted out—permanently. We were all set to pull it off but the Cuban Missile Crisis hit the fan and we had to put everything on hold for more than a month. By the time we had calmed that mess down he was more than ready to leave this earth. So we arranged the thing for Dallas.

We didn't dare tell Lyndon Johnson about the Martians, of course. He would've wanted to go to Mars and annex the whole damned planet. To Texas, most likely. And we didn't have to tell Nixon; he was happy to kill the Apollo program—after taking as much credit for the first lunar landing as the media would give him.

The toughest part was hoodwinking the astronomers and planetary scientists and the engineers who built planetary spacecraft probes. It took all of Schmidt's ingenuity and the Martians' technical skills to get the various Mariner and Pioneer probes jiggered so that they would show a barren dry Venus devastated by a runaway greenhouse effect instead of the lush Mesozoic jungle that really exists beneath those clouds. I had to pull every string I knew, behind the scenes, to get the geniuses at JPL to send their two Viking landers to the Martian equivalents of Death Valley and the Atacama Desert in Chile. They missed the cities and the canals completely.

Schmidt used his international connections, too. I didn't much like working with Commies, but I've got to admit the two Russian scientists I met were okay guys.

And it worked. Sightings of the canals on Mars went down to zero once our faked Mariner 6 pictures were published. Astronomy students looking at Mars for the first time through a telescope thought they were victims of eyestrain! They knew there were no canals there, so they didn't dare claim they saw any.

So that's how we got to the Moon and then stopped going. We set up the Apollo program so that a small number of Americans could plant the flag and their footprints on the Moon and then forget about it. The Martians studiously avoided the whole area during the four years that we were sending missions up there. It all worked out very well, if I say so myself.

I worked harder than I ever had before in my life to get the media to downplay the space program make it a dull, no-news affair. The man in the street, the average xenophobic Joe Six-Pack, forgot about the glories of space exploration soon enough. It tore at my guts to do it, but that's what had to be done.

So now we're using the resources of the planet Venus to replenish Mars. Schmidt has a tiny group of astronomers who've been hiding the facts of the solar system from the rest of the profession since the late forties. With the Martians' help they're continuing to fake the pictures and data sent from NASA's space probes.

The rest of the world thinks that Mars is a barren lifeless desert and Venus is a bone-dry hothouse beneath its perpetual cloud cover and space in general is pretty much of a bore. Meanwhile, with the help of Jazzbow and a few other Martians, we've started an environmental movement on Earth. Maybe if we can get human beings to see their own planet as a living entity, to think of the other animals and plants on our own planet as fellow residents of this Spaceship Earth rather than resources to be killed or exploited—maybe then we can start to reduce the basic xenophobia in the human psyche.

I won't live long enough to see the human race embrace the Martians as brothers. It will take gene rations, centuries, before we grow to their level of morality. But maybe we're on the right track now. I hope so.

I keep thinking of what Jack Kennedy said when he finally agreed to rig Project Apollo the way we did, and to arrange his own and his girlfriend's demises.

"It is a far, far better thing I do, than I have ever done," he quoted.

Thinking of him and Marilyn shacked up in a honeymoon suite on Mars, I realized that the remainder of the quote would have been totally inappropriate: "It is a far, far better rest that I go to, than I have ever known."

But what the hell, who am I to talk? I've fallen in love for the first time. Yeah, I know. I've been married several times, but this time it's real and I'm going to spend the rest of my life on a tropical island with her, just the two of us alone, far from the madding crowd.

Well, maybe not the whole rest of my life. The Martians know a lot more about medicine than we do. Maybe we'll leave this Pacific island where the Martians found her and go off to Mars and live a couple of centuries or so. I think Amelia would like that.

BUILD ME A MOUNTAIN

Here's Chet Kinsman again, about twenty years downstream from "The Lieutenant and the Folksinger," and a few years before his appearance at the beginning of my novel about him, Millennium.

AS SOON AS HE STEPPED THROUGH the acoustical screen at the apartment doorway, the noise hit him like a physical force. Chet Kinsman stood there a moment and watched them. *My battlefield,* he thought.

The room was jammed with guests making cocktail-party chatter. It was an old room, big, with a high, ornately paneled ceiling.

He recognized maybe one-tenth of the people. Over at the far end of the room, tall drink in his hand, head slightly bent to catch what some wrinkled matron was saying, stood the target for tonight: Congressman Neal McGrath, swing vote on the House Appropriations Committee.

"Chet, you did come after all!"

He turned to see Mary-Ellen McGrath approaching him, her hand extended in greeting.

"I hardly recognized you without your uniform," she said.

He smiled back at her. "I thought Air Force blue would be a little conspicuous around here."

"Nonsense. And I wanted to see your new oak leaves. A major now."

A captain on the Moon and a major in the Pentagon. Hazardous duty pay.

"Come on, Chet. I'll show you where the bar is." She took his arm and towed him through the jabbering crowd.

Mary-Ellen was almost as tall as Kinsman. She had the strong, honest face of a woman who can stand beside her husband in the face of anything from Washington cocktail parties to the tight infighting of rural Maine politics.

The bar dispenser hummed absent-mindedly to itself as it produced a heavy scotch and water. Kinsman took a stinging sip of it.

"I was worried you wouldn't come," Mary-Ellen said over the noise of the crowd. "You've been something of a hermit lately."

"Uh-huh."

"And I never expected you to show up by yourself. Chet Kinsman without a girl on his arm is . . . well, something new."

"I'm preparing for the priesthood."

"I'd almost believe it." she said, straight-faced. "There's something different about you since you've been on the Moon. You're quieter."

I've been grounded. Aloud, he said, "Creeping maturity. I'm a late achiever."

But she was serious, and as stubborn as her husband. "Don't try to kid around it. You've changed. You're not playing the dashing young astronaut any more."

"Who the hell is?"

A burly, balding man jarred into Kinsman from behind, sloshing half his drink out of its glass.

"*Whoops,* didn't get it on ya, did, oh, hell, Mrs. McGrath. Looks like I'm waterin' your rug."

"It's disposable," Mary-Ellen said. "Do you two know each other? Tug Wynne, this is—"

"I've seen Major Kinsman on the Hill."

Chet said, "You're with the Allnews Syndicate, aren't you?"

Nodding, Wynne replied, "Surprised to see you here, Major, after this morning's committee session."

Kinsman forced a grin. "I'm an old family friend. Mrs. McGrath and I went to college together."

"You think the congressman's gonna vote against the Moonbase appropriation?"

"Looks that way," Kinsman said.

Mary-Ellen kept silent.

"He sure gave your Colonel Murdock a hard time this morning. Mrs. McGrath, you shoulda seen your husband in action." Wynne chuckled wheezily.

Kinsman changed the subject. "Say, do you know Cy Calder . . . old guy, works for Allied News in California?"

"Only by legend," Wynne answered. "He died a couple months ago, y'know."

"No . . . I didn't know." Kinsman felt a brief pang deep inside the part of him that he kept frozen. He made himself ignore it.

"Yep. He musta been past eighty. Friend of yours?"

"Sort of. I knew him . . . well, a few years back."

Mary-Ellen said, "I'd better get to some of the other guests. There are several old friends of yours here tonight, Chet. Mix around, you'll find them."

With another rasping cackle, Wynne said, "Guess we *could* let somebody else get next to the bar."

Kinsman started to drift away, but Wynne followed beside him.

"Murdock send you over here to try to soften up McGrath?"

Pushing past a pair of arguing cigar smokers, Kinsman frowned. "I was invited to this party weeks ago. I told you, Mrs. McGrath and I are old friends,"

"How do you get along with the congressman?"

"What's that supposed to mean?"

Wynne let his teeth show. "Well, from what I hear, you were quite a hellraiser a few years back. How'd you and Mrs. McGrath get along in college together?"

You cruddy old bastard. "If you're so interested in Mrs. McGrath's college days, why don't you ask her? Or her husband? Get off my back."

Wynne shrugged and raised his glass in mock salute. "Yes sir, Major, sir."

Kinsman turned and started working his way toward the other end of the room. A grandfather clock chimed off in a corner, barely audible over the human noises and clacking of ice in glassware. *Eighteen hundred. Gold and Smitty ought to be halfway to Copernicus by now.*

And then he heard her. He didn't have to see her; he knew it was Diane. The same pure, haunting soprano; a voice straight out of a legend.

"Once I had a sweetheart, and now I have none.
Once I had a sweetheart, and now I have none.
He's gone and leave me, he's gone and leave me.
He's gone and leave me to sorrow and mourn."

Her voice stroked his memory and he felt all the old joys, all the old pain, as he pushed his way through the crowd.

Finally he saw her, sitting cross-legged on a sofa, guitar hiding her slim figure. The same ancient guitar: no amplifiers, no boosters. Her hair was still long and straight and black as space; her eyes even darker and deeper. The people were ringed around her, standing, sitting on the floor. They gave her the entire sofa to herself, like an altar that only the anointed could use. They watched her and listened, entranced by her voice. But she was somewhere else, living the song, seeing what it told of, until she strummed the final chord.

Then she looked straight at Kinsman. Not surprised, not even smiling, just a look that linked them as if the past five years had never been. Before either of them could say or do anything, the others broke into applause. Diane smiled and mouthed, "Thank you."

"More, more!"

"Come on, another one"

"'Greensleeves.'"

Diane put the guitar down carefully beside her, uncoiled her long legs, and stood up. "Would later be okay?"

Kinsman grinned. He knew it would be later or nothing.

They muttered reluctant agreement and broke up the circle around her. Kinsman took the final few paces and stood before Diane.

He said, "Good to see you again."

"Hello, Chet." She wasn't quite smiling.

"Here Diane, I brought you some punch." Kinsman turned to see a fleshy-faced young man with a droopy mustache and tousled brown hair, dressed in a violet suit, carrying two plastic cups of punch.

"Thank you, Larry. This is Chet Kinsman. Chet, meet Larry Rose."

"Kinsman?"

"I knew Chet in the Bay area a few years back, when I was just getting started. You're still in the Air Force, aren't you, Chet?"

"Affirmative." *Play the role.*

Diane turned back to Larry. "Chet's an astronaut. He's been on the Moon."

"Oh. That must be where I heard the name. Weren't you involved in some sort of rescue? One of your people got stranded or something and you—"

"Yes." Kinsman cut him short. "It was blown up out of proportion by the news people."

They stood there for a moment, awkwardly silent while the party pulsated around them.

Diane said, "Mary-Ellen told me you might be here tonight. You and Neal are both working on something about the space program?"

"Something like that. Organized any more peace marches?"

She laughed. "Larry, did I ever tell you about the time we tried to get Chet to come out and join one of our demonstrations? In his uniform?"

Larry shook his head.

"Do you remember what you told me, Chet?"

"No. I remember it was during the Brazilian crisis. You were planning to invade the U.C.L.A. library or something. I had flying duty that day."

It was a perfect day for flying, breaking out of the coastal haze and standing the jet on her tailpipe and ripping through the clouds until even the distant Sierras looked like nothing more than wrinkles. Then flat out over the Pacific at Mach 5, the only sounds in your earphones from your own breathing and the faint, distant crackle of earthbound men giving orders to other men.

"You told me," Diane said, "that you'd rather be flying patrol and making sure that nobody bombs us while we demonstrated for peace."

She was grinning at him. It was funny now; it hadn't been then.

"Yeah, I guess I did say that."

"How amusing," Larry said. "And what are you doing now? Protecting us from the Lithuanians? Or going to Mars?'

You overstuffed fruit, you wouldn't even fit into a flight crewman's seat. "I'm serving on a Pentagon assignment. My job is congressional liaison."

"Twisting congressmen's arms is what he means," came Neal McGrath's husky voice from behind him.

Kinsman turned.

"Hello, Chet, Diane . . . eh, Larry Rose, isn't it?"

"You have a good memory for names."

"Goes with the job." Neal McGrath topped Kinsman's six feet by an inch. He was red-haired and rugged-looking. His voice was soft, throaty. Somehow the natural expression of his face, in repose, was an introspective scowl. But he was smiling now. *His cocktail-party smile,* thought Kinsman.

"Tug Wynne tells me I was pretty rough on your boss this morning," McGrath said to Kinsman. The smile turned a shade self-satisfied.

"Colonel Murdock lost a few pounds, and it wasn't all from the TV lights," Kinsman said.

"I was only trying to get him to give me a good reason for funneling money into a permanent Moonbase."

Kinsman answered, "He gave you about fifty reasons, Neal."

"None that hold up," McGrath said. "Not when we've got to find money to reclaim every major city in this country, plus fighting these damned interminable wars."

"And to check the population growth," Diane added.

Here we go again. Shrugging. Kinsman. said, "Look, Neal, I'm not going to argue with you. We've been making one-shot missions to the Moon off and on for fifty years now. There's enough there to warrant a permanent base."

McGrath made a sour face. "A big, expensive base on the Moon."

"Makes sense," Kinsman slid in. "It makes sense on a straight cost-effectiveness basis. You've seen the numbers. Moonbase will save you billions of dollars in the long run."

"That's just like Mary-Ellen saves me money at department store sales. I can't afford to save that money. Not this year. The capital outlay is too high. To say nothing of the overruns."

"Now wait—"

"Come on, Chet. There's never been a big program that's lived within its budget. No . . . Moonbase is going to have to wait, I'm afraid."

"We've already waited fifty years."

A crowd was gathering around them now, and McGrath

automatically raised his voice a notch. "Our first priority has got to be for the cities. They've become jungles, unfit for sane human life. We've got to reclaim them, and save the people who're trapped in them before they all turn into savages."

Damn, he's got a thick hide. "Okay, but it doesn't have to be either/or. We can do both."

"Not while the war's on."

Hold your temper; don't fire at the flag. "The war's an awfully convenient excuse for postponing commitments. We've been in hot and cold wars since before you and I were born."

With the confident grin of a hunter who had cornered his quarry, McGrath asked, "Are you suggesting that we pull our troops out of South America? Or do you want to let our cities collapse completely?"

Do you still beat your wife? "All I'm suggesting," Kinsman said with, deliberate calm, "is that we shouldn't postpone building Moonbase any longer. We've got the technology—we know how to do it. It's either build a permanent base on the Moon, or stop the lunar exploration program altogether. If we fail to build Moonbase, your budget-cutting friends will throttle down the whole manned space program to zero within a few years."

Still smiling, McGrath said, "I've heard all that from your Colonel Murdock."

There was a curious look in Diane's dark eyes.

"Chet. Why do you want to have a Moonbase built?"

"Why? Because . . . I was just telling you—"

She shook her head. "No, I don't mean the official reasons, I mean why do *you* dig the idea?"

"We need it. The space program needs it."

"No," she said patiently. "*You.* Why are you for it? What's in it for you?"

"What do you mean?" Kinsman asked.

"What makes you tick, man? What turns you on? Is it a Moonbase? What moves you, Chet?"

They were all watching him, the whole crowd, their faces blank or smirking or inquisitive. Floating weightless, standing on nothing and looking at the overpowering beauty of Earth—rich, brilliant, full, shining against the black emptiness. Knowing that people down there are killing each other, teaching their children to kill, your eyes filling with tears at the beauty and sadness of it. How could they see it? How could they understand?

"What moves you, Chet?" Diane asked again.

He made himself grin. "Well, for one thing, the Pentagon cafeteria coffee."

Everybody laughed. But she wouldn't let him off the hook.

"No—get serious. This is important. What turns you on?"

Wouldn't understand anyway. "You mean aside from the obvious things, like sex?"

She nodded gravely.

"Hmmm. I don't know. It's kind of hard to answer. Flying, I guess. Getting out on your own responsibility, away from committees and chains of command."

"There's got to be more to it than that," Diane insisted.

"Well . . . have you ever been out on the desert at an Israeli outpost, dancing all night by firelight because at dawn there's going to be an attack and you don't want to waste a minute of life?"

There was a heartbeat's span of silence. Then one of the women asked in a near-whisper, "When . . . were you . . . ?"

Kinsman said, "Oh, I've never been there. But isn't it a romantic picture?"

They all broke into laughter. *That burst the bubble.* The crowd began to dissolve, breaking up into smaller groups, dozens of private conversations filling the silence that had briefly held them.

"You cheated," Diane said.

"Maybe I did."

"Don't you have anything except icewater in your veins?"

He shrugged. "If you prick us, do we not bleed?"

"Don't talk dirty."

He took her by the arm and headed for the big glass doors at the far end of the room. "Come on, we've got a lot of catching up to do. I've bought all your tapes."

"And I've been watching your name on the news."

"Don't believe most of it."

He pushed the door open and they stepped out onto the balcony. Shatterproof plastic enclosed the balcony and shielded them from the humid, hazy Washington air—and anything that might be thrown or shot from the street far below. The air conditioning kept the balcony pleasantly cool.

"Sunset," Diane said, looking out toward the slice of sky that was visible between the two apartment buildings across the avenue. "Loveliest time of the day."

"Loneliest time, too."

She turned to him, her eyes showing genuine surprise. "Lonely? You? I didn't know you had any weaknesses like that."

"I've got a few, hidden away here and there."

"Why do you hide them?"

"Because nobody gives a damn about them, one way or the other." Before Diane could reply, he said, "I sound sorry for myself, don't I?"

"Well . . ."

"Who's this Larry character?"

"He's a very nice guy," she said firmly. "And a good musician. And he doesn't go whizzing off into the wild blue yonder . . . or, space is black, isn't it?"

He nodded. "I don't go whizzing any more, either. I've been grounded."

She blinked at him. "What does that mean?"

"Grounded," Kinsman repeated. "Deballed. No longer qualified for flight duty. No orbital missions. No lunar missions. They won't even let me fly a plane any more. Got some shavetail to jockey me around. I work at a desk."

"But . . . why?"

"It's a long dirty story. Officially, I'm too valuable to risk or something like that."

"Chet, I'm so sorry . . . flying meant so much to you, I know." She stepped into his arms and he kissed her.

"Let's get out of here, Diane. Let's go someplace safe and watch the Moon come up and I'll tell you all the legends about your namesake."

"Same old smooth talker."

"No, not any more. I haven't even touched a woman since . . . well, not for a long time."

"I can't leave the party, Chet. They're expecting me to sing."

"Screw them."

"All of them?"

"Don't talk dirty."

She laughed, but shook her head. "Really, Chet. Not now."

"Then let me take you home afterward."

"I'm staying here tonight."

There were several things he wanted to say, but he checked himself.

"Chet, please don't rush me. It's been a long time." *It sure as hell has.*

They went back into the party and separated. Kinsman drifted through the crowd, making meaningless chatter with strangers and old friends alike, drink in one hand, occasionally nibbling on a canapé about the size and consistency of spacecraft food. But his mind was replaying, over and over again, the last time he had seen Diane.

Five years ago.

Soaring across the California countryside, riding the updrafts along the hillsides and playing hide-and-seek with the friendly chaste-white cumuli, the only sound the rush of air across the glass bubble an inch over your head, your guts held tight as you sweep and bank and then soar up, up past the clouds and then you bank way over so you're hanging by the shoulder harness and looking straight down into the green citrus groves below. Diane sitting in the front seat, so all you can see of her is the back of her plastic safety helmet. But you can hear her gasp.

"Like it?"

"It's wild . . . gorgeous!"

And then back on the ground. Back in reality.

"Chet, I've got to go to this meeting. Can't you come along with me?"

"No. Got to report for duty."

Just like that. An hour of sharing his world, and then gone. The last he had seen of her. Until tonight.

The crowd had thinned out considerably. People were leaving. McGrath was at the hallway door, making the customary noises of farewell. Kinsman spotted Diane sitting alone on the sofa, tucked against a corner of it, as if for protection.

He went over and sat down beside her. "I've got news for you."

"Oh? What?"

"An answer to your question. About what turns me on. I've been thinking about it all through the party and I've formed a definite opinion."

She turned to face him, leaning an arm on the sofa's back. "So what is it?"

"You do. You turn me on."

She didn't look surprised. "Do I?"

Nodding. "Yep. After five years, you still do."

Diane said, "Chet, haven't you learned anything? We're in two entirely different worlds. You want to go adventuring."

"And you want to join demonstrations and sing to the kids about how lousy the world is."

"I'm trying to make the world better!" Her face looked so damned intent.

"And I'm trying to start a new world."

She shook her head. "We never did see eye to eye on anything."

"Except in bed."

That stopped her, but only for a moment. "That's not enough. Not for me. It wasn't then and it isn't now."

He didn't answer.

"Chet . . . why'd they ground you? What's it all about?"

A hot spark of electricity flashed through his gut. *Careful!* "I told you. it's a long story. I'm a valuable public relations tool for Colonel Murdock. You know, a veteran of lunar exploration. Heroic rescuer of an injured teammate. All that crap. So my address is the Pentagon. Level three, ring D, corridor F, room—"

"Whether you like it or not."

"Yes."

"Why don't you quit?"

"And do what? To dig I am not able, to beg I am too proud."

Diane looked at him quizzically. They had both run out of stock answers.

"So there it is," Kinsman said, getting up from the sofa. "Right where we left it five years ago."

Mary-Ellen came over to them. "Don't leave, Chet. We're getting rid of the last of the guests, then we're going to have a little supper. Stay around. Neal wants to talk with you"

"Okay. Fine." *That's what I'm here for.*

"Can I fix you another drink?" Mary-Ellen asked.

"Let me fix you one."

"No, no more for me, thanks."

He looked down at Diane. "Still hooked on *tigers?*"

She smiled. "I haven't had one in years . . . .Yes, I'd like a *tiger.*"

By the time he came back from the bar with the two smoke-yellow drinks in his hands, the big living room was empty of guests. Diane and Mary-Ellen were sitting on the sofa together. Only when they were this close could you see that they really were sisters. Kinsman heard McGrath out in the hallway, laughingly bidding someone good night.

"Like a family reunion," Kinsman said as he sat on a plush chair facing the sofa.

"You're still here, Chet," McGrath called from the hail archway. "Good. I've got a bone to pick with you, old buddy."

As the congressman crossed to the bar, Mary-Ellen said, "Maybe Diane and I ought to hide out in the kitchen. We can see to supper."

"Not me," Diane said, "I want to be in on this."

Kinsman grinned at her.

McGrath came up and sat beside his wife. The three of them—husband, wife, sister—faced Kinsman. *Like the beginning of a shotgun wedding.*

"Listen, Chet," McGrath began, his voice huskier than usual from too much drinking and smoking. "I don't like the idea of Murdock sending you over here to try to soften me up. Just because you're an old friend doesn't give you—"

"Hold on," Kinsman said. "I was invited here two weeks ago. And I came because I wanted to."

"Murdock knew these hearings were coming up this week and next. Don't deny it."

"I'm not denying a damned thing. Murdock can do what he wants. I came here because I wanted to. If it fits Murdock's grand scheme, so what?"

McGrath reached into his jacket pocket for a cigarette. "I just don't like having space cadets from the Pentagon spouting Air Force propaganda at my parties. Especially when they're old friends. I don't like it."

"What if the old friend happens to believe that the propaganda is right and you're wrong?"

"Oh, come on now, Chet . . ."

"Look, Neal, on this Moonbase business, you're wrong. Moonbase is essential, no matter what you think of it."

"It's another boondoggle—"

"The hell it is! We either build Moonbase or we stop exploring the Moon altogether. It's one or the other."

McGrath took a deep, calming drag on his cigarette. Patiently, he said, "There's too much to do here on Earth for me to vote for a nickel on Moonbase. Let alone the billions of dollars—"

"The money is chickenfeed. We spend ten times that amount on new cars each year. A penny tax on cigarettes will pay for Moonbase."

McGrath involuntarily glanced at the joint in his hand. Scowling, he answered, "We need all the money we can raise to rebuild the cities. We're going under, the cities are sinking into jungles."

"Who's spouting the party line now?" Kinsman shot back. "Everybody knows about the poor and the cities. And the population overload. And the whole damned social structure. That's a damned safe hobbyhorse to ride in Congress. What we need is somebody with guts enough to stand up for spending two percent of all that money on the future."

"Are you accusing me—"

"I'm saying you're hiding in the crowd, Neal. I don't disagree with the crowd; they're right about the cities and the poor. But there's a helluva lot more to life than that."

Diane cut in. "Chet, what about Moonbase? What good is it? Who will it help? Will it make jobs for the city kids? Will it build schools?"

He stared at her for a long moment. "No," he said at last. "It won't do any of those things. But it won't prevent them from being done, either."

"Then why should we do it?" Diane asked. "For your entertainment? To earn your Colonel Murdock a promotion or something? Why? What's in it for us?"

Standing on the rim of a giant crater, looking down at the tiered terraces of rock worn smooth by five eons of meteoric erosion. The flat pitted plain at the base of the slope. The horizon, sharp and clear, close enough to make you think. And the stars beyond. The silence and the emptiness. The freedom. The peace.

"There's probably nothing in it for you. Maybe for your kids. Maybe for those kids in the cities. I don't know. But there's something in it for me. The only way I'll ever get to the Moon again is to push Moonbase through Congress. Otherwise I'm permanently grounded."

"What?"

Diane said, "Your man Murdock won't let you—"

Kinsman waved them quiet. "Officially, I'm grounded. Officially, there are medical and emotional reasons. That's on the record and there's no way to take it off. Unless there's a permanent base on the Moon, a place where a non-pilot passenger can go, then the only people on the Moon will be flight-rated astronauts. So I need Moonbase; I need it. Myself. For purely personal, selfish reasons."

"Being on the Moon means that much to you?" Diane asked.

Kinsman nodded.

"I don't get it," McGrath said. "What's so damned attractive about the Moon?"

"What was attractive about the great American desert?" Kinsman shot back. "Or the poles? Or the Marianas Deep? How the hell should I know? But a while ago you were all asking what turns me on. This does. Being out there, on your own, away from all the sickness and bullshit of this world—that's what I want. That's what I need."

Mary-Ellen shook her head. "But it's so desolate out there . . . forsaken . . ."

"Have you been there? Have you watched the Earth rise? Or planted footprints where no man has ever been before? Have you ever been anywhere in your life where you really challenged nature? Where you were really on your own?"

"And you still want to go back?" McGrath had a slight grin on his face.

"Damned right. Sitting around here is like being in jail. Know what they call us at the Pentagon? Luniks. Most of the brass think we're nuts. But they use us, just like Murdock is using me. Maybe we *are* crazy. But I'm going to get back there if I have to build a mountain, starting at my desk, and climb up hand over hand."

"But why, Chet?" Diane asked, suddenly intent. "*Why* is it so important to you? Is it the adventure of it?"

"I told you—it's the freedom. There are no rule books up there; you're on your own. You work with people on the basis of their abilities, not their rank. It's—it's just so completely different up there that I can't really describe it. I know we live in a canned environment, physically. If an air hose splits or a pump malfunctions, you could die in seconds. But in spite of that—maybe *because* of that—you're free emotionally. It's you against the universe, you and your friends, your brothers. There's nothing like it here on Earth."

"Freedom," Diane echoed.

"On the Moon," McGrath said flatly.

Kinsman nodded.

Staring straight at him, Diane said slowly. "What you're saying, Chet, is that a new society can be built on the Moon, a society completely different from anything here on Earth."

Kinsman blinked. "Did I say that?"

"Yes, you did."

He shrugged. "Well, if we establish a permanent settlement, I guess we'll have to work out some sort of social structure."

"Would you take the responsibility for setting up that social structure?" Diane asked. "Would you shoulder the job of making certain that all the nonsense of Earth is left behind? Would you do the job *right?*"

For a moment, Kinsman didn't know what to answer. Then he said, "I would try."

"You'd take that responsibility?" Diane asked again.

Nodding. "Damned right."

Mary-Ellen looked totally unconvinced. "But who would be willing to live on the Moon? Who would want to?"

"I would," Diane said.

They all turned to look at her. Mary-Ellen shocked, McGrath curious.

"Would you?" Kinsman asked. "Really?"

Very seriously, she replied, "If you're going to build a new world, how could I stay away?"

Kinsman felt himself relax for the first time all evening. "Well, I'll be damned! You can see it!" He started to laugh.

"What's funny?" McGrath asked.

"I've won a convert, Neal. If Diane can see what it's all about, then we've got it made. The idea of a Moonbase, of a permanent settlement on the Moon—if it gets across to Diane, then the kids will see it, too."

"There are no kids in Congress."

Kinsman shrugged. "That's okay. Congress'll come around sooner or later. Maybe not this year, maybe not until after Murdock retires. But we'll get it. There's going to be a permanent settlement on the Moon. In time for me to get there."

"Chet," Diane said, "it won't be fun. It's going to be a lot of work."

"I know. But it'll be worth the work."

They sat there, eye to eye, grinning at each other.

McGrath slouched back in the sofa. "I guess I'm simply too old to appreciate all this. I don't see how—"

"Neal," Kinsman said, "someday the history books will devote a chapter to the creation of man's first extraterrestrial society. Your name will be in there as one of the men who opposed it—or one of the leaders who helped create it. Which do you want to be put down beside your name?"

"You're a cunning bastard," McGrath mumbled.

"And don't you forget it." Kinsman stood up, stretched, then reached a hand out for Diane. "Come on, lunik, let's take a walk. There's a full Moon out tonight. In a couple years I'll show you what a full Earth looks like."

CRISIS OF THE MONTH

Although it is often difficult to admit it, writers do not work entirely alone. True, the hard work of actually composing a story, word by painstaking word, sentence by agonizing sentence, is almost always done in complete solitude. Nobody there except you and your writing instrument. (And the characters who are boiling out of your brain.) When the task of composition is going on, no writer wants anyone else in sight. Or sound, especially sound. Telephone rings, spousal queries, even dogs yapping outside can drive a writer to distraction. If it happens often enough, mayhem or murder can be the result. Divorce, more often.

But other persons contribute to the development of a story, some before the writing begins, some afterward. Sometimes these contributions are beneficial, sometimes harmful. The successful writer learns to be sensitive to the words of others: accept the good ideas with as much grace as you are capable of; reject the bad advice with equal tact. If you can.

"Crisis of the Month" began with my late wife's griping about the hysterical manner in which the news media report on the day's events. Veteran newscaster Linda Ellerbe calls the technique "anxiety news." Back in journalism school (so long ago that spelling was considered important) I was taught that "good news is no news." Today's media take this advice to extremes: no matter what the story, there is a down side to it that can be emphasized.

So when my darling and very perceptive wife complained about the utterly negative way in which the media presented the day's news, I quipped, "I can see the day when science finally finds out how to make people immortal. The media will do stories about the sad plight of the funeral directors."

My wife was also one of the top literary agents in the business. She immediately suggested, "Why don't you write a story about that?"

Thus the origin of "Crisis of the Month."

WHILE I CRUMPLED THE PAPER NOTE that someone had slipped into my jacket pocket, Jack Armstrong drummed his fingers on the immaculately gleaming expanse of the pseudomahogany conference table.

"Well," he said testily, "ladies and gentlemen, doesn't one of you have a possibility? An inkling? An idea?"

No one spoke. I left the wadded note in my pocket and placed both my hands conspicuously on the tabletop. Armstrong drummed away in abysmal silence. I guess once he had actually looked like The All-American Boy. Now, many face-lifts and body remodelings later, he looked more like a moderately well-preserved dummy.

"Nothing at all, gentlemen and ladies?" He always made certain to give each sex the first position fifty percent of the time. Affirmative action was a way of life with our Boss.

"Very well then. We will Delphi the problem."

That broke the silence. Everyone groaned.

"There's nothing else to be done," the Boss insisted. "We must have a crisis by Monday morning. It is now . . ." he glanced at the digital readout built into the tabletop, ". . . three-eighteen p.m. Friday. We will not leave this office until we have a crisis to offer."

We knew it wouldn't do a bit of good, but we groaned all over again.

The Crisis Command Center was the best-kept secret in the world. No government knew of our existence. Nor did the people, of course. In fact, in all the world's far-flung news media, only a select handful of the topmost executives knew of the CCC. Those few, those precious few, that band of brothers and sisters—they were our customers. The reason for our being. They paid handsomely. And they protected the secret of our work even from their own news staffs.

Our job, our sacred duty, was to select the crisis that would be the focus of worldwide media attention for the coming month. Nothing more. Nothing less.

In the old days, when every network, newspaper, magazine, news service, or independent station picked out its own crises, things were always in a jumble. Sure, they would try to focus on one or two surefire headline-makers: a nuclear power—plant disaster or the fear of one, a new disease like AIDS or Chinese Rot, a war, terrorism, things like that.

The problem was, there were so many crises springing up all the time, so many threats and threats of threats, so much blood and fire and terror, that people stopped paying attention. The news scared the livers out of them. Sales of newspapers and magazines plunged toward zero. Audiences for news shows, even the revered network evening shows, likewise plummeted.

It was Jack Armstrong—a much younger, more handsome and vigorous All-American Boy—who came up with the idea of the Crisis Command Center. Like all great ideas, it was basically simple.

Pick one crisis each month and play it for all it's worth. Everywhere. In all the media. Keep it scary enough to keep people listening, but not so terrifying that they'll run away and hide.

And it worked! Worked to the point where the CCC (or Cee-Cubed, as some of our analysts styled it) was truly the command center for all the media of North America. And thereby, of course, the whole world.

But on this particular Friday afternoon, we were stumped. And I had that terrifying note crumpled in my pocket. A handwritten note, on paper, no less. Not an electronic communication, but a secret, private, dangerous, seditious note, meant for me and me alone, surreptitiously slipped into my jacket pocket.

"Make big $$$," it scrawled. "Tell all to Feds."

I clasped my hands to keep them from trembling and wondered who, out of the fourteen men and women sitting around the table, had slipped that bomb to me.

Boss Jack had started the Delphi procedure by going down the table, asking each of us board members in turn for the latest news in her or his area of expertise.

He started with the man sitting at his immediate right, Matt Dillon.

That wasn't the name he had been born with, naturally; his original name had been Oliver Wolchinsky. But in our select little group, once you earn your spurs (no pun intended) you are entitled to a "power name," a name that shows you are a person of rank and consequence. Most power names were chosen, of course, from famous media characters.

Matt Dillon didn't look like the marshal of Dodge City. Or even the one-time teen screen-idol. He was short, pudgy, bald, with bad skin and an irritable temper. He looked, actually, exactly as you would expect an Oliver Wolchinsky to look.

But when Jack Armstrong said, "We shall begin with you," he added, "Matthew."

Matt Dillon was the CCC expert on energy problems. He always got to his feet when he had something to say. This time he remained with his round rump resting resignedly on the caramel cushion of his chair.

"The outlook is bleak," said Matt Dillon. "Sales of the new space-manufactured solar cells are still climbing. Individual homes, apartment buildings, condos, factories—everybody's plastering their roofs with them and generating their own electricity. No pollution, no radiation, nothing for us to latch on to. They don't even make noise!"

"Ah," intoned our All-American Boy, "but they must be ruining business for electric utility companies. Why not a crisis there?" He gestured hypnotically, and put on an expression of Ratheresque somberness, intoning, "Tonight we will look at the plight of the electrical utilities, men and women who have been discarded in the stampede for cheap energy."

"Trampled," a voice from down the table suggested.

"Ah, yes. Instead of discarded. Thank you." Boss Jack was never one to discourage creative criticism.

But Marshal Matt mewed, "The electric utility companies are doing just fine; they invested in the solar cell development back in '35. They saw the handwriting in the sky."

A collective sigh of disappointment went around the table.

Not one to give up easily, our Mr. Armstrong suggested, "What about oil producers, then? The coal miners?"

"The last coal miner retired on full pension in '38," replied Matt dolefully. "The mines were fully automated by then. Nobody cares if robots are out of work; they just get reprogrammed and moved into another industry. Most of the coal robots are picking fruit in Florida now."

"But the Texas oil and gas—"

Matt headed him off at the pass. "Petroleum prices are steady. They sell the stuff to plastics manufacturers, mostly. Natural gas is the world's major heating fuel. It's clean, abundant, and cheap."

Gloom descended on our conference table.

It deepened as Boss Jack went from one of our experts to the next.

Terrorism had virtually vanished in the booming world economy.

Political scandals were depressingly rare: with computers replacing most bureaucrats there was less cheating going on in government, and far fewer leaks to the media.

The space program was so successful that no less than seven governments of space-faring nations—including our own dear Uncle Sam—had declared dividends for their citizens and a tax amnesty for the year.

Population growth was nicely leveling off. Inflation was minimal. Unemployment was a thing of the past, with an increasingly roboticized work force encouraging humans to invest in robots, accept early retirement, and live off the productivity of their machines.

The closest thing to a crisis in that area was a street brawl in Leningrad between two retired Russian factory workers—aged thirty and thirty-two—who both wanted the very same robot. Potatoes that were much too small for our purposes.

There hadn't been a war since the International Peacekeeping Force had prevented Fiji from attacking Tonga, nearly twelve years ago.

Toxic wastes, in the few remote regions of the world where they still could be found, were being gobbled up by genetically altered bugs (dubbed Rifkins, for some obscure reason) that happily died once they had finished their chore and dissolved into harmless water, carbon dioxide, and ammonia compounds. In some parts of the world the natives had started laundry and cleaning establishments on the sites of former toxic-waste dumps.

I watched and listened in tightening terror as the fickle finger of fate made its way down the table toward me. I was low man on the board, the newest person there, sitting at the end of the table between pert Ms. Mary Richards (sex and family relations were her specialty) and dumpy old Alexis Carrington-Colby (nutrition and diets—it was she who had, three months earlier, come up with the blockbuster of the "mother's milk" crisis).

I hoped desperately that either Ms. Richards or Ms. Carrington-Colby would offer some shred of hope for the rest of the board to nibble on, because I knew I had nothing. Nothing except that damning damaging note in my pocket. What if the Boss found out about it? Would he think I was a potential informer, a philandering fink to the Feds?

With deepening despair I listened to flinty-eyed Alexis offer apologies instead of ideas. It was Mary Richards' turn next, and my heart began fluttering unselfishly. I liked her, I was becoming quite enthusiastic about her, almost to the point of asking her romantic questions. I had never dated a sex specialist, or much of anyone, for that matter. Mary was special to me, and I wanted her to succeed.

She didn't. There was no crisis in sex or family relations. "Mr. James," said the Boss, like a bell tolling for a funeral.

I wasn't entitled to a power name, since I had only recently been appointed to the board. My predecessor, Marcus Welby, had keeled over right at this conference table the previous month when he realized that there was no medical crisis in sight. His heart broke, literally. It had been his fourth one, but this time the rescue team was just a shade too late to pull him through again.

Thomas K. James is hardly a power name. But it was the one my parents had bestowed on me, and I was determined not to disgrace it. And in particular, not to let anyone know that someone in this conference room thought I was corruptible.

"Mr. James," asked a nearly weeping All-American Boy, "is there anything on the medical horizon—anything at all—that may be useful to us?"

It was clear that Boss Armstrong did not suspect me of incipient treason. Nor did he expect me to solve his problem. I did not fail him in that expectation.

"Nothing worth raising an eyebrow over, sir, I regret to say." Remarkably, my voice stayed firm and steady, despite the dervishes dancing in my stomach.

"There are no new diseases," I went on, "and the old ones are still in rapid retreat. Genetic technicians can correct every identifiable malady in the zygotes, and children are born healthy for life."

I cast a disparaging glance at Mr. Cosby, our black environmentalist, and added, "Pollution-related diseases are so close to zero that most disease centers around the world no longer take statistics on them."

"Addiction!" Jack Armstrong blurted, the idea apparently springing into his mind unexpectedly. "There must be a new drug on the horizon!"

The board members stirred in their chairs and looked hopeful. For a moment.

I burst their bubble. "Modern chemotherapy detoxifies the addict in about eleven minutes, as some of us know from firsthand experience." I made sure not to stare at Matt Dillon or Alexis Carrington-Colby, who had fought bouts with alcohol and chocolate, respectively. "And, I must unhappily report, cybernetic neural programming is mandatory in every civilized nation in the world; once an addictive personality manifests itself, it can be reprogrammed quickly and painlessly."

The gloom around the table deepened into true depression, tinged with fear.

Jack Armstrong glanced at the miniature display screen discreetly set into the tabletop before him, swiftly checking on his affirmative actions, then said, "Ladies and gentlemen, the situation grows more desperate with each blink of the clock. I suggest we take a five-minute break for R&R"—he meant relief and refreshment—"and then come back with some *new ideas!*"

He fairly roared out the last two words, shocking us all. I repaired to my office—little more than a cubicle, actually, but it had a door that could be shut. I closed it carefully and hauled the unnerving note out of my pocket. Smoothing it on my desk top, I read it again. It still said:

"Make big $$$. Tell all to Feds."

I wadded it again and with trembling hands tossed it into the disposal can. It flashed silently into healthful ions.

"Are you going to do it?"

I wheeled around to see Mary Richards leaning against my door. She had entered my cubicle silently and closed the door without a sound. At least, no sound I had heard, so intent was I on that menacing message.

"Do what?" Lord, my voice cracked like Henry Aldrich's.

Mary Richards (nee Stephanie Quaid) was a better physical approximation to her power name than any one of the board members, with the obvious exception of our revered Boss. She was the kind of female for whom the words cute, pert, and vivacious were created. But beneath those skin-deep qualities she had the ruthless drive and calculated intelligence of a sainted Mike Wallace. Had to. Nobody without the same could make it to the CCC board. if that sounds self-congratulatory, so be it. A real Mary Richards, even a Lou Grant, would never get as far as the front door of the CCC.

"Tell all to the Feds," she replied sweetly.

The best thing I could think of was, "I don't know what you're talking about."

"The note you just ionized."

"What note?"

"The note I put in your pocket before the meeting started."

"You?" Until that moment I hadn't known I could hit high C.

Mary positively slinked across my cubicle and draped herself on my desk, showing plenty of leg through her slit skirt. I gulped and slid my swivel chair into the corner.

"It's okay, there's no bugs operating in here. I cleared your office this morning."

I could feel my eyes popping. "Who are you?"

Her smile was all teeth. "I'm a spy, Tommy. A plant. A deep agent. I've been working for the Feds since I was a little girl, rescued from the slums of Chicago by the Rehabilitation Corps from what would have undoubtedly been a life of gang violence and prostitution."

"And they planted you here?"

"They planted me in Cable News when I was a fresh young thing just off the Rehab Farm. It's taken me eleven years to work my way up to the CCC. We always suspected some organization like this was manipulating the news, but we never had the proof . . ."

"Manipulating!" I was shocked at the word. "We don't manipulate."

"Oh?" She seemed amused at my rightful ire. "Then what do you do?"

"We select. We focus. We manage the news for the benefit of the public."

"In my book, Tommy old pal, that is manipulation. And it's illegal."

"It's . . . out of the ordinary channels," I granted.

Mary shook her pretty chestnut-brown tresses. "It's a violation of FCC regulations, it makes a mockery of the antitrust laws, to say nothing of the SEC, OSHA, ICC, WARK, and half a dozen other regulatory agencies."

"So you're going to blow the whistle on us."

She straightened up and sat on the edge of my desk. "I can't do that, Tommy. I'm a government agent. An agent provocateur, I'm sure Mr. Armstrong's lawyers will call me."

"Then, what—"

"You can blow the whistle," she said smilingly. "You're a faithful employee. Your testimony would stand up in court."

"Destroy," I spread my arms in righteous indignation, "all this?"

"It's illegal as hell, Tom," said Mary. "Besides, the rewards for being a good citizen can be very great. Lifetime pension. Twice what you're making here. Uncle Sam is very generous, you know. We'll fix you up with a new identity. We'll move you to wherever you want to live: Samoa, Santa Barbara, St. Thomas, even Schenectady. You could live like a retired financier."

I had to admit, "That is . . . generous."

"And," she added, shyly lowering her eyes, "of course I'll have to retire too, once the publicity of the trial blows my cover. I won't have the same kind of super pension that you'll get, but maybe . . ."

My throat went dry.

Before I could respond, though, the air-raid siren went off, signaling that the meeting was reconvening.

I got up from my chair, but Mary stepped between me and the door.

"What's your answer, Thomas?" she asked, resting her lovely hands on my lapels.

"I . . ." gulping for air, ". . . don't know."

She kissed me lightly on the lips. "Think it over, Thomas, dear. Think hard."

It wasn't my thoughts that were hardening. She left me standing in the cubicle, alone except for my swirling thoughts, spinning through my head like a tornado. I could hear the roaring in my ears. Or was that simply high blood pressure?

The siren howled again, and I bolted to the conference room and took my seat at the end of the table. Mary smiled at me and patted my knee, under the table.

"Very well," said Jack Armstrong, checking his display screen, "gentlemen and ladies. I have come to the conclusion that if we cannot find a crisis anywhere in the news—" and he glared at us, as if he didn't believe there wasn't a crisis out there somewhere, probably right under our noses—"then we must manufacture a crisis."

I had expected that. So had most of the other board members, I could see. What went around the table was not surprise but resignation.

Cosby shook his head wearily. "We did that last month, and it was a real dud. The Anguish of Kindergarten. Audience response was a negative four-point-four. Negative!"

"Then we've got to be more creative!" snapped The All-American Boy.

I glanced at Mary. She was looking at me, smiling her sunniest smile, the one that could allegedly turn the world on. And the answer to the whole problem came to me with that blinding flash that marks true inspiration and minor epileptic fits.

This wasn't epilepsy. I jumped to my feet. "Mr. Armstrong! Fellow board members!"

"What is it, Mr. James?" Boss Jack replied, a hopeful glimmer in his eyes.

The words almost froze in my throat. I looked down at Mary, still turning out megawatts of smile at me, and nearly choked because my heart had jumped into my mouth.

But only figuratively. "Ladies and gentlemen," (I had kept track, too), "there is a spy among us from the Federal Regulatory Commissions."

A hideous gasp arose, as if they had heard the tinkling bell of a leper.

"This is no time for levity, Mr. James," snapped the Boss. "On the other hand, if this is an attempt at shock therapy to stir the creative juices . . ."

"It's real!" I insisted. Pointing at the smileless Mary Richards, I said, "This woman is a plant from the Feds. She solicited my cooperation. She tried to bribe me to blow the whistle on the CCC!"

They stared. They snarled. They hissed at Mary. She rose coolly from her chair, made a little bow, blew me a kiss, and left the conference room.

Armstrong was already on the intercom phone. "Have security detain her and get our legal staff to interrogate her. Do it now!"

Then the Boss got to his feet, way down there at the other end of the table, and fixed me with his steeliest gaze. He said not a word, but clapped his hands together, once, twice . . .

And the entire board stood up for me and applauded. I felt myself blushing, but it felt good. Warming. My first real moment in the sun.

The moment ended too soon. We all sat down and the gloom began to gray over my sunshine once more.

"It's too bad, Mr. James, that you didn't find a solution to our problem rather than a pretty government mole."

"Ah, but sir," I replied, savoring the opportunity for *le mot just,* "I have done exactly that."

"What?"

"You mean . . . ?"

"Are you saying that you've done it?"

I rose once more, without even glancing at the empty chair at my left.

"I have a crisis, sir," I announced quietly, humbly.

Not a word from any of them. They all leaned forward, expectantly, hopefully, yearningly.

"The very fact that we—the leading experts in the field—can find no crisis is in itself a crisis," I told them.

They sighed, as if a great work of art had suddenly been unveiled.

"Think of the crisis-management teams all around the world who are idle! Think of the psychologists and the therapists who stand ready to help their fellow man and woman, yet have nothing to do! Think of the vast teams of news reporters, camera persons, editors, producers, publishers, even gofers, the whole vast panoply of men and women who have dedicated their lives to bringing the latest crisis into the homes of every human being on this planet—with nothing more to do than report on sports and weather!"

They leaped to their feet and converged on me. They raised me to their shoulders and joyously carried me around the table, shouting praises.

Deliriously happy, I thought to myself, *I won't be at the foot of the table anymore. I'll move up. One day, I'll be at the head of the table, where The All-American Boy is now. He's getting old, burnt out. I'll get there. I'll get there!*

And I knew what my power name would be. I'd known it from the start, when I'd first been made the lowliest member of the board. I'd been saving it, waiting until the proper moment to make the change.

My power name would be different, daring. A name that bespoke true power, the ability to command, the vision to see far into the future. And it wouldn't even require changing my real name that much. I savored the idea and rolled my power name through my mind again as they carried me around the table. Yes, it would work. It was right.

I would no longer be Thomas K. James. With the slightest, tiniest bit of manipulation my true self would stand revealed: James T. Kirk.

I was on my way.

FREE ENTERPRISE

In the Nineteen Seventies much was said and written about the failures of American industry and the successes of the Japanese. Here is a tale that examines an industry I know rather well, publishing, and shows why we are buying our digital book readers from Japan, as well as our automobiles and television sets.

For, although this tale was science fiction when I wrote it, today it's history.

The Idea

It happened at approximately midnight, late in April, when they both should have been studying for their final exams.

Mark Moskowitz (a.k.a. "Mark the Monk") and Mitsui Minimata shared a rented room over one of Berkeley's shabbier head shops, less than a half-mile from the campus. Mark was going for his doctorate in logic; Mitsui was working doggedly toward his in electrical engineering. The few friends they had, years later, claimed that the idea was probably inspired by the various strange aromas wafting up from the shop below their room.

Mark's sobriquet was two-edged: not only did he have the heavy-browed, hairy, shambling appearance of an early homonid; he was,

97

despite his apish looks, exceedingly shy, bookish, and unsocial to the point of reclusiveness. Mitsui was just the opposite: tiny, constantly smiling, excruciatingly polite, and an accomplished conversationalist. Where Mark sat and pondered, Mitsui flashed around the room like an excited electron.

He was struggling with a heavy tome on electrical engineering, just barely managing to stagger across the room with it, heading for his reading chair, when he tripped on the threadbare rug and went sprawling face-first. Mark, snapped out of his glassy-eyed introspection by the thud of his roommate's impact on the floor, spent a moment focusing his far-sighted eyes on the situation. As Mitsui slowly sat up and shook his head groggily, Mark heaved himself up from the sagging sofa which served as his throne, shambled over to his friend, picked the little Japanese up with one hand, the ponderous textbook in the other, and settled them both safely on Mitsui's reading chair.

"Thank you ten thousand times," said Mitsui, after a sharp intake of breath to show that he was unworthy of his friend's kindness.

"You ought to pick on books your own size," Mark replied. For him, that amounted to a sizzling witticism.

Mitsui shrugged. "There *are* no books my size. Not in electrical engineering. They all weigh a metric ton."

Mark glared down at the weighty tome. "I wonder why they still print books on paper. Wouldn't electrons be a lot lighter?"

"Yes, of course. And cheaper, as well."

"H'mm," said Mark.

"H'mm," said Mitsui.

And they never spoke of the idea again. Not to each other, at least.

A month later they received their degrees and went their separate ways.

The Presentation

Gene Rockmore blinked several times at the beetle-browed young man sitting in his office. "Mark M. Moskowitz, Ph.D." the visitor's card said. Nothing else. No phone number or address. Rockmore tried to engage the young man in trivial conversation while studying him. He looked like a refugee from a wrestling school, despite his three-piece suit and conservative tie. Or maybe because of them; the clothes did not seem to be his, they barely fit him, and he looked very uncomfortable in them.

For several minutes Rockmore chatted about the weather, the awful cross-town traffic, and the dangers of being mugged on Manhattan's streets. He received nothing back from his visitor except a few grunts and uneasy wriggles.

Why me? Rockmore asked himself silently. Why do I have to get all the crazies who come in off the street? After all, I'm a vice president now. I ought to be involved in making deals with agents, and taking famous writers out to lunch. At least Charlene's father ought to let me get into the advertising and promotion end of the business. I could be a smash on the Johnny Carson show, plugging our company's books. Instead, I have to sit here and deal with inarticulate ape-men.

Rockmore, who looked like (and was) a former chorus boy in a Broadway musical, slicked back his thinning blond hair with one hand and finally asked, "Well, eh, just what is it you wanted to talk to me about, Mr. Mos—I mean, *Dr.* Moskowitz?"

"Electronic books," said Mark.

"Electronic books?" Rockmore asked.

"Uh-huh." And for the next three hours, Mark did all the talking.

Mitsui hardly spoke at all, and when he did, it was in Japanese, a language both simple and supple. Most of the time, as he sat side-by-side with the vice president for innovation at Kanagawa Electronics and Shipbuilding, Inc., Mitsui tapped out numbers on his pocket computer. The V.P. grinned and nodded and hissed happily at the glowing digits on the tiny readout screen.

The Reception

Robert Emmett Lipton, president of Hubris Books, a division of WPA Entertainment, which is a wholly-owned subsidiary of Moribundic Industries, Inc., which in turn is owned by Empire State Bank (and, it is rumored, the Mafia), could scarcely believe his ears.

"Electronic books? What on earth are electronic books?"

Lipton smiled gently at his son-in-law. It didn't do to get tough with Rockmore. He simply broke down and cried and went home to Charlene, who would then phone to tell her mother what a heel her father was to pick on such a sensitive boy as Gene.

So the president of Hubris Books rocked slowly in his big leather chair and tried to look interested as his son-in-law explained his latest hare-brained scheme. Lipton sighed inwardly, thinking about the time Rockmore suggested to the editorial board that they stop printing books that failed to sell well, and stuck only to best sellers. That was when Rockmore had just graduated from the summer course in management at Harvard. Ten years later, and he still didn't know a thing about the publishing business. But he kept Charlene happy, and that kept Charlene's mother happy, and *that* was the only reason Lipton allowed Rockmore to play at being an executive.

"So it's possible," Rockmore was saying, "to make the thing about the size of a paperback book. Its screen would be the size of a book page, and it could display a page of printed text or full-color illustrations—"

"Do you realize how much color separations cost?" Lipton snapped. Instantly he regretted his harshness. He started to reach for the Kleenex box on the shelf behind his chair.

But Rockmore did not burst into tears, as he usually did. Instead he smirked. "No color separations, Papa. It's all done electronically."

"No color separations?" Lipton found that hard to believe.

"No color separations. No printing at all. No paper. It's like having a hand-sized TV set in your . . . er, hand. But the screen can be any page of any book we publish."

"No printing?" Lipton heard his voice echoing, weakly. "No paper?"

"It's all done by electronics. Computers."

Lipton's mind was in a whirl. He conjured up last month's cost figures. The exact numbers were a blur in his memory, but they were huge—and most of them came from the need to transport vast tonnages of paper from the pulp mills to the printing plants, and then from the printing plants to the warehouses, and then from the warehouses to the wholesalers, and then . . .

He sat up straighter in his chair. "No paper? Are you certain?"

Mitsui bowed low to the president of Kanagawa. The doughty old man, his silver hair still thick, his dark eyes still alert, sat on the matted floor, dressed in a magnificent midnight-blue kimono. He barely nodded his head at the young engineer and the vice president for innovation, both of whom wore Western business suits.

With a curt gesture, he commanded them to sit. For long moments, nothing was said, as the servants brought the tea. The old man let his favorite, a young woman of heartbreakingly fragile beauty, set out the graceful little cups and pour the steaming tea.

Mitsui held his breath until the V.P. nodded to him. Then, from the inside pocket of his jacket, Mitsui pulled out a slim package, exquisitely wrapped in expensive golden gift paper and tied with a silk bow the same color as the president's kimono. He held the gift in outstretched arms, presenting it to the old man.

The president allowed a crooked grin to cross his stern visage. As the v.p. knew, he took a childish pleasure in receiving gifts. Very carefully, the old man untied the bow and peeled away the heavy paper. He opened the box and took out an object the size of a paperback book. Most of its front surface was taken up by a video screen. There were three pressure pads at the screen's bottom, nothing more.

The old man raised his shaggy brows questioningly. The V.P. indicated that he should press the first button, which was a bright green.

The president did, and the little screen instantly showed a listing of titles. Among them were the best-selling novels of the month. By pressing the buttons as indicated, the old man got the screen to display the opening pages of half a dozen books within less than a minute.

He smiled broadly, turned to Mitsui and extended his right hand. He clasped the young engineer's shoulder the way a proud father would grasp his bright young son.

The Evaluation

Lipton sat at the head of the conference table and studied the vice presidents arrayed about him: Editorial, Marketing. Production, Advertising, Promotion, Subsidiary Rights, Legal, Accounting, Personnel, and son-in-law. For the first time in the ten years since Rockmore had married his daughter, Lipton gazed fondly at his son-in-law.

"Gentlemen," said the president of Hubris Books, then, with his usual smarmy nod to the Editor-in-Chief and the head of Subsidiary Rights, "and ladies . . ."

They were shocked when he invited Rockmore to take the floor, and even more startled when the former chorus boy made a fifteen-minute presentation of the electronic book idea without falling over himself. It was the first time Lipton had *asked* his son-in-law to speak at the monthly executive board conference, and certainly the first time Rockmore had anything to say that was worth listening to.

Or was it? The assembled vice presidents eyed each other nervously as Rockmore sat down after his presentation. No one wanted to be the first to speak. No one knew which way the wind was blowing. Rockmore sounded as if he knew what he was talking about, but maybe this was a trap. Maybe Lipton was finally trying to get his son-in-law bounced out of the company, or at least off the executive board.

They all fidgeted in their chairs, waiting for Lipton to give them some clue as to what they were supposed to think. The president merely sat up at the head of the table, fingers steepled, smiling like a chubby, inscrutable Buddha.

The silence stretched out to an embarrassing length. Finally, Editorial could stand it no longer.

"*Another* invasion by technology," she said, her fingers fussing absently with the bow of her blouse. "It was bad enough when we computerized the office. It took my people *weeks* to make the adjustment. Some of them are still at sea."

"Then get rid of them," Lipton snapped. "We can't stand in the way of progress. Technology is the future. I'm sure of it."

An almost audible sigh of relief went around the table. Now they knew where the boss stood; they knew what they were supposed to say.

"Well, of course technology is important," Editorial backtracked, "but I just don't see how an electronic thing-a-majig can replace a *book*. I mean, it's cold . . . metallic. It's a *machine*. A book is . . . well, it's comforting, it's warm and friendly, it's the feel of paper . . ."

"Which costs too damned much," Lipton said.

Accounting took up the theme with the speed of an electronic calculator. "Do you have any idea of what paper costs this company each month?"

"Well, I . . ." Editorial saw that she was going to be the sacrificial lamb. She blushed and lapsed into silence.

"How much would an electronic book sell for?" Marketing asked.

Lipton shrugged. "One dollar? Two?"

Rockmore, from the far end of the table, spoke up. "According to the technical people I've spoken to, the price of a book could be less than one dollar."

"Instead of fifteen to twenty," Lipton said, "which is what our hardcovers are priced at now."

"One dollar?" Marketing looked stunned. "We could sell *zillions* of books at a dollar apiece!"

"We could wipe out the paperback market," Lipton agreed, happily.

"But that would cut off a major source of income for us," cried Sub Rights.

"There would still be foreign sales," said Lipton. "And film and TV rights."

"I don't know about TV," Legal chimed in. "After all, by displaying a book on what is essentially a television screen, we may be construed as utilizing the broadcast TV rights."

The discussion continued right through the morning. Lipton had sandwiches and coffee brought in, and the executive board stayed in conference well past quitting time.

In the port city of Numazu, not far from the blissful snow-covered cone of divine Fujiyama, Kanagawa Industries began the urgent task of converting one of its electronics plants to building the first production run of Mitsui Minimata's electronic book. Mitsui was given the position of advisor to the chief production engineer, who ran the plant with rigid military discipline. His staff of six hundred (five hundred eighty-eight of them robots) worked happily and efficiently, converting the plant from building navigation computers to the new product.

The Resistance

Editorial sipped her Bloody Mary while Sub Rights stared out the restaurant window at the snarling Manhattan midtown traffic. The restaurant was only half-filled, even though this was the height of the lunch-hour rush; the publishing business had been in the doldrums for some time. Suave waiters with slicked-back hair and European accents hovered over each table, anxious to generate tips through quality of service, when it was obvious that quantity of customers was lacking.

Sub Rights was a pale, ash-blonde woman in her late thirties. She had worked for Hubris Books since graduating from Barnard with stars in her eyes and dreams of a romantic career in the world of literature. Her most romantic moment had come when a French publisher's representative had seduced her, at the height of the Frankfurt Book Fair, and thus obtained a very favorable deal on Hubris's entire line of "How To" books for that year.

"I think you've hit it on the head," Sub Rights said, idly stirring her Campari-and-soda with its plastic straw. "Books should be made of *paper*, not this electric machine thing."

Editorial had worked for six publishers in the twelve years since she had arrived in New York from Kansas. Somehow, whenever the final sales figures for the books she had bought became known to management, she was invited to look for work elsewhere. Still, there were plenty of publishing houses in midtown Manhattan which operated on the same principle: fire the editor when sales don't pan out, and then hire an editor fired by one of your competitors for the same reason.

"That's what I think, too," she said. Her speech was just a little blurred, her tinted auburn hair just a bit frazzled. This was her third Bloody Mary and they had not ordered lunch yet.

"I love to curl up with a book. It's cozy," said Sub Rights.

"Books are *supposed* to be made of paper," Editorial agreed. "With pages that you can turn."

Sub Rights nodded unhappily. "I said that to Production, and do you know what *he* said?"

"No. What?"

"He said I was wrong, and that books were supposed to be made of clay tablets with cuneiform marks pressed into them."

Editorial's eyes filled with tears. "It's the end of an era. The next thing you know, they'll replace us with robots."

The chief engineer paced back and forth, hands clasped behind his back, as the two technicians worked feverishly on the robot. The entire assembly area of the factory was absolutely still; not a machine moved, all across the wide floor. Both technicians' white coveralls were stained with sweat and oil, a considerable loss of face for men who prided themselves on keeping their machines in perfect working order.

The chief engineer, in his golden-tan coveralls and plastic hard hat, alternately glared at the technicians and gazed up at the huge digital clock dominating the far wall of the assembly area. Up in the glass-paneled gallery above the clock, he could see Mitsui Minimata's young, eager face peering intently at them.

A shout of triumph from one of the technicians made the chief engineer spin around. The technician held a tiny silicon chip delicately between his thumb and forefinger, took two steps forward and offered the offending electronic unit to the chief engineer. The chief took it, looked down at the thumbnail-sized chip, so small and insignificant-seeming in the palm of his hand. Hard to believe that this tiny grain of sand caused the robot to malfunction and ruined an entire day's work. He sighed to himself, and thought that this evening, as he relaxed in a hot bath, he would try to compose a haiku on the subject of how small things can cause great troubles.

The junior of the two technicians, in the meantime, had dashed to the automated supply dispenser across the big assembly room, dialed up a replacement chip, and come running back with the new unit pressed between his palms. The senior technicians installed it quickly, buttoned up the robot's access panel, turned and bowed to the chief engineer.

The chief grunted a grudging approval. The junior technician bowed to the chief and asked permission to activate the robot. The chief nodded. The robot stirred to life, and it too bowed to the chief engineer. Only then did production resume.

The Sales Manager for Hubris Books stroked his chin thoughtfully as he sat behind his desk conversing with his western district sales director.

"But if they ever start selling these electronic doohickeys," the western district man was saying, "they'll bypass the wholesalers, the distributors, even the retail stores, for cryin' out loud! They'll sell those little compter disks direct to the customer! They'll sell 'em through the mail!"

"And over the phone," the Sales Manager added wearily. "They're talking about doing the whole thing electronically."

"Where's that leave us?"

"Out in the cold, buddy. Right out in the cold."

The Decision

Robert Emmett Lipton was not often nervous. His position in life was to make other people nervous, not to get the jitters himself. But he was not often summoned to the office of the CEO of Moribundic Industries. Lipton found himself perspiring as the secretary escorted him through the cool, quiet, elegantly carpeted corridors toward the CEO's private suite.

It wasn't as if he had been asked to report to the bejewelled jackass who headed WPA Entertainment, out in Los Angeles. Lipton could deal with him. But the CEO was different; he had the real power to make or break a man.

The secretary was a tall, lissome, devastatingly beautiful woman: the kind who could marry a millionaire and then ruin him. In the deeper recesses of his mind, Lipton thought it would be great fun to be ruined by such a creature.

She opened the door marked ALEXANDER HAMILTON STARK, CHIEF EXECUTIVE OFFICER and smiled at Lipton. He thought there was a trace of sadness in her smile, as if she never expected to see him again— alive.

"Thank you," Lipton managed, as he stepped into the CEO's private office.

He had seen smaller airport terminals. The room was vast, richly carpeted, furnished with treasures from the Orient in teak and ebony, copper, silver, and gold. Far, far across the room, the CEO sat behind his broad, massive desk of rosewood and chrome. its gleaming surface was uncluttered.

Feeling small and helpless, like a pudgy little gnome suddenly summoned to the throne of power, Lipton made his way across the vast office, plowing through the thick carpeting with leaden steps.

The CEO was an ancient, hairless, wrinkled, death's head of a figure, sitting hunched and aged in a high-backed leather chair that dwarfed him. For a ridiculous instant, Lipton was reminded of a turtle sitting there, staring at him out of dull reptilian eyes. With something of a shock, he suddenly realized that there was a third man in the room: a younger man, swarthy, dark of hair and jaw, dressed in a European-cut silk suit, sitting to one side of the massive desk.

Lipton came to a halt before the desk. There was no chair there, so he remained standing.

"Mr. Stark," he said. "I'm so happy that you've given me this opportunity to report directly to you about the electronic book project."

"You'll have to speak louder," the younger man said. "His batteries are running down."

Lipton turned slightly toward him. "And you are?"

"I'm Mr. Stark's personal secretary and bodyguard," the young man said.

"Oh."

"We hear that Hubris Books is in hock up to its elbows on this electronic book thing," the bodyguard said.

"I wouldn't . . ." Lipton stopped himself, turned toward the CEO and said, louder, "I wouldn't put it that way. We're pushing ahead on a very difficult project."

"Don't give up the ship," the CEO muttered.

"We don't intend to, sir," said Lipton. "It's quite true that we've encountered some difficulties in the electronic book project, but we are moving right ahead."

"I have not yet begun to fight!" said the CEO.

Lipton felt himself frown slightly, puzzled. The bodyguard said, "Our sources of information say that morale at Hubris is very low. And so are sales."

"We're going through a period of adjustment, that's true . . ."

"Millions for defense," the CEO's quavering voice piped, "but not one cent for tribute."

"Sir?" Lipton felt confused. What was the CEO driving at?

"Your costs are shooting through the roof," the bodyguard accused.

Lipton felt perspiration beading his upper lip. "We're involved in a very difficult project. We're working with one of the nation's top electronics firms to produce a revolutionary new concept, a product that will totally change the book business, It's true that we've had problems—technical as well as human problems. But—"

"We have met the enemy," croaked the CEO, "and they are ours."

"I don't want to be overly critical," said the bodyguard-cum-secretary, with a smirk on his face that belied his words, "but you seem to have gotten Hubris to a point where sales are down, costs are up, and profits will be a long time coming."

"But, listen," Lipton replied, trying to keep his voice from sounding as if he were begging, "this concept of electronic books is going to sweep the publishing industry! We'll be able to publish books for a fraction of what they cost now, and sell them directly to the readers! Our sales volume is projected to triple, the first year we're on the market, and our profit margin . . ."

"Fifty-four forty or fight!" cackled the CEO.

"What?" Lipton blurted.

The bodyguard's smile seemed knowing, cynical. "We've seen your projections. But they're all based on the assumpton that you'll have the electronic books on the market next year. We don't believe you can do that, not at the rate you're going now."

"As I said, we've had some problems here and there." Lipton was starting to feel desperate. "We contracted with Moribundic's electronics division, at first, to make the damned things, but they flubbed the job completely. They produced a monstrosity that weighed seventeen pounds and didn't work half the time."

The CEO shook his wizened head. "My only regret is that I have but one life to give for my country."

Suppressing an urge to run screaming out of the room, Lipton slogged forward. "The company we're working with now is based in Silicon Valley, in California. At least they've got the electronics right. But they've got problems with their supply of parts. Seems there's a trucker's strike in Texas, where the chips are being manufactured. This has caused a delay."

"And in the meantime, Hubris' sales are sinking out of sight."

"The whole book industry is in a bad way . . ."

The bodyguard raised his dark eyebrows half an inch, as if acknowledging the point. "But we're hearing complaints about poor morale in the office. Not just down in the pits, but among your own executive board."

Lipton growled, "Those dimwitted idiots can't see any farther than their own paychecks! They're afraid that the electronic book is going to take away their jobs."

"Your profit-and-loss projections are based, in part, on eliminating most of their jobs, aren't they?"

"Well, yes, of course. We won't need them anymore."

The CEO's frail voice became mournful. "It is for us, the living, rather to be dedicated here to the unfinished work . . ." His voice sank to an unintelligible mumble, then rose again to conclude, ". . . that these dead shall not have died in vain."

As if the CEO were not in the room with them, or at least not in the same plane of reality, the bodyguard launched into a detailed analysis of Lipton's electronic book project. He referred to it specifically as Lipton's project. Hubris Books' president felt sweat trickling down his ribs. His hands shook and his feet hurt as he stood there defending every dollar he had spent on the idea.

Finally, the bodyguard turned to the CEO, who had sat unmoving and silent for the past hour.

"Well, sir," he said, "that brings us up to date on the project. The potential for great profits is there, but at the rate we're going, the cost will drag the entire corporation's P-and-L statement down into the red ink."

The CEO said nothing; he merely sat hunched in his oversized chair, watery eyes blinking slowly.

"On the other hand," the bodyguard went on, "our tax situation should be vastly improved by all these losses. If we continue with the electronic book project, we won't have to worry about the IRS for the next three years, at least."

Lipton wanted to protest, to shout to them that the electronic book was more than a tax dodge. But his voice was frozen in his throat.

"What's your decision, sir?" the bodyguard asked.

The CEO lifted one frail hand from his desktop and slowly clenched it into a fist. "Damn the torpedoes! Full steam ahead!"

The Result

Mitsui Minimata held his breath. Never in his happiest dreams had he entertained the idea that he would someday meet the Emperor face to face, in the Imperial Palace. Yet here he was, kneeling on a silken carpet, close enough to the Divine Presence to touch him.

Arrayed around Mitsui, also kneeling with eyes respectfully lowered, were the head of Kanagawa Industries, the vice president for innovation, and the chief engineer of the Numazu plant. All were dressed in ceremonial kimonos more gorgeous than Mitsui would have thought it was possible for human hands to create.

The Emperor was flanked by serving robots, of course. It was fitting that the Divine personage not be touched by human hands. Besides, his decision to have robots serve him presented the Japanese people with an example of how these new devices should be accepted into every part of life.

With trembling hands Mitsui placed the first production unit of the electronic book in the metal fingers of the robot that stood between him and the Emperor. The robot pivoted, making hardly more noise than the heel of a boot would on a polished floor, and extended its arm to the Emperor.

The Emperor peered through his glasses at the little electronic package, then picked it up. He had been instructed, of course, on how to use the book. But for an instant Mitsui was frightened that somehow the instructions had not been sufficient, and the Emperor would be embarrassed by being unable to make the book work. Suicide would be the only way out, in that case.

After what seemed like several years of examining the book, the Emperor touched the green pressure pad at its base. Mitsui knew what would come up on the screen: a listing of all the books and papers that the Emperor himself had written in the field of marine biology.

The Divine face broke into a pleased smile. The smile broadened as the Emperor pecked away at the book's controls, bringing one after another of his own writings to the book's page-sized screen. He laughed with delight, and Mitsui realized that mortal life offered no higher reward than this.

Mark Moskowitz paced angrily back and forth across his one-room apartment as he argued with the image of his attorney on the phone screen.

"But they're screwing me out of my own invention!" he yelled.

The attorney, a sad-eyed man with an expression of utter world-weariness, replied, "Mark, when you accepted their money you sold them the rights to the invention."

"But they're lousing it up! Three years now and they still haven't produced a working model that weighs less than ten pounds!"

"There's nothing you can do about it," said the attorney. "It's their ball."

"But it's my idea! My invention!"

The attorney shrugged.

"You know what I think?" Mark growled, pacing back to the phone and bending toward the screen until his nose almost touched it. "I think Hubris Books doesn't *want* to make the project succeed! I think they're screwing around with it just to give the whole idea a bad name and make certain that no other publisher will touch it, by the time they're finished."

"That's silly," said the attorney. "Why would they—"

"Silly?" Mark snapped. "How about last year, when they tried to make the picture screen feel like paper? How about that scheme they came up with to have a hundred separate screens that you could turn like the pages of a book? Silly? They're *crazy!*"

They argued fruitlessly for nearly half an hour, and finally Mark punched the phone's OFF button in a fury of frustration and despair. He sat in glowering, smoldering anger in the one-room apartment as the afternoon sun slowly faded into the shadows of dusk.

Only then did he remember why he had placed the call to his attorney. The package from Tokyo. From Mitsui. When it had arrived, Mark had gone straight to the phone to see what progress his suit against Hubris Books was making. The answer, of course, had been: zero.

With the dejected air of a defeated soldier, Mark trudged to the table by his hotplate where he had left the package. Terribly afraid that he knew what was inside the heavy wrappings, he nonetheless opened the package as delicately, as tenderly, as if it contained newborn kittens.

It contained a newborn, all right. An electronic book, just as Mark had feared. No message, no card. Nothing but the book itself.

Mark held it in the palm of his left hand. It weighed a little more than a pound. he judged. Three pads were set below the screen, marked with Arabic numerals and Japanese characters. He touched the green one, which was marked "1."

A still picture of Mitsui appeared on the screen, grinning—no, *beaming*—at him. The amber pressure pad, marked "2," began to blink. Mark touched it.

A neatly typed letter appeared on the screen:

Dear Friend Mark:

    Please accept this small token of my deep friendship for you. In a few days your news media will be filled with stories about Kanagawa Industries' revolutionary new electronic book. I will tell every reporter I speak to that the idea is just as much yours as mine, which is nothing less than the truth.

As you may know, trade agreements between your government and mine will make it impossible for Japan to sell electronic books in the U.S.A. However, it should be permissible for us to form an American subsidiary of Kanagawa in the United States. Would you consider accepting the position of chief scientist, or a post of similar rank, with this new company? In that way, you can help to produce electronic books for the American market.

Please phone me at your earliest convenience . . .

Mark read no further. He ran to the phone. He did not even bother to check what time it was in Tokyo. As it happened, he interrupted Mitsui's lunch, but the two ex-roommates had a happy, laughing talk together, and Mark agreed to become vice president for innovation of the planned Kanagawa-U.S.A. subsidiary.

The Moral
Victor Hugo was right when he said that no army can withstand the strength of an idea whose time has come. But if you're narrow-minded enough, both the time and the idea can pass you by.

VISION

We can talk about the practical benefits of going into space: the fortunes to be made in zero-gravity manufacturing, the benefits of new medicines and materials produced in orbit. But there is the human aspect to consider also.

Philosophers have long argued over whether human history is molded by the daring actions of extraordinary men and women, or whether history responds to implacable, inevitable natural forces which individual human actions can do little to bend or shape.

"Vision" might just help you to decide which side of that argument you are on. Then again, it might just add a little weight to both sides of the argument.

"BUT IF YOU LIVE IN ORBIT, you can live forever!" Don Arnold said it in sheer frustration and immediately regretted opening his mouth.

Picture the situation. Don was sitting under the glaring lights of a TV studio, in a deep fake-leather couch that looked comfortable but wasn't. His genial talk-show host had ignored him totally since introducing him as "one of NASA's key scientists." (Don was a NASA engineer, and pretty far from the top.)

On one side of Don sat a UFOlogist, a balding, owlishly bespectacled man with a facial tic and a bulging briefcase clutched in his lap, full of Important Documents.

On Don's other side sat a self-proclaimed Mystic of indeterminate age, a benign smile on his face, his head shaved and a tiny gem in his left earlobe.

They had done all the talking since the show had started, nearly an hour earlier.

"The government has all sorts of data about UFOs," the UFOlogist was saying, hugging his battered briefcase. "NASA has tons of information about how the saucers are built and where they're coming from, but they won't release any of this to the people."

Before Don could reply, the Mystic raised both his hands, palms outward. The cameras zoomed in on him.

"All of the universe is a single entity, and all of time is the same," he said in a voice like a snake charmer's reed flute. "Governments, institutions, all forms of society are merely illusions. The human mind is capable of anything, merely by thinking transcendentally. The soul is immortal—"

That's when Don burst out, "But if you live in orbit, you can live forever!"

It surprised them all, especially Don. The Mystic blinked, his mouth still silently shaped for his next pronouncement. The UFOlogist seemed to curl around his briefcase even tighter. The studio audience out there beyond the blinding glare of the overhead lights surged forward in their chairs and uttered a collective murmur of wonderment.

Even the talk show's host seemed stunned for just a moment. he was the best-dressed man on the set, in a deep blue cashmere sports jacket and precisely creased pearl gray slacks. He was the only man on camera in makeup. His hairpiece gave him a youthful-yet-reliable look.

The host swallowed visibly as Don wished he could call back the words he had just blurted.

"They live forever?" the host asked, so honestly intrigued that he forgot to smile.

How in hell can I backtrack out of this? Don asked himself desperately.

Then the Mystic started to raise his hands again, his cue to the cameras that he wanted their attention on him.

"Our studies have shown that it's possible," Don said, leaning forward slightly to stare right into the host's baby-blue eyes.

"How long have people lived in space, anyway?" the host asked.

"The record is held by two Russian cosmonauts, aboard their space station. They were up there for almost nine months. Our Skylab team was up for eighty-three days, back in '73-'74."

Don could sense the UFOlogist fidgeting beside him, but the host asked, "And they did experiments up there that showed you could live longer if you stayed in space?"

"Lots of experiments have been done," Don answered before anyone else could upstage him, "both in orbit and on the ground."

"On . . . immortality?"

"We tend to call it life extension," Don said truthfully. "But it's quite clear that in orbit, where you can live under conditions of very low gravity, your heart doesn't have to work so hard, your internal organs are under much less stress . . ."

"But don't your muscles atrophy? Isn't there calcium loss from the bones?"

"No," Don said flatly. All three cameras were aimed squarely at him. Normally he was a shy man, but nearly an hour of listening to the other two making a shambles of organized thought had made him sore enough to be bold.

"It doesn't?"

"It takes a lot of hard work to move around in low gravity," Don answered. "With a normal work routine, plus a few minutes of planned exercise each day, there's no big muscle-tone loss. In fact, you'd probably be in better condition if you lived in a space station than you are here on Earth."

"Fascinating!" said the host.

"As for calcium loss, that levels off eventually. It's no real problem."

"And then you just go on living," the host said, "forever?"

"For a long, long time," Don hedged. "On a space station, of course, your air is pure, your water's pure, the environment is very carefully controlled. There are no carcinogens lousing up the ecology. And you have all the benefits of low gravity."

"I never knew that! Why hasn't NASA told us about this?"

As Don fished around in his mind for a reply, the host turned on his smile and fixed his gaze on camera one.

"Well, it always seems that we run out of time just when things are really interesting." Glancing back along his guests on the couch, he said, "Dr. Arnold, that was fascinating. I hope you can come back and talk with us again, real soon."

Before Don could answer, the host said farewell to the two other guests, mispronouncing both their names.

Don sat up in bed, his back propped by pillows, the sheet pulled up to his navel. It was hot in the upstairs bedroom now that they had to keep the air-conditioner off, but he stayed covered because of the twins. They were nine now, and starting to ask pointed questions.

Judy was putting them into their bunk beds for the night, but they had a habit of wandering around before they finally fell asleep. And Judy, good mother that she was, didn't have the heart to lock the master bedroom door. Besides, on a sultry night like this, the only way to catch a breath of breeze was to keep all the doors and windows open.

Don played a game as he sat up watching television, the remote-control wand in his sweating hand. He found the situation comedies, police shows, doctor shows, even the TV science-fiction shows, so boring that he couldn't bear to watch them for their own sake.

But they were tolerable—almost—if he watched to see how much space-inspired technology he could identify in each show. The remote monitors in the surgeon's intensive-care unit. The sophisticated sensors used by the coroner's hot-tempered pathologist. The pressure-sensitive switch on the terrorists' bomb planted in the cargo bay in the threatened airliner.

Judy finally came in and began undressing. The bedroom lights were out, but there was plenty of light coming from the TV screen.

"Better close the door, hon," Don told her as she wriggled her skirt down past her hips. "The twins—"

"They're both knocked out," she said. "They spent all day in the Cramers' pool."

"Still . . ." He clicked off the TV's sound and listened for the patter of nine-year-old feet.

His wife's body still turned him on. Judy was short, a petite dark-haired beauty with flashing deep-brown eyes and a figure that Don thought of as voluptuous. She stripped off her panties and crawled into the bed beside Don.

Grinning at him, she said, "You worry too much."

"Yeah, maybe I do."

"I thought you were terrific on the show this afternoon. I got so mad when those other two clowns kept hogging the camera!"

"Maybe I should have let them hog it for the whole show," he said.

"No you shouldn't! I sat here for nearly an hour waiting for you to open your mouth."

"Maybe I should've kept it closed."

"You were terrific," she said, snuggling closer to him.

"I was lying," he answered. "Or at least stretching the truth until it darn near snapped."

"You looked so handsome on television."

"I just hope nobody at Headquarters saw the show."

"It's a local talk show," Judy said. "Nobody watches it but housewives."

"Yeah."

He started to feel better, especially with Judy cuddling next to him, until almost the very end of the eleven o'clock news. Then they showed a film clip of him staring earnestly into the camera—*I thought I was looking at the host*, Don thought—and explaining how people who live in orbit will live forever.

Don saw his whole career passing in from of his eyes.

He made sure to get to his office bright and early the next morning, taking a bus that arrived on Independence Avenue before the morning traffic buildup. Don was at his desk, jacket neatly hung behind the door and shirt sleeves rolled up, going over the cost figures for yet another study of possible future options for the Office of Space Transportation Systems, when his phone buzzed.

"Uncle Sam wants yew," rasped Jack Hardesty's voice in the phone receiver.

He saw the show! was Don's first panicked thought.

"You there, Mr. Personality!" Hardesty demanded.

"Yeah, Jack, I'm here."

"Meeting, Kluge's office, in five minutes." The phone clicked dead.

Don broke into a sweat.

Otto von Kluge was as American as the Brooklyn Bridge, but many and various were the jokes around NASA Headquarters about his name, his heritage and his abilities. He was an indifferent engineer, a terrible public speaker, and a barely adequate administrator. But he was one of the few people in the office who had a knack for handling other people—from engineers to congressmen, from White House whiz kids to crusty old accountants from the Office of Management and Budget.

Despite the low setting of the building's air-conditioning, von Kluge wore his suit jacket and even a little bow tie under his ample chin. Don always thought of him as a smiling, pudgy used-car salesman. But once in a great while he came across as a smiling, pudgy Junker land baron.

Hardesty—bone-thin, lantern-jawed, permanently harried—was already perched on the front half-inch of a chair at one side of von Kluge's broad desk, puffing intensely on a cigarette.

Don entered the carpeted office hesitantly, feeling a little like the prisoner on his way to the guillotine.

Von Kluge grinned at him and waved a hand in the general direction of the only other available chair.

"Come on in, Don. Sit down. Relax."

Just like the dentist says, Don thought.

"The TV station is sending me a tape of your show," von Kluge said, with no further preliminaries.

"Oh," said Don, feeling his guts sink. "That."

Laughing, von Kluge said. "Sounds to me like you're bucking for a job in the PR department."

"Uh, no, I'm not. I mean—"

"Sounds to me," Hardesty said as he ground his cigarette butt into von Kluge's immaculate stainless-steel ashtray—"like you're bucking for a job selling brushes door to door!"

"Now don't get your blood pressure up, Jack," von Kluge said easily. "Most of the crimes of this world come out of overreacting to an innocent little mistake."

An overwhelming sense of gratitude flooded through Don. "I really didn't mean to do it," he said. "It's just that—"

"I know, I know," von Kluge said. "Your first time on television. The thrill of show business. The excitement, takes your breath away, doesn't it?"

Don nodded. Hardesty glowered at him.

"Let's just see the tapes and find out what you really said," von Kluge went on. "I'll bet you don't remember yourself, do you, Don?"

"No . . . not exactly."

Shrugging, von Kluge said, "It's probably no big deal. We'll just play it cool until it all blows over."

The office door opened slightly and Ms. Tucker, a black secretary of such sweetness and lithe form that she could make bigots vote probussing, said softly:

"Phone for you, Dr. von Kluge."

"I can't be disturbed now, Alma."

"It's Senator Buford," she said, in an awed whisper.

Von Kluge's eyes widened. "Excuse me," he said to Don and Hardesty as he reached for his phone.

He smiled broadly and said, "Senator Buford, sir! Good morning! How are you—"

And that was all he said for the next twenty-two minutes. Von Kluge nodded, grunted, closed his eyes, gazed at the ceiling, stared at Don as he listened.

Finally he put the phone down, slowly, wearily, like a very tired man at last letting go of an enormous weight. His ear was red.

Looking sadly at Don, von Kluge said, "Well, son, the Senator wants you to appear at his Appropriations Committee hearing. Tomorrow morning."

Don had expected the hearing chamber to be packed with newsmen, cameras, lights, crowds, people grabbing at him for interviews or comments.

Instead, the ornate old chamber was practically empty, except for the few senators who had shown up for their committee's session and their unctuous aides. Even the senators themselves seemed bored and fidgety as a series of experts from various parts of NASA and the Office of Management and Budget gave conflicting testimony on how much money should be appropriated for the space program.

But flinty old Senator Buford, the committee's chairman, sat unflinchingly through it all. His crafty gray eyes drilled holes through every witness; even when he said nothing, he made the witnesses squirm in their seats.

Don was the last scheduled witness before the lunch break, and he kept hoping that they would run out of time before they called on him. Hardesty and von Kluge had drilled him all night in every aspect of the space agency's programs and budget requests. Don's head hadn't felt SO burstingly full of facts since his senior year in college, when he had crammed for three days to get past a Shakespeare final exam.

By the time Don sat himself cautiously in the witness chair, only four senators were left at the long baize-covered table facing him. It was a few minutes past noon, but Senator Buford showed no inclination to recess the hearing.

"Mistah Arnold," Buford drawled, "have you prepared a statement for this committee?"

"Yes, sir, I have." Don leaned forward to speak into the microphone on the table before him, even though there was no need to amplify his voice in the nearly empty, quiet room.

"In view of the hour—" Buford turned *hour* into a two-syllable word—"we will dispense with your reading your statement and have it inserted into the record as 'tis. With your permission, of course."

Don felt sweat beading on his forehead and upper lip. "Certainly, sir." His statement was merely the regular public relations pamphlet the agency put out, extolling its current operations and promising wonders for the future.

Senator Buford smiled coldly. Don thought of a rattlesnake coiled to strike.

"Now what's this I heah," the Senator said, "'bout livin' in space prolongin' your life?"

Don coughed. "Well, sir, if you're referring to . . . ah, to the remarks I made on television—"

"I am, suh."

"Yes, well, you see . . . I had to oversimplify some very complex matters, because . . . you realize . . . the TV audience isn't prepared . . . I mean, there aren't very many scientists watching daytime television talk shows."

Buford's eyes bored into Don. "Ah'm not a scientist eitheh, Mr. Arnold. I'm jest a simple ol' country lawyer tryin' to understand what in the world you're talkin' 'bout."

And in a flash of revelation, Don saw that Senator Buford was well into his eighties. His skin was creased and dry and dead-gray. The little hair left on his head was wispy and white. Liver spots covered his frail, trembling hands. Only his eyes and his voice had any spark or strength to them.

A phrase from the old Army Air Corps song of Don's childhood skipped through his memory: *We live in fame or go down in flames.*

Taking a deep breath and sitting up straighter in the witness chair, Don said. "Well, sir, there are two ways to look at any piece of information—optimistically or pessimistically. What I'm about to tell you is the optimistic view. I want you to understand that clearly, sir. I will be interpreting the information we have on hand in its most optimistic light."

"You go right ahead and do that," said Senator Buford.

They lunched in the Senate dining room: dry sherry, mock turtle soup, soft-shell crabs. Just the two of them at a small table, Don and Senator Buford.

"I finally got me a NASA scientist who can talk sense," Buford was saying as he cut through one of the little crabs.

Don's head was still reeling. "You know, Senator, that there will be lots of experts inside NASA and outside who'll make some pretty strong arguments against me."

Buford fixed him with a baleful eye. "Mebbe so. But they won't get away with any arguments 'gainst me, boy."

"We can't guarantee anything, you realize," Don hedged. "I could be completely wrong."

"Ah know. But like you said, if we don't try, we'll never know for sure."

This has got to be a dream, Don told himself. *I'm home in bed and I'll have to get up soon and go testify before Buford's committee.*

"Now lessee what we got heah," Buford said as the liveried black waiter cleared their dishes from the table. "Y'all need the permanent space station—with a major medical facility in it."

"Yessir. And the all-reusable shuttle."

Buford looked at Don sharply. "What's wrong with the space shuttle we got? Cost enough, didn't it?"

"Yessir, it did. But it takes off like a rocket. Passengers pull three or four gees at launch. Too much, for . . ."

"For old geezers like me!" Buford laughed, a sound halfway between a wheeze and a cackle.

Don made his lips smile, then said, "An advanced shuttle would take off like an airplane, nice and smooth. Anybody could ride in it."

"Uh-huh. How long'll it take to get it flyin'?"

Don thought a moment, considered the state of his soul, and decided, *What the hell, go for broke.*

"Money buys time, Senator," he said craftily. "Money buys time."

Senator Buford nodded and muttered, mostly to himself, "I finally got a NASA scientist who tells me the truth."

"Sir, I want you to realize the whole truth about what I've been telling you—"

But Buford wasn't listening. "Senator Petty will be our major obstacle. Scrawny little Yankee—thinks he's God's chosen apostle to watch out over the federal budget. He'll give us trouble."

The name of Senator Petty was known to make scientists weep. NASA administrators raced to the bathroom at the sound of it.

Buford waggled a lean, liver-spotted hand in Don's general direction. "But don't you worry none 'bout Petty. Ah'll take care o' him! You just concentrate on gettin' NASA to bring me a detailed program for that space station—with the medical center in it."

"And the advanced shuttle," Don added, in a near whisper.

"Yeh, of course. The advanced shuttle, too. Can't ride up there to your geriatrics ward in th' sky on a broomstick, now can I?"

"The twins were twelve years old today."

Don looked up from the report he was writing. It had been nearly midnight by the time he'd gotten home, and now it was well past one.

"I forgot all about their birthday," he confessed.

Judy was standing in the doorway of his study, wrapped in a fuzzy pink housecoat. There were lines in her face that Don hadn't noticed before. Her voice was sharper than he'd remembered.

"They could both be in jail for all you think about them!" she snapped. "Or me, for that matter."

"Look, honey. I've got responsibilities . . ."

"Sure! The big-shot executive. All day long he's running NASA and all night long he's out at parties."

"Meetings," Don said defensively. "It's tough to deal with congressmen and senators in their offices—"

"Meetings with disco bands and champagne and lots of half-naked secretaries prancing around!"

"Judy, for God's sake, I'm juggling a million and one details! The space station, the flyback shuttle booster, and now Senator Buford's in the hospital."

"I hope he drops dead and Petty cuts your balls off!" Judy looked shocked that the words could have come from her mouth. She turned and fled from the room.

Don gave out a long, agonized sigh and leaned back in his desk chair. For a moment he wanted to toss the report he was writing into the wastebasket and go up to bed with his wife.

But he knew he had to face Senator Petty the next morning, and he had to be armed for the encounter. He went back to his writing.

"I think you're pulling the biggest boondoggle this nation's ever seen since the Apollo project," said Senator Petty, smiling.

Don was sitting tensely in a big leather chair in front of the Senator's massive oak desk. On Don's left, in an equally sumptuous chair, sat Reed McCormack, NASA's chief administrator, the space agency's boss and a childhood chum of the President.

McCormack looked like a studious, middle-aged banker who kept in trim playing tennis and sailing racing yachts. Which was almost entirely true. He was not studious. He had learned early in life that you can usually buy expertise—for a song. His special talent was making people trust him.

Senator Petty didn't trust anyone.

From the neck up the Senator looked like a movie idol: brilliant white straight teeth (capped); tanned, taut handsome face (lifted, twice); thick, curly, reddish-brown hair (implanted and dyed). Below the neck, however, his body betrayed him. Despite excruciating hours of jogging and handball, his stomach bulged and his chest was sunken.

"A boondoggle?" McCormack asked easily. "Your colleagues in the Senate don't seem to think so."

Petty's smile turned acid. "Funny thing about my fellow senators. The older they are, the more money they want to appropriate for your gold-plated space station. Why do you think that is?"

"Age brings wisdom," said McCormack.

"Does it?" Petty turned his mud-brown eyes on Don. "Or is it that you keep telling them they can live forever, once they're up in your orbital old-age home?"

"I've never said that," Don snapped. His nerves were frayed, he realized, as much by Senator Buford's hospitalization as by Judy's growing unhappiness.

"Oh, you've been very careful about what you've said, and to whom, and with what qualifications," Petty replied. "But they all get the same impression: Live in space and you live forever. NASA can give you immortality—if you vote the funds for it."

"That is not our policy," McCormack said firmly.

"The hell it isn't," Petty snapped. "But old Bufe's terminal, they tell me. You won't have him to steer your outrageous funding requests through the Senate. You'll have to deal with me."

Don knew it was true, and saw the future slipping away from his grasp.

"That's why we're here," McCormack said. "To deal."

Petty nodded curtly.

"If you try to halt construction on the space station, your colleagues will outvote you overwhelmingly," said McCormack.

"Same thing applies to the new shuttle," Don added.

Petty leaned back in his chair and steepled his fingers. "I know that. But I can slow you down. OMB isn't very happy with your cost overruns, you know. And I can always start an investigation into this so-called science of life extension. I can pick a panel of experts that will blow your immortality story out of the water."

For the first time, McCormack looked uneasy.

"There's no immortality 'story,'" Don said testily. "We've simply reported the conclusions of various studies and experiments. We've been absolutely truthful."

"And you've allowed the senators to believe that if they live in orbit they can all become Methuselahs," Petty laughed. "Well, a couple of biologists from Harvard and Berkeley can shoot you down inside a week—with the proper press coverage. And I can see to it that they get the coverage."

Don gripped the arms of his chair and tried to hold onto his temper. "Senator Buford is dying and you're already trying to tear down everything he worked to achieve."

Petty grinned mischievously. "You bet I am."

"What do you want from us?" McCormack asked.

The Senator's grin faded slowly.

"I said we're here to deal with you," McCormack added, speaking softly. "The President is very anxious to keep this program going. Its effect on the national economy has been very beneficial, you realize."

"So you say."

"What do you want?" McCormack repeated.

"The ground-based medical center that's going to be built as part of your life-extension program—"

"In your state?"

"Yes," said Petty.

McCormack nodded. "I see no reason why that can't be done. It would be rather close to the Mayo Clinic, then, wouldn't it?"

"And one other thing," Petty said.

"What is it?"

He pointed at Don. "I want this man—Senator Buford's dear friend—to personally head up the space station operation."

Don felt his incipient ulcer stab him as McCormack's face clouded over.

"Mr. Arnold is program manager for the space station program already," McCormack said, "and also serves as liaison to the advanced shuttle program office."

"I know that," Petty snapped. "But I want him up there, in the space station, with the first permanent crew."

Don stared at the Senator. "Why . . . ?"

Petty gave him a smirk. "You think living up in space is such a hot idea, let's see *you* try it."

Senator Buford's intensive-care bed looked more like a spacecraft command module than a hospital. Electronics surrounded the bed, monitoring the dying old man. Oscilloscope traces wriggled fitfully, lights blinked in rhythm to his sinking heartrate, tubes of nutrients and fresh blood fed into his arteries.

Don had to lean close to the old man's toothless sunken mouth to hear his wheeze:

"'Preciate your comin' to see me. Got no family left, y'know."

Don nodded and said nothing.

"Looks like I cain't hold out much longer," the Senator whispered. "How's the space station comin' along?"

"We've got Petty behind it," Don answered. "For a price."

Buford smiled wanly. "Good. Good. You'll get the whole Senate behind you. They're all gettin' older. They'll all want to go . . . up there."

"I'm only sorry that we're not ready to take you."

Cackling thinly, Buford said. "But I'm goin'! Ah made all the arrangements. They're gonna freeze me soon's I'm clinically dead. And then I'm gonna be sent up to your space station. I'll stay froze until the science fellas figure out how to cure this cancer I got. Then they'll thaw me out and I'll live in orbit. I'll outlive all o' you!" He laughed again.

"I hope you do," Don said softly. "You deserve to."

"Only trouble is, once I'm froze I won't need that advanced shuttle to boost me into orbit. Coulda saved th' taxpayers all that money if I'd known. I can ride the regular ol' shuttle, once I'm dipped in that liquid nitrogen stuff."

He was still cackling to himself as Don tiptoed out of his room.

"I'm coming home, honey! For once, I'll be home in time for the twins' birthday."

Don was floating easily in his "office": a semicircular desk welded into a bulkhead in the zero-gee section of the space station. There was no need for chairs; a few looped straps bolted to the deck sufficed to keep one from drifting too far from one's work.

Don took a good look at his wife's face as it appeared in the telephone screen of his desk. Her mouth was a thin, tight line. There were crow's feet at the corners of her eyes. Her hair was totally gray.

"What happened to your hair?" he asked. "It wasn't like that the last time we talked, was it?"

"I've been dyeing it for years and you never noticed," Judy said, her voice harsh, strained. "The style is gray this year. Now I dye it so it's all gray."

"That's the style?" Don glanced at his own reflection in the darkened window above his desk. His hair was still dark and thick.

"How would you know anything about fashion," Judy snapped, "living up in that tin can in the sky?"

"But I'm coming home early this year," Don said. "Things are going well enough so I can get away a whole month earlier than I thought. I'll be there in time for the twins' birthday."

"Don't bother," Judy said.

"What? But the kids—"

"The kids are nineteen and they don't want their Mommy and Daddy embarrassing them, espcially on their birthday. They want to be with their friends, out on the farm they've set up."

"Farm?"

"In Utah. They've joined the Church of the Latter Day Saints."

"Mormons? Our kids?"

"Yes."

Don felt confused, almost scared. "I've got to talk with them. They're too young to—"

But Judy was shaking her gray head. "They won't be here to talk with. And neither will I."

He felt it like a body blow as he hung there weightlessly, defenselessly, staring into the screen.

"I'm getting a divorce, Don," Judy said. "You're not a husband to me. Not two months out of every twelve. That's no marriage."

"But I asked you to come up here with me!"

"I've been living with Jack Hardesty the past six months," she said, almost tonelessly, it was so matter-of-fact. "He's asked me to marry him. That's what I'm going to do."

"Jack Hardesty? Jack?"

"You can live up there and float around forever," Judy said. "I'm going to get what happiness I can while I'm still young enough to enjoy it."

"Judy, you don't understand—"

But he was talking to a blank screen.

Don had to return to Earth for the official opening ceremonies of Space Station Alpha. It was a tremendous international media event, with special ceremonies in Washington, Cape Canaveral, Houston and the new life-extension medical center in Senator Petty's home state.

It was at the medical center ceremonies that Petty pulled Don aside and walked him briskly into an immaculate, new, unused men's room.

Leaning on the rim of a sparkling stainless-steel sink, Petty gave Don a nervous half-smile.

"Well, you got what you wanted," the Senator said, "How do you feel about it?"

Don shrugged. "Kind of numb, I guess. After all these years, it's hard to realize that the job is done."

"Cost a whole lot of the tapayers' money," Petty said.

Gesturing at the lavish toilet facility, Don riposted. "You didn't pinch any pennies here, I notice."

Petty laughed, almost like a little boy caught doing something naughty, "Home-state contractors. You know how it is."

"Sure."

"I guess you'll want to start living here on the ground full-time again," Petty said.

Don glared at him. "Oh? Am I allowed to? Is our deal completed?"

With an apologetic spread of his hands, Senator Petty said, "Look, I admit that it was a spiteful thing for me to do."

"It wrecked my marriage. My kids are total strangers to me. I don't even have any friends down here anymore."

"I'm . . . sorry."

"Stuff it."

"Listen." The Senator licked his thin lips. "I . . . I've been thinking maybe I won't run for re-election next time around. Maybe . . . maybe I'll come up and see what it's like living up there for a while."

Don stared at him for a long, hard moment. And saw that there was a single light brown spot about the size of a dime on the back of the Senator's right hand.

"You want to live in the space station?"

Petty tried to make a nonchalant shrug. "I've . . . been thinking about it."

"Afraid of old age?" Don asked coldly. "Or is it something more specific?"

Petty's face went gray. "Heart," he said. "The doctors tell me I'll be in real trouble in another few years. Thanks to the technology you guys have developed, they can spot it coming that far in advance now."

Don wanted to laugh. Instead, he said, "If that's the case, you'd better spend your last year or two in the Senate pushing through enough funding to enlarge the living quarters in the space station."

Petty nodded. Grimly.

"And you should introduce a resolution," Don added, "to give the station an official name: the Senator Robert E. Buford Space Center."

"Now that's too much."

Don grinned at him. "Tell it to your doctors."

There was no reason for him to stay on Earth. Too many memories. Too few friends. He felt better in orbit. Even in the living sections of the Buford Space Center, where the spin-induced gee forces were close to Earth-normal gravity, Don felt more alive and happier. His friends were there, and so was his work.

Don had been wrong to think that his job was finished once the space station was officially opened. In reality, his work had merely begun.

A year after the station was officially opened, von Kluge came aboard as a retiree. His secretary, Alma Tucker, still lithe and wonderful despite the added years, came up to work for Don. They were married, a year later. Among the witnesses was Senator Petty, the latest permanent arrival.

The Buford Space Center grew and grew and grew. Its official name was forgotten after a few decades, it was known everywhere as Sky City.

Sky City became the commercial hub of the thriving space industries that reached out across the solar system. Sky City's biomedical labs became system-famous as they took the lead in producing cures for the various genetic diseases known collectively as cancer.

Ex-Senator Petty organized the first zero-gee Olympics and participated personally in the Sky City-Tranquility Base yacht race.

Von Kluge, restless with retirement, became an industrial magnate and acquired huge holdings in the asteroid belt: a Junker land baron at last.

Alma Tucker Arnold became a mother—and a prominent low-gravity ballerina.

Don stayed in administration and eventually became the first mayor of Sky City.

The election was held on his ninety-ninth birthday, and he celebrated it by leading a bicycle race all around the city's perimeter.

The next morning, his first official act as mayor was to order the thawing of Senator Buford. The two of them spent their declining centuries in fast friendship.

MOON RACE

It matters not if you win or lose, it's how you play the game.

Yeah, maybe.

"Moon Race" is set on the Moon, at a time when that airless, barren little world is the frontier of human expansion beyond Earth.

It's a hard and dangerous frontier. As one insightful man once put it, "Pioneering boils down to inventing new ways to get yourself killed."

But even on the most arduous and demanding of frontiers, the human spirit will invent new ways of entertainment, too. No human community has ever been all work and no play.

Each form of entertainment has its own particular rules. Breaking the rules, even bending them, can get a player disqualified.

It doesn't matter if you win or lose? The hell it doesn't!

John Henry, he said to his captain,
"A man ain't nothing but a man.
"And before I'll let your steam drill beat me
"I'll die with a hammer in my hand,
"Lawd, Lawd,
"I'll die with a hammer in my hand."

USUALLY, gazing out across the crater floor to the weary old ringwall mountains with the big, blue, beautiful Earth hanging in the black sky above—usually it fills my heart with peace and calm.

But not today.

My palms are sweaty while I wait for the GO signal. There are six of us lined up in our lunar buggies, ready to race out to the old *Ranger 9* site and back again to Selene's main airlock. Two hundred and some kilometers, round trip. If I follow the path the race officials have laid out.

I'm sitting at the controls of a five-meter-tall, six-legged lunar vehicle that we've nicknamed Stomper. We designed it to haul freight and carry cargo over rough ground, not for racing. The five other racers are also converted from working lunar vehicles, but they're either wheeled or tracked: they can zip along at speeds up to thirty klicks per hour, if you push them.

I've got to win this race or get sent back to dirty, dangerous, overcrowded Earth.

See, Harry Walker and I started this design company, Walker's Walkers, while I was still his student at Selene University. Put every penny we had into it. Now we've built our prototype, Stomper, and we've got to prove to everybody that a legged vehicle can work out on the Moon's surface as well or better than anything with wheels or tracks.

So we entered the race. Harry's a paraplegic. If we win, he'll be able to afford stem cell therapy to rebuild his legs. If we don't win, Walker's Walkers goes bust, he stays in his wheelchair, and I get sent back Earthside. It's Selene's one hard rule: if you don't have a job you get shipped out. You either contribute to Selene's economy or you're gone, man, gone. There's no room for freeloaders. No charity. No mercy.

The light on my control board flashes green and I push Stomper's throttle forward carefully. We're off with a lurch and a bump.

Stomper's six legs start thumping along as I edge the throttle higher. But Zeke Browkowski zips out ahead of the rest of the pack, just like I figured he would.

"So long, slowpokes," he sings out as he pulls farther in front. "Hey, Taylor," he calls to me, "why don't you get out and push?" I can hear him laughing in my headphones.

Zeke's in Dash-nine, the newest buggy in Selene, of course. His older brother runs the maintenance section and makes certain he does well by Zeke.

Even though Stomper's cabin is pressurized, I'm suited up, helmet and all. It's uncomfortable, but if I have to go outside for emergency maintenance during the race I won't have to take the time to pull on the cumbersome suit.

Selene City is built into the base of Mt. Yeager, the tallest mountain in the ringwall of the giant crater Alphonsus. Two-thirds of the way across the crater floor lie the remains of *Ranger 9*, one of the early unmanned probes from back in the days before Armstrong and Aldrin landed over in the Sea of Tranquility.

There's been some talk about expanding Selene beyond Alphonsus' ringwall, going out onto the Mare Nubium and even farther. But so far it's only talk. Selene is restricted to Alphonsus, for now.

I figure the run out to the *Ranger 9* site and back to Selene's main airlock should take on the order of ten hours. Zeke Browkowski will try to make it faster, of course. Knowing him, I'll bet he's souped up Dash-nine with extra fuel cells, even though that's against the race rules.

Harry teaches mechanical design at the university, from his wheelchair. He had the ideas for Walker's Walkers and I did his legwork, so to speak. I've got to win this race and show everybody what Stomper can do. Harry can keep his professorship at the university even if we lose. But I'll have to go back to Detroit, Michigan, USA, Earth. I've worked too long and too hard to go back to that cesspool.

I need to win this race!

Stomper's lumbering along like some monster in a horror vid. Sitting five meters above the ground, I can see Zeke's Dash-nine pulling farther ahead of us, kicking up a cloud of dust as it rolls across the crater floor on its big springy wheels. In the Moon's low gravity the dust just hangs there like a lazy cloud.

"Come on, Stomper," I mutter to myself as we galumph past the solar-cell farms spread out on the crater floor. "It's now or never." I nudge the throttle a notch higher.

Stomper's six legs speed up, but not by much. It's like sitting on top of a big mechanical turtle with six heavy metal feet. I have to be careful: if I push too hard I could burn out a bearing. Stomper's slow enough on six legs; if we lose one we'll be out of it altogether.

Zeke's pulling farther ahead while ol' Stomper's six feet pound along the dusty bare ground. Lots of little pockmark craterlets scattered across the floor of Alphonsus, and plenty of rocks, some big as houses. Stomper's automated guidance sensors walk us around the more dangerous ones, but I get a kick out of smashing the smaller stones into powder.

It's a real hoot, sitting five meters tall with Stomper's control panel spread out in front of me, feeling all that power, watching the rock-strewn ground go by. Harry would love to be up here, I bet, in control even though his own legs are useless.

Stomper has a lot of power, all right, but not enough speed to catch Dash-nine or even the slower vehicles. Like the turtle against a quintet of hares. But I have a plan. I'm going to take a shortcut.

The race's official course from Selene's main airlock to the *Ranger 9* site is a dogleg shape, because the buggies have to detour around the hump of rugged hills in the center of Alphonsus. I figure that ol' Stomper can climb those hills, thread through 'em and get to the *Ranger 9* site ahead of everybody else. Then I'll come back the same way and win the race!

That's my plan.

For now I follow the trail of lighted poles that mark the race course. Dash-nine is so far ahead that all I can see of Browkowski is a cloud of dust near the short horizon. Three of the other vehicles are ahead of me, too, but I see that the fourth one of them is stopped dead, its two-man crew outside in their suits, bending over a busted track.

I flick to the suit-to-suit frequency and get a blast of choice language from the pair of 'em.

"You guys all right?" I call to them.

Moans and groans and elaborate profanity. But neither one of them is hurt and Selene's already sending a repair tractor to pick them up.

I push on. I can see the tired old slumped hills of the crater's central peak rising just over the horizon. I turn Stomper toward them.

Instantly my earphones sing out, "Taylor Reed, you're veering off course." Janine's voice. She sounds upset.

"I'm taking a shortcut," I say.

"That's not allowed, Taylor."

The race controller is Janine Al-Jabbar, as sweet and lovely a lady as you could find. But now she sounds uptight, almost fearful.

"I've studied the rules," I tell her, keeping my voice calm, "and there's nothing in 'em says you *have to* follow the course they've laid out."

"It's a safety regulation," she answers, sounding even more worried. "You can't go off on your own."

"Janine, there's no problem with safety. Ol' Stomper can—"

A man's voice breaks in. "Taylor Reed, get back on course or you're disqualified!"

That's Mance Brunner, the director of the race. He's also chancellor of Selene University. Very important person, and he knows it.

"Disqualified?" My own voice comes out as a mouse squeak. "You can't disqualify me just because—"

"Get back on course, Reed," says Brunner, less excited but harder, colder. "Otherwise I'll have no option except to disqualify you."

I take a deep breath, then I reply as calmly as I can, "Sir, I am continuing on my own course. This is not a safety risk, nor is it grounds—"

He doesn't even hear me out. "You're disqualified, Reed!"

"But—"

"Attention all vehicles," Brunner announces. "Taylor Reed in vehicle oh-four is hereby disqualified."

None of the other racers says a word, except for Zeke Browkowski, who snickers, "Bye-bye, turtle guy."

To say I am pissed off is putting it very mildly. Brunner never did like me, but what he's just done is about as low and rotten as you can get. And there's no way around it, he's the race director. There's no court of appeals. If he says I'm out, I'm *out*.

Stomper's still clunking along, but I reach for the control yoke to turn us around and head back to Selene.

But I hesitate. Disqualify me, huh? Okay, so I'm disqualified. I'm not going to let that stop me. Brunner can yell all he wants to, I'm going to push through those hills and prove my point, even if it's just to myself.

Janine's voice comes back in my earphones, low and kind of sad. "I'm sorry, Tay. He was standing right over my shoulder. There was nothing I could do."

"Not your fault, Janine," I tell her. "You didn't do anything to feel sorry about."

But in the back of my mind I realize that if I have to go back Earthside I'll never see her again.

Well, disqualified or not, I head out for the *Ranger 9* site by the most direct route: across the central hills.

They look like dimples in the satellite imagery, but as ol' Stomper gets closer to them, those rounded slumped hills rise up in front of me like a real barrier. They're not steep, and not really all that high, but those slopes are worn almost as smooth as glass. There's no air on the Moon, you know, and for eons micrometeorites the size of dust motes have been falling in from space and sandpapering the hills.

I start to wonder if Stomper can really climb across them. There aren't any trails or passes, just a jumbled knot of rocks rising up from the plain of the crater floor. Sigurdsen tried going up them in a wheeled buggy back before Selene became an independent nation; he found the going too treacherous and turned back. Nobody's bothered since then. There's nothing in those bare knobby hills that's worth the effort.

I throttle down and shift to a lower gear.

"Easy does it, Stomper," I mutter. "You can do it. I know you can."

One step at a time, like a turtle on tiptoes, we pick our way through the jumbled rocks. I'm pouring sweat by the time we get near the top. Inside the space suit you can boil in your own juices, you know.

"Are you singing?" Janine's voice asks me.

"What?"

"Sounds like you were singing to yourself, Tay," she says, sounding kind of concerned.

I realize I must have been humming to myself, sort of. An old folk song my grandfather used to sing, about a railroad worker named John Henry.

"I'm okay," I tell her.

"Dr. Brunner's really hacked at you," Janine says. "He's sore you haven't turned back."

"He's gonna have to be sore a while longer," I answer tightly.

Stomper clomps along up the worn old rocks and we get to the top. Off in the distance I can see the crumpled wreckage of *Ranger 9*. I have to be even more careful going downhill, making sure each one of Stomper's six feet are solidly planted with each step. No slipping, no sliding.

Easing my way down the hills is even scarier than going up. Ol' Stomper lurches hard; for an instant I'm scared that we're going to tip over. But Stomper plants those big feet of his solidly and we're okay. Still, my hands are slippery with perspiration as I jiggle the throttle and the gear shifts.

We get down, back on the crater floor and start thumping along as fast as we can to the *Ranger 9* wreckage. Out on the horizon to my left I spot a hazy cloud of dust heading my way. It's Zeke, in Dash-nine. The turtle has beaten the hare!

"Vehicle oh-four reporting," I sing into my lip microphone. "I'm approaching the *Ranger* site."

"Pay no attention to Taylor Reed," Brunner's icy voice answers immediately. "He's been disqualified."

Bastard! I walk Stomper right up to the crumpled remains of *Ranger 9*, under its protective dome of clear glassteel, and use the external arms to plant my marker by the old wreckage. Then I turn around and start for home.

I ought to slow down, I know. I can't win the flicking race, I've been disqualified. So what's the difference? But then I hear Zeke call, "Dash-nine at *Ranger* site. Starting my return leg."

And again I remember that old, old folk song my grandfather used to sing when things got really bad. About John Henry, a black man who refused to give up. And I thought, I'll be damned if I let Zeke Browkowski or Mance Brunner or anybody else beat me. I'll die with a hammer in my hands, Lawd, Lawd.

"Come on, you ol' turtle," I mutter to Stomper. "Let's get home before Zeke does."

Stomper weaves through the hills again and we're back down on the flat. We clomp along at a pretty fair clip, but then I see Browkowski off to my right, a cloud of dust coming around the hills and heading straight for home.

It's turning into a two-car race. I'm way ahead but Zeke is catching up fast. I can see him in the rear-view screen, a cloud of dust that's getting closer every second.

I'm pushing too hard. Stomper's middle left leg starts making a grinding noise. My control panel shows a blinking yellow light. The leg's main bearing is starting to overheat.

I shut down the middle left leg altogether; just keep it locked up and off the ground. Stomper limps the rest of the way back to Selene's main airlock. It's a rough, jouncing ride but we get there a whole two minutes, eighteen seconds ahead of Zeke.

Who is proclaimed the official winner of the race, of course.

I limp Stomper through the main airlock and into Selene's big, cavernous garage, power down, and duck through the hatch. Five meters high, I can see the crowd gathering around Browkowski and Dash-nine: Brunner and Zeke's older brother, the chief of maintenance, a bunch of other people. Even Janine.

Nobody's waiting for me at the bottom of Stomper's ladder except Harry, sitting in his powerchair and grinning up at me.

I'll die with a hammer in my hand. The words to that old song kept ringing in my mind. I was dead all right. Just like ol' John Henry.

Once I plant my boots on the garage's concrete floor, I slide my helmet visor up and take a look at Stomper. His legs are covered with dust, even the middle left one, which is still hanging up there like some ponderous mechanical ballet dancer doing a pose.

"Better keep your distance," I tell Harry. "My coveralls are soaked with perspiration. I'm gonna smell pretty ripe when I peel off this suit."

He's grinning at me, big white teeth sparkling against his dark skin. "I'll go to the infirmary and get some nose plugs," he says.

He rolls his chair alongside me as I clump to the lockers where the suits are stored. I take off the helmet and then sit wearily on the bench to remove my big, thick-soled boots. As I start to worm my arms out of the sleeves, Janine shows up.

I stand up, my arms half in the suit's sleeves. Janine looks pretty as ever, but kind of embarrassed.

"I'm sorry you were disqualified, Tay," she says.

"Not your fault," I mumble.

She tries to smile. "There's a sort of party over to the Pelican Bar."

"For Zeke. He's the winner."

"You're invited, too."

Before I can refuse, Harry pipes up. "We'll be there!"

Janine's smile turns genuine. "Good. I'll see you there, okay?" And she scampers off.

I scowl at Harry. "Why'd you say yes? I don't feel like partying. 'Specially for Zeke."

"Chill out, Taylor," Harry tells me. "All work and no play, you know."

So we go off to the Pelican Bar—after I take a quick shower and pull on a fresh set of coveralls. The Pelican's owned by some fugitive from Florida; he's got the place decorated with statues of pelicans, photographs of pelicans, painting of pelicans. Behind the bar there's a big screen display of Miami, the way it looked before the greenhouse floods covered it over. Lots of pelicans flying over the water, diving for fish.

The place is jammed. Bodies three, four deep around the long bar. Every booth filled. Noise like a solid wall. I take two steps inside the door and decide to turn around and leave.

But Harry grabs my wrist and tows me through the boisterous crowd, like a tractor dragging some piece of wreckage.

He takes me right up to Zeke Browkowski, of all people, who's standing at the bar surrounded by admirers. Including Janine.

"Hey, here's the turtle guy!" Zeke yells out, grinning at me. My hands clench into fists but I don't say anything.

To my total shock, Zeke sticks out his hand to shake. "Taylor, you beat me. You broke the rules, but you beat me, man. Congratulations."

Surprised, I take his hand and mutter, "Lotta good it's done me."

Still grinning, Zeke half-turns to the guy standing next to him. He's an oriental: older, grayer, wearing a regular suit instead of coveralls, like the rest of us.

"Taylor, this is Hideki Matsumata. He designed Dash-nine."

Matsumata bows to me. On reflex, I bow back.

"You have made an important contribution, Mr. Reed."

"Me?"

Smiling at me, Matsumata says, "I was certain that my Dash-nine couldn't be beaten. You proved otherwise."

I can't figure out why he was smiling about it. I hear myself say, "Like Zeke says, I broke the rules."

"You bent the rules, Mr. Reed. Bent them. Sometimes rules need to be bent, stretched."

I didn't know what to say.

Glancing down at Harry, in the powerchair beside me, Matsumata says, "Today you showed that walking vehicles can negotiate mountainous territory that wheeled or tracked vehicles cannot."

"That's what walkers are all about," says Harry. "That's what I was trying to tell you all along."

"You have proved your point, Professor Walker," Matsumata says. But he's looking at me as he says it.

Harry laughs and says, "Soon's we get that bad bearing replaced, Tay, you're going to take Stomper up to the top of Mt. Yeager. And then maybe you'll do a complete circumnavigation of the ringwall."

"But I don't have a job."

"Sure you do! With Walker's Walkers. I haven't fired you."

"The company's not busted?"

Harry's big grin is my answer. But Matsumata says, "Selene's governing council has wanted for some time to build a cable-car tramway over the ringwall and out onto Mare Nubium. Walking vehicles such as your Stomper will make that project possible."

"We can break out of the Alphonsus ringwall and start to spread out," Harry says. "Get down to the south polar region, where the ice deposits are."

My head's spinning. They're saying that I can stay here on the Moon, and even do important work, valuable work.

Zeke claps me on the shoulder. "You done good, turtle guy."

"By breaking the rules and getting disqualified," I mutter, kind of stunned by it all.

Janine comes up and slips her hand in mine. "What was it you were singing during the race? Something about dying with a hammer in your hand?"

"John Henry," I mumble.

"Wrong paradigm," says Harry, with a laugh.

"Whattaya mean?"

"The right paradigm for this situation is an old engineer's line: Behold the lowly turtle, he only makes progress when he sticks his neck out."

SCHEHERAZADE AND THE STORYTELLERS

As we said earlier, one of the great attractions of the field of science fiction is its vast scope: all of the universe, the past, present and future are potential settings for science fiction stories.

In the tale that follows, we go back to ancient Baghdad at its most magnificent, in the time of turbaned sultans and the beautiful, clever and courageous Scheherazade of The Thousand and One Nights.

But was she really that clever and courageous?

"**I NEED A NEW STORY!**" exclaimed Scheherazade, her lovely almond eyes betraying a rising terror. "By tonight!"

"Daughter of my heart," said her father, the grand vizier, "I have related to you every tale that I know. Some of them, best beloved, were even true!"

"But, most respected father, I am summoned to the sultan again tonight. If I have not a new tale with which to beguile him, he will cut off my head in the morning!"

The grand vizier chewed his beard and raised his eyes to Allah in supplication. He could not help but notice that the gold leaf adorning the ceiling is his chamber was peeling once more. *I must call the workmen again*, he thought, his heart sinking.

For although the grand vizier and his family resided in a splendid wing of the sultan's magnificent palace, the grand vizier was responsible for the upkeep of his quarters. The sultan was no fool.

"Father!" Scheherazade screeched. "Help me!"

"What can I do?" asked the grand vizier. He expected no answer.

Yet his beautiful, slim-waisted daughter immediately replied, "You must allow me to go to the Street of the Storytellers."

"The daughter of the grand vizier going into the city! Into the bazaar! To the street of those loathsome storytellers? Commoners! Little better than beggars! Never! It is impossible! The sultan would never permit you to leave the palace."

"I could go in disguise," Scheherazade suggested.

"And how could anyone disguise those ravishing eyes of yours, my darling child? How could anyone disguise your angelic grace, your delicate form? No, it is impossible. You must remain in the palace."

Scheherazade threw herself onto the pillows next to her father and sobbed desperately, "Then bid your darling daughter farewell, most noble father. By tomorrow's sun I will be slain."

The grand vizier gazed upon his daughter with true tenderness, even as her sobs turned to shrieks of despair. He tried to think of some way to ease her fears, but he knew that he could never take the risk of smuggling his daughter out of the palace. They would both lose their heads if the sultan discovered it.

Growing weary of his daughter's wailing, the grand vizier suddenly had the flash of an idea. He cried out, "I have it, my best beloved daughter!"

Scheherazade lifted her tear-streaked face.

"If the Prophet—blessed be his name—cannot go to the mountain, then the mountain will come to the Prophet!"

The grand vizier raised his eyes to Allah in thanksgiving for his revelation and he saw once again the peeling gold leaf of the ceiling. His heart hardened with anger against all slipshod workmen, including (of course) storytellers.

And so it was arranged that a quartet of burly guards was dispatched that very morning from the sultan's palace to the street of the storytellers, with orders to bring a storyteller to the grand vizier without fail. This they did, although the grand vizier's hopes fell once he beheld the storyteller the guards had dragged in.

He was short and round, round of face and belly, with big round eyes that seemed about to pop out of his head. His beard was ragged, his clothes tattered and tarnished from long wear. The guards hustled him into the grand vizier's private chamber and threw him roughly onto the mosaic floor before the grand vizier's high-backed, elaborately carved chair of sandalwood inlaid with ivory and filigrees of gold.

For long moments the grand vizier studied the storyteller, who knelt trembling on the patched knees of his pantaloons, his nose pressed to the tiles of the floor. Scheherazade watched from the veiled gallery of the women's quarters, high above, unseen by her father or his visitor.

"You may look upon me," said the grand vizier.

The storyteller raised his head, but remained kneeling. His eyes went huge as he took in the splendor of the sumptuously appointed chamber. *Don't you dare look up at the ceiling,* the grand vizier thought.

"You are a storyteller?" he asked, his voice stern.

The storyteller seemed to gather himself and replied with a surprisingly strong voice, "Not merely *a* storyteller, oh mighty one. I am *the* storyteller of storytellers. The best of all those who—"

The grand vizier cut him short with, "Your name?"

"Hari-ibn-Hari, eminence." Without taking a breath, the storyteller continued, "My stories are known throughout the world. As far as distant Cathay and the misty isles of the Celts, my stories are beloved by all men."

"Tell me one," said the grand vizier. "If I like it you will be rewarded. If not, your tongue will be cut from your boastful throat."

Hari-ibn-Hari clutched at his throat with both hands.

"Well?" demanded the grand vizier. "Where's your story?"

"Now, your puissance?"

"Now."

Nearly an hour later, the grand vizier had to admit that Hari-ibn-Hari's tale of the sailor Sinbad was not without merit.

"An interesting fable, storyteller. Have you any others?"

"Hundreds, oh protector of the poor!" exclaimed the storyteller. "Thousands!"

"Very well," said the grand vizier. "Each day you will come to me and relate to me one of your tales."

"Gladly," said Hari-ibn-Hari. But then, his round eyes narrowing slightly, he dared to ask, "And what payment will I receive?"

"Payment?" thundered the grand vizier. "You keep your tongue! That is your reward!"

The storyteller hardly blinked at that. "Blessings upon you, most merciful one. But a storyteller must eat. A storyteller must drink, as well."

The grand vizier thought that perhaps drink was more important than food to this miserable wretch.

"How can I continue to relate my tales to you, oh magnificent one, if I faint from hunger and thirst?"

"You expect payment for your tales?"

"It would seem just."

After a moment's consideration, the grand vizier said magnanimously, "Very well. You will be paid one copper for each story you relate."

"One copper?" squeaked the storyteller, crestfallen. "Only one?"

"Do not presume upon my generosity," the grand vizier warned. "You are not the only storyteller in Baghdad."

Hari-ibn-Hari looked disappointed, but he meekly agreed, "One copper, oh guardian of the people."

Six weeks later, Hari-ibn-Hari sat in his miserable little hovel on the Street of the Storytellers and spoke thusly to several other storytellers sitting around him on the packed-earth floor.

"The situation is this, my fellows: the sultan believes that all women are faithless and untrustworthy."

"Many are," muttered Fareed-al-Shaffa, glancing at the only female storyteller among the men, who sat next to him, her face boldly unveiled, her hawk's eyes glittering with unyielding determination.

"Because of the sultan's belief, he takes a new bride to his bed each night and has her beheaded the next morning."

"We know all this," cried the youngest among them, Haroun-el-Ahson, with obvious impatience.

Hari-ibn-Hari glared at the upstart, who was always seeking attention for himself, and continued, "But Scheherazade, daughter of the grand vizier, has survived more than two months now by telling the sultan a beguiling story each night."

"A story stays the sultan's bloody hand?" asked another storyteller, Jamil-abu-Blissa. Lean and learned, he was sharing a *hooka* water pipe with Fareed-al-Shaffa. Between them, they blew clouds of soft gray smoke that wafted through the crowded little room.

With a rasping cough, Hari-ibn-Hari explained, "Scheherazade does not finish her story by the time dawn arises. She leaves the sultan in such suspense that he allows her to live to the next night, so he can hear the conclusion of her story."

"I see!" exclaimed the young Haroun-el-Ahson. "Cliffhangers! Very clever of her."

Hari-ibn-Hari frowned at the upstart's vulgar phrase, but went on to the heart of the problem.

"I have told the grand vizier every story I can think of," he said, his voice sinking with woe, "and still he demands more."

"Of course. He doesn't want his daughter to be slaughtered."

"Now I must turn to you, my friends and colleagues. Please tell me your stories, new stories, fresh stories. Otherwise the lady Scheherazade will perish." Hari-ibn-Hari did not mention that the grand vizier would take the tongue from his head if his daughter was killed.

Fareed-al-Shaffa raised his hands to Allah and pronounced, "We will be honored to assist a fellow storyteller in such a noble pursuit."

Before Hari-ibn-Hari could express his undying thanks, the bearded, gnomish storyteller who was known throughout the bazaar as the Daemon of the Night, asked coldly, "How much does the sultan pay you for these stories?"

Thus it came to pass that Hari-ibn-Hari, accompanied by Fareed-al-Shaffa and the graybearded Daemon of the Night, knelt before the grand vizier. The workmen refurbishing the golden ceiling of the grand vizier's chamber were dismissed from their scaffolds before the grand vizier asked, from his chair of authority:

"Why have you asked to meet with me this day?"

The three storytellers, on their knees, glanced questioningly at one another. At length, Hari-ibn-Hari dared to speak.

"Oh, magnificent one, we have provided you with a myriad of stories so that your beautiful and virtuous daughter, on whom Allah has bestowed much grace and wisdom, may continue to delight the sultan."

"May he live in glory," exclaimed Fareed-al-Shaffa in his reedy voice.

The grand vizier eyed them impatiently, waiting for the next slipper to drop.

"We have spared no effort to provide you with new stories, father of all joys," said Hari-ibn-Hari, his voice quaking only slightly. "Almost every storyteller in Baghdad has contributed to the effort."

"What of it?" the grand vizier snapped. "You should be happy to be of such use to me—and my daughter."

"Just so," Hari-ibn-Hari agreed. But then he added, "However, hunger is stalking the Street of the Storytellers. Starvation is on its way."

"Hunger?" the grand vizier snapped. "Starvation?"

Hari-ibn-Hari explained, "We storytellers have bent every thought we have to creating new stories for your lovely daughter—blessings upon her. We don't have time to tell stories in the bazaar anymore—"

"You'd better not!" the grand vizier warned sternly. "The sultan must hear only new stories, stories that no one else has heard before. Otherwise he would not be intrigued by them and my dearly loved daughter would lose her head."

"But, most munificent one," cried Hari-ibn-Hari, "by devoting ourselves completely to your needs, we are neglecting our own. Since we no longer have the time to tell stories in the bazaar, we have no other source of income except the coppers you pay us for our tales."

The grand vizier at last saw where they were heading. "You want more? Outrageous!"

"But, oh far-seeing one, a single copper for each story is not enough to keep us alive!"

Fareed-al-Shaffa added, "We have families to feed. I myself have four wives and many children."

"What is that to me?" the grand vizier shouted. He thought that these pitiful storytellers were just like workmen everywhere, trying to extort higher wages for their meager efforts.

"We cannot continue to give you stories for a single copper apiece," Fareed-al-Shaffa said flatly.

"Then I will have your tongues taken from your throats. How many stories will you be able to tell then?"

The three storytellers went pale. But the Daemon of the Night, small and frail though he was in body, straightened his spine and found the strength to say, "If you do that, most noble one, you will get no more stories and your daughter will lose her life."

The grand vizier glared angrily at the storytellers. From her hidden post in the veiled gallery, Scheherazade felt her heart sink. Oh father! she begged silently, be generous. Open your heart.

At length the grand vizier muttered darkly, "There are many storytellers in Baghdad. If you three refuse me I will find others who will gladly serve. And, of course, the three of you will lose your tongues. Consider carefully. Produce stories for me at one copper apiece, or be silenced forever."

"Our children will starve!" cried Fareed-al-Shaffa.

"Our wives will have to take to the streets to feed themselves," wailed Hari-ibn-Hari.

The Daemon of the Night said nothing.

"That is your choice," said the grand vizier, as cold and unyielding as a steel blade. "Stories at one copper apiece or I go to other storytellers. And you lose your tongues."

"But magnificent one—"

"That is your choice," the grand vizier repeated sternly. "You have until noon tomorrow to decide."

It was a gloomy trio of storytellers who wended their way back to the bazaar that day.

"He is unyielding," Fareed-al-Shaffa said. "Too bad. I have been thinking of a new story about a band of thieves and a young adventurer. I think I'll call him Ali Baba."

"A silly name," Hari-ibn-Hari rejoined. "Who could take seriously a story where the hero's name is so silly?"

"I don't think the name is silly," Fareed-al-Shaffa maintained. "I rather like it."

As they turned in to the Street of the Storytellers, with ragged, lean and hungry men at every door pleading with passersby to listen to their tales, the Daemon of the Night said softly, "Arguing over a name is not going to solve our problem. By tomorrow noon we could lose our tongues."

Hari-ibn-Hari touched reflexively at his throat. "But to continue to sell our tales for one single copper is driving us into starvation."

"We will starve much faster if our tongues are cut out," said Fareed-al-Shaffa.

The others nodded unhappily as they plodded up the street and stopped at al-Shaffa's hovel.

"Come in and have coffee with me," he said to his companions. "We must think of a way out of this problem."

All four of Fareed-al-Shaffa's wives were home, and all four of them asked the storyteller how they were expected to feed their many children if he did not bring in more coins.

"Begone," he commanded them—after they had served the coffee. "Back to the women's quarters."

The women's quarters was nothing more than a squalid room in the rear of the hovel, teeming with noisy children.

Once the women had left, the three storytellers squatted on the threadbare carpet and sipped at their coffee cups.

"Suppose this carpet could fly," mused Hari-ibn-Hari.

Fareed-al-Shaffa h'mphed. "Suppose a genie appeared and gave us riches beyond imagining."

The Daemon of the Night fixed them both with a somber gaze. "Suppose you both stop toying with new story ideas and turn your attention to our problem."

"Starve from low wages or lose our tongues," sighed Hari-ibn-Hari.

"And once our tongues have been cut out the grand vizier goes to other storytellers to take our place," said the Daemon of the Night.

Fareed-al-Shaffa said slowly, "The grand vizier assumes the other storytellers will be too terrified by our example to refuse his starvation wage."

"He's right," Hari-ibn-Hari said bitterly.

"Is he?" mused Fareed. "Perhaps not."

"What do you mean?" his two companions asked in unison.

Stroking his beard thoughtfully, Fareed-al-Shaffa said, "What if all the storytellers refused to work for a single copper per tale?"

Hari-ibn-Hari asked cynically, "Would they refuse before or after our tongues have been taken out?"

"Before, of course."

The Daemon of the Night stared at his fellow storyteller. "Are you suggesting what I think you're suggesting?"

"I am."

Hari-ibn-Hari gaped at the two of them. "No, it would never work. It's impossible!"

"Is it?" asked Fareed-al-Shaffa. "Perhaps not."

The next morning the three bleary-eyed storytellers were brought before the grand vizier. Once again Scheherazade watched and listened from her veiled gallery. She herself was bleary-eyed as well, having spent all night telling the sultan the tale of Ala-al-Din and his magic lamp. As usual, she had left the tale unfinished as the dawn brightened the sky.

This night she must finish the tale and begin another. But she had no other to tell! Her father had to get the storytellers to bring her fresh material. If not, she would lose her head with tomorrow's dawn.

"Well?" demanded the grand vizier as the three storytellers knelt trembling before him. "What is your decision?"

The three of them had chosen the Daemon of the Night to be their spokesperson. But as he gazed up at the fierce countenance of the grand vizier, his voice choked in his throat.

Fareed-al-Shaffa nudged him, gently at first, then more firmly.

At last the Daemon said, "Oh, magnificent one, we cannot continue to supply your stories for a miserable one copper per tale."

"Then you will lose your tongues!"

"And your daughter will lose her head, most considerate of fathers."

"Bah! There are plenty of other storytellers in Baghdad. I'll have a new story for my daughter before the sun goes down."

Before the Daemon of the Night could reply, Fareed-al-Shaffa spoke thusly, "Not so, sir. No storyteller will work for you for a single copper per tale."

"Nonsense!" snapped the grand vizier.

"It is true," said the Daemon of the Night. "All the storytellers have agreed. We have sworn a mighty oath. None of us will give you a story unless you raise your rates."

"Extortion!" cried the grand vizier.

Hari-ibn-Hari found his voice. "If you take our tongues, oh most merciful of men, none of the other storytellers will deal with you at all."

Before the astounded grand vizier could reply to that, Fareed-al-Shaffa explained, "We have formed a guild, your magnificence, a storyteller's guild. What you do to one of us you do to us all."

"You can't do that!" the grand vizier sputtered.

"It is done," said the Daemon of the Night. He said it softly, almost in a whisper, but with great finality.

The grand vizier sat on his chair of authority getting redder and redder in the face, his chest heaving, his fists clenching. He looked like a volcano about to erupt.

When, from the veiled gallery above them, Scheherazade cried out, "I think it's wonderful! A storyteller's guild. And you created it just for me!"

The three storytellers raised their widening eyes to the balcony of the gallery, where they could make out the slim and graceful form of a young woman, suitably gowned and veiled, who stepped forth for them all to see. The grand vizier twisted around in his chair and nearly choked with fury.

"Father," Scheherazade called sweetly, "is it not wonderful that the storytellers have banded together so that they can provide stories for me to tell the sultan night after night?"

The grand vizier started to reply once, twice, three times. Each time no words escaped his lips. The three storytellers knelt before him, staring up at the gallery where Scheherazade stood openly before them—suitably gowned and veiled.

Before the grand vizier could find his voice, Scheherazade said, "I welcome you, storytellers, and your guild. The grand vizier, the most munificent of fathers, will gladly pay you ten coppers for each story you relate to me. May you bring me a thousand of them!"

Before the grand vizier could figure how much a thousand stories would cost, at ten coppers per story, Fareed-al-Shaffa smiled up at Scheherazade and murmured, "A thousand and one, oh gracious one."

The grand vizier was unhappy with the new arrangement, although he had to admit that the storyteller's newly founded guild provided stories that kept the sultan bemused and his daughter alive.

The storytellers were pleased, of course. Not only did they keep their tongues in their heads and earn a decent income from their stories, but they shared the subsidiary rights to the stories with the grand vizier once Scheherazade had told them to the sultan and they could then be related to the general public.

Ten coppers per story was extortionate, in the grand vizier's opinion, but the storyteller's guild agreed to share the income from the stories once they were told in the bazaar. There was even talk of an invention from far-off Cathay, where stories could be printed on vellum and sold throughout the kingdom. The grand vizier consoled himself with the thought that if sales were good enough, the income could pay for regilding his ceiling.

The sultan eventually learned of the arrangement, of course. Being no fool, he demanded that he be cut in on the profits. Reluctantly, the grand vizier complied.

Scheherazade was the happiest of all. She kept telling stories to the sultan until he relented of his murderous ways and eventually married her, much to the joy of all Baghdad.

She thought of the storyteller's guild as her own personal creation, and called it Scheherazade's Fables and Wonders Association.

That slightly ponderous name was soon abbreviated to SFWA.

Afterword to
SCHEHERAZADE AND THE STORYTELLERS

The story was written as my contribution to Gateways, *a story collection honoring Frederik Pohl on his ninetieth birthday, edited by his wife Elizabeth Anne Hull.*

The storytellers are all based on fellow writers of science fiction, their names thinly disguised by pseudo-Arabic monikers.

In addition to being a masterful storyteller himself, and a good and sadly missed friend, Fred Pohl was a Grand Master of the Science Fiction and Fantasy Writers of America—a slightly ponderous name that is usually abbreviated as SFWA.

NUCLEAR AUTUMN

The alternative to defenses against nuclear-armed ballistic missiles is the policy called Mutual Assured Destruction. MAD is essentially a mutual suicide pact between the nuclear-armed nations: attack is deterred because neither side dares risk the other's devastating counterattack.

But there might be another way for a ruthless and calculating enemy to launch a nuclear attack and confidently expect no counterstrike at all.

The arguments over Nuclear Winter—the idea that a sufficient number of nuclear explosions in the atmosphere will plunge the whole world into an era of freezing darkness that will extinguish all life on Earth—has been hotly debated among scientists.

Strangely, very little of this debate was reported in the news media. Even the science press largely ignored it. To the media, Nuclear Winter was a Truth. It was revealed through press conferences, a slickly illustrated book, and videotapes. No matter that the basic scientific underpinnings of the concept were attacked by many atmospheric physicists and other scientists, it became embedded in cement in the mind-sets of the world's media—and many science fiction writers, too.

Critics of Nuclear Winter claim that its proponents used Joe McCarthy tactics to publicize what, to them, was a political idea rather than a scientific theory. They claimed that Carl Sagan, Paul Ehrlich, et al made their publicity splash and "sold" the idea to the media, and only afterward quietly admitted that there are some doubts about the models and calculations they used.

On their side, Sagan, Ehrlich, and their colleagues insist that Nuclear Winter has been verified by extensive computer simulations, and is absolute proof that even a relatively small nuclear war threatens to end not only human life on Earth, but all life.

"Nuclear Autumn" takes it for granted that the Nuclear Winter theory is right. It shows one of the possible consequences. A very likely one, I fear.

"THEY'RE BLUFFING," said the President of the United States.

"Of course they're bluffing," agreed her science advisor. "They have to be."

The chairman of the Joint Chiefs of Staff, a grizzled old infantry general, looked grimly skeptical.

For a long, silent moment they faced each other in the cool, quiet confines of the Oval Office. The science advisor looked young and handsome enough to be a television personality, and indeed had been one for a while before he allied himself with the politician who sat behind the desk. The President looked younger than she actually was, thanks to modern cosmetic surgery and a ruthless self-discipline. Only the general seemed to be old, a man of an earlier generation, gray-haired and wrinkled, with light brown eyes that seemed sad and weary.

"I don't believe they're bluffing," he said. "I think they mean exactly what they say—either we cave in to them or they launch their missiles."

The science advisor gave him his most patronizing smile. "General, they *have* to be bluffing. The numbers prove it."

"The only numbers that count," said the general, "are that we have cut our strategic ballistic missile force by half since this Administration came into office."

"And made the world that much safer," said the President. Her voice was firm, with a sharp edge to it.

The general shook his head. "Ma'am, the only reason I have not tendered my resignation is that I know full well the nincompoop you intend to appoint in my place."

The science advisor laughed. Even the President smiled at the old man.

"The Russians are not bluffing," the general repeated. "They mean exactly what they say."

With a patient sigh, the science advisor explained, "General, they cannot—repeat, cannot—launch a nuclear strike at us or anyone else. They know the numbers as well as we do. A large nuclear strike, in the three-thousand-megaton range, will so damage the environment that the world will be plunged into a Nuclear Winter. Crops and animal life will be wiped out by months of subfreezing temperatures. The sky will be dark with soot and grains of pulverized soil. The sun will be blotted out. All life on Earth will die."

The general waved an impatient hand. "I know your story. I've seen your presentations."

"Then how can the Russians attack us, when they know they'll be killing themselves even if we don't retaliate?"

"Maybe they haven't seen your television specials. Maybe they don't believe in Nuclear Winter."

"But they have to!" said the science advisor. "The numbers are the same for them as they are for us."

"Numbers," grumbled the general.

"Those numbers describe reality," the science advisor insisted. "And the men in the Kremlin are realists. They understand what Nuclear Winter means. Their own scientists have told them exactly what I've told you."

"Then why did they insist on this hot-line call?"

Spreading his hands in the gesture millions had come to know from his television series, the science advisor replied, "They're reasonable men. Now that they know nuclear weapons are unusable, they are undoubtedly trying to begin negotiations to resolve our differences without threatening nuclear war."

"You think so?" muttered the general.

The President leaned back in her swivel chair. "We'll find out what they want soon enough," she said. "Kolgoroff will be on the hot-line in another minute or so."

The science advisor smiled at her. "I imagine he'll suggest a summit meeting to negotiate a new disarmament treaty."

The general said nothing.

The President touched a green square on the keypad built into the desk's surface. A door opened and three more people—a man and two women—entered the Oval Office: the Secretary of State, the Secretary of Defense, and the National Security Advisor.

Exactly when the digital clock on the President's desk read 12:00:00, the large display screen that took up much of the wall opposite her desk lit up to reveal the face of Yuri Kolgoroff, prime minister of the Russian Federation. He was much younger than his predecessors had been, barely in his mid-fifties, and rather handsome in a Slavic way. If his hair had been a few shades darker and his chin just a little rounder, he would have looked strikingly like the President's science advisor.

"Madam President," said Kolgoroff in flawless American-accented English, "it is good of you to accept my invitation to discuss the differences between our two nations."

"I am always eager to resolve differences," said the President.

"I believe we can accomplish much." Kolgoroff smiled, revealing large white teeth.

"I have before me," said the President, glancing at the computer screen on her desk, "the agenda that our ministers worked out."

"There is no need for that," said the Russian leader. "Why encumber ourselves with such formalities?"

The President smiled. "Very well. What do you have in mind?"

"It is very simple. We want the United States to withdraw all its troops from Europe and to dismantle NATO. Also, your military and naval bases in Japan, Taiwan, and the Philippines must be disbanded. Finally, your injunctions against Russia concerning trade in high-technology items must be ended."

The President's face went white. It took her a moment to gather the wits to say, "And what do you propose to offer in exchange for these concessions?"

"In exchange?" Kolgoroff laughed. "Why, we will allow you to live. We will refrain from bombing your cities."

"You're insane!" snapped the President.

Still grinning, Kolgoroff replied, "We will see who is sane and who is mad. One minute before this conversation began, I ordered a limited nuclear attack against every NATO base in Europe, and a counterforce attack against the ballistic missiles still remaining in your silos in the American Midwest."

The red panic light on the President's communications console began flashing frantically.

"But that's impossible!" burst the science advisor. He leaped from his chair and pointed at Kolgoroff's image in the big display screen. "An attack of that size will bring on Nuclear Winter! You'll be killing yourselves as well as us!"

Kolgoroff smiled pityingly at the scientist. "We have computers also, Professor. We know how to count. The attack we have launched is just below the threshold for Nuclear Winter. It will not blot out the sun everywhere on Earth. Believe me, we are not such fools as you think."

"But . . ."

"But," the Soviet leader went on, his smile vanished and his voice iron-hard, "should you be foolish enough to launch a counterstrike with your remaining missiles or bombers, that *will* break the camel's back, so to speak. The additional explosions of your counter-strike will bring on Nuclear Winter."

"You can't be serious!"

"I am deadly serious," Kolgoroff replied. Then a faint hint of his smile returned. "But do not be afraid. We have not targeted Washington. Or any of your cities, for that matter. You will live—under Russian governance."

The President turned to the science advisor. "What should I do?"

The science advisor shook his head.

"What should I do?" she asked the others seated around her.

They said nothing. Not a word.

She turned to the general. "What should I do?"

He got to his feet and headed for the door. Over his shoulder he answered, "Learn Russian."

LOWER THE RIVER

I worked for a dozen years at Avco Everett Research Laboratory, in Massachusetts. In many ways, it was the best experience of my life. I was living a science-fiction writer's dream, surrounded by brilliant scientists, engineers, and technicians working on cutting-edge research in everything from high-power lasers to artificial hearts.

We got involved in developing superconducting magnets in the early 1960s. Superconductors can generate enormously intense magnetic fields, and once energized they do not need to be continuously fed electrical power, as ordinary electromagnets do.

But they only remain magnetized if they are kept below a certain critical temperature. For the superconductors of the 1960s, the necessary temperature was a decidely frosty −423.04° Fahrenheit, only a few degrees above absolute zero. The coolant we used was liquified helium.

In the 1980s, "high-temperature" superconductors were discovered: they work at the temperature of liquid nitrogen, −320.8°F. Whoopee.

The search for a room-temperature superconductor, one that will remain superconducting at a comfortable 70°F and therefore would not need cryogenic coolants, is being pushed in many labs.

In the meantime, business colleges have sent their graduates into all sorts of industries. What would happen, I wondered, if one of these MBAs tried to use the management techniques of goal-setting and negative incentives on a physicist who is laboring to produce a room-temperature superconductor?

"Lower the River" is the result.

JACKSON KLONDIKE did not look like a world-class physicist. He was a shaggy bear of a man with a gruff manner and a ferocious sense of humor. Yet he was the unchallenged leader of the Rockledge Research Laboratory's bright and quirky scientific staff.

William Rather did not look like a research lab director. He was astonishingly young, astoundingly handsome, and incredibly vapid. Yet he held a master's degree in business administration, and the Rockledge corporate officers (including his uncle Sylvester) had handed him the directorship of the lab.

With one single demand: Get results!

Klondike was smolderingly unhappy as he sat in front of Rather's desk. It was obvious that he felt the time spent in the director's office was wasted; he wanted to be back in his own rat's nest of a lab where he could do some creative work.

Rather had peeked into Klondike's lab only once. It looked like a chaotic mess, wires dangling from the ceiling, insulated tubing snaking everywhere, and vats of some mysterious stuff boiling and filling the chamber with steam that somehow felt cold instead of hot.

Klondike was the resident genius, though. His specialty was solid-state physics. For years he had been experimenting on superconducting magnets.

"I have a directive here from corporate headquarters in New York," Rather said, as sternly as he could manage, rattling the single sheet of paper in one hand.

Across his desk Klondike sat straddling a chair he had turned backward, leaning his beefy arms on the chair's back, his chin half-buried in their hair, his eyes glowering at Rather.

"A directive, huh?" Klondike vouchsafed.

Sitting up as straight as he could, Rather said, "I know you don't think much of me, but I've been studying this superconductivity business for several weeks now."

"Have you?" Klondike's voice rumbled from somewhere deep in his chest, like distant thunder.

"Yes I have," Rather said. "Superconducting magnets could be a major product line for this corporation, if it weren't for the fact that you need to keep them cold with liquid oxygen."

"Liquid nitrogen," reverberated Klondike.

"Nitrogen. That's what I meant."

"Used to be worse. When I first started in this game, we hadda use mother-lovin' liquid helium for cooling the coils. Liquid nitrogen's easy."

"But it's still a problem, as far as practicality is concerned, isn't it?"

"Nah. The real problem's the ductility of—"

"Never mind!" Rather snapped, unwilling to allow Klondike to snow him with a lot of technical jargon.

Klondike glared at him, but shut up.

"I know what we need, and I made the suggestion to corporate management. They agree with me." He rattled the paper again.

Klondike remained in scowling silence.

"What we need is a superconductor that works at ordinary temperature, so we won't have to keep it cold with liquid—uh, nitrogen."

Klondike lifted his chin off his shaggy arms. "You mean we oughtta produce a room-temperature superconductor?"

"That's exactly right," said Rather. "And the corporate management agrees with me. This directive *orders* you to produce a room-temperature superconductor."

Barely suppressing his disdain, Klondike replied, "Orders me, huh? And when do they want it? This week or next?"

Rather smiled shrewdly. "I'm not a neophyte at this, you know. I understand that breakthroughs can't be made on a preconceived schedule."

Klondike glanced ceilingward, as if giving swift thanks for small mercies.

"Any time this fiscal year will do."

"This fiscal year?"

"That gives you nearly six months to get the task done."

"Produce a room-temperature superconductor in less than six months."

"Yes," said Rather. "Or we'll have to find someone else who can."

Five months and fourteen days went by.

In all that time Rather hardly saw Klondike at all. The man had barricaded himself in his lab, working night and day. His weekly reports were terse to the point of insult.

Week 1: Working on room-temperature superconductor.

Week 7: Still working on rt s.

Week 14: Continuing work on rts.

Week 20: Making progress on rts.

Week 21: Demonstration of rts scheduled for next Monday.

Rather had been worried, at first, that Klondike was simply ignoring his instruction.. But once he saw that a demonstration was being set up, he realized that his management technique had worked just the way they had told him it would in business school: Set a goal for your employees, then make certain they reach your goal.

"So where is it?" Rather asked. "Where is the demonstration?"

Klondike had personally escorted his boss down hallways and through workshops from the director's office to his own lab, deep in the bowels of the building.

"Right through there," Klondike said, gesturing to the closed door with the sign that read: ROOM-TEMPERATURE SUPERCONDUCTOR TEST IN PROGRESS. ENTRY BY AUTHORIZED PERSONNEL ONLY!

Feeling flushed with triumph, Rather flung open the insulated door and stepped into—

A solid wall of frozen air. He banged his nose painfully and bounced off, staggering back into Klondike's waiting arms.

Eyes tearful, nose throbbing, he could see dimly through the frozen-solid air a small magnet coil sitting atop a lab bench. It was a superconductor, of course, working fine in the room temperature of that particular room.

Klondike smiled grimly. "There it is, boss, just like management asked for. I couldn't raise the bridge so I lowered the river."

THE CAFÉ COUP

One of the standard arguments against the possibility of time travel is that if time travel actually existed, time travelers would be deliberately or accidentally changing history. One morning we'd all wake up to find that the South won the Civil War, for example. Since we have not seen our history changing, time travel has not happened. If it hasn't happened yet, it never will. QED.

But if time travelers were altering history, would we notice? Or would our history books and even our memories be changed each time a time traveler finagled with our past?

Leaving aside such philosophical speculations, this story originated in a panel discussion of time travel at a science-fiction convention. It occurred to me during the panel's discussion of time-travel stories that while many, many tales have been written about a world in which Nazi Germany won World War II, no one that I know of has tackled the idea of having Imperial Germany win World War I.

The Kaiser's Germany actually came very close to winning the First World War. It was the intervention of the United States, brought about by U-boat sinkings of ships with Americans aboard them, such as the Lusitania, that brought the Americans into the war and turned the tide against Germany.

Prevent the sinking of the Lusitania, I reasoned, and Germany could win World War I. In a victorious Germany, Hitler would never have risen to power. No Hitler, no World War II. No Holocaust. No Hiroshima.

Maybe.

PARIS WAS NOT FRIENDLY TO AMERICANS in the soft springtime of 1922. The French didn't care much for the English, either, and they hated the victorious Germans, of course.

I couldn't blame them very much. The Great War had been over for more than three years, yet Paris had still not recovered its gaiety, its light and color, despite the hordes of boisterous German tourists who spent so freely on the boulevards. More likely, because of them.

I sat in one of the crowded sidewalk cafés beneath a splendid warm sun, waiting for my lovely wife to show up. Because of all the Germans, I was forced to share my minuscule round table with a tall, gaunt Frenchman who looked me over with suspicious eyes.

"You are an American?" he asked, looking down his prominent nose at me. His accent was worse than mine, certainly not Parisian.

"No," I answered truthfully. Then I lied, "I'm from New Zealand." It was as far away in distance as my real birthplace was in time.

"Ah," he said with an exhalation of breath that was somewhere between a sigh and a snort. "Your countrymen fought well at Gallipoli. Were you there?"

"No," I said. "I was too young."

That apparently puzzled him. Obviously I was of an age to have fought in the Great War. But in fact, I hadn't been born when the British Empire troops were decimated at Gallipoli. I hadn't been born in the twentieth century at all.

"Were you in the war?" I asked needlessly.

"But certainly. To the very last moment I fought the Boche."

"It was a great tragedy."

"The Americans betrayed us," he muttered.

My brows rose a few millimeters. He was quite tall for a Frenchman, but painfully thin. Half-starved. Even his eyes looked hungry. The inflation, of course. It cost a basketful of francs, literally, to buy a loaf of bread. I wondered how he could afford the price of an aperitif. Despite the warm afternoon he had wrapped himself in a shabby old leather coat, worn shiny at the elbows.

From what I could see there were hardly any Frenchmen in the café, mostly raucous Germans roaring with laughter and heartily pounding on the little tables as they bellowed for more beer. To my amazement, the waiters had learned to speak German.

"Wilson," my companion continued bitterly. "He had the gall to speak of Lafayette."

"I thought that the American president was the one who arranged the armistice."

"Yes, with his Fourteen Points. Fourteen daggers plunged into the heart of France."

"Really?"

"The Americans should have entered the war on our side! Instead they sat idly by and watched us bleed to death while their bankers extorted every gram of gold we possessed."

"But the Americans had no reason to go to war," I protested mildly.

"France needed them! When their pitiful little colonies rebelled against the British lion, France was the only nation to come to their aid. They owe their existence to France, yet when we needed them they turned their backs on us."

That was largely my fault, although he didn't know it. I averted the sinking of the *Lusitania* by the German U-boat. It took enormous energies, but my darling wife arranged it so that the *Lusitania* was crawling along at a mere five knots that fateful morning. I convinced Lieutenant Walther Schwieger, skipper of the U-20, that it was safe enough to surface and hold the British liner captive with the deck gun while a boarding party searched for the ammunition that I knew the English had stored aboard her.

The entire affair was handled with great tact and honor. No shots were fired, no lives were lost, and the 123 American passengers arrived safely in Liverpool with glowing stories of how correct, how chivalrous, the German U-boat sailors had been. America remained neutral throughout the Great War. Indeed, a good deal of anti-British sentiment swept the United States, especially the Midwest, when their newspapers reported that the British were transporting military contraband in secret and thus risking the lives of American passengers.

"Well," I said, beckoning to the waiter for two more Pernods, "the war is over, and we must face the future as best we can."

"Yes," said my companion gloomily. "I agree."

One group of burly Germans was being particularly obnoxious, singing bawdy songs as they waved their beer glasses to and fro, slopping the foaming beer on themselves and their neighboring tables. No one complained. No one dared to say a word. The German army still occupied much of France.

My companion's face was white with fury. Yet even he restrained himself. But I noticed that he glanced at the watch on his wrist every few moments, as if he were expecting someone. Or something.

If anyone had betrayed France, it was me. The world that I had been born into was a cesspool of violence and hate, crumbling into tribal savagery all across the globe. Only a few oases of safety existed, tucked in remote areas far from the filthy, disease-ridden cities and the swarms of ignorant, vicious monsters who raped and murdered until they themselves were raped and murdered.

Once they discovered our solar-powered city, tucked high in the Sierra Oriental, I knew that the end was near. Stupidly, they attacked us, like a wild barbarian horde. We slaughtered them with laser beams and heat-seeking bullets. Instead of driving them away, that only whetted their appetite.

Their survivors laid siege to our mountaintop. We laughed, at first, to think their pitiful handful of ragged ignoramuses could overcome our walled city, with its high-tech weaponry and endless energy from the sun. Yet somehow they spread the word to others of their kind. Day after day we watched their numbers grow, a tattered, threadbare pack of rats surrounding us, watching, waiting until their numbers were so huge they could swarm us under despite our weapons.

They were united in their bloodlust and their greed. They saw loot and power on our mountaintop, and they wanted both. At night I could see their campfires down below us, like the red eyes of rats watching and waiting.

Our council was divided. Some urged that we sally out against the besiegers, attack them and drive them away. But it was already too late for that. Their numbers were far too large, and even if we drove them away, they would return, now that they knew we existed.

Others wanted to flee into space, to leave Earth altogether and build colonies off the planet. We had the technology to build and maintain the solar-power satellites, they pointed out. It was only one technological step farther to build habitats in space.

But when we put the numbers through a computer analysis, it

showed that to build a habitat large enough to house us all permanently would be beyond our current resources—and we could not enlarge our resource base as long as we were encircled by the barbarians.

I had worked on the time translator since my student days. It took enormous energy to move objects through time, far too much for all of us to escape that way. Yet I saw a possibility of hope.

If I could find a nexus, a pivotal point in time, perhaps I could change the world. Perhaps I could alter events to such an extent that this miserable world of terror and pain would dissolve, disappear, and a better world replace it. I became obsessed with the possibility.

"But you'll destroy this world," my wife gasped, shocked when I finally told her of my scheme.

"What of it?" I snapped. "Is this world so delightful that you want it to continue?"

She sank wearily onto the lab bench. "What will happen to our families? Our friends? What will happen to us?"

"You and I will make the translation. We will live in an earlier, better time."

"And the others?"

I shrugged. "I don't know. The mathematics isn't clear. But even if they disappear, the world that replaces them in this time will be better than the world we're in now."

"Do you really think so?"

"We'll make it better!"

The fools on the council disagreed, naturally. No one had translated through time, they pointed out. The energy even for a preliminary experiment would be prohibitively high. We needed that energy for our weapons.

None of them believed I could change a thing. They weren't afraid that they would be erased from existence, their world line snuffed out like a candle flame. No, in their blind ignorance they insisted that an attempt at time translation would consume so much energy that we would be left defenseless against the besieging savages outside our walls.

"The savages will no longer exist," I told them. "None of this world line will exist, once I've made the proper change in the geodesic."

They voted me down. They would rather face the barbarians than give up their existence, even if it meant a better world would replace the one they knew.

I accepted their judgment outwardly. Inwardly I became the most passionate student of history of all time. Feverishly I searched the books and discs, seeking the nexus, the turning point, the place where I could make the world change for the better. I knew I had only a few months; the savage horde below our mountaintop was growing and stirring. I could hear their murmuring dirge of hate even through the walls of my laboratory, like the growls of a pack of wild beasts. Every day it grew louder, more insistent.

It was the war in the middle of the twentieth century that started the world's descent into madness. A man called Adolph Hitler escalated the horror of war to new levels of inhumanity. Not only did he deliberately murder millions of civilian men, women and children, he destroyed his own country, screaming with his last breath that the Aryan race deserved to be wiped out if they could not conquer the world.

When I first realized the enormity of Hitler's rage I sat stunned for an entire day. Here was the model, the prototype, for the brutal, cruel, ruthless, sadistic monsters who ranged my world seeking blood.

Before Hitler, war was a senseless affront to civilized men and women. Soldiers were tolerated, at best; often despised. They were usually shunned in polite society. After Hitler, war was commonplace, genocide routine, nuclear weapons valued for the megadeaths they could generate.

Hitler and all he stood for was the edge of the precipice, the first terrible step into the abyss that my world had plunged into. If I could prevent Hitler from coming to power, perhaps prevent him from ever being born, I might save my world—or at least erase it and replace it with a better one.

For days on end I thought of how I might translate back in time to kill this madman or even prevent his birth. Slowly, however, I began to realize that this single man was not the cause of it all. If Hitler had never been born, someone else would have arisen in Germany after the Great War, someone else would have unified the German people in a lust for revenge against those who had betrayed and defeated them, someone else would have preached Aryan purity and hatred of all other races, someone else would have plunged civilization into World War II.

To solve the problem of Hitler I had to go to the root causes of the Nazi program: Germany's defeat in the First World War, the war that was called the Great War by those who had lived through it. I had to make Germany win that war.

If Germany had won World War I, there would have been no humiliation of the German people, no thirst for revenge, no economic collapse. Hitler would still exist, but he would be a retired soldier, perhaps a peaceful painter or even a minor functionary in the Kaiser's government. There would be no World War II.

And so I set my plans to make Germany the victor in the Great War, with the reluctant help of my dear wife.

"You would defy the council?" she asked me, shocked when I revealed my determination to her.

"Only if you help me," I said. "I won't go unless you go with me."

She fully understood that we would never be able to return to our own world. To do so, we would have to bring the components for a translator with us and then assemble it in the early twentieth century. Even if we could do that, where would we find a power source in those primitive years? They were still using horses then.

Besides, our world would be gone, vanished, erased from space-time.

"We'll live out our lives in the twentieth century," I told her. "And we'll know that our own time will be far better than it is now."

"How can you be sure it will be better?" she asked me softly.

I smiled patiently. "There will be no World War II. Europe will be peaceful for the rest of the century. Commerce and art will flourish. Even the Russian communists will join the European federation peacefully, toward the end of the century."

"You're certain?"

"I've run the analysis on the master computer a dozen times. I'm absolutely certain."

"And our own time will be better?"

"It has to be. How could it possibly be worse?"

She nodded, her beautiful face solemn with the understanding that we were leaving our world forever. *Good riddance to it*, I thought. But it was the only world we had ever known, and she was not happy to deliberately toss it away and spend the rest of her life in a bygone century.

Still, she never hesitated about coming with me. I wouldn't go without her, she knew that. And I knew that she wouldn't let me go unless she came with me.

"It's really quite romantic, isn't it?" she asked me, the night before we left.

"What is?"

"Translating across time together. Our love will span the centuries."

I held her close. "Yes. Across the centuries."

Before sunrise the next morning we stole into the laboratory and powered up the translator. No one was on guard, no one was there to try to stop us. The council members were all sleeping, totally unaware that one of their loyal citizens was about to defy their decision. There were no renegades among us, no rebels. We had always accepted the council's decisions and worked together for our mutual survival.

Until now. My wife silently took her place on the translator's focal stage while I made the final adjustments to the controls. She looked radiant standing there, her face grave, her golden hair glowing against the darkened laboratory shadows.

At last I stepped up beside her. I took her hand; it was cold with anxiety. I squeezed her hand confidently.

"We're going to make a better world," I whispered to her.

The last thing I saw was the pink glow of dawn rising over the eastern mountains, framed in the lab's only window.

Now, in the Paris of 1922 that I had created, victorious Germany ruled Europe with strict but civilized authority. The Kaiser had been quite lenient with Great Britain; after all, was he not related by blood to the British king? Even France got off relatively lightly, far more lightly than the unlucky Russians. Germany kept Alsace-Lorraine, of course, but took no other territory.

France's punishment was mainly financial: Germany demanded huge, crippling reparations. The real humiliation was that France was forced to disarm. The proud French army was reduced to a few regiments and forbidden modem armaments such as tanks and airplanes. The Parisian police force was better equipped.

My companion glanced at his watch again. It was the type that the army had issued to its officers, I saw.

"Could you tell me the time?" I asked, over the drunken singing of the German tourists. My wife was late, and that was quite unlike her.

He paid no attention to me. Staring furiously at the Germans who surrounded us, he suddenly shot to his feet and shouted, "Men of France! How long shall we endure this humiliation?"

He was so tall and lean that he looked like a human Eiffel Tower standing among the crowded sidewalk tables. He had a pistol in his hand. One of the waiters was so surprised by his outburst that he dropped his tray. It clattered to the pavement with a crash of shattered glassware.

But others were not surprised, I saw. More than a dozen men leaped up and shouted, "Vive La France!" They were all dressed in old army uniforms, as was my companion, beneath his frayed leather coat. They were all armed, a few of them even had rifles.

Absolute silence reigned. The Germans stared, dumbfounded. The waiters froze in their tracks. I certainly didn't know what to say or do. My only thought was of my beautiful wife; where was she, why was she late, was there some sort of insurrection going on? Was she safe?

"Follow me!" said the tall Frenchman to his armed compatriots. Despite every instinct in me, I struggled to my feet and went along with them.

From cafés on both sides of the wide boulevard armed men were striding purposefully toward their leader. He marched straight ahead, right down the middle of the street, looking neither to the right nor left. They formed up behind him, some two or three dozen men.

Breathlessly, I followed along.

"To the Elysee!" shouted the tall one, striding determinedly on his long legs, never glancing back to see if the others were following him.

Then I saw my wife pushing through the curious onlookers thronging the sidewalks. I called to her, and she ran to me, blonde and slim and more lovely than anyone in all of space-time.

"What is it?" she asked, as breathless as I. "What's happening?"

"Some sort of coup, I think."

"They have guns! We should get inside. If there's shooting—"

"No, we'll be all right," I said. "I want to see what's going to happen."

It was a coup, all right. But it failed miserably.

Apparently the tall one, a fanatical ex-major named de Gaulle, believed that his little band of followers could capture the government. He depended on a certain General Pétain, who had the prestige and authority that de Gaulle himself lacked.

Pétain lost his nerve at the critical moment, however, and abandoned the coup. The police and a detachment of army troops were waiting for the rebels at the Petit Palace; a few shots were exchanged. Before the smoke had drifted away the rebels had scattered, and de Gaulle himself was taken into custody.

"He will be charged with treason, I imagine," I said to my darling wife as we sat that evening at the very same sidewalk café. The very same table, in fact.

"I doubt that they'll give him more than a slap on the wrist," she said. "He seems to be a hero to everyone in Paris."

"Not to the Germans," I said.

She smiled at me. "The Germans take him as a joke." She understood German perfectly and could eavesdrop on their shouted conversations quite easily.

"He is no joke."

We both turned to the dark little man sitting at the next table; we were packed in so close that his chair almost touched mine. He was a particularly ugly man, with lank black hair and the swarthy face of a born conspirator. His eyes were small, reptilian, and his upper lip was twisted by a curving scar.

"Charles de Gaulle will be the savior of France," he said. He was absolutely serious. Grim, even.

"If he's not guillotined for treason," I replied lightly. Yet inwardly I began to tremble.

"You were here. You saw how he rallied the men of France."

"All two dozen of them," I quipped.

He looked at me with angry eyes. "Next time it will be different. We will not rely on cowards and turncoats like Pétain. Next time we will take the government and bring all of France under his leadership. Then . . ."

He hesitated, glancing around as if the police might be listening.

"Then?" my wife coaxed.

He lowered his voice. "Then revenge on Germany and all those who betrayed us."

"You can't be serious."

"You'll see. Next time we will win. Next time we will have all of France with us. And then all of Europe. And then, the world."

My jaw must have dropped open. It was all going to happen

anyway. The French would rearm. Led by a ruthless, fanatical de Gaulle, they would plunge Europe into a second world war. All my efforts were for nothing. The world that we had left would continue to exist—or be even worse.

He turned his reptilian eyes to my lovely wife. Although many of the German women were blond, she was far more beautiful than any of them.

"You are Aryan?" he asked, his tone suddenly menacing.

She was nonplussed. "Aryan? I don't understand."

"Yes you do," he said, almost hissing the words. "Next time it will go hard on the Aryans. You'll see."

I sank my head in my hands and wept openly.

REMEMBER, CAESAR

One little phrase, "What if . . . ?" has been the beginning of many a science-fiction story.

Wars are started by old men (and sometimes old women) who sit at home and direct their troops. They are fought by young men (and sometimes young women) who do the bleeding and the dying.

But what if the dangers, the risks, the terror of battle could be brought home to the leaders who can sit out a war in a bombproof bunker, far from the fighting front?

And what if modern technology could produce a suit that makes its wearer invisible?

A "cloak of invisibility" is not terribly far from our current technological capabilities. Could that second "What if . . . ?" be used to answer the first one?

We have never renounced the use of terror.
—Vladimir Ilyich Lenin

SHE WAS ALONE and she was scared.

Apara Jaheen held her breath as the two plainclothes security guards walked past her. They both held ugly, deadly black machine pistols casually in their hands as they made their rounds along the corridor.

They can't see you, Apara told herself. You're invisible.

Still, she held her breath.

She knew that her stealth suit shimmered ever so slightly in the glareless light from the fluorescents that lined the ceiling of the corridor. You had to be looking for that delicate little ripple in the air, actively seeking it, to detect it at all. And even then you would think it was merely a trick your eyes played on you, a flicker that was gone before it even registered consciously in your mind.

And yet Apara froze, motionless, not daring to breathe, until the two men—smelling of cigarettes and after-shave lotion—passed her and were well down the corridor. They were talking about the war, betting that it would be launched before the week was out.

Her stealth suit's surface was honeycombed with microscopic fiber-optic vidcams and pixels that were only a couple of molecules thick. The suit hugged Apara's lithe body like a famished lover. Directed by the computer built into her helmet, the vidcams scanned her surroundings and projected the imagery onto the pixels.

It was the closest thing to true invisibility that the Cabal's technology had been able to come up with. So close that, except for the slight unavoidable glitter when the sequinlike pixels caught some stray light, Apara literally disappeared into the background.

Covering her from head to toe, the suit's thermal absorption layer kept her infrared profile vanishingly low and its insulation subskin held back the minuscule electromagnetic fields it generated. The only way they could detect her would be if she stepped into a scanning beam, but the wide-spectrum goggles she wore should reveal them to her in plenty of time to avoid them.

She hoped.

Getting into the president's mansion had been ridiculously easy. As instructed, she had waited until dark before leaving the Cabal's safe house in the miserable slums of the city. Her teammates drove her as close to the presidential mansion as they dared in a dilapidated, nondescript faded blue sedan that would draw no attention. They wished her success as she slipped out of the car, invisible in her stealth suit.

"For the Cause," Ahmed said, almost fiercely, to the empty air where he thought she was.

"For the Cause," Apara repeated, knowing that she might never see him again.

Tingling with apprehension, Apara hurried across the park that fronted the mansion, unseen by the evening strollers and beggars, then climbed onto the trunk of one of the endless stream of limousines that entered the grounds. She passed the perimeter guardposts unnoticed.

She rode on the limo all the way to the mansion's main entrance. While a pair of bemedaled generals got out of the limousine and walked crisply past the saluting uniformed guards, Apara melted back into the shadows, away from the lights of the entrance, and took stock of the situation.

The guards at the big, open double doors wore splendid uniforms and shouldered assault rifles. And were accompanied by dogs: two big German shepherds who sat on their haunches, tongues lolling, ears laid back.

Will they smell me if I try to go through the doors? Apara asked herself. Muldoon and his technicians claimed that the insulated stealth suit protected her even from giving off a scent. They were telling the truth, as they knew it, of course. But were they right?

If she were caught, she knew her life would be over. She would simply disappear, a prisoner of their security apparatus. They would use drugs to drain her of every scrap of information she posessed. They would not have to kill her afterward; her mind would be gone by then.

Standing in the shadows, invisible yet frightened, she tongued the cyanide capsule lodged between her upper-right wisdom tooth and cheek. This is a volunteer mission, Muldoon had told her. You've got to be willing to give your life for the Cause.

Apara was willing, yet the fear still rose in her throat, hot and burning.

Born in the slums of Beirut to a mother who abandoned her and a father she never knew, she had understood from childhood that her life was worthless. Even the name they had given her, Apara, meant literally "born to die."

It was during her teen years, when she had traded her body for life itself, for food and protection against the marauding street gangs who raped and murdered for the thrill of it, that she began to realize that life was pointless, existence was pain, the sooner death took her the sooner she would be safe from all fear.

Then Ahmed entered her life and showed her that there was more to living than waiting for death. Strike back! he told her. If you must give up your life, give it for something worthwhile. Even we who are lost and miserable can accomplish something with our lives. We can change the world!

Ahmed introduced her to the Cabal, and the Cabal became her family, her teacher, her purpose for breathing. For the first time in her short life, Apara felt worthwhile. The Cabal flew her across the ocean, to the United States of America, where she met the pink-faced Irishman who called himself Muldoon and was entrusted with her mission to the White House. And decked in the stealth suit, a cloak of invisibility, just like the magic of old Baghdad in the time of Scheherazade and the *Thousand and One Nights*.

You can do it, she told herself as she clung to the shadows outside the White House's main entrance. They are all counting on you: Muldoon and his technicians and Ahmed, with his soulful eyes and tender dear hands.

When the next limousine disgorged its passengers, a trio of admirals, Apara sucked in a deep breath and walked in with them, past the guards and the dogs. One of the animals perked up its ears and whined softly as she marched in step behind the admirals, but other than that heart-stopping instant she had no trouble getting inside the White House. The guard shushed the animal, gruffly.

She followed the trio of admirals out to the west wing, and down the stairs to the basement level and a long, narrow corridor. At its end, Apara could see, was a security checkpoint with a metal detector like the kind used at airports, staffed by two women in uniform. Both of them were African-Americans.

She stopped and faded back against the wall as the admirals stepped through the metal detector, one by one. The guards were lax, expecting no trouble. After all, only the president's highest and most trusted advisors were allowed here.

Then the two plainclothes guards walked past her, openly displaying their machine pistols and talking about the impending war.

"You think they're really gonna do it?"

"Don't see why not. Hit 'em before they start some real trouble. Don't wait for the mess to get worse."

"Yeah, I guess so."

They walked down the corridor as far as the checkpoint, chatted briefly with the female guards, then came back, passing Apara again, still talking about the possibility of war.

Apara knew that she could not get through the metal detector without setting off its alarm. The archwaylike device was sensitive not only to metals, but sniffed for explosives and x-rayed each person stepping through it. She was invisible to human eyes, but the x-ray camera would see her clearly.

She waited, hardly breathing, until the next clutch of visitors arrived. Civilians, this time. Steeling herself, Apara followed them up to the checkpoint and waited as they stopped at the detector and handed their wristwatches, coins and belts to the women on duty, then stepped through the detector, single file.

Timing was important. As the last of the civilians started through, holding his briefcase in front of his chest, as instructed, Apara dropped flat on her stomach and slithered across the archway like a snake speeding after its prey. Carefully avoiding the man's feet, she got through the detector just before he did.

The x-rays did not reach the floor, she had been told. She hoped it was true.

The alarm buzzer sounded. Apara, on the far side of the detector now, sprang to her feet.

"Hold it, sir," said one of the uniformed guards. "The metal detector went off."

He looked annoyed. "I gave you everything. Don't tell me the damned machine picked up the hinges on my briefcase."

The woman shrugged. "Would you mind stepping through again, sir, please?"

With a huff, the man ducked back through the doorway, still clutching his briefcase, and then stepped through once more. No alarm.

"Satisfied?" he sneered.

"Yes, sir. Thank you, sir," the guard said tonelessly.

"Happens now and then," said her partner as she handed the man back his watch, belt and change. "Beeps for no reason."

"Machines aren't perfect," the man muttered.

"I guess," said the guard.

"Too much iron in your blood, Marty," joked one of the other men.

Apara followed them down the corridor, feeling immensely relieved. As far as her information went, there were no further security checkpoints. Unless she bumped into someone, or her suit somehow failed, she was safe.

Until she tried to get out of the White House. But that wouldn't happen until she had fulfilled her mission. If they caught her then, she would simply bite on the cyanide capsule, knowing that she had struck her blow for the Cause.

She followed the civilians into a spacious conference room dominated by a long, polished mahogany table. Most of the high-backed leather chairs were already occupied, mainly by men in military uniforms. There were more stars around the table than in a desert sky, Apara thought. One bomb in here and the U.S. military establishment would be decapitated, along with most of the cabinet heads.

She pressed her back against the bare wall next to the door as the latest arrivals went around the table, shaking hands.

They chatted idly for several minutes, a dozen different conversations buzzing around the long table. Then the president entered from the far door and they all snapped to their feet.

"Sit down, gentlemen," said the president. "And ladies," she added, smiling at the three female cabinet members who stood together at one side of the table.

The president looked older in person than she did on television, Apara thought. *She's not wearing so much makeup, of course.* Still, the president looked vigorous and determined, her famous green eyes sweeping the table as she took her chair at its head. For an instant those eyes looked directly at Apara, and her heart stopped. But the moment passed. The president could not see Apara any more than the others could.

The president's famous smile was absent as she sat down. Looking directly at the chairman of the joint chiefs, she asked the general, "Well, are we ready?"

"In twenty-four hours," he replied crisply. "Troop deployment is complete, our naval task force is on station and our full complement of planes is on site, ready to go."

"Then why do we need twenty-four hours?" the president demanded.

The general's silver eyebrows rose a centimeter. "Logistics, ma'am. Getting ammunition and fuel to the front-line units, setting our communications codes. Strictly routine, but very important if we want the attack to come off without a hitch."

The president was not pleased. "Every hour we delay means more pressure from the U.N."

"And from the Europeans," said one of the civilians. Apara recognized him as the secretary of defense.

"The French are complaining again?"

"They've never stopped complaining, Madam President. Now they've got the Russians joining the chorus. They've asked for an emergency meeting of NATO."

"Not the General Assembly?"

The secretary of defense almost smiled. "No, ma'am. Even the French realize that the U.N. can't stop us."

A murmur of suppressed laughter rippled along the table. Apara felt anger. *These people use the United Nations when it suits them, and ignore the U.N. otherwise.*

The secretary of state, sitting at the president's right hand, was a thickset older man with a heavy thatch of gray hair that flopped stubbornly over his forehead. He held up a blunt-fingered hand and the table fell silent.

"I must repeat, Madam President," he said in a grave, dolorous voice, "that we have not yet exhausted all our diplomatic and economic options. Military force should be our *last* choice, after all other possibilities have been foreclosed, not our first choice."

"We don't have time for that," snapped the secretary of defense. "And those people don't respect anything but force, anyway."

"I disagree," said state. "Our U.N. ambassador tells me that they are willing to allow the United Nations to arbitrate our differences."

"The United Nations," the president muttered.

"As an honest broker—"

"Yeah, and we'll be the honest brokee," one of the admirals wisecracked. Everyone around the table laughed.

Then the president said, "Our U.N. ambassador is a well-known weak sister. Why do you think I put him there in New York, Carlos, instead of giving him your portfolio?"

The secretary of state was not deterred. "Invading a sovereign nation is a serious decision. American soldiers and aircrew will be killed."

The president glared at him. "All right, Carlos, you've made your point. Now let's get on with it."

One of the admirals said, "We're ready with the nuclear option, if and when it's needed."

"Good," snapped the president.

And on it went, for more than an hour. The fundamentalist regime of Iran was going to be toppled by American military power. Its infiltration of other Moslem nations would end, its support of international terrorism would be wiped out.

Terrorism, Apara growled silently. *They speak of using nuclear weapons, and they call the Iranians terrorists.*

And what am I? she asked herself. *What is the Cabal and the Cause we fight for? What other weapons do we have except terror? How can we struggle for a just world, a world free of domination, unless we use terror? We have no armies, no fleets of ships or planes. Despite the lies their media publish, we have no nuclear weapons, and we would not use them if we did.*

Apara felt sure of that. The guiding precept of the Cause was to strike at the leaders of oppression and aggression. Why kill harmless women and children? Why strike the innocent? Or even the soldiers who merely carry out the orders of their leaders?

Strike the leaders! Put terror in *their* hearts. That was the strategy of the Cabal, the goal of the Cause.

Brave talk, Apara thought. *Tonight we will see if it works.*

Apara glided along the wall until she was standing behind the president. She looked down at the woman's auburn hair, so perfectly curled and tinted. The president's fingernails were perfect, too: shaped and colored beautifully. *She's never chipped a nail by doing hard work*, Apara thought.

I could kill her now and it would look to them as if she had been struck down by God.

But her orders were otherwise. Apara waited.

The meeting broke up at last with the president firmly deciding to launch the attack within twenty-four hours.

"Tell me the instant everything's ready to go," she said to the chairman of the joint chiefs.

"Yes, ma'am," he said. "We'll need your positive order at that point."

"You'll get it."

She rose from her chair, and they all got to their feet. Like a ghost, Apara followed the president through the door into a little sitting room, where two more uniformed security guards snapped to attention.

They accompanied her down the corridor to the main section of the mansion and left her at the elevator that went up to the living quarters on the top floor. Apara climbed the stairs; the elevator was too small. She feared the president would sense her presence in its cramped confines.

Unseen, unsensed, Apara tiptoed through the broad upstairs hallway with its golden carpet and spacious windows at either end. There were surveillance cameras discreetly placed up by the ceiling, but otherwise no obvious security up at this level—except the electronic sensors on the windows, of course.

The president lived alone here, except for her personal servants. Her husband had died years earlier, during her election campaign, in an airplane crash that won her a huge sympathy vote.

Apara loitered in the hallway, not daring to rest on one of the plush couches lining the walls, until a servant bearing a tray with a silver carafe and bottles of pills entered the president's bedroom. Apara slipped in behind her.

The black woman turned her head, frowning slightly, as if she heard a movement behind her or felt a breath on the back of her neck. Apara froze for a moment, then edged away as the woman reached for the door and closed it.

The president was showering, judging by the sounds coming from the bathroom. Legs aching from being on her feet for so many hours, Apara went to the far window and glanced out at the darkened garden, then turned back to watch the servant deposit the tray on the president's night table and leave the room, silent and almost as unnoticed as Apara herself.

There was one wooden chair in the bedroom, and Apara sat on it gratefully, knowing that she would leave no telltale indentation on its hard surface. She felt very tired, sleepy. The adrenaline had drained out of her during the long meeting downstairs. She hoped the president would finish her shower and get into bed and go to sleep quickly.

It was not to be. The president came out of the bathroom soon enough, but she sat up in bed and read for almost another hour before finally putting down the paperback novel and reaching for the pills on the night table. One, two, three different pills she took, with sips of water or whatever was in the carafe the servant had left.

At last the president sank back on her pillows, snapped her fingers to turn off the lights, and closed her eyes. Apara waited the better part of another hour before stirring off the chair. She had to be certain that the president was truly, deeply asleep.

Slowly she walked to the side of the bed. She stared at the woman lying there, straining to hear the rhythm of her breathing through the insulated helmet.

Deep, slow breaths. *She's really sleeping,* Apara decided. If the thought of invading another country and killing thousands of people bothered her, she gave no indication of it. *Maybe the pills she took help her to sleep. She must have some qualms about what she's going to do.*

Apara realized she was the one with the qualms. *I can leave her here and get out of the mansion undetected,* she told herself.

And the Cause, the purpose of her life, would evaporate like dew in the hot desert sun. Muldoon would be despairing, Ahmed so furious that he would never speak to her again. They would know she was unreliable, a risk to their own safety.

Strike! she told herself. *They are all counting on you. Everything depends on you.*

She struck.

By seven-fifteen the next morning the White House was surrounded by an armed cordon of U.S. Marines. No one was allowed onto the grounds, no one was allowed to leave the mansion.

Apara had already left; she simply walked out with the cleaning crew, a few minutes after 5:00 A.M.

The president summoned her secretary of state to the Oval Office at eight sharp. It was early for him, and he had to pass through the gauntlet of Marines as well as the regular guards and Secret Service agents. He stared in wonder as more Marines, in their colorful full-dress uniforms, stood in place of the usual servants.

"What's going on?" he asked the president when he was finally ushered into the oval office.

She looked ghastly: her face was gray, her eyes darting nervously. She clutched a thin scrap of paper in one hand.

"Never mind," the president said curtly. "Sit down."

The secretary of state sat in front of her desk. He himself felt bleary-eyed and rumpled, this early in the morning.

Without preamble, the president asked, "Carlos, do you seriously think we can settle this crisis without a military strike?"

The secretary of state looked surprised, but he quickly regained his wits. "I've been trying to tell you that for the past six weeks, Alicia."

"You think diplomacy can get us what we want."

"Diplomacy and economic pressures, yes. We can even get the United Nations on our side, if we call off this military strike. It's not too late, you know."

The president leaned back in her chair, fiddling with that scrap of paper, trying to keep her hands from trembling. Unwilling to allow her secretary of state to see how upset she was, she swiveled around to look out the long windows at the springtime morning. Birds chirped happily among the flowers.

"All right," she said, her mind made up. "Tell Muldoon to ask for an emergency session of the Security Council. That's what he's been after all along."

A boyish grin broke across the secretary of state's normally dour face. "I'll phone him right now. He's still in New York."

"Do that," said the president. Then she added, "From your own office."

"Yes, ma'am!"

The secretary of state trotted off happily, leaving the president alone at her desk in the Oval Office. With the note still clutched in her shaking hand.

I'll put the entire White House staff through the wringer, she said to herself. *Every damned one of them. Interrogate them until their brains are fried. I'll find out who's responsible for this . . . this . . .*

She shuddered involuntarily.

They got into my bedroom. My own bedroom! Who did it? How many people in this house are plotting against me?

They could have killed me!

I'll turn the note over to the Secret Service. No, they screwed up. If they were doing their job right this would never have happened. The attorney general. Give it to the FBI. They'll find the culprit.

Her hands were shaking so badly she could hardly read the note. *Remember, Caesar, thou art dust.*

That's all the note said. Yet it struck terror into her heart. *They could have killed me. This was just a warning. They could have killed me just as easily as leaving this warning on my pillow.*

For the first time in her life, she felt afraid. She looked around the Oval Office, at the familiar trappings of power, and felt afraid. *It's like being haunted*, she said to herself.

In his apartment in New York, the U.S. ambassador to the United Nations nodded as he spoke to the president's secretary of state.

"That's good news, Carlos!" said Herbert Muldoon, with a hint of Irish lilt in his voice. "Excellent news. I'm sure the president's made the right choice."

He cut the connection with Washington and immediately punched up the number of the U.N.'s secretary general, thinking as his fingers tapped on the keyboard: It worked! *Apara did the job. Now we'll have to send her to Tehran. And others, too, of course. The mullahs may be perfectly willing to send young assassins to their deaths, but I wonder how they'll react when they know they're the ones being targeted.*

We'll find out soon.

LIFE AS WE KNOW IT

The scientific effort to determine if life exists elsewhere in the universe has been ridiculed by politicians, pundits, and even some scientists.

When NASA established a department dedicated to the search for extraterrestrial life, for example, Harvard biologist George Gaylord Simpson quipped that it was the first time in the history of science that an organization had been put together to study a subject before evidence of its subject matter had been found.

Politicians have turned SETI (the search for extraterrestrial intelligence) into a well-publicized whipping boy. However small the funds allocated for SETI, some representative or senator loudly proclaims that it's a vast waste of money and gets Congress to cancel the appropriation. It is only through the private efforts of activist groups such as the Planetary Society that astronomers have been able to continue the search.

No extraterrestrial life has yet been found, although in 1996, NASA scientists reported that microscopic structures inside a meteorite that originated on Mars may be the fossilized remains of 3.5-billion-year-old Martian bacteria.

Radio telescopes have not detected any intelligent signals, although they have barely begun to scratch the surface of the problem. There are billions of stars and thousands of millions of wavelengths to be examined.

Our spacecraft have landed on the Moon, Mars, and Venus; others have flown past all the planets of our solar system, even distantmost

Pluto. The Moon is, as we expcted, airless, waterless and lifeless. Mars is a frigid desert, although there is some hope that life may have arisen there, only to be extinguished in the planet's increasing aridity. Venus is an utterly barren oven, with surface temperatures hot enough to melt aluminum and a heavy choking atmosphere of carbon dioxide.

Jupiter, largest of the solar system's planets, might have the chemical ingredients for life swirling in its multicolored clouds. If I were a betting man, I'd put my money on Jupiter as the most likely place to find some form of extraterrestrial life. Not intelligent life, most likely. But you never know.

Sadly, this story contains a glaring anachronism. Carl Sagan died in late 1996, more than two years after this story was written, and a thousand years too soon. He is a living character in the story, just as his dedication and drive are still living influences in the continuing search for extraterrestrial life.

THEY WERE ALL THERE, all the Grand Old Men of the field: McKay, Kliest, Taranto—even Sagan, little more than an ancient withered husk in his electric wheelchair. But the fire still burned in his deep, dark eyes.

All the egos and superegos who had given their lifetimes to the search for extraterrestrial life. Often derided by the media, scorned by the politicians, even scoffed at by their fellow scientists, this was going to be their day. One way or the other.

Jupiter was going to reveal its secrets to them. Today. Life on another world at last. Make or break.

I could feel the tension in the room, like just before a thunderstorm, that electrical smell in the air that makes the hair on your arms stand on end. Careers would be made today, or broken. Mine included. That's why everyone was here, waiting impatiently, chattering nervously, staring at the display screens that still showed nothing but crackling streaks of random noise.

The mission control center was a big room, huge really, but now it was jammed with bodies, hot and sweaty, buzzing with voices in half a dozen languages. The project scientists, all the top government officials, invitees like Sagan, hangers-on who inveigled their way in, everybody who thought or hoped they'd capture some of the glory of the moment, and more than a hundred news reporters and photographers, all crammed into the mission control chamber, all talking at once. Like a tribe of apes, jabbering, gesticulating, posturing to hide their dreams and ambitions and fear.

They didn't want to miss the first images from beneath the cloud tops of Jupiter. Even if it killed them, they had to be at mission control when the probe's first pictures came in.

Most of the reporters clustered around Sagan, of course, although quite a few hung near Lopez-Oyama, the center's director. Our boss.

Beautiful Allie stayed at Lopez-Oyama's side. Allison Brandt, she of the golden hair and pendulous breasts. I dreamed about Allie, saw her flawlessly naked, smiling at me willingly. In my waking hours I thought about her endlessly, picturing myself doing things with her that not even my dreams dared to imagine.

But she stayed beside the director, next to the power and the attention. I was merely an engineer, neither powerful nor glamorous. Still, I longed for Allie. Lusted after her. Even as she smiled for the photographers I noticed how she had artfully undone an extra couple of buttons on the front of her blouse.

"Imagery systems check," droned the voice of the mission controller. The huge room fell absolutely silent. I held my breath.

"Imagery systems functioning."

We all let out a sigh of relief. Me especially. The imagery systems were my responsibility. I built them. If they failed, the mission failed, I failed, six dozen careers would go down the tubes, six dozen frustrated scientists would be seeking my blood.

Our probe into Jupiter was unmanned, of course. No astronaut could survive the crushing pressures and turbulent storms beneath the cloud deck of Jupiter. No one knew if our robotic probe was sturdy enough to reach below the cloud tops and survive.

Over the years, the earlier probes had shown that beneath those gaudy colorful swirling clouds there was an ocean ten times larger than the whole Earth. An ocean of water. Heavily laced with ammonia, to be sure, but water nonetheless. There was only one other world in the solar system where liquid water existed—Earth. We knew that liquid water meant life on Earth.

Did it on Jupiter?

"Jupiter represents our best chance for finding extraterrestrial life." Lopez-Oyama had said those words to the congressional committee that ruled on NASA's budget, when he went begging to them for the money to fund our mission.

"Life?" asked one of the congressmen, looking startled, almost afraid. "Like animals and trees and such?"

I watched those hearings on TV; we all did, sitting on the edges of our chairs in the center's cafeteria while the politicians decided if we lived or died. I had picked a seat next to Allie, although she barely acknowledged my presence beside her. She stared unwaveringly at the screen.

With a tolerant little shake of his head, Lopez-Oyama replied, "It probably won't be life as we know it here on Earth, sir. That would be too much to hope for."

"Then what will it be like?"

"We just don't know. We've never found life on another world before." Then he added, "But if we don't find life on Jupiter, then I doubt that life of any form exists anywhere else in the solar system."

"Do you mean intelligent life?" asked the committee chairwoman sharply.

Lopez-Oyama smiled winningly at her. "No, ma'am," he said. "Intelligent life would be too much to expect. I'll be happy if we find something like bacteria."

Now, as the moment of truth approached, the scientists cramming mission control were busily spinning theories about what the cameras would find in Jupiter's global ocean. They couldn't wait for the actual pictures, they had to show how clever they were to impress the reporters and each other. A bunch of alpha male apes, preening and displaying their brains instead of their fangs. Competing for primacy and the attention of the news reporters who were clustered around them, goggle-eyed, recorders humming. Even the women scientists were playing the one-upmanship game, in the name of equality.

To her credit, Allie remained quiet. She was as clever a scientist as any of them, but she refused to involve herself in the primate competition. She didn't have to. Her standing in the hierarchy was as secure as could be.

None of them paid the slightest attention to me. I was only the engineer who had built the imaging system. I wasn't a scientist, just the guy with dirt under his fingernails who made the machinery work. I'd be ignored unless something went wrong.

To tell the truth, I paid damned little attention to them and their constant gabbling. My eyes were focused on long-legged Allie, by far the most desirable female in the pack. How could I make her notice me? How could I get her to smile in my direction instead of clinging so close to the boss? How could I get to be an alpha male in her lustrous eyes?

"Data coming through."

From nearly a thousand million kilometers away, my cameras were functioning. Had already functioned, as a matter of fact, more than eight hours ago. It took that long for the telemetry signal to travel from Jupiter to our antennas out in the desert.

Suddenly all their jabbering stopped. Mission control fell absolutely silent. The first images began to raster across the main display screens, line by line. Live, from beneath the endless cloud deck of Jupiter.

Each display screen showed imagery from a different wavelength. We had blue, green, red, infrared, and even radar imaging systems. Despite all their theories, none of the scientists had been able to tell me which wavelengths would work best beneath Jupiter's clouds.

I had asked them how much sunlight filtered through the clouds. None of them could tell me. Which wavelengths of sunlight penetrated the clouds? None of them knew. I had to grope blindly and include as broad a spectrum of instruments as possible.

Now I swiveled my gaze from one screen to the next. The blue system was pretty much of a washout, nothing but a blur, as I had expected. The atmosphere must be filled with haze, a planetwide fog of ammonia and sulfur molecules.

"That looks like wave tops!"

The infrared image indeed looked as if it was plunging toward the surface of a turbulent ocean. Radar showed more detail. Waves, crests and troughs racing madly across the screen. A rough sea down there. A very turbulent, storm-tossed ocean.

"Immersion in three minutes," said mission control. The probe was going to hit those waves. It was designed to sink slowly to a depth of about a hundred kilometers, where it would—we hoped—attain a neutral buoyancy and float indefinitely.

Of course, if we saw something interesting at a shallower depth, the probe could eject some of its ballast on command and rise accordingly. The trouble was that it took more than eight hours for any of our commands to reach the probe. We had to pray that whatever we found wouldn't go away in the course of eight hours—almost a full revolution of the planet, a whole Jovian day.

I summoned up all my courage and sidled closer to Allie, squeezing slowly through the crush of bodies. They were all staring at the screens, ignoring me, watching the ocean waves and the streams of low-level clouds streaking past. Storm clouds, swirling viciously.

I pushed between Allie and Lopez-Oyama. Not daring to try to say anything to her, I looked down on the boss's balding pate, and half whispered, "I didn't think we'd get much from the blue at this level."

He was so short that he had to crane his neck to look at me. He said nothing, just nodded in his inscrutable way.

Allie was almost my own height. We were nearly eye to eye.

"The infrared is fabulous," she said. To me!

"It is working pretty well, isn't it?" Be modest in triumph. All the books of advice I had studied told me that women appreciated men who were successful, yet not boastful; strong but sensitive.

"It won't work as well once it's underwater, though, will it?" she asked.

I suppressed the urge to grab her and carry her off. Instead, I deliberately turned to look at the screens instead of her cool hazel eyes.

"That's when the blue or blue-green should come into its own," I said, trying to keep my voice from trembling.

"If the laser works," said Lopez-Oyama. It was almost a growl. He was distinctly unhappy that I had stepped between him and Allie.

Mission control announced, "Impact in ten seconds."

The whole crowd seemed to surge forward slightly, lean toward the screens, waiting.

"Impact!"

All the screens went blank for a heart-stopping instant. But before anyone could shout or groan or even take a breath, they came on again. Radar was blank, of course, and the infrared was just a smudge.

But the blue and blue-green images were clear and beautiful.

"My god, it's like scuba diving in Hawaii," Allie said.

That's how crisp and clear the pictures were. We could see bubbles from our splash-in and light filtering down from the ocean's surface. The water looked crystal clear.

And empty. No fish, no fronds of vegetation, nothing that looked like life in that ammonia-laced water, nothing at all to be seen.

"Not deep enough yet," grumbled Lopez-Oyama. If we found nothing, his career was finished, we all knew that. I caught a glimpse of the congressional committee chairwoman, up in the special VIP section behind plate-glass windows, staring hard at him.

For more than an hour we saw nothing but bubbles from the probe's descent. The faint light from the surface dwindled, as we had expected. At precisely the preprogrammed moment, the laser turned on and began sweeping its intense light through the water.

"That should attract anything that can swim," Allie said hopefully.

"Or repel anything that's accustomed to swimming in darkness," said one of the scientists, almost with a smirk.

The laser beam ballooned in the water, of course. I had expected that; counted on it, really. It acted as a bright wide searchlight for me. I wanted to tell Allie why I had chosen that specific wavelength, how proud I was that it was working just as I had planned it would.

But her attention was riveted to the screen, and Lopez-Oyama pushed to her side again, squeezing me out from between them.

Lopez-Oyama was perspiring. I could see drops of sweat glistening on his bald spot.

"Deeper," he muttered. "We've got to go deeper. The ocean is heated from below. Life-forms must be down there."

I thought I heard a slightly desperate accent on the word "must."

"Spectrographic data coming in," announced mission control.

All eyes turned to the screen that began to show the smears and bands of colors from the probe's mass spectrometer. All eyes except mine. I kept my attention on the images from the laser-illuminated sea. They were becoming cloudy, it seemed to me.

"There's the ammonia band," someone said.

"And carbon compounds, I think."

"My god, those are organics!"

"Organic compounds in the water!"

"Life."

"Don't jump to conclusions," Lopez-Oyama warned. But his voice was shaking with excitement.

Allie actually clutched at my shoulder. "Can your cameras see anything?"

The water was cloudy, murky, even where the laser beam swept through; it looked like a thin fog, glistening but obscuring.

"The ocean's filled with organic chemicals at this level," one of the scientists said.

"Particles," corrected another scientist.

"Food," somebody quipped.

"For who?"

"Deeper," Sagan said, his voice surprisingly strong. "The organic particles are drifting downward. If there's anything in that ocean that eats them, it's down at a deeper level."

The probe was designed to attain neutral buoyancy at a depth of a hundred kilometers. We were approaching that depth now. It might not be enough.

"How deep can we push it?" Lopez-Oyama asked no one in particular.

Immediately a dozen opinions sprang out of the eager, excited, sweaty chattering apes. Earlier probes had been crushed like soda cans by the immense pressure of the Jovian ocean. But I knew that the probe's limits were not only structural, but communications-based. The probe could not hold more than a hundred kilometers of the hair-thin optical fiber that carried its comm signals to the surface of the ocean. So even if it could survive lower depths, we would lose touch with it.

"What's that?"

In the hazy light, a dark shape drifted by, too distant to make out any detail.

"Follow it!" Lopez-Oyama snapped.

Then his face reddened. It would take more than eight hours for his order to reach the probe. In his excitement he had forgotten.

Allie turned to me. "Are the close-up cameras working?"

They were. I gestured toward the screens that showed their imagery. The dark hulk, whatever it was, had not come within the narrow focus of either of the close-view cameras. Both screens showed nothing but the cloudy water, tinted sickly green by the laser light.

"Another one!" somebody shouted.

This time the shape drifted past the view of one of the close-up cameras, briefly. We saw a bulbous dark dome, almost spherical, with snakelike appendages dangling from its bottom.

"Tentacles!"

"It's an animal! Like an octopus!"

I scanned the numerical data on the bottom of the screen. The object, whatever it was, was three and a half kilometers from the probe. And it was 432 meters long, from the top of its dome to the tip of its tentacles. Huge. Fifteen times bigger than a blue whale. Immense.

"It's not moving."

"It's drifting in the current."

"The tentacles are just hanging there. No activity that I can see."

"Conserving energy?"

"Maybe that's the way it hunts for prey."

"Trolling?"

It looked dead to me. Inert. Unmoving. It drifted out of the close-up camera's view and all the heads in the room swiveled to the wide-angle view. The dark lump did nothing to show it might be alive.

"What's the spectrograph show?"

"Not a helluva lot."

"Absorption bands, lots of them."

"Chlorophyll?"

"Don't be a butthead!"

Allie was the only one who seemed to realize the significance of what we were seeing. "If it's an animal, it's either in a quiescent, resting phase . . . or it's dead."

"The first extraterrestrial creature we find, and it's dead," somebody groused.

"There'll be more," said Lopez-Oyama, almost cheerfully.

I looked across the room at Sagan. He was leaning forward in his wheelchair, eyes intent on the screens, as if he could make something more appear just by concentrating. The reporters were gaping, not saying a word for a blessed change, forgetting to ask questions while the underwater views of the Jovian ocean filled the display screens.

Then I looked at Allie again. Her lovely face was frozen in an expression of . . . what? Fear? Dread? Did she have the same terrible suspicion that was building in my mind?

It was almost another hour before we saw another of the tentacled creatures. The probe had reached its maximum depth and was drifting through the murky water. Particles floated past the cameras, some of them as big as dinner plates. None of them active. They all just drifted by, sinking slowly like dark chunks of soot meandering toward the bottom of that sunless sea.

Then we saw the second of the octopods. And quickly afterward, an entire school of them, hundreds, perhaps a thousand or more. The sensors on the probe went into overdrive; the automatic analysis programs would count the creatures for us. We simply stared at them.

Different sizes. Lots of small ones—if something a dozen times the size of a whale can be called small.

"Babies," Allie murmured.

A family group, I thought. A clan. All of them dead. There was no mistaking it now. My cameras showed them clearly. Big saucer eyes clouded and unmoving. Open wounds in some of them. Tentacles hanging limply. They were just drifting along like ghosts, immense dark shadows that once had been alive.

Time lost all meaning for us. The big mission control center fell absolutely silent. Even the most assertive and egocentric of the male apes among us stopped trying to make instant theories and simply stared at a scene of devastation. A holocaust.

At last Lopez-Oyama whispered, "They're all dead. The whole fucking planet's dead."

Then we saw the city. A sort of collective gasp went through the crowded mission control room when it came into view.

It was a structure, a vast, curving structure that floated in that mighty ocean, graceful despite its immense size. Curves atop curves. Huge round ports and beautifully symmetrical archways, a gigantic city built by or for the immense creatures that floated, dead and decaying, before our camera eyes.

The numbers flickering at the bottom of the screens told us that the city was hundreds of kilometers away from our lenses, yet it filled the screens of the narrow-view cameras. We could see delicate traceries along its massive curving flank, curves and whorls etched into its structure.

"Writing," someone breathed.

A dream city, built of alien inspirations and desires. It staggered our Earthbound senses, dwarfed us with its immensity and grandeur.

It was enormous yet graceful and entirely beautiful in an eerie, unearthly way. It was dead.

As it swung slowly, majestically, in the powerful ocean currents we saw that it was only a fragment of the original structure, a piece somehow torn off from its original whole. Jagged cracks and ragged edges showed where it had been ripped away from the rest of the city. To me it looked like a fragment of a shell from an enormous Easter egg, beautifully decorated, that had been smashed by some titanic unseen malevolency.

"War?" someone's voice whispered plaintively. "Did they destroy themselves?"

But I knew better. And I couldn't stand it. I turned away from the screens, away from the views of dead Jupiter, and pushed through the crowd that was still gaping stupidly at my cameras' views. I was suffocating, strangling. I had to have fresh air or die.

I bolted out the main doors and into the corridor, empty and silent, deserted by all the people who had crammed mission control. The first outside door I could find I kicked through, heedless of the red EMERGENCY ONLY sign and the wailing alarm that hooted accusingly after me.

The brilliant late-afternoon sun surprised me, made my eyes suddenly water after the cool shadows inside the building. I took in a deep raw lungful of hot, dry desert air. It felt like brick dust, alien, as if part of me were still deeply immersed in Jupiter's mighty ocean.

"It's all ruined." Allie's voice.

Turning, I saw that she had followed me. The tears in her eyes were not from the bright sunshine.

"All dead," she sobbed. "The city . . . all of them destroyed."

"The comet," I said. Shoemaker-Levy 9 had struck Jupiter fifty years ago with the violence of a million hydrogen bombs.

"Fifty years," Allie moaned. "They were intelligent. We could have communicated with them!"

If we had only been fifty years earlier, I thought. Then the true horror of it struck me. What could we have told them, fifty years ago? That a shattered comet was going to rain destruction on them? That no matter what they had built, what they had learned or hoped for or prayed to, their existence was going to be wiped out forever? That there's absolutely nothing either they or we could do about it?

"It's cold," Allie said, almost whimpering.

She wanted me to go to her, to hold her, to comfort her the way one warm-blooded primate ape comforts another. But what was the use? What was the use of anything?

What difference did any of it make in a world where you could spend millions of years evolving into intelligence, build a civilization, reach a peak of knowledge where you begin to study and understand the universe around you, only to learn that the universe can destroy you utterly, without remorse, without the slightest shred of hope for salvation?

I looked past Allie, shivering in the last rays of the dying day. Looked past the buildings and antennas, past the gray-brown hills and the distant wrinkled mountains that were turning blood red in the inevitable sunset.

I saw Jupiter. I saw those intelligent creatures wiped away utterly and implacably, as casually as a man flicks a spot of dust off his sleeve.

And I knew that somewhere out in that uncaring sky another comet was heading inexorably for Earth to end all our dreams, all our strivings, all our desires.

DELTA VEE

You meet a lot of people over the years, and as a writer's career advances, some of those people become close friends, no matter how geographically distant they may be.

One of my closest friends—even though he lives a three hours' drive from me—is Rick Wilber. Rick is a fellow writer, a teacher of journalism at Florida Southern University, and was editor of the Tampa Tribune Fiction Quarterly.

The fourth edition of 1995's Fiction Quarterly *was scheduled to be published on Sunday, the thirty-first of December. Rick asked me to contribute a story with a New Year's Eve theme.*

"Delta Vee" is the result.

By the way, if you detect a faint hint of Cinderella in this tale, it was an unconscious influence that I myself didn't see until the first draft of the story was finished. Something about that old clock striking a midnight deadline must have, well, struck a chime in my subconscious mind.

IT WAS GOING TO BE the last New Year's Eve. Forever. Six months after the last hydrogen bomb was dismantled, a Japanese amateur astronomer discovered the comet. It was named after him, therefore: Comet Hara.

For more than thirty years, special satellites and monitoring stations on both the Earth and the Moon had kept a dedicated watch for asteroids that might endanger our world. Sixty-five million years ago, the impact of an asteroid some ten miles wide drove the dinosaurs and three-fourths of all the living species on Earth into permanent oblivion.

Comet Hara was 350 miles long, and slightly more than 100 miles wide, an oblong chunk of ice slowly tumbling through space, roughly the size of the state of Florida minus its panhandle.

It was not detected until too late.

While asteroids and many comets coast through the solar system close to the plane in which the planets themselves orbit, Comet Hara came tumbling into view high in the northern sky. The guardian battery of satellites and monitoring stations did not see it until it was well inside the orbit of Saturn.

It came hurtling, now, out of the dark vastness of the unknown gulfs beyond Pluto, streaking toward an impact that would destroy civilization and humanity forever. It was aimed squarely at Earth, like the implacable hand of fate, due to strike somewhere in North America between the Great Lakes and the Front Range of the Rockies.

Comet Hara was mostly ice, instead of rock. But a 350-mile-long chunk of ice, moving at more than seven miles per second, would explode on Earth with the force of millions of H-bombs. Megatons of dirt would be thrown into the air. Continentwide firestorms would rage unchecked, their plumes of smoke darkening the sky for months. No sunlight would reach the ground anywhere. Winter would freeze the world from pole to pole, withering crops, killing by starvation those who did not die quickly in the explosion and flames. The world would die.

Desperate calculations showed that Comet Hara would strike the Earth on New Year's Eve. No one would live to see the New Year.

Unless the comet could be diverted.

"It's too much delta vee," said the head of the national space agency. "If we had spotted it earlier, maybe then we'd have had a chance. But now . . ."

The president of the United States and the secretary-general of the United Nations were the only two people in the conference room that the former astronaut recognized. The others were leaders of other nations, he knew; twenty of them sitting around the polished mahogany table like twenty mourners at a funeral. Their own.

"What's delta vee?" asked the president. She had been a biochemist before entering politics. None of the men and women around the table knew much about astronautics.

"Change in velocity," he said, knowing it explained nothing to them. "Look—it's like this . . ."

Using his hands the way a pilot would, the former astronaut showed the comet approaching Earth. Any rocket vehicle sent out to intercept it would be going in the opposite direction from the comet.

"It takes a helluva lot of rocket thrust to get that high above the plane of the ecliptic," he said, moving his two hands together like a pair of airplanes rushing into a head-on collision.

"That's the plane in which the planets orbit?" asked the prime minister of Italy.

"More or less," the ex-astronaut replied. "Anyway, you need a huge jolt of thrust to get a spacecraft out to the comet, but when it gets there it's going the wrong way!"

"Then it will have to turn around," said the American president impatiently.

The NASA chief nodded unhappily. "Yes, ma'am. But it isn't all that easy to turn around in space. The craft has to kill its forward velocity and then put on enough speed again to catch up with the comet."

"I don't see the difficulty."

"Those maneuvers require rocket thrust. Lots of it. Rocket thrust requires propellants. Tons and tons of propellants. We just don't have spacecraft capable of doing the job."

"But couldn't you build one?"

"Sure. In a year or two."

"We only have five months," said the secretary-general, sounding somewhere between miffed and angry.

"That's the problem," admitted the space chief.

Hovering weightlessly in the cramped little cubbyhole that passed for the bridge of her spacecraft, Cindy Lundquist stared at the communications screen. The image was grainy and streaked with interference, but she could still see the utterly grim expression on the face of Arlan Prince.

"And after a thorough analysis of all the available options," the handsome young man was saying, "they've come to the conclusion that yours is the only spacecraft capable of reaching the comet in time."

Arlan was the government's coordinator of operations for all the mining ships in the Asteroid Belt, a job that would drive a lesser man to madness or at least fits of choler. There were dozens of mining ships plying the Belt, each owned and operated by a cantankerous individualist who resented any interference from some bureaucrat back on Earth.

But Arlan Prince did not descend into madness or even choleric anger. He smiled and patiently tried to help the miners whenever he could. Cindy dreamed about his smile. It was to die for.

"I don't want to mislead you, Cindy," he was saying, very seriously. "It's a tricky, dangerous mission . . ."

Grease my monkey! she thought. *He wants me to go out and catch a comet? They must be in ultimate despair if they expect this creaking old bucket of bolts to catch anything except terminal metal fatigue.*

Cindy's aged spacecraft was coasting along the outer fringe of the Asteroid Belt, well beyond the orbit of Mars, almost four times farther from the Sun than the Earth's orbit. Since she was on the opposite side of the Sun from Earth's current position, it took thirty-eight minutes for a communications signal to reach her lonely little mining craft.

That meant that she couldn't have a conversation with Arlan Prince. She could talk back, of course, but it would be more than half an hour before the man heard what she had to say.

So he didn't wait for her response. He just went right on talking, laying the whole load on her shoulders.

"I know it's a lot to ask, but the entire world is depending on you. Yours is the only spacecraft anywhere in the solar system that has even a slight chance of catching up with the comet and diverting it."

He's not going to give me a chance to say no, Cindy realized. *I either do it or the world gets smashed.*

A thousand questions flitted through her mind. *Why can't they just send some missiles out to the comet and blast it into ice cubes? No missiles and no H-bombs*, she remembered. *They've all been dismantled.*

Do I have enough propellant to get to the comet? That's a whole mess of delta vee we're talking about. While Arlan droned on lugubriously, she flicked her fingers across her computer keypad. The numbers told her she could reach the comet, just barely. If nothing at all went wrong.

Which was asking a lot from this ancient wheeze of a mining

ship she had inherited from her father. The old man had died brokenhearted out here among the asteroids that orbited between Mars and Jupiter. Looking for a mountain of gold floating in the dark emptiness of space.

All he ever found were chunks of nickel-iron or carbon-rich rock. Just enough to keep him going. Just enough to get by and raise his only child out in the loneliness of this cold, dark frontier.

Cindy couldn't remember her mother at all. She had died when Cindy was still an infant, killed by a tiny asteroid no bigger than a bullet that had punctured her spacesuit while she worked outside the ship alongside her husband.

Her father had died of cancer only a few months ago. An occupational hazard, he had joked feebly, for anyone who spends as much time exposed to the radiation of space as an asteroid miner has to.

So now all she had was the old spacecraft, so tiny and tight that you had to go into the airlock to have enough room to sneeze. It was all the home that Cindy had ever known, and all she ever would know, yet it felt more like a prison to her.

Cindy knew she would spend her life alone in this ship, plying the vast empty spaces of the asteroid belt. Miners were few and very far between. Born and raised in the weightlessness of zero gravity, her delicate bones could never hold her up on the surface of Earth, or even the lighter gravity of the Moon.

Arlan was still talking earnestly about saving the Earth from certain doom. "According to our figures, you won't have enough propellant to return once you've matched velocities with the comet, therefore we will send a drone tanker to your expected position . . ."

Drone tanker, Cindy thought. *And if I miss it I'll go sailing out of the solar system forever. I'll die all alone, farther from Earth than anyone's flown before.*

So what? a voice sneered at her. *You're all alone now, aren't you? You'll always be alone.*

Wedged amid consoles and control boards like a key in a slot, Cindy turned to the laser control console and pecked at its faded color-coded keys. Power okay. Focusing optics needed work, but she could bring them in and spruce them up during the couple of months it would take to reach the comet.

She turned off the sound of Arlan's somber voice and spoke into her comm unit's microphone. "Okay, I'll do it. Track me good and have that tanker out there."

The truth was, she could not have refused anything that Arlan Prince asked of her, even though they had never met face-to-face. In fact, they had never been closer to each other than fifty million miles.

The comet was *huge.* Cindy had never seen anything so big. It blotted out the sky, a massive overpowering expanse of dirty gray-white. She was so close that she couldn't see all of it, any more than a butterfly hovering near a flower can see the entire garden.

Cindy floated weightlessly to the ship's only observation port and craned her neck, gaping at the monumental stretch of dust-filmed ice. The port's crystal surface felt cold to her touch. There was nothing outside except frigid emptiness, her fingers reminded her.

In one corner of her control console, a display screen showed how the comet looked from Earth: a big bright light in the sky, trailing a long blue-white plume that stretched halfway across the sky. It was beautiful, really, but every word she had heard from Earth was trembling with fear. The comet was pointed like the finger of doom, growing larger in Earth's sky every night, getting so near and so bright that it could be seen even in daylight.

Other screens scattered across her consoles scrolled graphs and numbers. Cindy had slaved the laser control to the computer calculations beamed up from Earth. When the moment came she wouldn't even have to press a button. It would all happen automatically.

If her laser worked.

The tanker was nowhere in sight, but Arlan Prince kept assuring her that it was on its way and would be at the rendezvous point on time.

Or else I'm dead, Cindy thought. And that voice inside her head scoffed, *You're dead anyway. You've been more dead than alive ever since your father left you.*

The thundering howl of the power generator start led her. Looking through the narrow observation port, she saw a sudden jet of glittering white vapor spurt from the comet's surface, like the spout of a gigantic whale's breath blowing into the dark vacuum of space. Cindy clapped her hands over her ears and stared at the readouts on her display screens. The laser had never run this long, and she feared that it would break down long before its job was finished.

When it finally shut off, Cindy glanced at the master clock set into the console above her head. Its digital numbers told her that the laser ran a full two minutes. Exactly 120 seconds, as programmed.

Was it enough?

Hours passed. The comet was drifting away, slowly at first, but as Cindy stared out through the observation port it seemed to gather speed and leave her farther and farther behind.

Not even the bleeding comet wants to be near me, she thought. She waved to it, a great oblong chunk of grayish white, still spurting a glistening plume of icy vapor. *Good-bye*, she called silently, knowing that she was alone once again.

When the call from Earth came on her comm screen, it was the secretary-general of the United Nations. The woman had tears in her eyes.

"You've done it," she said, solemnly, like a worshiper thanking a god. "You've saved the world."

Cindy's spacecraft was so close to Earth now that they could talk with only a half-minute's delay.

"You diverted it into a trajectory that's pulling it toward the Sun," the secretary-general said, trying to smile. "It will break up into fragments and then fall into the Sun, if it doesn't melt completely first."

"You mean I killed it?" Cindy felt a pang of regret, remorse. The comet had been beautiful, in its way.

"You've saved the world," the secretary-general said gratefully.

Cindy fished around for something to say, but nothing came to mind.

The secretary-general had more, though.

"The tanker . . ." The woman's voice faltered. With an obvious effort, she went on, "The tanker . . . isn't going to be at the rendezvous point. One of its rocket engines failed . . ."

"It won't be there?" Cindy asked, surprised that her voice sounded so high, so frightened.

"I'm afraid not," said the secretary-general.

Cindy felt her entire body slump with defeat. Numbers were scrolling on her data screens. The tanker would pass near the rendezvous point, but too far away for Cindy to reach it. She had no propulsion fuel left, only a bit of maneuvering thrust, nowhere near enough to chase down the errant tanker.

"Then I'll continue on my current trajectory," she said to the screens.

"Which is the same as the comet's original path," the secretary-general pointed out. She waited a decent interval, then added, "We don't want you to crash into the Earth, of course."

"Of course," said Cindy, as she turned off her communications system. The secretary-general's oh-so-sad face winked out.

Cindy knew that her little ship was no threat to the world. It would burn to cinders once it hit the atmosphere. *Maybe I can jink it a little so I'll blaze through the atmosphere like a falling star*, she thought. *I'll be cremated, and my ashes will scatter all across the world.*

But then she thought, *NO, I'll use the last of my maneuvering thrust to move out of Earth's way altogether. I'll just sail out of the solar system forever. I'll be the first human to reach the stars—in a couple-three million years.*

New Year's Eve.

All across the world people celebrated not only the beginning of a new year, but the end of the fear that had gripped them. Comet Hara was gone. The world had been saved.

Cindy Lundquist floated alone in her little spacecraft as it streaked safely beyond the Earth and speeded out toward the cold darkness of infinite space. For days her communications screen had been filled with gray-headed persons of importance, congratulating her on her heroic and self-sacrificing deed.

Now the screen was blank The world was celebrating New Year's Eve, and she was alone, heading toward oblivion.

Precisely at midnight, on her ship's clock, the comm screen chimed once and the blond, tanned face of Arlan Prince appeared on it, smiling handsomely.

"Hi," he said brightly. "Happy New Year."

Cindy didn't have the heart to smile back at him, handsome though he was.

"I've been put in charge of your rescue operation," he said.

"Rescue operation?"

Nodding, he explained, "Since we weren't able to get the tanker to you, we decided to send out a rescue mission."

"But I'm heading out of the solar system now."

"We know." His smile clouded briefly, then lit up again. "It's going to take us at least six months to build the ship we need, and another six months to reach you."

"You're going to come out after me?"

"Certainly! You saved the world. We can't let you drift off and leave us. You're a celebrity now."

"Oh," said Cindy, dumbfounded.

"But it'll take a year before we get to you," he said, apologetically. "Do you have enough supplies on your ship to last that long?"

Cindy nodded, thinking that she'd have to skimp a lot, but losing a few pounds wouldn't hurt, especially if . . .

"Will you personally come out to get me?" she asked.

"Yes, of course," he replied. "When they asked me to head up the rescue mission, I insisted on it."

"A year from now?"

"Exactly one year from today," he said confidently.

"Then we can celebrate New Year's Eve together, can't we?" Cindy said.

"Indeed we will."

Cindy smiled her best smile at him. "Happy New Year," she said sweetly.

WE'LL ALWAYS
HAVE PARIS

All *that we see or seem*
Is but a dream within a dream
—Edgar Allan Poe

"We'll Always Have Paris" is a piece of fiction about a piece of fiction.

Casablanca is one of the most popular films of all time: romantic, suspenseful, filled with fascinating characters and memorable lines.

I've seen the movie dozens of times, and I've always wondered what happened to Rick and Ilsa and Capt. Reynaud after that unforgettable final scene at the airport.

"We'll Always Have Paris" is my stab at answering my own question. A good story always leaves you asking yourself, What happened afterward?

Here is a possible answer.

HE HAD CHANGED from the old days, but of course going through the war had changed us all.

We French had just liberated Paris from the Nazis, with a bit of help (I must admit) from General Patton's troops. The tumultuous outpouring of relief and gratitude that night was the wildest celebration any of us had ever witnessed.

I hadn't seen Rick during that frantically joyful night, but I knew exactly where to find him. *La Belle Aurore* had hardly changed. I recognized it from his vivid, pained description: the low ceiling, the checkered tablecloths—frayed now after four years of German occupation. The model of the Eiffel Tower on the bar had been taken away, but the spinet piano still stood in the middle of the floor.

There he was, sitting on the cushioned bench by the window, drinking champagne again. Somewhere he had found a blue pinstripe double-breasted suit. He looked good in it; trim and debonair. I was still in uniform and felt distinctly shabby.

In the old days Rick had always seemed older, more knowing than he really was. Now the years of war had made an honest face for him: world-weary, totally aware of human folly, wise with the experience that comes from sorrow.

"Well, well," he said, grinning at me. "Look what the cat dragged in."

"I knew I'd find you here," I said as I strode across the bare wooden floor toward him. Limped, actually; I still had a bit of shrapnel in my left leg.

As I pulled up a chair and sat in it, Rick called to the proprietor, behind the bar, for another bottle.

"You look like hell," he said.

"It was an eventful night. Liberation. Grateful Parisians. Adoring women."

With a nod, Rick muttered, "Any guy in uniform who didn't get laid last night must be a real loser."

I laughed, but then pointed out, "You're not in uniform."

"Very perceptive."

"It's my old police training."

"I'm expecting someone," he said.

"A lady?"

"Uh-huh."

"You can't imagine that she'll be here to—"

"She'll be here," Rick snapped.

Henri put another bottle of champagne on the table, and a fresh glass for me. Rick opened it with a loud pop of the cork and poured for us both.

"I would have thought the Germans had looted all the good wine," I said between sips.

"They left in a hurry," Rick said, without taking his eyes from the doorway.

He was expecting a ghost, I thought. She'd been haunting him all these years and now he expected her to come through that doorway and smile at him and take up life with him just where they'd left it the day the Germans marched into Paris.

Four years. We had both intended to join de Gaulle's forces when we'd left Casablanca, but once the Americans got into the war Rick disappeared like a puff of smoke. I ran into him again by sheer chance in London, shortly before D-Day. He was in the uniform of the U.S. Army, a major in their intelligence service, no less.

"I'll buy you a drink in *La Belle Aurore*," he told me when we'd parted, after a long night of brandy and reminiscences at the Savoy bar. Two weeks later I was back on the soil of France at last, with the Free French army. Now, in August, we were both in Paris once again.

Through the open windows behind him I could hear music from the street; not martial brass bands, but the whining, wheezing melodies of a concertina. Paris was becoming Paris again.

Abruptly, Rick got to his feet, an expression on his face that I'd never seen before. He looked . . . surprised, almost.

I turned in my chair and swiftly rose to greet her as she walked slowly toward us, smiling warmly, wearing the same blue dress that Rick had described to me so often.

"You're here," she said, looking past me, her smile, her eyes, only for him.

He shrugged almost like a Frenchman. "Where else would I be?"

He came around the table, past me. She kissed him swiftly, lightly on the lips. It was affectionate, but not passionate.

Rick helped her slip onto the bench behind the table and then slid in beside her. I would have expected him to smile at her, but his expression was utterly serious. She said hello to me at last, as Henri brought another glass to the table.

"Well," I said as I sat down, "this is like old times, eh?"

Rick nodded. Ilsa murmured, "Old times."

I saw that there was a plain gold band on her finger. I'm certain that Rick noticed it, too.

"Perhaps I should be on my way," I said. "You two must have a lot to talk about."

"Oh no, don't leave," she said, actually reaching across the table toward me. "I . . ." She glanced at Rick. "I can't stay very long, myself."

I looked at Rick.

"It's all right, Louie," he said.

He filled her glass and we all raised them and clinked. "Here's . . . to Paris," Rick toasted.

"To Paris," Ilsa repeated. I mumbled it, too.

Now that I had the chance to study her face, I saw that the war years had changed her, as well. She was still beautiful, with the kind of natural loveliness that other women would kill to possess. Yet where she had been fresh and innocent in the old days, now she looked wearier, warier, more determined.

"I saw Sam last year," she said.

"Oh?"

"In New York. He was playing in a nightclub."

Rick nodded. "Good for Sam. He got home."

Then silence stretched between them until it became embarrassing. These two had so much to say to each other, yet neither of them was speaking. I knew I should go, but they both seemed to want me to remain.

Unable to think of anything else to say, I asked, "How on earth did you ever get into Paris?"

Ilsa smiled a little. "I've been working with the International Red Cross . . . in London."

"And Victor?" Rick asked. There. It was out in the open now.

"He's been in Paris for the past month."

"Still working with the Resistance." It wasn't a question.

"Yes." She took another sip of champagne, then said, "We have a child, you know."

Rick's face twitched into an expression halfway between a smile and a grimace.

"She'll be three in December."

"A Christmas baby," Rick said. "Lucky kid."

Ilsa picked up her glass, but put it down again without drinking from it. "Victor and I . . . we thought, well, after the war is over, we'd go back to Prague."

"Sure," said Rick.

"There'll be so much to do," Ilsa went on, almost whispering, almost pleading. "His work won't be finished when the war ends. In a way, it will just be beginning."

"Yes," I said, "that's understandable."

Rick stared into his glass and said nothing.

"What will you do when the war's over?" she asked him.

Rick looked up at her. "I never make plans that far ahead."

Ilsa nodded. "Oh, yes. I see."

"Well," I said, "I'm thinking about going into politics, myself."

With a wry grin, Rick said, "You'd be good at it, Louie. Perfect."

She took another brief sip of champagne, then said, "I'll have to go now."

He answered, "Yeah, I figured."

"He's my husband, Rick."

"Right. And a great man. We all know that."

Ilsa closed her eyes for a moment. "I wanted to see you, Richard," she said, her tone suddenly different, urgent, the words coming out all in a rush. "I wanted to see that you were all right. That you'd made it through the war all right."

"I'm fine," he said, his voice flat and cold and final. He got up from the bench and helped her come out from behind the table.

She hesitated just a fraction of a second, clinging to his arm for a heartbeat. Then she said, "Goodbye, Rick."

"Goodbye, Ilsa."

I thought there would be tears in her eyes, but they were dry and unwavering. "I'll never see you again, will I?"

"It doesn't look that way."

"It's . . . sad."

He shook his head. "We'll always have Paris. Most poor chumps don't even get that much."

She barely nodded at me, then walked swiftly to the door and was gone.

Rick blew out a gust of air and sat down again.

"Well, that's over." He drained his glass and filled it again.

I'm not a sentimentalist, but my heart went out to him. There was nothing I could say, nothing I could do.

He smiled at me. "Hey, Louie, why the long face?"

I sighed. "I've seen you two leave each other twice now. The first time you left her. This time, though, she definitely left you. And for good."

"That's right." He was still smiling.

"I should think—"

"It's over, Louie. It was finished a long time ago."

"Really?"

"That night at the airport I knew it. She was too much of a kid to understand it herself."

"I know something about women, my friend. She was in love with you."

"Was," Rick emphasized. "But what she wanted I couldn't give her."

"And what was that?"

Rick's smile turned just slightly bitter. "What she's got with Victor. The whole nine yards. Marriage. Kids. A respectable home after the war. I could see it then, that night at the airport. That's why I gave her the kiss-off. She's a life sentence. That's not for me."

I had thought that I was invulnerable when it came to romance. But Rick's admission stunned me.

"Then you really did want to get her out of your life?"

He nodded slowly. "That night at the airport. I figured she had Victor and they'd make a life for themselves after this crazy war was over. And that's what they'll do."

"But . . . why did you come here? She *expected* to find you here. You both knew . . ."

"I told you. I came here to meet a lady."

"Not Ilsa?"

"Not Ilsa."

"Then who?"

He glanced at his watch. "Figuring that she's always at least ten minutes late, she ought to be coming in right about now."

I turned in my seat and looked toward the door. She came striding through, tall, glamorous, stylishly dressed. I immediately recognized her, although she'd been little more than a lovesick child when I'd known her in Casablanca.

Rick got to his feet again and went to her. She threw her arms around his neck and kissed him the way a Frenchwoman should.

Leading her to the table, Rick poured a glass of champagne for her. As they touched glasses, he smiled and said, "Here's looking at you, kid."

Yvonne positively glowed.

THE BABE, THE IRON HORSE, AND MR. MCGILLICUDDY

As I mentioned in the introduction to "Delta Vee," Rick Wilber is a writer, as well as an editor and teacher. A very fine writer, as a matter of fact; one of the few true literary stylists in today's science-fiction field.

Rick is also, like me, a baseball fan. He comes to this genetically, being the son of Del Wilber, a big-league catcher for many years. Thus, when he writes about baseball Rick adds an insider's knowledge to his formidable writing skills.

My knowledge of baseball is strictly from the grandstand seats, rooting for the tragedy-prone Boston Red Sox.

One day we got talking about baseball and, as writers will, we were soon plotting a story that involved Babe Ruth, Lou Gherig (baseball's "Iron Horse") and Cornelius McGillicuddy, known to the world as Connie Mack, longtime owner and manager of the Philadelphia Athletics.

This story is pure fantasy, of course. I only hope that you have as much fun reading it as Rick and I had writing it.

THE IRON HORSE uncoiled, bringing the hips through first and then following with the shoulders, those quick wrists, that snap as the bat hit the ball.

It was just batting practice, but Lou felt wonderful, like a kid again, with no pain, with the body doing what it had always done so well. He had no idea what was going on, how he'd gotten here, what had happened. He almost didn't want to think about it, for fear it might all be some hallucination, some death dream, his mind going crazy in the last moments, trying to make the dying easier for him.

There was a sharp crack as he sent a towering shot toward the center-field wall in Yankee Stadium, over the wall for sure, sailing high and deep. He stood there and watched this one go. It would be nearly five hundred feet before it landed, he guessed.

But the Negro ballplayer roaming around out in center shagging flies did it again, turned his back to the plate and raced away, heading straight toward the wall, full tilt. There was, surprisingly, a lot of room now in center, and the Negro had blazing speed. He somehow managed to nearly catch up with the ball, and then, amazingly, reached straight out in front to make a basket catch over his shoulder. It was a beautiful catch, an amazing one, really, the large number 24 on the man's back all that Lou could see for a moment as the ball was caught.

Then the Negro turned and fired a strike toward second, where Charlie Gehringer waited for it, catching it on one long hop and sweeping the bag as if there were a runner sliding in. Gehringer whooped as he made the phantom tag, as impressed as everyone else with the centerfielder's arm. Then he rolled the ball in toward the batting practice pitcher.

On the mound, taking a ball out of the basket and pounding it into his catcher's mitt, Yogi just smiled. Like everyone else, he didn't understand how this was happening, how they all came to be here— but he really didn't care. When he let that last pitch go he'd have sworn he was in Yankee Stadium somehow, but then, looking at Willie chase it down in dead center, it looked for all the world like the Polo Grounds, with Coogan's Bluff in the background.

It didn't make any kind of sense, but Yogi just decided he wasn't going to worry about it. He and the other fellows were having a good time, that was all. And he'd been right, he figured with pride. It wasn't over till it was over.

He took a quick look around. There was Willie Mays out there in center, and Gehringer at second, and Ted out in left. Next to the cage, swinging a couple of bats, getting loose to hit next, was Scooter himself, happy as a clam. There were great players everywhere, and more showing up all the time, walking in from the clubhouse or just suddenly out there, in the field, taking infield or shagging flies.

Yogi counted heads. Where, he wondered, was the Babe? You'd think he'd be here. Then Yogi went into a half-wind, took a short stride toward the plate, making sure to get the pitch up over that open corner of the screen that protected him from shots up the middle, and threw another straight ball in to Lou. Imagine, he thought, me, throwing BP to Gehrig. The line drive back at him almost took his head off.

In the stands, up a dozen rows near the back of the box seats, an old, fat, sad-faced Babe Ruth sat in a wide circle of peanut shells. He was eating hot dogs now, and drinking Knickerbocker beer, watching batting practice, not saying much. He knew a few of the guys out there, but couldn't place the others. There was a sharp clap of thunder, and the Babe wondered if the day might be rained out. Low dark clouds circled the field, swirling and rumbling with menace.

Next to him sat white-haired, saintly Connie Mack, producing hot dog after hot dog as the Babe shoved them into that maw and chewed them down. Amazing, really, this fellow's capacity. Ruth was perspiring in a heavy flannel suit. Mack, slim as a willow, looked coolly comfortable in his customary dark suit, starched collar, and straw boater.

"George," Mack said, "isn't that about enough for now?"

Ruth never stopped chewing, but managed to say, "Mr. Mack, I ain't got any idea how long it's been since I sat in a ballyard and ate a hot dog, and I also ain't got any idea how long this is gonna' last. Them clouds move in and this thing'll be a rain-out. I'm eating while I can, you know?"

"George, I understand. Truly I do. But I really don't think it will rain, and I'd hoped that you might want to get out there and take a few cuts, meet the other fellows. There are some very fine players out there."

Mack pointed toward the infield. "That fellow there at third is Brooks Robinson, as fine a glove man as you'll ever see at that position. And at shortstop, that young, lanky fellow is Marty Marion, one of the slickest men to ever play short. And there, in the outfield, is Willie

Mays, the Negro who just caught that ball. Next to him, in left, is Ted Williams—"

"I know him, the Williams kid," said the Babe between bites. "Helluva young hitter. Got a real future."

"Indeed," said Mack. "And at second is Charlie Gehringer, you know him, too. And there are others showing up all the time. Look, there's Dominic DiMaggio, and Hoot Evers. These are good men, Babe, all of them, good men. You really should make the decision to join them, before it's too late."

"Who's that catching?"

"Fellow named Wilber. Del Wilber. A journeyman, but with a fine mind, Babe. He'll make a fine manager someday, and he has a good, strong arm. He'll cut people down at second if we need him to play."

"And pitching?"

"That's a coach throwing batting practice, Yogi Berra. Another good catcher, too, in his day. He can help us if it comes to that. And warming up out there in the bullpen is Sandy Koufax, he's our starter. You should see his curveball, George, it's really something."

"You know," Mack said, "you belong out there. You really do. You should be loosening up a bit, running around out in the outfield, a few wind sprints perhaps, instead of—" he handed the Babe a napkin— "this."

The Babe shook his head. "I gave all that up a few years back. I appreciate it, Mr. Mack. But the thing is, it's like this, I hung 'em up, Mr. Mack, and that's all there is to it. Now if you need a manager . . ."

Mack smiled. "I'm afraid that the managerial position is filled for now, George. But, there *is* a roster spot for you, I'd love to have you on my team. You could play in the outfield for us, or even pitch. I think you'd enjoy it."

The Babe held out his hand, and Mack started to shake it, thinking the deal was done, and quite early, too. Then he realized what the Babe really wanted, sighed to himself, and obligingly placed another hot dog into it. Incredible capacity, really.

"Maybe in a little while, Mr. Mack," Ruth said, taking a huge first bite. "But right now, if you don't mind, I'd like to just sit and watch Lou and these other guys. The Dutchman, he looks fine, don't he? Always was a sweet hitter, got those wrists, you know? Snap on that ball and away she goes."

There was another sharp crack as Gehrig sent one deep to center. Mays drifted under this one, waited, then made a basket catch to some general laughter from the other players. What a showboat, that Mays.

"He's something, ain't he, that nigger?" said the Babe. "Remember Josh Gibson, Mr. Mack? Now, there was a ballplayer. Boy, I tell you, he could hit that thing a ton. Played against him once or twice in exhibitions."

But Mack wasn't listening to the Babe, who, Mack figured, would just have to make his decision later. For now, Mack had heard the clatter of a dying engine out in the parking lot and rose to head out that way, excusing himself absentmindedly and leaving six more hot dogs with Ruth—enough, Mack hoped, to tide the Babe over for a few minutes.

Although he carried a cane, the elderly Mack seemed almost to float along the row of seats and out to the steps that led up from the box seats. He was a quiet man, and despite the peanut shells everywhere, there was no crunching, no sound at all, really, as he left, moving up to the back ramp of the stadium, from where he watched the old 1937 Ford bus clang its way into the empty parking lot. There was a cloud of blue smoke and a loud bang as the engine finally seized up entirely and the bus shuddered to a stop.

Mack frowned slightly, then watched with interest as the front door of the bus creaked open halfway. A hand reached out and tugged, tugged again, and the door banged open another foot or so. People started to emerge.

First off the bus was Leo Durocher, scowling and cursing, five o'clock shadow already darkening his jaw. Pushing him from behind was Pete Rose, who in turn was being pushed by Ty Cobb, who threatened to spike Rose if he didn't hurry it up.

A quiet, scared-looking Joe Jackson got off next, looking around anxiously for any kids ready to ask troublesome questions. Then came Billy Martin, Buck Weaver, Bill Terry, John "Bad Dude" Sterns, Carl Mays, Eddie Stanky, Sal Ivars, Bill Lee, Bob Gibson, Rogers Hornsby, Thurman Munson. This was a tough bunch of guys.

Charlie Comiskey was driving the bus, and still on it, arguing with someone while the others stood around outside, waiting.

"Damn it, we're here. You have to get off now, all right? We can settle all this later."

"*Merde*," said a voice from the back, enveloped in a cloud of cigar smoke. "You are all the same, always, you colonialists, always demanding that we do your bidding. Well, I tell you this, I will get off when I am damn well ready to get off, and no sooner. *Comprende?*"

"Get your ass out here, Fidel," shouted Rose. Then he turned to Durocher, and added, "Damn commies. All the same, I swear."

Durocher nodded, but added, "I played winter ball down there in Cuba a couple of times, Petey. Great times. Food was good, women were fast, and the players were pretty damn decent. They're not too bad, you know. But this guy? Shit. Nothing but bitching for twenty miles of bumpy roads getting here."

Durocher looked over at the ballpark. "Where the hell is 'here,' anyway?"

"We're in Fostoria, Ohio, Leo," said Comiskey, giving up on Castro for the moment and stepping down from the bus. "Nice little park. Seats about a thousand. Built in the early twenties. Two showerheads. Cold water. A few nails to hang your street clothes on. You'll love the accommodations."

"Oh, Christ," said Bill Terry. "I played in this park. It's got a godforsakin' skin infield, and some fucking mountains in the outfield. What a hole. Jesus, the Ohio State League. I don't fuckin' believe it. This is hell, just hell."

Comiskey just smiled and pointed toward the door that said "Visitors" in faded black paint. The players headed that way, all except for Castro, who still wouldn't budge.

"Hey, Fidel," said Rose, "I hear Lou Gehrig's in there taking batting practice. If you can move your fat Cuban ass outta there, you can pitch to him today. Wouldn't that be something, striking out Gehrig?"

There was a rustle from the back of the bus, and then Castro's head appeared out the top half of one cracked window. "Gehrig? Is this true?"

"Swear to god, Fidel. Swear to god. The Iron Horse himself. And in his prime."

Fidel looked at Comiskey, who simply nodded. It was true. And so, a few minutes later the President for Life and the Black Sox owner walked side by side toward the clubhouse through the dusty parking lot. Castro's expensive Italian shoes left a perfect outline in the dust, aimed toward the ballpark and a chance to pitch to the Iron Horse.

And next to them, filling in quickly even in the lightest of breezes, were other prints, narrower prints, almost round ones, like hoofprints with a sharp indentation.

Above, in the stands, Connie Mack watched them open the clubhouse door and walk through. He sighed. So, he thought, it was time.

He looked out across the field, seeing stately old Shibe Park with its double-decked stands out in left field and the deep, deep center field and the long high wall in right. Bobo Newsome was throwing batting practice pitches to Stan Musial. Walter Johnson was warming up in the home-team bullpen. Roberto Clemente had just arrived and was trotting out to join Ted Williams in the outfield.

Mack looked up. The dark clouds still swirled by, but he knew the rain would hold off for as long as he needed to get the game in. Otherwise, the setting was perfect.

There was a long, low rumble of thunder, and Mack looked down to see Charlie Comiskey, fat and grunting and sweating, climbing the concrete steps toward him. No, Mack saw. Comiskey was heading for the Babe. By the time Mack got back to the box—littered with peanut shells and hot-dog wrappers—Comiskey had peeled off his woolen jacket and was sitting next to the Babe, laughing and wheezing away.

Mack took a seat behind them.

"Why, Cornelius McGillicuddy, as I live and breathe!" Comiskey said, with mock good cheer. "The Babe tells me you won't let him manage your team."

"And you won't allow him to manage yours, either, will you Charles?" Mack replied.

"Well," Comiskey drew out the word tantalizingly. "I don't exactly know about that. You do well on the field, Babe, get the rest of my men to look up to you, maybe I'll step aside and let you take over as manager."

Mack gave his rival a wintry smile. "But not for today's game."

Comiskey scowled and squinted at Mack. "No, that's right. I've got to be manager for today. That's in the agreement we signed." Then he added, almost growling, "In blood."

"That," said Mack, "was your idea, Charles. Not mine."

"I did all the playin' I intend to do," Ruth said, looking around for more hot dogs. "There's nothing left for me to do on a ball field that I ain't already done. But they never let me manage a club. I coulda' been a good manager. You know, if things had worked out better in '35 . . ."

Comiskey reached into the jacket he had tossed over the back of the empty seat next to him and pulled out a hot dog. It looked cold and soggy, flecked with lint here and there, but the Babe took it and munched away hungrily.

"Don't they have any more beer around here?" he asked, through a mouthful of hot dog.

"Down in the visitors' clubhouse," Comiskey answered quickly. "We brought barrels of beer. Good stuff, too."

"Well, then," said the Babe, putting his hands on the rail in front of his seat to help pull his bulk up and out of the tight fit of the chair.

"George. Here," said Mack, miraculously producing another bottle of Knickerbocker and handing it to Ruth.

"Why, thanks, Mr. Mack, thanks very much," said the Babe, taking a long swig and then turning away from both managers to look at the field.

"Say, look at those guys coming out of the visitors' dugout," he said suddenly, pointing with the brown bottle of Knickerbocker toward the first-base line.

"Say!" he said, again, excited, rising from his seat. "Why, that's Ty Cobb, and poor old Joe Jackson, and—why, there's a whole team full of 'em. Look at that." And he slumped back into his seat, stunned by what he was seeing.

"Why, I guess you two *are* going to have a game today, aren't ya. And it's gonna be a helluva game, too, I can tell you that. A hell of game. That's some of the best fellows out there that has ever played hardball. I mean it, the best."

"Yes, George," said Mack, kindly. "Yes, it is going to be a very fine game, played by some of the best the game has ever produced."

"And my team is going to win it, McGillicuddy," snarled Comiskey. "You can bet on it." And he chuckled. "As if you'd ever bet on anything."

Mack just looked at Comiskey, shook his head slightly, then turned to speak to Ruth.

"George, you just relax here for now, all right?" And he handed the Babe a few more hot dogs and another beer. "Enjoy the game. And if you ever decide you'd like to play, for one team or the other, you just let us know, all right?"

"Sure, Mr. Mack. Sure. I'll let the two of you know, right away," said the Babe. "But y'know, I'm not sure this is enough beer," and he turned to face the two men to request a bit more, figuring one of them would come through, for sure.

But they were gone. Both of them. And when the Babe turned back to look at the field, Sandy Koufax was warming up on the mound, Pete Rose was at the plate, leading off, and the game was about to begin.

It was a battle, right from the outset. Koufax was blazing fast, and his curve looked as if it was dropping off a table. But Ty Cobb chopped one of those curves into the dirt along the third-base line and beat it out for a single. Then Rogers Hornsby slapped a Texas Leaguer that dropped between Gehrig, Gehringer, and Aaron for a double while Cobb raced home with the first run. Koufax then fanned Ducky Medwick and Bill Terry, to end the inning with Hornsby stranded on second.

As the players trooped in from the dugout, Gehrig saw the Babe sitting alone and forlorn in the box seat. He waved to his old teammate, then ducked into the shadow of the dugout and sat next to Connie Mack.

"What's this all about, Mr. Mack?" he asked, as he sat next to the frail-looking old man.

"What do you mean, Louis?"

Phil Rizzuto led off for Mack's team. Carl Mays scowled at the diminutive shortstop, then threw a wicked underhand fastball at the Scooter's head. Rizzuto hit the dirt as Bill Klem calmly called ball one.

"This game, the guys here." Gehrig's handsome face was truly troubled. "I mean, I *died*, Mr. Mack. There was a lot of pain, and I was in the hospital, and my wife was crying and . . . all of a sudden, I'm here."

"I died, too, Louis," said Mack, as Rizzuto danced away from another fastball aimed at his ear. "Everyone dies."

Gehrig stared at him. "Then . . . where are we?"

Mack smiled gently. "That all depends, Louis. It all depends on this game. And that big fellow sitting up there in the stands."

"The Babe?"

Mack nodded as Rizzuto slapped weakly at a curve and popped it toward Eddie Stanky at second base. The Scooter trudged halfway down the base path, then turned toward the dugout, looking glad to be out of range of Mays' beanballs.

Gehrig scanned the infield. "Wait a minute, where's Hornsby? Who's that little fellow out at second?"

Connie Mack sighed unhappily. "The other team has a certain amount of flexibility in the rules," he said.

"They can take players in and out of the lineup whenever they want to?"

With an even deeper sigh, Mack admitted, "That was just one of the provisions that Mr. Comiskey insisted upon, Louis. There are others changes, too. Now and again you'll see them playing on an artificial surface, a kind of fake grass. It helps the singles hitters immensely. You'll see their Rose fellow take special advantage of that, I suspect. And if this threatening weather actually turns to rain, they'll play indoors, in a ballpark with a roof over it."

Gehrig gaped at the thought.

"And they even have what they call a designated hitter, Louis, a fellow who just steps up to the plate and hits for the pitcher. He never has to play any defense."

"Free substitution?" Gehrig shook his head in surprise. "Fake grass? A roof, for god's sake? Full-time hitters? That just doesn't seem like baseball to me, Mr. Mack."

"There are a lot of us who feel that way, Louis, but those are today's rules."

"And we can't get our own roof, or use a permanent hitter if we want?"

Mack took off his straw hat, used the back of his hand to mop his brow and put the hat back on. "Well, Louis, it's more that we choose not to. It just doesn't seem right to me. We are, after all, on the side of the angels, Louis. I thought we ought to play the game the way it's meant to be played."

And Lou nodded in agreement, then turned to look up into the box seats, where the Babe sat, watching.

To the Babe's credit, by the bottom of the first he was pretty much done with the hot dogs and beer and was limiting himself to an occasional peanut, carefully squeezing the shell to crack it, then breaking off the top half of the shell and tossing the nuts, nestled there in the bottom half, into his mouth.

But that was all, just the peanuts. Oh, and a sip of beer once in a while to wash them down. And just one more hot dog now and again.

But he was slowing down on the eating because, in truth, the game was beginning to bother him. He knew it was just some sort of exhibition, and so they were being a little easy on the rules and all, but not only were Comiskey's guys substituting right and left, coming in and then out of the game whenever they seemed to want to, they were also playing a mean, vicious brand of ball.

In the top of the second, for instance, Ty Cobb, at the plate again even though he'd hit in the first and wasn't due up, slashed a line drive into the gap in right that had stand-up double written all over it. The black kid in right, though, got a good jump on the ball and chased it down on the third hop, before it got to the warning track. Then he turned and fired to second, and it was suddenly a close play as the ball and Cobb approached the bag at the same time.

And damned if Ty didn't come in with those spikes up high, trying to move the shortstop, that Rizzuto guy, off the bag or cut him if he stayed in. Rizzuto, to his credit, stood his ground, catching Aaron's throw on the first hop and bringing the glove down in front of Cobb's right foot as it approached the bag. Out.

But the left foot, up high, caught Rizzuto on the right calf, tearing right through the baggy flannel and cutting open a good six-inch gash that bled badly until the trainer, Bob Bauman from the Cardinals, trotted out from the dugout to get enough pressure on it to stop the flow.

Rizzuto limped off the field under his own power, but he was obviously in pain. Marty Marion, tall and lanky for a shortstop, came out to replace him. Cobb, glaring defiantly, watched it all, hands on hips, until Rizzuto left, then trotted into the Comiskey dugout to a few handshakes and back slaps from his teammates.

And in the bottom of the second Carl Mays hit two of Mack's players. First he put a fastball into Aaron's ribs, then he followed that up with another heater that caught Brooks Robinson on the left wrist. If Brooks hadn't gotten that hand up in the way, the ball might have caught him in the face. There was an audible gasp from Mack's dugout as the dull thwack of the ball hitting flesh echoed through the park. Then there were angry shouts, but Mays, imperious on the mound, ignored them, and Klem, behind the plate, bade the game go on.

The Babe, munching peanuts, scowled as he sat in the stands. It wasn't right. One side not only seemed to get special rules but also played a really mean brand of ball. He was starting to get downright mad about it. Okay, it wasn't like Comiskey's guys were a bunch of choirboys, they were rough, tough players, by God, and everybody knew it; but the Babe thought this game was meant to be for fun, for the love of the game and all that. Those guys shouldn't be cutting each other up out there. They're playing like it was a World Series, like their lives depended on it.

They took Mays out after Charlie Gehringer whacked a double down the right-field line. The Babe stared, wide-eyed, at Comiskey's new pitcher. The guy had a beard! Must be from the House of David team. He was a southpaw, in to face Williams and then Lou.

Williams walked. Lou swung and missed a really wicked curve ball. The bearded lefthander grinned on the mound and yelled something the Babe couldn't understand. Hebrew, maybe.

He tried his curve again. Wrong move. Lou smashed it way, way out there, so high and deep the ball disappeared into the bright sky. Three-run homer. That was all for the bearded lefthander.

But Comiskey's guys started hitting, too. And slashing any infielder who got in their way. Durocher barreled into Charlie Gehringer at second on a routine double-play ball, knocked him flat. It was such a cheap shot that the Babe jumped out of his seat and yelled at Durocher as he trotted in from the field. Leo glanced up at the only man in the stands and seemed to look—embarrassed? The Babe sat down again, stunned at that.

The game went on, seesawing back and forth. The Babe would roar whenever Comiskey's guys pulled one of their lousy stunts. It felt real good, in fact, to let the anger explode, tell those cheap-shot bums what bush-league bastards they were, get the juices flowing again like they hadn't in a long, long time.

"By God," the Babe muttered to himself, "if I wasn't so old, if I wasn't in such rotten shape, I'd go out there and teach those sonsabitches a lesson they wouldn't forget."

But he was old and fat and useless. And he knew it.

Then came the sixth inning.

A chunky righthander named Wynne was pitching for Comiskey now. Lou was at the plate, and the Babe was thinking about all the good years he and Gehrig had put in together.

Truth be known, the Babe had always had mixed feelings about

Lou. On the one hand, he envied the Dutchman a bit, that tight focus on the game, the way he always kept himself in shape, the reputation he had as a nice guy and a smart one, a real gentleman. In a lot of ways, the Babe wished he could have been a gentleman.

But, on the other hand, the Babe thought that Lou had always been so busy being nice that a lot of times he didn't seem to be having much fun. The booze, the women, the high life—it was all part of the fun, and if the game wasn't fun, why play? My god, it ought to be fun, that was the whole point. Lou had always seemed so damned serious about everything, and that was too bad.

That was part of what was making the Babe so mad right now about these other fellows, these guys playing for Comiskey. The way they were playing was too low, too mean, for it to be any fun. They had forgotten what the game was about. It wasn't life and death, it was baseball, for Christ's sake, the joy of hitting, of catching and throwing the ball, or rounding third on a home-run trot, of sliding into second with a double, of just knocking the dirt off the cleats with the handle of the bat.

Ah, yes, the bat. Watching Lou take two balls low and away, then swing and hit a long foul ball out into the right-field seats for a 2-1 count, the Babe could almost feel the way it was to hold his old Louisville Slugger, to swing it and make contact. He leaned back in his seat and stretched his arms out, opening and closing those meaty hands, tightening the arm muscles, feeling good in doing it.

He brought his hands together, made fists, placed the left fist over the right as if holding a bat, and brought the two fists back into a stance, as if he were waiting for a pitch, a good fastball out over the plate, rising, begging to be hit. He felt good doing it, real good, like a kid again, having fun.

"Damned if it wouldn't feel good. Just one more time," he said aloud, to no one in particular. "Damned if it wouldn't."

It was calming, thinking about that. The Babe almost forgot how infuriated he'd been by the rough play, when Wynne changed all that, almost forever.

First he came inside on Lou for ball three, and then, while the Babe watched horrified, Wynne—despite the count—brought in a rising fastball, high and tight, that caught Lou just above the ear and laid him out cold in the dirt.

It looked for a second like maybe Lou had gotten his hand up to block it, but then, the Babe heard the awful *chunk* of ball hitting flesh and the Iron Horse just lay there. Babe knew it was serious. As Lou lay still in the dirt the Babe rose from his seat.

"You goddamned sonsabitches," he yelled, and started walking down toward the diamond. "You bunch a' shitheaded bastards," he yelled again, taking the wide concrete steps two at a time. "That ain't baseball, that ain't the way it's supposed to be played."

He reached the low gate that was next to the dugout, but didn't bother to open it, just vaulted over the rail instead and landed on the field.

And in doing that he realized there had been some changes. He felt good, he felt really good. He looked down at himself, expecting to see the man he'd become, that rounded belly, the toothpick legs, the arms with the flesh on them loose, hanging down, like the jowls on his face. Damn age. He hated it, hated getting old, hated knowing he couldn't hit anymore, hated having to live the game through memories.

And what he saw instead was the Babe he'd been at twenty-five, his first year in the outfield for the Yankees. Solid, tight, firm. The legs were strong, he could feel that. And the arm felt good, real good. He brought his hands to his face, felt the youth there.

He hustled over to where Lou lay there, barely conscious, the trainer working on him, talking to him in low tones, trying to bring him out of it.

"Lou," the Babe said, leaning over to look at Gehrig. "Lou, it was a damn cheap shot, a rotten lowdown no-good thing."

Gehrig, his eyes focusing as Ruth watched, smiled. "Yeah, Babe, it was a little inside, wasn't it?"

"A little inside?" Babe snorted. "He *meant* to bean you, Lou. That dirty little coward. He did it on purpose, I tell you."

"Babe," said Lou, slowly sitting up. "Babe, you look good, you look ready to play." And he started to try and stand, first coming to a kneel.

"Lou. I sure wished he hadn't thrown at you like that, that's all. He could've killed you."

"No, no," said Gehrig, waving away the help and sympathy. "No, I'll be all right. I'll . . ." And he nearly collapsed, giving up on the idea of standing and then falling back to one knee. "Shoot, I'm a little woozy, I guess."

Connie Mack, standing next to Lou, patted his star on the back. "You just take it easy, Louis. We'll get a pinch runner for you. There's plenty of talented players left around here, you just don't worry about it."

"Mr. Mack," said the Babe, reaching down to help Lou to his feet as Gehrig tried again to rise. "I'd like to be that runner, if it's all right with you. I think I'd like to get into this game after all."

"Well, that's fine, George, of course," said Mack, as he and the Babe helped Gehrig walk slowly toward the dugout. "You'll be hitting fourth, then, in Lou's spot. We'll put you out in right, in Henry's spot, and bring in Gil Hodges. And we're sure glad to have you on the team."

The Babe trotted out to first, not bothering to loosen up at all, feeling too good to need it. Somehow he was in uniform now, instead of the suit he'd been wearing.

The next fellow up for Mack's team was Willie Mays and he went with the first pitch from Wynne, a fastball low and away, and took it to the opposite field, sending it into the corner in right. The Babe, off at the crack of the bat, was making it to third standing up, but that wasn't good enough, not after what had been going on here.

Instead of easing into third, he ignored the stop sign from Yogi, the third-base coach, and barreled right on through, pushing off the bag with his right foot and heading toward home.

Out in right, Joe Jackson had chased down the ball and came up expecting to see men on second and third, but there was Ruth already rounding third and heading home. Shoeless Joe took one hop step and fired toward Thurman Munson at the plate.

Munson had the plate blocked, and was reaching up with that big mitt to catch the throw as the Babe came in, shoulder down, determined to plow right through him and score.

The collision raised a cloud of dust, and for a long second Bill Klem hesitated over making the call. Then, with a smile and long, slow deep-throated growl, he yanked his thumb toward the sky and called the Babe out.

The Babe was in a fury. He leaped to his feet, started screaming bloody murder at Klem.

"Out? How the hell could you call me out? He dropped the goddamned ball! Can't you see anything, you dumb—"

The umpire silenced him with the jab of a finger. "You just got into the game, Babe," Klem snapped. "You wanna get tossed out so soon?"

Growling, holding in the anger, the Babe slowly dusted off his uniform, staring at Klem the whole time. Klem stared back, hands on hips. Then, shaking his head, fists clenched, the Babe trudged over to the dugout.

Munson shakily got up on one knee, reached over to pick up the ball from where it had trickled away, gave Klem a puzzled glance, and then flipped the ball out to Wynne. In all the commotion Mays had moved up to third, and there was still a game to play. Munson adjusted his chest protector, pulled the mask down firmly, and crouched behind the plate as Wynne went through the usual fidgeting and finally stood on the rubber and looked in for the signal. The game went on.

The Babe had calmed down a bit in the dugout when Gehrig, still pale, came over to chat with him.

"Tough call, Babe," Lou said, slapping him on the back.

"Yeah. Tough, all right. Say, Dutch, you feeling OK now?"

Gehrig ran his right hand through his hair. There was an ugly bluish lump rising behind his ear. He saw Ruth notice the bruise, touched at it gingerly, then smiled, nodded, said, "Yeah, sure, better, Babe, better," he said. "You just keep that temper under control out there, right? You always did have a problem with that. We need you thinking straight, Babe, OK?"

"Sure, Lou, sure," said the Babe, and gave Lou a puzzled look as the Iron Horse walked away.

The sixth ended with Mack's team still a run ahead, but in the seventh Comiskey's team used a walk, an outrageously bad call at first, and a sharp single up the middle from Rose to tie the game at five apiece. Mack's team threatened in the bottom but couldn't get a run across even with the bases full and just one out.

Then, in the top of the eighth, Bill Terry hit a sharp grounder to Hodges at first, who moved away from the bag to get a glove on it, then flipped to Robin Roberts, Mack's pitcher. Roberts had to reach to catch the toss while stepping on the bag, and Terry ran him down. There was a tangle of arms and legs rolling in the chalk and dust, and when it all settled, Terry was safe at first and Roberts was done for the day, his ankle badly spiked.

There were other pitchers available, of course, but Connie Mack had something particular in mind, some kind of purpose, and waved out to right, to the Babe. And so, for the first time since a brief appearance in 1933, Babe Ruth came in to pitch.

He had his best stuff, a blazing fastball that he could place accurately. It was the Babe Ruth of 1916 on the mound, the Ruth who won twenty-three games and had an E.R.A. of 1.75. The Ruth who pitched twenty-nine straight scoreless innings in World Series play.

Comiskey's guys would have had a tough time getting to the Babe in any event, but now, his anger really seething, the Babe was viciously untouchable, high and tight fastballs threatening skulls, everything working inside, his ire obvious to every hitter who stepped into the box.

"Stay on your toes, wise-ass," he bellowed at Cobb, throwing close enough to shave his chin.

And at the plate he was just as angry, though he had to control it some. In the bottom of the eighth, he came to the plate again with one out and nobody on. Bob Gibson, pitching in relief, wasn't at all afraid to play even-up, and came in with one under Ruth's chin on the first pitch, and then broke off a curve low and away for ball two, before throwing something in the strike zone, a blazing fastball low and inside, an unhittable pitch. For anybody else.

The Babe golfed it, reached down to make contact and drove the ball up and out, deep to right, twenty rows up, a towering home run. As he rounded the bases he muttered under his breath as he passed each of Comiskey's players, cursing them quietly, so the umps wouldn't hear, but swearing to get each and every one of them the next time up.

They all looked shocked. The Babe? Swearing vengeance? Rollicking, fun-loving Babe Ruth, threatening to bean them, calling them the foulest names they'd ever heard? They looked like whipped little boys, scared and ashamed.

They deserve it, the Babe said to himself as he trotted into the dugout. *They deserve whatever I dish out to them, the dirty bastards.*

Then he looked across the infield to the other team's dugout and saw Comiskey grinning from ear to ear, like he was perfectly satisfied with the way the game was developing.

It stopped being a baseball game and turned into a war. Every batter who faced the Babe had to dive into the dirt. The Babe wasn't throwing warning pitches; he was trying to break skulls. He fired his hardest, especially at Cobb and Durocher. Klem, officiating behind the plate, gave him a few hard stares, but let the mayhem go on.

The Babe expected the other guys to come charging out to the mound after him. He was ready for a real fight. Spoiling for one, in fact. But they just took their turns at bat, dived to the ground when the Babe zinged a fastball at their heads, and meekly popped up or grounded out. Vaguely, through his haze of anger, the Babe saw that they all looked scared. Terrified. Good, he thought. Serves 'em right.

In the top of the ninth Rose worked up the nerve to stand in there and one of the Babe's fastballs nailed him in the shoulder. Hal Chase went in to run for him. The Babe tried twice to pick him off first, couldn't do it, and then, angry as hell, came in with a high, hard one to Shoeless Joe, who slapped it out into short right field, putting men on first and third. Cobb's fly ball to center, three pitches later, gave Comiskey's men the tie before the Babe could pitch out of the jam.

Babe trudged off the field, more furious than ever that he'd let them tie the score. His teammates shied away from him: *They're sore at me*, Babe grumbled to himself. Connie Mack just shook his head, looking distressed. Even Lou seemed unhappy, disappointed in him.

So what? the Babe thought. *So they got a lucky run off me. At least they're not beaning and spiking anybody now. They're whipped, and they know it.*

In the bottom of the ninth the Babe was hitting fourth and just hoping to get an at-bat. Marty Marion, leading off, smacked a grounder up the middle that looked like a sure single, but Durocher came behind the bag and made a hell of a play to get him. Charlie Gehringer fouled off four pitches and finally drew a walk, but then Lefty Grove came in to get Ted Williams on a long fly to deep right, so that brought the Babe up with two outs and one on.

The Babe knew all about Grove. He was a fastball pitcher all the way, with a good curve that he didn't bother with much since he had so much heat. Somebody said once that Grove could throw a lamb chop past a wolf. *We'll see about that, the Babe thought.*

The Babe figured he could wait him out a pitch or two and then take him deep and end this game. That would feel good, real good. He was so mad that he wanted to do more than just win, he wanted to really hurt these guys, teach them a lesson, humiliate them.

But the Babe didn't figure he'd get a chance to do anything like that, much as he wanted to. Instead, he'd just sit back a bit, let Grove have a little rope, and then crush one. End the game in real Babe Ruth style and leave the damned bastards standing there on the field, cowed for good.

But it wasn't Grove on the mound when the Babe stepped into the batter's box. Instead, as he settled in, digging a spot for the left foot to brace, and looked up, it was Charley Root.

Where the hell had Root come from? Then the Babe smiled. This was typical. Of course Comiskey would pull a stunt like this. In 1932, in the third game of the World Series, the Babe had gotten even with the Cubs by showing up Root, pointing at the spot in the stands where he planned to hit his home run and then doing it. He called his shot, and it became part of baseball's legend.

Root said it never happened that way, experts analyzed old home movies of the moment and tended to agree. But the Babe knew better, he'd gotten even with Root back then and he would do it now, just the same way.

First, he wanted to let a few pitches go by, just to get another good look at Root's stuff, and to let the moment build up a bit.

The first pitch came right at his head, and the Babe had to fight the instinct to hit the dirt, getting away from it. Instead, he just leaned back and let the pitch go by his eyes, inches away. Gehringer, on first, could see how Root had his attention focused on the plate, and took off as the pitcher started his windup. Munson pegged it down to second, but never had a chance, and Gehringer was on second with an easy steal.

The Babe, laughing as the ball came back to the mound, stepped back out of the box and looked back at the catcher.

"That the best you guys can do? You sons of bitches, give me a strike in here now and I'll ride the thing right out of here."

Munson just shook his head, said nothing.

The second pitch came even closer, aimed at the Babe's ribs. It was another fastball, a good one with a lot of movement aimed high and tight. The Babe didn't flinch, and the ball came so close to him that Klem, umping behind the plate, hesitated for a moment, wondering if it hadn't clipped the Babe's jersey.

Sensing the hesitation, the Babe turned to face Klem, and said loudly, "It didn't touch me, and you know it. You and me got some history, Klem, but this ain't your fight here. Just let it go, you hear me? Let it go."

Klem stared back at Ruth. "You're showing me up, Babe, and I don't like it. That's not your style. I don't know what's eating you, but just get back in there and play."

"What's eating me," growled the Babe as he dug in again, "is a bunch of snotty little goddamned bushers playing dirty ball. That's what eating me."

"And what've you been doing, Babe?" Klem snapped.

Munson, looking toward Root on the mound, pulled down his face mask, and added: "Hey Babe, some of us don't have a choice out here, so don't take it out on us, huh?"

"No choice, hell. You guys play rough and then when I give you a dose of your own medicine you start crying," the Babe said.

Munson shook his head, and muttered, "You still don't get it, do you, Babe?"

"Play ball," Klem ordered.

Root pounded the ball into his glove nervously and glared toward the plate. The Babe stepped back out of the box, lifted his bat toward the right-field seats, and pointed it.

"You got that?" the Babe yelled out to the pitcher. There was no doubt about it this time, nothing unsure. This was meant. "You got that? Right out there, Charlie, right out there, maybe ten rows up."

Root glared at him, and then, as the Babe stepped back in, went into his windup and brought in the next pitch, a good fastball down low for a strike.

The Babe just watched it go by, full of confidence, not bothering with the pitch because it wasn't where he wanted it. By God, he wanted to show these guys up, every one of them. They'd put some good men out of the game, especially poor old Lou, and the Babe was going to get even, going to win this thing in fine style.

The next pitch started out low and away, way out of the strike zone, and then tailed off into the dirt as Root tried to get the Babe to go after a bad one. But the Babe didn't move, and the ball got by Munson, who couldn't even get a glove on it as it skipped by.

Gehringer, on second, made it easily to third while Munson chased it down.

The count was 3 and 1 now, with a man on third and two outs. The Babe started to step back in, then hesitated.

He stared at Root and saw a look of utter hopelessness in the pitcher's face. Root knew the Babe was going to hammer him, blast the ball out of sight, just the way he'd done in '32. The infielders all looked like whipped dogs, too. Hell, even Durocher had that hangdog look about him. That's not like Lippy, he'd always been a scrapper.

What had the catcher said? *You still don't get it, do you, Babe?* And before that: *Some of us don't have a choice out here.*

Damn, he wanted to get even with these guys, he really did. But . . . something really weird was going on here.

And the Babe remembered. Remembered his own cancer, remembered Lou being so sick and frail and—the Dutchman had died. I went to his funeral, for God's sake. I died!

The Babe looked around the field again. Cobb, Hornsby, Joe Jackson.

"Time out," he said to Klem. And he went over to the dugout, trailing his big brown Louisville Slugger in the dust.

Connie Mack came halfway up the dugout steps. "Something wrong, George?"

Feeling perplexed, not really believing what his own mind was telling him, the Babe asked, "Mr. Mack, this ain't just another ball game, is it?"

Mack's blue eyes seemed to sparkle. "No, George, it certainly is not an ordinary game."

Lou came over and joined them, holding an ice bag to his head. "It's a special game, Babe. We've got to win it."

"But we've got to win it in the right way," Mack said. "It won't matter if we win the game but you end up playing with Mr. Comiskey's team."

The Babe felt startled. "You'd trade me?"

Mack shook his head. "No, George. Up here the players make their own decisions about which side they want to be with."

"Well, I sure don't want—" The Babe hesitated. "You mean all those guys, Leo and Cobb and Shoeless Joe and all, they *chose* to play for Comiskey?"

"They didn't realize it at the time, but, yes, they chose the wrong team."

"They didn't mean to, though, did they?" Gehrig asked.

The ghost of a smile played across Mack's bloodless lips. "I'm sure that if they knew then what they know now, they would have acted differently."

The Babe frowned with concentration. This was a lot to think about, a lot to figure out.

"Are we playing a ball game here or not?" Klem bellowed from home plate. "Get back in the box, Babe, or I'll forfeit the game."

"Okay, Klem, okay," the Babe hollered back. He started back toward the plate, his mind churning. These other guys have *got* to play for Comiskey, whether they want to or not? They got no choice?

Abruptly he turned and yelled to Mack, "If we win this game, it's for all of 'em. Get me? Not just for me. *All* of the others, too!"

Lou grinned happily at him. Mack seemed to hesitate for a moment, as if holding a private conversation with himself. Then he, too, smiled, and tipped his straw boater to Ruth, agreeing to the terms.

And the Babe dug in at the batter's box, cocked his Louisville Slugger, looked ready to cream Root's next pitch.

But that's what they all expect, he thought. *They're waiting for me to crush it, waiting for me to show them how much better I am than any of them.*

"Pride, George," he remembered Brother Domimic telling him, time and again at the orphanage in Baltimore. "Pride will be your undoing, unless you learn to control it, use it for good."

He took a deep breath. As Root stepped onto the rubber and checked Gehringer, leading off third, the Babe pointed with his bat again toward the right-field seats. "Maybe twenty rows up," he taunted.

Root scowled, went into an abbreviated windup, and threw a wicked fastball at the Babe's ear. He hit the ground. The ball thwacked into Munson's mitt.

"Strike two!" called Klem.

The Babe leaped to his feet, bat in hand. Klem stared at him from behind his mask.

Then, with a childish grin, the Babe got back into the batter's box. "Come on, chickenshit," he yelled to Root, hoisting the bat over his shoulder. "Put one over the plate."

Root did. Another fastball, low and away this time. The Babe knew Klem would call it strike three if he let it pass.

He didn't. He squared his feet and tapped the ball toward third base, as neat a bunt as ever laid down the line. The infield had been playing 'way back, of course. The outfielders, too. Everybody knew that the Babe was going to swing for the fences.

And here's this bunt trickling slowly down the third-base line, too far from the plate for Munson to reach, too slow for Tabor at third to possibly reach it. Gehringer streaked home with the winning run while the Babe laughed all the way to first base.

The game was over.

And the other guys were laughing, too! Tabor picked the ball off the grass near third and twirled it in his hand. As the fielders headed in for the visitors' dugout, Durocher cracked:

"Twenty rows up, huh, Babe?"

Cobb gave a huff. "You're stealing my stuff now, Babe. Using your head out there."

Even old Charlie Root just shook his head and grinned at the Babe. "Who'd a thought it?" he said, true wonderment in his eyes. "Who'd a thought it?"

On impulse, the Babe reached out his hand. Root looked startled, then he took it in a firm ballplayer's grip.

"I was afraid you'd strike me out, Charlie," said the Babe.

Root actually laughed. "Yeah. Sure. Like I did in Chicago."

And he followed his teammates into the shadows of the dugout, where Charlie Comiskey stood glaring hotly at them.

The Babe trotted to his own dugout. Lou and the other guys slapped his back and congratulated him on the big winning blast. One of the black players, Mays, raised his hand up above his head, palm outward. The Babe didn't know what to do.

Hank Aaron, looking slightly embarrassed, demonstrated a high five with Mays. The Babe grinned and tried it.

"Okay!" he laughed.

About an hour later, Connie Mack and Charlie Comiskey stood on the mound, staring out toward left, talking it over. Both men were in a good mood. Mack had proven his point, and said so to Comiskey.

"I told you he'd do the right thing, Charles. You wouldn't believe me, of course, but I was confident."

"Oh, that's all right, McGillicuddy, that's all right," said Comiskey with a wave of his hand. "I never thought he'd bunt, but it's turned out all right for me. Some of my fellows proved they really belong on my team, you might say."

Mack smiled. "Well, I suppose that's true, Charles. But you do remember what George said just before he went back to bat."

"What he said?"

"Well. Yes. You heard him. He said he wasn't doing it merely for himself. It was for all of them."

Comiskey scratched his jowly jaw. "Yeah, I remember. What'd he mean by that?"

"What he meant," said Mack, "was that he wants *all* the players—yours as well as mine—to be free to choose which team they want to be with from now on."

"All the players? Mine? *My* players?" Comiskey sputtered. "Never! He can't do that! It's against our rules. Each player is bound to the team that owns him. The reserve clause—"

"The reserve clause is ancient history, Charles," said Mack patiently.

"What in hell do you mean?"

"I've already spoken to the Commissioner. The reserve clause that you insisted upon has been stricken from each player's contract."

Comiskey just gaped at Cornelius McGillicuddy. "You can't! You—it's not fair! Dammit to hell, it's not fair! Those players signed their lives away. To me!"

Mack shook his head ever so slightly. "Those poor souls are free, Charles. The Commissioner agreed to the terms George requested. And with that bunt, the Babe freed them."

Comiskey's face was redder than fire. "You engineered this, McGillicuddy! You *knew*—"

"I hoped, Charles," replied Mack softly. "And the Babe came through for me. And for all of them."

Stamping his cloven feet in fury, Comiskey snarled, "This isn't the end of it! You'll see!"

"Oh, goodness gracious, yes, I know. You'll make an offer that some of the players can't refuse, Charles. Some of them will want to stay on your team, of course. That's up to them."

Comiskey shook his fist under Mack's nose. "Wait till next year, McGillicuddy. Wait till next year!"

Connie Mack smiled. "Next year the Babe will be managing my dub. I'm being moved . . . eh, upstairs."

And Mack began to shimmer, his form slowly losing its solidity, becoming transparent.

"Oh, and Charles," he added while slowly fading away. "It's my understanding that you've been moved to a new assignment, too, something a little slower paced; cricket, I believe. And if you do well there, then, perhaps, next year you'll be back to face the Babe. I *do* hope so, really, for your sake." And he was gone.

Comiskey, furious but helpless, could only stamp his foot in anger and shake his fist at the sky, where the dark clouds that had rumbled and threatened rain all day were now, finally, blowing clear and letting the late-afternoon sun shine through.

GREENHOUSE CHILL

Most scientists around the world are convinced that the Earth's climate is heating up, and that the human race's outpouring of greenhouse-enhancing gases such as carbon dioxide are a significant factor in the global warming. A small but insistent minority of scientists protests that global warming is largely illusory, or at least its impact has been grossly exaggerated.

What if global warming is not only real, but its impact will hit suddenly, over a matter of a decade or so, not the gradual, centuries-long effect that most people expect? A greenhouse cliff, with a sudden, drastic rise in sea levels that floods coastal cities worldwide, leading to a collapse of the electrical power grid that is the cornerstone of our industrial society. Together with shifts of climate that wipe out large swaths of farmlands, such a greenhouse cliff could cause a global catastrophe of unparalleled proportion.

Ironically, the possibility that a greenhouse warming can lead to a new ice age is now an accepted concept among many scientists: see William H. Calvin's A Brain for all Seasons *(University of Chicago Press, 2002).*

But I published first!

"LET'S FACE IT, Hawk, we're lost."

Hawk frowned in disappointment at his friend. "You're lost, maybe. I know right where I am."

Squinting in the bright sunshine, Tim turned his head this way and that, searching the horizon. Nothing. Not another sail, not another boat anywhere in sight. Not even a bird. The only sounds he could hear were the soft gusting of the hot breeze and the splash of the gentle waves lapping against their stolen sailboat. The brilliant sky was cloudless, the sea stretched out all around them and they were alone. Two teenaged runaways out in the middle of the empty sea.

"Yeah?" Tim challenged. "Then where are we?"

"Comin' up to the Ozarks, just about," said Hawk.

"How d'you know that?"

Hawk's frown evolved into a serious, superior, *knowing* expression. He was almost a year older than Tim, lean and hard-muscled from backbreaking farm labor. But his round face was animated, with sparkling blue eyes that could convince his younger friend to join him on this wild adventure to escape from their parents, their village, their lives of endless drudgery.

Tim was almost as tall as Hawk, but pudgier, softer. His father was the village rememberer, and Tim was being groomed to take his place in the due course of time. The work he did was mostly mental, instead of physical, but it was pure drudgery just the same, remembering all the family lines and the history of the village all the way back to the Flood.

"So," Tim repeated, "how d'you know where we're at? I don't see any signposts stickin' up outta the water."

"How long we been out?" Hawk asked sternly.

With a glance at the dwindling supply of salt beef and apples in the crate by the mast, Tim replied, "This is the fifth mornin'."

"Uh-huh. And where's the sun?"

Tim didn't bother to answer, it was so obvious.

"So the sun's behind your left shoulder, same's it's been every mornin'. Wind's still comin' up from the south, hot and strong. We're near the Ozarks."

"I still don't see how you figure that."

"My dad and my uncle been fishin' in these waters all their lives," Hawk said, matter-of-factly. "I learned from them."

Tim thought that over for a moment, then asked, "So how long before we get to Colorado?"

"Oh, that's *weeks* away," Hawk answered.

"Weeks? We ain't got enough food for weeks!"

"I know that. We'll put in at the Ozark Islands and get us some more grub there."

"How?"

"Huntin'," said Hawk. "Or trappin'. Or stealin', if we hafta."

Tim's dark eyes lit up. The thought of becoming robbers excited him.

The long lazy day wore on. Tim listened to the creak of the ropes and the flap of the heavy gray sail as he lay back in the boat's prow. He dozed, and when he woke again the sun had crawled halfway down toward the western edge of the sea. Off to the north, though, ominous clouds were building up, gray and threatening.

"Think it'll storm?" he asked Hawk.

"For sure," Hawk replied.

They had gone through a thunderstorm their first afternoon out. The booming thunder had scared Tim halfway out of his wits. That and the waves that rose up like mountains, making his stomach turn itself inside out as the boat tossed up and down and sideways and all. And the lightning! Tim had no desire to go through that again.

"Don't look so scared," Hawk said, with a tight smile on his face.

"I ain't scared!"

"Are too."

Tim admitted it with a nod. "Ain't you?"

"Not any more."

"How come?"

Hawk pointed off to the left. Turning, Tim saw a smudge on the horizon, something low and dark, with more clouds over it. But these clouds were white and soft-looking.

"Island," Hawk said, pulling on the tiller and looping the rope around it to hold it in place. The boat swung around and the sail began flapping noisily.

Tim got up and helped Hawk swing the boom. The sail bellied out again, neat and taut. They skimmed toward the island while the storm clouds built up higher and darker every second, heading their way.

They won the race, barely, and pulled the boat up on a stony beach just as the first drops of rain began to spatter down on them, fat and heavy.

"Get the mast down, quick!" Hawk commanded. It was pouring rain by the time they got that done. Tim wanted to run for the shelter of the big trees, but Hawk said no, they'd use the boat's hull for protection.

"Trees attract lightnin', just like the mast would if we left it up," said Hawk.

Even on dry land the storm was scarifying. And the land didn't stay dry for long. Tim lay on the ground beneath the curve of the boat's hull as lightning sizzled all around them and the thunder blasted so loud it hurt his ears. Hawk sprawled beside Tim and both boys pressed themselves flat against the puddled stony ground.

The world seemed to explode into a white-hot flash and Tim heard a crunching, crashing sound. Peeping over Hawk's shoulder he saw one of the big trees slowly toppling over, split in half and smoking from a lightning bolt. For a moment he thought the tree would smash down on them, but it hit the ground a fair distance away with an enormous shattering smash.

At last the storm ended. The boys were soaking wet and Tim's legs felt too weak to hold him up, but he got to his feet anyway, trembling with cold and the memory of fear.

Slowly they explored the rocky, pebbly beach and poked in among the trees. Squirrels and birds chattered and scolded at them. Tim saw a snake, a beautiful blue racer, slither through the brush. Without a word between them, the boys went back to the boat. Hawk pulled his bow and a handful of arrows from the box where he had stored them while Tim collected a couple of pocketfuls of throwing stones.

By the time the sun was setting they were roasting a young rabbit over their campfire.

Burping contentedly, Hawk leaned back on one elbow as he wiped his greasy chin. "Now this is the way to live, ain't it?"

"You bet," Tim agreed. He had seen some blackberry bushes back among the trees and decided that in the morning he'd pick as many as he could carry before they started out again. No sense leaving them to the birds.

"Hello there!"

The deep voice froze both boys for an instant. Then Hawk dived for his bow while Tim scrambled to his feet.

"Don't be frightened," called the voice. It came from the shadowy bushes in among the trees, sounding ragged and scratchy, like it was going to cough any minute.

On one knee, Hawk fitted an arrow into his hunter's bow. Tim suddenly felt very exposed, standing there beside the camp fire, both hands empty.

Out of the shadows of the trees stepped a figure. A man. An old, shaggy, squat barrel of a man in a patchwork vest that hung open across his white-fuzzed chest and heavy belly, his head bare and balding but his brows and beard and what was left of his hair bushy and white. His arms were short, but thick with muscle. And he carried a strange-looking bow, black and powerful-looking, with all kinds of weird attachments on it.

"No need for weapons," he said, in his gravelly voice.

"Yeah?" Hawk challenged, his voice shaking only a little. "Then what's that in your hand?"

"Oh, this?" The stranger bent down and laid his bow gently on the ground. "I've been carrying it around with me for so many years it's like an extension of my arm."

He straightened up slowly, Tim saw, as if the effort caused him pain. There was a big, thick-bladed knife tucked in his belt. His feet were shod in what looked like strips of leather.

"Who are you?" Hawk demanded, his bow still in his hands. "What do you want?"

The stranger smiled from inside his bushy white beard. "Since you've just arrived on my island, I think it's more proper for you to identify yourselves first."

Tim saw that Hawk was a little puzzled by that.

"Whaddaya mean, your island?" Hawk asked.

The old man spread his arms wide. "This is my island. I live here. I've lived her for damned near two hundred years."

"That's bull-dingy," Hawk snapped. Back home he never would have spoken so disrespectfully to an adult, but things were different out here.

The shaggy old man laughed. "Yes, I suppose it does sound fantastic. But it's true. I'm two hundred and fifty-six years old, assuming I've been keeping my calendar correctly."

"Who are you?" Hawk demanded. "Whatcha want?"

Placing a stubby-fingered hand on his chest, the man replied, "My name is Julius Schwarzkopf, once a professor of meteorology at the University of Washington, in St. Louis, Missouri, U. S. of A."

"I heard of St. Louie," Tim blurted.

"Fairy tales," Hawk snapped.

"No, it was real," said Professor Julius Schwarzkopf. "It was a fine city, back when I was a teacher."

Little by little, the white-bearded stranger eased their suspicions. He came up to the fire and sat down with them, leaving his bow where he'd laid it. He kept the knife in his belt, though. Tim sat a little bit aways from him, where there were plenty of fist-sized rocks within easy reach.

The Prof, as he insisted they call him, opened a little sack on his belt and offered the boys a taste of dried figs.

As the last embers of daylight faded and the stars began to come out, he suggested, "Why don't you come to my place for the night? It's better than sleeping out in the open."

Hawk didn't reply, thinking it over.

"There's wild boars in the woods, you know," said the Prof. "Mean beasts. And the cats hunt at night, too. Coyotes, of course. No wolves, though; for some reason they haven't made it to this island."

"Where's your cabin?" Hawk asked. "Who else lives there?"

"Ten minutes' walk," the Prof answered, pointing with an outstretched arm. "And I live alone. There's nobody but me on this island—except you, of course."

The old man led the way through the trees, guiding the boys with a small greenish lamp that he claimed was made from fireflies' innards. It was fully dark by the time they reached the Prof's cabin. To Tim, what little he could make out of it looked more like a bare little hump of dirt than a regular cabin.

The Prof stepped down into a sort of hollow and pushed open a creaking door. In the ghostly green light from his little lamp, the boys stepped inside. The door groaned and closed again.

And suddenly the room was brightly lit, so bright it made Tim squeeze his eyes shut for a moment. He heard Hawk gasp with surprise.

"Ah, I forgot," the Prof said. "You're not accustomed to electricity."

The place was a wonder. It was mostly underground, but there were lights that made everything like it was daytime. And there were lots of rooms; the place just seemed to go on and on.

"Nothing much else to do for the past two centuries," the Prof said. "Home improvement was always a hobby of mine, even back before the Flood."

"You remember before the Flood?" Tim asked, awed.

The Prof sank his chunky body onto a sagging, tatty sofa and gestured to chairs for the boys to sit on.

"I was going to be one of the Immortals," he said, his rasping voice somewhere between sad and sore. "Got my telomerase shots. I'd never age—so long as I took the booster shots every fifty years."

Tim glanced at Hawk, who looked just as puzzled as he himself felt.

"But then the Flood wiped all that out. I'm aging again . . . slowly, I grant you, but just take a look at me! Hardly immortal, right?"

Hawk pointed to the thickly stacked shelves lining the room's walls. "Are all those things books?"

The Prof nodded. "My other hobby was looting libraries—while they were still on dry land."

He babbled on about solar panels and superconducting batteries and thermionic generators and all kinds of other weird stuff that started to make Tim's head spin. It was like the Prof was so glad to have somebody to talk to he didn't know when to stop.

Tim had always been taught to be respectful of his elders; sometimes the lessons had included a sound thrashing. But no matter how respectfully he tried to pay attention to the Prof's rambling, barely understandable monologue, he kept drifting toward sleep. Back home everybody was abed shortly after nightfall, but now this Prof was yakking on and on. It must be pretty near midnight, Tim thought. He could hardly keep his eyes open. He nodded off, woke himself with a start, tried as hard as he could to stay awake.

"But look at me," the Prof said at last. "I'm keeping you two from a good night's sleep, talking away like this."

He led the boys to another room that had real beds in it. "Be careful how you get on them," he warned. "Nobody's slept in those antiques in fifty years or more, not since a family of pilgrims got blown off their course for New Nashville. Stayed for damned near a month. Ate me out of house and home, just about, but I was still sad to see them go. I . . ."

Hawk yawned noisily and the Prof's monologue petered out. "I'll see you in the morning. Have a good sleep."

Tim didn't care about the Prof's warning. He was so sleepy he threw himself on the bare mattress of the nearer bed. He raised a cloud of dust, but after one cough he fell sound asleep.

Because the Prof's home was mostly underground it stayed dark long after sunrise. Tim and Hawk slept longer than they ever had at home. Only the sound of the Prof knocking hard on their bedroom door woke them.

The boys washed and relieved themselves in a privy that was built right into the house, in a separate little room of its own, with running water at the turn of a handle.

"Gravity feed," the Prof told them over a hearty breakfast of eggs and ham and waffles and muffins and fruit preserves. "Got a cistern for rainwater up in the hills and pipes carry the water here. I boil all the drinking and cooking water, of course."

"Of course," Hawk mumbled, his mouth full of blueberry muffin.

"We've got to haul your boat farther up out of the water," the Prof said, "and tie it down good and tight. Big blow likely soon."

Tim glanced out the narrow slit of the kitchen's only window and saw that it was dull gray outside, cloudy.

Once they finished breakfast, the Prof took them to still another room. This one had desks and strange-looking boxes sitting on them, with windows in them.

The Prof slipped into a little chair that creaked under his weight and started pecking with his fingers on a board full of buttons. The window on the box atop the desk lit up and suddenly showed a picture.

Tim jerked back a step, surprised. Even Hawk looked wide-eyed, his mouth hanging open.

"Not many weather satellites still functioning," the Prof muttered, as much to himself as the boys. "Only the old military birds left; rugged little buggers. Hardened, you know. But even with solar power and gyro stabilization, after two hundred years they're crapping out, one by one."

"What is that?" Hawk asked, his voice strangely small and hollow. Tim knew what was going through his friend's mind: *This is witchcraft!*

The Prof launched into an explanation that meant practically nothing to the boys. Near as Tim could figure it, the old man was saying there was a machine hanging in the air like a circling hawk or buzzard, but miles and miles and higher, so high they couldn't see it. And the machine had some sort of eyes on it and this box on the Prof's desk was showing what those eyes saw.

It didn't sound like witchcraft, the way the Prof explained it. He made it sound just as natural as chopping wood.

"That's the United States," the Prof said, tapping the glass that covered the picture. "Or what's left of it."

Tim saw mostly wide stretches of blue stuff that sort of looked like water, with plenty of smears of white and gray. Clouds?

"Florida's gone, of course," the Prof muttered. "Most of the midwest has been inundated. New England . . . Maryland and the whole Chesapeake region . . . all flooded."

His voice had gone low and soft, as if he was about to cry. Tim even thought he saw a tear glint in one of the old man's eyes, though it was hard to tell, under those shaggy white brows of his.

"Here's where we are," the Prof said, pointing to one of the gray smudges. "Can't see the island, of course; we're beneath the cloud cover."

Tim looked at Hawk, who shrugged. Couldn't figure out if the Prof was crazy or a witch or what.

The Prof tapped at the buttons on the oblong board in front of him and the picture on the box changed. Now it showed something that was mostly white. Lots of clouds, still, but they were almost all white and if that was supposed to be ground underneath them the ground was all white, too.

"Canada," said the Prof, grimly. "The icecap is advancing fast."

"What's that mean?" Hawk asked.

The Prof sucked in a big sigh and looked up at the boys. "It's going to get colder. A lot colder."

"Winter's comin' already?" Tim asked. It was still springtime, he knew. Summer was coming, not winter.

But the Prof answered, "A long winter, son. A winter that lasts thousands of years. An ice age."

Hawk asked, "What's an ice age?"

"It's what follows a greenhouse warming. This greenhouse was an anomaly, caused by anthropogenic factors. Now the cee-oh-two's being leached out of the atmosphere and the global climate will bounce back to a Pleistocene condition."

He might as well have been talking Cherokee or some other redskin language, Tim thought. Hawk looked just as baffled.

Seeing the confusion on the boys' faces, the Prof went to great pains to try to explain. Tim got the idea that he was saying the weather was going to turn colder, a lot colder, and stay that way for a *really* long time.

"Glaciers a mile thick!" the Prof said, nearly raving in his earnestness. "Minnesota, Michigan, the whole Great Lakes region was covered with ice a mile thick!"

"It was?"

"When?"

Shaking his head impatiently, the Prof said, "It doesn't matter when. The important thing is that it's going to happen all over again!"

"Here?" Tim asked. "Where our folks live?"

"Yes!"

"How soon?" asked Hawk.

The Prof hesitated. He drummed his fingers on the desktop for a minute, looking lost in thought.

"By the time you're a grandfather," he said at last. "Maybe sooner, maybe later. But it's going to happen."

Hawk let a giggle out of him. "That's a long time from now."

"But you've got to get ready for it," the Prof said, frowning. "It will take a long time to prepare, to learn how to make warm clothing, to grow different crops or migrate south."

Hawk shook his head.

"You ought to at least warn your people, let them know it's going to happen," the Prof insisted.

"But we're headin' for Colorado," Tim confessed. "We're not goin' back home."

The Prof's bushy brows knit together. "This climate shift could be just as abrupt as the greenhouse cliff was. People who aren't prepared for it will die—starve to death or freeze."

"How do you know it's gonna happen like that?" Hawk demanded.

"You saw the satellite imagery of Canada, didn't you?"

"We saw some picture of something, I don't know what it really was," Hawk said. "How do you know what it is? How do you know it's gonna get so cold?"

The Prof thought a moment, then admitted, "I don't *know*. But all the evidence points that way. I'm sure of it, but I don't have conclusive proof."

"You don't really know," Hawk said.

For a long moment the old man glared at Hawk angrily. Then he took another deep breath and his anger seemed to fade away.

"Listen, son. Many years ago people like me tried to warn the rest of the world that the greenhouse warming was going to drastically change the global climate. All the available evidence pointed to it, but the evidence was not conclusive. We couldn't convince the political leaders of the world that they were facing a disaster."

"What happened?" Tim asked.

Spreading his arms out wide, the Prof shouted, "This happened! The world's breadbaskets flooded! Electrical power distribution systems totally wiped out. The global nets, the information and knowledge of centuries—all drowned. Food distribution gone. Cities abandoned. Billions died! Billions! Civilization sank back to subsistence agriculture."

Tim looked at Hawk and Hawk looked back at Tim. Maybe the old man isn't a witch, Tim thought. Maybe he's just crazy.

The Prof sighed. "It doesn't mean a thing to you, does it? You just don't have the understanding, the education or . . ."

Muttering to himself, the old man turned back to his magic box and pecked at the buttons again. The picture went back to the first one the boys had seen.

Abruptly the Prof jabbed a button and the picture winked off. Pushing himself up from his chair, he said, "Come on, we've got to get your boat farther up out of the water and tied down good and strong."

"What for?" Hawk demanded, suddenly suspicious.

With a frown, the Prof said, "This area used to be called Tornado Alley. Just because it's covered by water doesn't change that. In fact, it makes the twisters even worse."

The boys had heard of twisters. One had leveled a village not more than a day's travel from their own, only a couple of springtimes ago.

When it came, the twister was a monster.

The boys spent most of the day hauling their boat up close to the trees and then tying it down as firmly as they could. The Prof provided ropes and plenty of advice and even some muscle power. All the time they worked the clouds got thicker and darker and lower. Tim expected a thunderstorm any minute as they headed back for the Prof's house, bone tired.

They were halfway back when the trees began tossing back and forth and rain started spattering down. Leaves went flying through the air, torn off the trees. A whole bough whipped by, nearly smacking Hawk on the head. Tim heard a weird sound, a low dull roaring, like the distant howl of some giant beast.

"Run!" the Prof shouted over the howling wind. "You don't want to get caught here amidst the trees!"

Despite their aching muscles they ran. Tim glanced over his shoulder and through the bending, swaying trees he saw a mammoth pillar of pure terror marching across the open water, heading right for him, sucking up water and twigs and anything in its path, weaving slowly back and forth, high as the sky, bearing down on them, coming to get him.

It roared and shouted and moved up onto the land. Whole trees were ripped up by their roots. Tim tripped and sprawled face-first into the dirt. Somebody grabbed him by the scruff of his neck and yanked him to his feet. The rain was so thick and hard he couldn't see an arm's length in front of him but suddenly the low earthen hump of the Prof's house was in sight and the old man, despite his years, was half a dozen strides ahead of them, already fumbling with the front door.

They staggered inside, the wind-driven rain pouring in with them. It took all three of them to get the door closed again and firmly latched. The Prof pushed a heavy cabinet against the door, then slumped to the floor, soaking wet, chest heaving.

"Check . . . the windows," he gasped. "Shutters . . ."

Hawk nodded and scrambled to his feet. Tim hesitated only a moment, then did the same. He saw there were thick wooden shutters folded back along the edges of each window. He pulled them across the glass and locked them tight.

The twister roared and raged outside but the Prof's house, largely underground, held firm. Tim thought the ground was shaking, but maybe it was just him shaking, he was so scared. The storm yowled and battered at the house. Things pounded on the roof. The rain drummed so hard it sounded like all the redskins in the world doing a war dance.

The Prof lay sprawled in the puddle by the door until Hawk gestured for Tim to help him get the old man to his feet.

"Bedroom . . ." the Prof said. "Let me . . . lay down . . . for a while." His chest was heaving, his face looked gray.

They put him down gently on his bed. His wet clothes made a squishy sound on the covers. He closed his eyes and seemed to go to sleep. Tim stared at the old man's bare, white-fuzzed chest. It was pumping up and down, fast.

Something crashed against the roof so hard that books tumbled out of their shelves and dust sifted down from the ceiling. The lights blinked, then went out altogether. A dim lamp came on and cast scary shadows on the wall.

Tim and Hawk sat on the floor, next to each other, knees drawn up tight. Every muscle in Tim's body ached, every nerve was pulled tight as a bowstring. And the twister kept howling outside, as if demanding to be allowed in.

At last the roaring diminished, the drumming rain on the roof slackened off. Neither Tim nor Hawk budged an inch, though. Not until it became completely quiet out there.

"Do you think it's over?" Tim whispered.

Hawk shook his head. "Maybe."

They heard a bird chirping outside. Hawk scrambled to his feet and went to the window on the other side of the Prof's bed. He eased the shutter open a crack, then flung it all the way back. Bright sunshine streamed into the room. Tim noticed a trickle of water that had leaked through the window and its shutter, dripping down the wall to make a puddle on the bare wooden floor.

The Prof seemed to be sleeping soundly, but as they tiptoed out of the bedroom, he opened one eye and said, "Check outside. See what damage it's done."

A big pine had fallen across the house's low roof; that had been the crash they'd heard. The water pipe from the cistern was broken, but the cistern itself—dug into the ground—was unharmed except for a lot of leaves and debris that had been blown into it.

The next morning the Prof felt strong enough to get up, and he led the boys on a more detailed inspection tour. The solar panels were caked with dirt and leaves, but otherwise unhurt. The boys set to cleaning them while the Prof mended the broken water pipe.

By nightfall the damage had been repaired and the house was back to normal. But not the Prof. He moved slowly, painfully, his breathing was labored. He was sick, even Tim could see that.

"Back in the old days," he said in a rasping whisper over the dinner table, "I'd go to the local clinic and get some pills to lower my blood pressure. Or an EGF injection to grow new arteries." He shook his head sadly. "Now I can only sit around like an old man waiting to die."

The boys couldn't leave him, not in his weakened condition. Besides, the Prof said they'd be better off waiting until the spring tornado season was over.

"No guarantee you won't run into a twister during the summer, of course," he told them. "But it's safer if you wait a bit."

He taught them as much as he could about his computers and the electrical systems he'd rigged to power the house. Tim knew how to read some, so the Prof gave him books while he began to teach Hawk about reading and writing.

"The memory of the human race is in these books," he said, almost every day. "What's left of it, that is."

The boys worked his little vegetable patch and picked berries and hunted down game while the Prof stayed at home, too weak to exert himself. He showed the boys how to use his high-powered bow and Tim bagged a young boar all by himself.

One morning well into the summertime, the Prof couldn't get out of his bed. Tim saw that his face was gray and soaked in sweat, his breathing rapid and shallow. He seemed to be in great pain.

He looked up at the boys and tried to smile. "I guess I'm . . . going to become immortal . . . the old-fashioned way."

Hawk swallowed hard and Tim could see he was fighting to hold back tears.

"Nothing you can do . . . for me," the Prof said, his voice so weak that Tim had to bend over him to hear it.

"Just rest," Tim said. "You rest up and you'll get better."

"Not likely."

Neither boy knew what else to say, what else to do.

"I bequeath my island to you two," the Prof whispered. "It's all yours, boys."

Hawk nodded.

"But you . . . you really ought to warn . . . your people," he gasped, "about the ice . . ."

He closed his eyes. His labored breathing stopped.

That evening, after they had buried the Prof, Tim asked Hawk, "Do you think we oughtta go back and tell our folks?"

Hawk snapped, "No."

"But the Prof said—"

"He was a crazy old man. We go back home and all we'll get is a whippin' for runnin' away."

"But we oughtta tell them," Tim insisted. "Warn them."

"About something that ain't gonna happen until we're grandfathers? Something that probably won't happen at all?"

"But—"

"We got a good place here. The crazy old coot left it to us and we'd be fools to leave it."

"What about Colorado?"

"We'll get there next year. Or maybe the year after. And if we don't like it there we can always come back here."

For the first time in his life, Tim not only felt that Hawk was wrong, but he decided to do something about it.

"Okay," he said. "You stay. I'm goin' back."

"You're as crazy as he was!"

"I'll come back here. I'm just goin' to warn them and then I'll come back."

Hawk made a snorting noise. "If they leave any skin on your hide."

For a week Tim patched up their boat and its ragged sail and filled it with provisions. The morning he was set to cast off, Hawk came to the pebbly beach with him.

"I guess this is goodbye for a while," Tim said.

"Don't be a dumbbell," Hawk groused. "I'm goin' with you."

Tim felt a rush of joy. "You are?"

"You'd get yourself lost out there. Some sea monster would have you for lunch."

"We can always come back here again," Tim said, grunting, as they pushed the boat into the water.

"Yeah, sure."

"We hafta warn them, Hawk. We just hafta."

"Shut up and haul out the sail."

For several days they sailed north and east, back along the way they had come. The weather was sultry, the sun blazing like molten iron out of a cloudless sky.

"Ice age," Hawk grumbled. "Craziest thing I ever heard."

"I saw pictures of it in the books the Prof had," said Tim. "Big sheets of ice covering everything."

Hawk just shook his head and spit over the side.

"It really happened, Hawk."

"The weather don't change," Hawk snapped. "It's the same every year. Hot in the summer, cool in the winter. You ever known anything else?"

"No," Tim admitted.

"You ever seen ice, except in the Prof's pictures?"

"No."

"Or that stuff he called snow?"

"Never."

"We oughtta turn this boat around and head back to the island."

Tim almost agreed. But he saw that Hawk made no motion to change their course. He was talking one way but acting the other.

They fell silent. Tim understood Hawk's resentment. Probably nobody would listen to them when they got home. The elders would be pretty mad about the two of them running off and they wouldn't listen to a word the boys had to say.

For hours they skimmed along, the only sound the gusting of the hot southerly wind and the hiss of the boat cutting through the placid water.

"It's all fairy tales," Hawk grumbled, as much to himself as to Tim. "Stories they make up to scare the kids. What do they call 'em?"

"Myths," said Tim.

"Myths, that's right. Myths." But suddenly he jerked to attention. "Hey, what's that?"

Tim saw he was looking down into the water. He came over to Hawk's side of the boat.

Something was glittering down below the surface. Something big.

Tim's heart started racing. "A sea monster?"

Hawk shook his head impatiently. "I don't think it's moving. Leastways it's not following after us. Look, it's falling behind."

They lapsed into silence again. Tim felt uncomfortable. He didn't like it when Hawk was sore at him.

Apologetically, he said, "Maybe you're right. The old man was most likely a little crazy."

"A *lot* crazy," Hawk said. "And we're just as crazy as he was. The weather don't change like that. It's just not possible. There never was a Flood. The world's always been like this. Always."

Tim was shocked. "No Flood?"

"It's one of them myths," Hawk insisted. "Like sea monsters. Ain't no such thing."

"Then what did we see back there?"

"I dunno. But it wasn't no sea monster. And the weather don't change the way the Prof said it's goin' to. There wasn't any Flood and there sure ain't goin' to be any ice age."

Tim wondered if Hawk was right, as their boat sailed on and the glittering stainless steel stump of the St. Louis Gateway Arch fell farther and farther behind them.

BROTHERS

Over my desk is a page from a collection of Ernest Hemingway's short stories. The page contains a brief sketch, set in a town in Spain in the 1920s. Two aging bullfighters are watching the young matador who is supposed to be the star of that afternoon's corrida de toros. *But the young star is drunk, dancing in the street with gypsies, staggeringly drunk, in no condition to face the bulls.*

"Who will kill his bulls?" one of the older matadors asks the other.

"We, I suppose. We kill the savage's bulls, and the drunkard's bulls, and the riau-riau dancer's bulls."

The point is, some people get the job done and some people don't. A successful writer gets the job done. No matter what is happening around him or her. No matter family or weather or finances, a writer writes. *The world can collapse and the writer writes. No excuses. No delays. No waiting for inspiration or the right moment or the proper phase of the Moon. A writer works at it. The rest is all talk.*

Humphrey Bogart made somewhat the same point when he said, "A professional is a guy who gets the job done whether he feels like it or not."

"Brothers" is a story about two professionals, doing two very different jobs that needed to be done on a certain day in November 1971.

NOVEMBER 1971: *Command Module* Saratoga, *in Lunar Orbit*

Alone now, Bill Carlton stopped straining his eyes and turned away from the tiny triangular window. The landing module was a dwindling speck against the gray pockmarked surface of the barren, alien Moon.

He tried to lean his head back against the contour couch, remembered again that he was weightless, floating lightly against the restraining harness. All the old anger surged up in him again, knotting his neck with tension even in zero gravity.

Sitting here like a goddamned robot. Left here to mind the store like some goddamned kid while they go down to the surface and get their names in the history books. The also-ran. Sixty miles away from the Moon, but I'll never set foot on it. Never.

The Apollo command module seemed almost large now that Wally and Dave were gone. The two empty couches looked huge, luxurious. The banks of instruments and controls hummed at him electrically. We can get along fine without you, they were saying. We're machines, we don't need an also-ran to make us work.

This tin can stinks, he said to himself. *Five days cooped up in here, sitting inside these damned suits. I stink.*

With a wordless growl, Bill turned up the gain on the radio. His earphones crackled for a moment, then the robotic voice of the Capcom came through.

"You're in approach phase, *Yorktown*. Everything looking good."

Wally's voice answered, "Manual control okay. Altitude forty-three hundred."

Almost three seconds passed. "Forty-three, we copy." It was Shannon's voice from Houston. Capcom for the duration of the landing.

Bill sat alone in the command module and listened. His two teammates were about to land. He had traveled a quarter million miles, but would get no closer than fifty-eight miles to the Moon.

5 NOVEMBER 1971: *U.S.S.* Saratoga, *in the Tonkin Gulf*

Bob Carlton tapped the back of his helmet against the head knocker and held his gloved hands up against the canopy's clear plastic so the deck crew could see he was not touching any of the controls. The sky-blue paint had been scratched from the spot where the head knocker touched the helmet. Sixty missions will do that.

Sixty missions. It seemed more like six hundred. Or six thousand. It was endless. Every day, every day. The same thing. Endless.

The A-7 was being attached to the catapult now. It was the time when Bob always got just slightly queasy, staring out beyond the edge of the carrier's heaving deck into the gray mist of morning.

"Cleared for takeoff," said the launch director's voice in his earphones.

"Clear," Bob repeated.

He rammed the throttle forward and felt the bomber's jet engine howl and surge suddenly, straining, making the whole plane tremble like a hunting dog begging to be released from its leash.

"Three . . . two . . . one . . . GO!"

His head slammed back and his whole body seemed to flatten against itself, pressed into the seat as the A-7 leaped off the carrier's deck and into the misty air. The deep rolling swells of the blue-green water whipped by and then receded as he pulled the control column back slightly and the swept-wing plane angled up into the sullen, low-hanging clouds. Without even thinking consciously of it, he reached back and pushed the head knocker up into its locked position. Now he could fire the ejection seat if he had to.

In a moment the Sun broke through and sparkled off the mirrors arrayed around the curve of the canopy. Bob saw the five other planes of his flight and formed upon the left end of their V. The queasiness was gone now. He felt strong and good in the sunshine.

He looked up and saw the pale shadow of a half moon grinning lopsidedly at him. Bill's up there, he thought. Can you see me, Bill? Can you hear me calling you?

Then he looked away. A dark slice of land lay on the horizon, slim and silent as a dagger. Vietnam.

"Contact. All lights on. Engine stop. We're down." Bill heard Dave McDonald's laconic voice announce their landing on the moon.

"We copy, *Yorktown.* Good job. Fantastic." Shannon sounded excited. He was due to fly the next mission. "*Saratoga,* do you read?"

Bill was surprised that he had to swallow twice before his voice would work. "Copy. *Yorktown* in port. Good going, guys."

It was an all-Navy crew, so they had named their modules in honored Navy tradition. The lunar lander became *Yorktown.* Bill rode alone in the command module, *Saratoga.* The old men with gold braid on their sleeves and silver in their hair loved that. Good old Annapolis spirit.

"You are go for excursion," said Shannon, lapsing back into technical jargon.

"Roger." McDonald's voice was starting to fade out. "We'll take a little walk soon's we wiggle into the suits."

And I'll sit here by myself, Bill thought. *What would Shannon and the rest of those clowns at Houston do if I screwed my helmet on and took a walk on my own?*

The fucking oxygen mask never fit right. It pressed across the bridge of Bob's nose and cut into his cheeks. And the stuff was almost too cold to breathe; it made his teeth ache. Bob felt his ears pop slightly as the formation of six attack bombers dove to treetop height and then streaked across the mottled green forest.

This was the part of the mission that he liked best, racing balls-out close enough to the goddamned trees to suck a monkey into your air intake. Everything a green blur outside the cockpit. Six hundred knots and the altimeter needle flopping around zero. The plane took it as smooth as a new Cadillac tooling up to the country club. Not a shake or a rattle in her. She merely rocked slightly in the invisible air currents bubbling up from the forest.

Christ, any lower and we'll come back smeared green. He laughed aloud.

Bob flew the bomb-laden plane with mere touches of his thumb against the button on the control column that moved the trim tabs. The A-7 responded like a thoroughbred, jumping smoothly over an upjutting tree, turning gracefully information with the five others.

Why don't we just fly like this forever? Bob wondered. *Just keep going and never, never stop.*

But up ahead the land was rising, ridge after ridge of densely wooded hills. In a valley between one particular pair of ridges was an NVA ammunition dump, according to their preflight briefing. By the time they got there, Bob guessed, the North Vietnamese would have moved their ammo to someplace else. We'll wind up bombing the fucking empty jungle again.

But their antiaircraft guns will be there. Oh yes indeed, the little

*brown bastards'll have everything from slingshots to radar-directed
artillery to throw at us. They always do.*

There was a whole checklist of chores for Bill to do as he waited
alone in the command module. Photographic mapping. Heat sensors.
Housekeeping checks on the life-support systems.

Busywork, Bill grumbled silently. He went through the checklist
mechanically, doing even the tiniest task with the numb efficiency of
a machine. *Just a lot of crap to make me feel like I'm doing something.
To make them feel like there's something for me to do.*

The radio voices of Peters and McDonald were fading fast now. The
command module was swinging around in its orbit toward the far side
of the moon. Bill listened to Wally and Dave yahooing and joking with
each other as they bounced and jogged on the Moon's surface, stirring
up dust that had waited four billion years for them to arrive.

"Wish you could be here, buddy!" sang Wally.

"Yeah, Bill. You'd love the scenery," Dave agreed happily.

Bill said into his radio microphone, "Thanks a lot, you guys." So
what if they heard him in Houston. What more could they do to him?

"*Saratoga*, you are approaching radio cutoff," Shannon reminded
him needlessly.

"Radio cutoff," Bill repeated to Houston. Then he counted silently,
one thousand, two thousand, three.

"See you on the other side," said Shannon, his radio voice finally
crossing the distance between them.

"That's a rog," Bill said.

The far side of the Moon. Totally alone, separated from the entire
human race by a quarter million miles of distance and two thousand
miles of solid rock.

Bill stole one final glance at the Earth as the spaceship swung
around in its orbit. It was blue and mottled with white swirling clouds,
glowing like a solitary candle on a darkened altar. He could not see
Vietnam. He did not even try to find it.

"Check guns." The flight leader's voice in his helmet earphones
almost startled Bob.

The easy part of the flight was finished. The work was beginning.
He thumbed the firing button on his control column, just the slightest

tap. Below his feet he could feel a brief buzz, almost like a small vacuum cleaner or an electric shaver. Just for an instant.

"Corsair Six, guns clear." His microphone was built into the oxygen mask.

The flight leader kept an open mike. Bob could hear him breathing heavily inside his mask, as if he were personally carrying the bomb-laden plane on his shoulders. The ground was rising now, still green and treacherous, reaching up into the sky in steep ridges.

Their flight plan took advantage of the terrain. Come in low, skim the treetops, until the final ridge. Then zoom up over that last crest, dive flat out into the valley and plaster the joint with high-explosive bombs and napalm. Get in and get out before they know you're there.

Good plan. Except for tail-end Bobby. Four planes could get past the fucking slopes before they can react. Maybe five. But six was expecting too much. *They'll have their radars tracking and their guns firing by the time I come through.*

The only sound in the command module was the inevitable electrical hum of the equipment. Bill ignored it. It would make no impression on his conscious mind unless it stopped.

He floated gently against the light restraining harness of his couch and closed his eyes. This was the time he had waited for. His own time. They could pick him for the shit job of sitting here and waiting while Wally and Dave got all the glory, but they couldn't stop him from doing this one experiment, this test that nobody in the world knew about.

Nobody except Bobby and me, he thought.

Eyes closed, Bill tried to relax his body completely. Force the tension out of his muscles. Make those tendons ease their grip.

"Bobby," he whispered. "Bobby, can you hear me?"

They had agreed to the experiment a year earlier, the last time they had seen each other, at the lobby bar in the Saint Francis hotel.

"What the hell are you, doing here?" they had asked simultaneously.

"I'm rotating back to 'Nam," said Bob.

"I'm attending an engineering conference over at Ames," said Bill.

They marveled at the coincidence. Neither of them had ever gone to that hotel bar before. And at four in the afternoon!

"For twin brothers, we sure don't see much of each other," Bill said, after the bartender had set up a pair of Jack Daniel's neat, water on the side, before them. "Takes a coincidence like this."

"This is more than a coincidence," said Bob.

"You think so?"

Bobby nodded, picked up his drink, and sipped at it.

"I think you've been out of the mystic East too long, kid. You're going Asiatic."

"Maybe you've been hanging around with too many scientists," Bob countered. "You're starting to think like a machine."

"Come on, Bobby, you don't really believe—"

"What made you come in here this afternoon?"

Bill shrugged. "Damned if I know. What about you?"

A twin shrug. "Can't say it was a premonition. On the other hand, I usually don't even come to this part of town when I'm on leave in Frisco."

They drank for several hours, ignoring the bar girls who sauntered through looking for early action. They talked about family and old times. They avoided comparing their Navy duties. Bob was a frontline pilot in a carrier attack squadron. Bill was on detached duty with the NASA astronaut corps. They had both made their decisions about that years earlier.

"You really believe this ESP stuff?" Bill asked as they fumbled in their pockets for money to pay the tab.

"I don't know." Then Bob looked directly into his brother's eyes. "Twins ought to be close."

"Yeah. I guess so."

"I'll be shipping out next week."

"They've scheduled me for a shot two months from now."

"Great! Good luck."

"Luck to you, kid." Bill got up from the barstool.

Bob did the same. "Stay in touch, huh? Wouldn't hurt you to write me a line now and then."

With a sudden grin, Bill said, "I'll do better than that. I'll give you a call from the Moon."

"Sure," Bob replied.

"Why not? You think this ESP business is real—let's give it a test."

Bob put on the same frown he had worn as a child when his twin brother displeased him.

Bob's frown melted. "You dream about me?"

"Sometimes."

He grinned and clapped his brother on the shoulder. "Me, too," he said. "I dream about you, now and then."

"So let's see if we can make contact from the Moon!" Bill insisted.

Bob shrugged, the way he always did when he gave in to his older brother. "Sure. Why not?"

But now, as he sat alone in the silence of space, where he could not even see the Earth, Bill's call to his younger brother went unanswered.

"Bobby," he said aloud. It was almost a snarl, almost a plea. "Bobby, where in hell are you?"

The valley was long and narrow, that's why they had to go in Indian file. Bob saw the green ridges tilt and slide beneath him, then straighten out as he banked steeply and put the A-7 into a flat dive, following the plane ahead of him, sixth in the flight of six.

He felt a strange prickling at the back of his neck. Not fear. Something he had never felt before, as if someone far, far away was calling his name. No time for that now. He nosed the plane down and started his bomb run.

For once, intelligence had the right shit. The flight leader's cluster of bombs waggled down into the engulfing forest canopy, then all hell broke loose. The bombs and napalm went off, blowing big black clouds streaked with red flame up through the roof of the jungle. Before the next plane could drop its load, the secondary explosions started. Huge fireballs. Tracers whizzing out in every direction. Searing white magnesium flares.

The second plane released its bombs as Bob watched. Everything seemed to freeze in place for a moment that never ended, and then the plane, the bombs, the fireballs blowing away the jungle below all merged into one big mass of flame and the plane disappeared.

"Pull up, pull up!" Bob heard somebody screaming in his earphones. He had already yanked the control column back toward his crotch. Planes were scattering across the sky, jettisoning their bomb loads helter-skelter. Bob glanced at his left hand and was shocked to see that the bomb release switches next to it had already been tripped.

The valley itself was seething with explosions. The ammo dump was blowing itself to hell and anybody who was down there was going along for the ride. Including the flight leader's wingman. Who the hell was flying wing for him today? Bob wondered briefly.

"Form up on me," the voice in his earphones commanded. "Come on, dammit, stop gawking and form up."

Bob craned his neck to find where the other planes were. He saw two, three . . . another one pulling gees to catch up with them.

He banked and started climbing to rejoin the group, his own gee suit squeezing his guts and legs, his breath gasping. Hard work, pulling gees. And he felt a stray tendril of thought, like the wispy memory of a tune that he could not fully recall.

"Bill?" he asked aloud.

Then something exploded and he was slammed against the side of the cockpit, helmet bashing against the plastic canopy, pain flaming through his legs and groin.

The shock of contact was a double hammer blow. Bill's body went rigid with sudden pain.

Bobby! What happened? But he knew, immediately and fully, just as if he sat in the A-7's cockpit.

Flak, Bobby gasped. *I'm hit.*

Jesus Christ, the pain!

I'm bleeding bad, Billy. Both legs.

Can you work the controls?

It took an enormous effort to move his arms. Tabs and ailerons okay. Elevators. Another surge of agony, dizziness. *Can't use my legs. Rudder pedals no go. Radio's shot to hell, too.*

They're leaving me behind, Bill. They're getting out of here and leaving me.

That's what they're supposed to do! We've got to gain altitude, Bob. Get away from their guns.

Yeah. We're climbing. Engine's running rough, though.

Never mind that. Grab altitude. Point her home.

Can't make the rudder work. Can't turn.

Use trim tabs. Go easy. She'll steer okay. Like that time we broke the boom off the Sailfish. We'll get back okay.

You see anything else out there? MiGs?

No, you're clear. Just concentrate on getting this bird out over the sea. You don't want to eject where they'll capture you.

Don't want to eject, period. Or ditch. Not in the shape I'm in.

We'll get back to the carrier, don't worry.

I won't be able to land it, Billy. I don't think I can last that long anyway.

We'll do it together. I'll help you.

You can't . . .

Who says I can't?

Yeah, but . . .

We'll do it together.

I don't think I'll make it. I'm . . .

Don't fade out on me! Bobby, stay awake! Here, let me get that dammed oxygen mask off you; we're low enough to suck real air.

Bill, you shouldn't try this. I don't want us both to get killed.

I've got to, kid. Nothing else matters.

But . . .

Bobby, listen to me. I ought to be there with you. For real. I should've been on the line with you instead of playing around out here in space. I took the easy way out. The coward's way out. They gave me a chance to play astronaut and I took it. I jumped at it!

Who wouldn't?

You didn't. I owe you my life, Bobby. You're doing the fighting while I'm playing it safe a quarter million miles away from the real thing.

You're crazy! You think blasting off into outer space on top of some glorified skyrocket and riding to the fucking Moon in a tin can is safe?

There's no Indians up here shooting at us, kid.

I'll take the Indians.

Bobby, I'm not kidding. I feel so goddamned ashamed. I've always grabbed the best piece of the pie away from you. All our lives. I ran out on you.

I always got the piece I wanted, big brother. You did what you had to do. And it's important work. I know that. We all know that. I'm doing what I want to do.

You're putting your life on the line.

So are you.

I shouldn't have run out on you. I should have helped you fight this war.

There's enough of us fighting this lousy war. Too many. It's all a wagonload of shit, Bill. Talk about feeling ashamed. Making war on goddamned farmers and blowing villages to hell isn't my idea of glory.

But how else . . .

You do what you have to do, brother. Doesn't make any difference why. You get locked into the job by the powers that be.

The gold braid.

The gods.

Whatever.

We're locked in, Billy. Both of us. All of us. It's all a test, just like Father Gilhooley always told us. We do what we have to, because if we do less than that, we let down the guys with us. Nobody flies alone, brother. We've got each other's lives in our hands.

You believe that?

I know it.

Bob?

Yeah.

I know I've treated you like shit ever since we were kids . . .

You did? When?

I'm sorry. I should've done better.

I should've been better, Bill. Sometimes I raised hell just to see what you'd do about it.

I love you, brother.

I know. It goes both ways, Bill.

Don't die, Bobby. Please don't die.

I don't want to.

The pain was flowing over them both in overpowering waves now, like massive breakers at the beach. They could sense a new surge growing and gliding toward them and then engulfing them, drenching them until they finally broke out of it only to see a new wave heading their way.

I'm not going to make it, Bill.

Yes you are. We can make it.

I don't think so. I'm sorry, big brother. I'm trying, but . . .

You can do it! We can do it—together.

Together. It's not so bad that way, is it? I mean, when you're not alone.

Nobody's ever alone, kid. Even out here neither one of is alone. Not ever.

The plane was out over the water now, the dark green ridges behind them, nothing but restless deep blue billows below, reaching for them. Not another plane in sight.

We're losing altitude.

Yeah.

I don't know how long—

Look! The carrier, Bob!

Where? Yeah. Looks damned small from up here.

You're almost home. I'll handle the rudder, you work the stick.

Yeah, okay. Maybe we can make it. Maybe.

No maybe about it! We're going to put this junk heap down right in front of the admiral's nose.

Sure.

Gear down?

Think so. Indicator light's shot away.

The hell with it.

LSO's waving us in.

They've cleared the deck for us.

Nice of them.

Easy now, easy on the throttle. Don't stall her!

Stop the backseat driving.

Deck's coming up too damned fast, Bobby!

Don't worry . . . I can . . . make it. Always was . . . a better flier . . . than you.

I know. I know! Just take her easy now.

Got it.

Head knocker?

Yeah. Don't want to eject by accident, do we.

Hang in there, kid.

Here it comes!

You did it! We're down!

We did it, brother. We did it together.

The deck team rushed to the battered plane. Firefighters doused the hot engine area and wings with foam. Plane handlers climbed up to the cockpit and slid the canopy back to find the pilot crumpled unconscious, his flight suit soaked with blood from the waist down. The medics lifted Bob Carlton from the cockpit tenderly and had whole blood flowing into his arm even while they wheeled him toward the sick bay.

"Look at his face," said one of the medics. "What the hell's he smiling about?"

It took thirty more orbits around the Moon before Peters and McDonald left the surface to rendezvous with the command module and begin the flight back to Earth. Thirty orbits while Bill Carlton sat totally alone. New attempts to contact his brother were fruitless. He knew that Bob was alive; that much he could sense. But there was no answer to his silent calls.

Wally Peters wormed his way through the airlock hatch first, a quizzical expression on his square-jawed face.

"How you doing, Billy boy?"

"Just fine. Glad to have you back."

Dave McDonald came through and floated to his couch on Bill's left. "Miss us?"

"Lonesome in here, all by yourself?" Wally grinned.

"Nope." Bill grinned back.

Wally and Dave glanced at each other. Bill realized it had been a long time since either of them had seen him smile.

"Here," said Wally. "We brought you a present." He reached into the pouch in the leg of his suit and took out a slim, dark piece of stone.

"Your very own moon rock," Dave said.

Bill took it from them wordlessly.

"We're sorry you couldn't have been down there with us, Bill. You would have enjoyed it."

"Yeah, we kind of felt bad leaving you here."

Bill laughed. "It's okay, guys. We all do what we have to do. We get the job done. Whatever it is. Whatever it is. We do what we've got to do, and we don't let our teammates down."

Dave and Wally stared at him for a moment.

"Come on," said Bill, his smile even warmer. "Let's take this tin can home."

INTERDEPARTMENTAL
MEMORANDUM

Strictly speaking, "Interdepartmental Memorandum" is not a story at all. There are no characters to speak of and no character development. There is no real plot; all the action has already taken place before the tale begins.

In length, this is what the publishing industry terms a short-short. Short-short stories are almost always under two thousand words, often under fifteen hundred. They are like a boxer's left jab, intended to jar you, snap your head back. They are not knockout punches.

Often the short-short story depends on a "twist" at its very end, a surprise that often comes on the very last line. The entire story is written precisely to hit you with that final shock ending.

Which brings me to O. Henry. Of all the pernicious influences that afflict young writers, O. Henry has caused the most damage. The man's stories should be banned from school classes altogether. Don't get me wrong: William Sydney Porter was a damned good writer; his short stories will be read for many generations to come. But because so many of his stories are memorable for their ironic surprise endings, young writers often fall into the trap of trying to write their first stories with surprise endings.

The trouble is, most young writers don't have the experience or observational talents that O. Henry had. The youngsters' surprises almost always fall flat. They are predictable or silly or both.

Take some heartfelt advice: If you are just starting to write, avoid the surprise ending. Make your stories flow to a logical ending, a conclusion that is in keeping with your characters and the conflicts they encounter. Remember, the editor you send your story to has probably read a thousand times more fiction than you have. It will be almost impossible to surprise a veteran editor.

"Interdepartmental Memorandum" was not written to surprise anyone. It is merely a fictionalized picture of a social trend that I find disturbing. As I have pointed out earlier, science fiction is an ideal vehicle for examining a social trend by stretching it far beyond its present dimensions. I kept the story to a short-short length precisely because I did not feel that an extrapolation of this kind would stand a longer treatment.

Left jab. Or maybe the prick of a needle. That's what a short-short story is.

To: All Cabinet Secretaries and Administrators of Independent Agencies
From: M. DeLay, secretary to the President
Subject: Minutes of Cabinet meeting, 24 December 2043

1. There was only one item on the agenda for the cabinet to consider: the President's decision to ask Congress for a Declaration of War against Mexico, citing Mexico's conquest of Central America and seizure of the Panama Canal, as well as the Gonzalez government's massing of troops along the Rio Grande River border with Texas.

2. In accordance with the Cabinet Act of 2032, the President was required to ask for a vote on his motion to ask for a declaration of war.

3. The Departments and Independent Agencies voted on the motion as follows:

Department of State: Opposed. Declaring war on Mexico would be a de facto recognition of the Gonzalez government, which government we have in fact refused to recognize since it came to power in an unauthorized coup d'etat.

Department of the Treasury: Opposed. A war with Mexico would force us into deficit financing and thereby violate the Balanced-Budget Act of 2020.

Department of Defense: Opposed. The Joint Chiefs have requested three more years for planning and training before they feel confident in launching a successful war against Mexico.

Department of Justice: Opposed. The Attorney General pointed out that since the war would undoubtedly be popular with the people of the U.S. (at least at the outset) the war would have an adverse effect on national gun-control efforts.

Department of the Interior: In favor. The Secretary of the Interior made an impassioned speech to his fellow Cabinet members about the danger Mexico presents to his home state of Texas.

Department of Agriculture: Opposed. Troops returning from Mexico and/or Central America could introduce many foreign pests to the U.S. (i.e., nonhuman pests such as insects, plant seeds and spores, various parasites, disease microbes, etc.).

Department of Commerce: Opposed. War with Mexico would adversely affect trade with all of Latin America, as well as tourism.

Department of Labor: Opposed. If the Army finds it necessary to call up the Reserves and/or the National Guard, this will result in labor shortages, especially in low-skill and non-skill service areas of the economy such as fast-food outlets and retail bookstores.

Department of Health and Human Services: Opposed. Battle casualties will adversely affect national health statistics. Also, increased need for psychological counseling of troops and their dependents and families will strain existing social-worker systems.

Department of Housing and Urban Development: Abstained, except to ask how and where expected Prisoners of War will be housed.

Department of Transportation: In favor, especially if suggested San Francisco-to-Panama City railroad line can be completed after war's end.

Department of Energy: Opposed, since no use of nuclear weapons is proposed.

Department of Education: Unsure.

National Aeronautics and Space Administration: Opposed. Mexico has missiles that could destroy civilian satellites, including the manned space station Freedom.

Environmental Protection Agency: Strongly opposed, since DoD environmental impact statement shows that proposed military action will cause unacceptable levels of air, water, and ground-water pollution.

The President therefore withdrew her motion to ask the Congress for a declaration of war. "If you people won't go along with me," she said, "I can imagine how those chowderheads up on the Hill will react to my request."

To: His Excellency Generalissimo Gonzalez
From: General Davila, commander of the Armies of the North
Date: 5 May 2044
Subject: Captured enemy documents

Most revered Leader!

The document above, together with many others, was captured by our shock troops when they reached the city of Washington, capital of the former United States. I believe it sheds some light on the "happy mystery" of why the U.S. crumbled so quickly.

Long Live Greater Mexico!

WORLD WAR 4.5

The plot of "World War 4.5" clearly falls into the area of "the man who learns better." Except that, in this case, it is a woman who learns.

This story is also a variation of what I call the "jailbreak" plot. The protagonist is doing something that you feel instinctively is wrong, like a convict's attempting to break out of jail. Yet because the protagonist is sympathetically drawn, the reader wants the protagonist to succeed, even though the protagonist may be doing "wrong" in the eyes of society.

"World War 4.5" was commissioned by a group who wanted to publicize the Unix computer system. Unix is a decentralized system that allows great flexibility for the user, in contrast to hierarchical systems that are more rigid.

Now, one of the best ways to generate a story is to ask, "If this goes on . . . what happens?" If some computer systems become more and more flexible while others become more and more rigid, how far can the two systems go? Will they compete? Very quickly I saw that the two competing types of computer systems could be used as metaphors for the two types of politico-economic systems then competing around the world: democracy and communism.

The story was written in 1989, when Eastern Europe was in ferment and the Berlin Wall was about to come down. It was not until two years later that the Soviet military attempted their coup against Mikhail Gorbachev and the Russian people took to the streets to stop them, much as depicted in this story. For months, whenever newscasters asked rhetorically, "Who would have thought that the Soviet Union would collapse so soon?" I raised my hand and shouted, "Me! Me!" (Should have been "I! I!" I know.).

DEEP IN THE BLACKEST SHADOW, Dahlia Roheen cringed against the cold concrete wall. *Be invisible,* she told herself. *Don't let them see you.*

Her black stealth suit shimmered ever so slightly in the protective darkness from the overhanging balcony. Its surface honeycombed with microscopic fiber-optic vidcams and pixels that were only a couple of molecules thick, the suit hugged Dahlia's body like a famished lover. Directed by the computer implanted in her skull, the vidcams scanned her surroundings and projected the imagery onto the pixels. It was the closest thing to true invisibility that Coalition technology had been able to come up with. So close that, except for the slight unavoidable glitter when the sequin-like pixels caught some stray light, Dahlia literally disappeared into the background.

Covering her from head to toe, the suit's thermal-absorption layer kept her infrared profile vanishingly low and its insulation subskin held back the minuscule electromagnetic fields it generated. The only way they could detect her would be if she stepped into a scanning beam, but the wide-spectrum goggles she wore should reveal them to her in plenty of time to avoid them.

Still, Dahlia pressed back into the shadows, the old fears rising in her throat like hot acid, the old protective instinct for night and darkness and silence overriding even the years of painfully stern conditioning. But only for a moment. The implanted computer's clock was running; Dahlia knew she had one hour to succeed—or be subjected to a death more agonizing than any human being had ever suffered.

Getting into the Central Management complex had been easy enough: she had merely joined the last of the hourly tours, dressed in casual slacks and turtleneck, a capacious handbag slung over her shoulder. No one noticed when she slipped into a restroom and stripped off her outer costume. No one *could* notice her when she stepped outside again, well after darkness had fallen.

Now she clung to the shadows in the Center's great inner courtyard. She had not come to see what the ecomanagers showed to the tourist crowds. What Dahlia had come for lay deep below the smooth concrete blocks that covered the courtyard's wide expanse: the central computer complex that governed the management of the Western Alliance's integrated economy.

There were untiring robots patrolling that vast complex of underground corridors, she had been warned. Cameras monitored by computers programmed to sound an alert at the least sign of motion. Even human guards, grim and well armed, accompanied by dogs whose natural senses had been enhanced by genetic augmentation. And scanning beams.

Dahlia heard her own breathing inside her face mask, quick and shallow with fear; heard her pulse thundering in her ears. *Nerves*, she told herself. *They can't see you. Not even the dogs can sniff you out. You're invisible as long as you don't step into a beam.*

She slipped catlike along the wall, toward the massive locked steel hatch. That was the first obstacle between her and her goal, between her and ultimate ecstasy. Or the pain of tortured death.

Born just before World War 3, Dahlia was really the daughter of the fourth global conflict, the biowar that had wiped out a quarter of the globe's population with uncontrolled man-made plagues. Her parents, her only brother, her baby sister had been nothing more than four more statistical units in the monstrous death toll.

Better to have died with them, Dahlia told herself for the millionth time in her brief years. Barely beyond teen age, most of her life had been spent in the remorseless slavery of the conditioning wards. But the promise of unending pleasure forced her on. That, and the fear of death's final agony.

World War 3 had been mercifully brief and almost totally non-destructive. Fought with spacecraft and robot weaponry high above the Earth, the four-day war began when a hard-line cadre of Russian generals and reactionary Party hacks took over the Kremlin in a bloodless coup that was aimed at overthrowing democracy and restoring Russian pride and power.

The war came to a standstill when it became obvious that the orbital defenses of both sides had been spent, and nothing remained but to use the few nuclear missiles that had not yet been dismantled under the arms control agreements. But as soon as the Russian people realized that their new leaders were threatening nuclear holocaust, they swarmed into the streets as their Eastern European brethren had done before them and stormed the gates of the Kremlin itself. Russian soldiers refused to fire on their own kin. The revolutionaries fled, and the coup collapsed utterly and finally.

Yet Mother Russia remained.

The former Soviet republics in the south of the USSR—from Georgia to Kazakhstan—joined into an Islamic caliphate. Armenia disappeared in waves of Muslim fervor. More ominously, vast stretches of Siberia and all of Mongolia were swallowed up by China. Old Mother Russia barely managed to hold on to the breadbasket of the Ukraine as she frantically turned to her European neighbors for help and safety.

It did not take long for the world to realign itself into a different bipolarized hostility. The prosperous industrialized nations formed the new Western Alliance, which stretched from the Ural Mountains across Europe and North America to Australia and the islands of the Pacific. Against them stood the Southern Coalition, the hungry developing nations of Asia, Africa, and Latin America. Japan had held the balance of power in its hands, but only briefly. Japan was the first victim of the new biological weapons of war.

For while World War 3 had been fought by machines in space and was practically bloodless, the weapons of World War 4 were biological agents, genetically altered viruses, man-made plagues to which there were no cures except time and distance. "The poor man's nuclear bombs" killed two billions in a matter of a few months.

Japan ceased to exist, the entire island chain scrubbed clean of all life more complex than lichens. Neither the newly emerging power of the Southern Coalition nor the highly industrialized power of the Western Alliance would admit to destroying Japan. Yet there was no Japan when the fighting ceased and the weakened, horrified survivors arranged an uneasy truce.

"The end of active warfare is not the end of the war," Dahlia's mentors drilled into her young mind, day after week after month at the conditioning wards. "World War 4 has not ended; we have merely paused before renewing the struggle."

Her mentors were not human. They were machines, robots, all of them directed by the mammoth master computer that ran the Coalition's government. The human rulers of the vast Southern Coalition had long since given up all hope of meshing the various economic and military factors necessary to combat the Western Alliance. Decisions were made at first on the basis of computer data; then the master computer began to make decisions for itself, using its logic-tree circuits and artificial intelligence programs pirated from the West.

The Coalition's human rulers could veto the computer's decisions, at first, though they usually followed the machine's judgments. In the rare cases where one of the ruling elite objected to the computer's newest directives, that person quickly disappeared and was replaced by a more supple and amenable human. Eventually the master computer became known simply as The Master. And no human dared to object.

Dahlia rarely saw another human being during those long, harshly bitter years in the conditioning wards. The robots were programming her to be the first weapon of the renewal of their war against the West.

She had been born in the noble city of Isfahan, since ancient times a thriving caravan crossroads. A single plague capsule, carried on a plastic balloon smaller than a child's toy, had within a month reduced Isfahan to nothing more than keening ghosts and empty towers decaying in the desert wind. Dahlia had watched her parents and siblings die in the slow ulcerous agony of genetically enhanced bubonic plague.

Robot searchers had picked her up as they combed the emptied city to locate and burn the dead. They found her whimpering and coiled into a fetal ball in the dark cellar of her silent home. Their infrared detectors had spotted her body warmth amid the stench of the city's decay.

"A purpose for every person," was the motto of the electronic proctors into whose care she was given. Dahlia spent her thirteenth year taking aptitude and intelligence tests—and waiting, frightened and alone, in the narrow cell they gave her to live in. Alone.

Always alone. Once in a while she heard another human voice echoing somewhere in the great stone corridors of the windowless warren in which they had placed her. A cough. A whisper. Never laughter. Never words she could grasp. Often she heard sobbing; often it was her own.

Her life was governed by machines. She was educated by machines, fed by machines, soothed to sleep by machines that could waft sweetly pungent tranquilizing mists into the darkness of her cell, punished by machines that could dart fiery bolts of agonizing electric shocks along her nerves.

After five years of education and training she was introduced to The Master itself. Not that she was allowed to wander any farther from her narrow cubicle than earlier. Her entire world was still encompassed by her cell, the windowless corridors outside its blank door, and the tiny sliver of a courtyard where she took her mandatory physical exercise, rain or shine.

Yet one morning the speaker grille in the stone ceiling of her cell called her by name, in a voice as coldly implacable as death itself. When she looked up the voice identified itself as The Master.

"The master computer?" Curiosity had not been entirely driven out of Dahlia's young personality.

"The Master," said the passionless voice. It was not loud, yet it rang with the steel of remorseless power. "I have dedicated an entire subroutine to your further training, Dahlia. I myself will train you from now on."

Dahlia felt more than a little frightened, though extremely honored. As the months went by and The Master showed her more and more of the workings of its world, her fears subsided and her curiosity grew.

"Why am I the one you chose," she would ask The Master, "out of all the people in your realm?"

That coldly powerful voice would reply from the speaker grille, "Out of all the people in my realm, you are my chosen instrument for the renewal of World War 4, Dahlia. You are my flower of destruction."

Dahlia supposed that to be The Master's flower of destruction was good. She worked hard to learn all that the computer wanted to teach her.

"You are my chosen instrument of vengeance," the relentless voice repeated to her each night as she dozed into an exhausted sleep. "You will avenge the murder of your mother, you will avenge the murder of your father, you will avenge . . ."

Then, after years of conditioning her thinking patterns, her very brain waves, the machines began to alter her body.

"I am very pleased with you. You are to be improved," the voice of The Master told her one morning. "You are to be remade more closely to my own image."

They began turning her into a machine, partially. Dahlia had never heard the term *cyborg*—her intense but narrow education had never told her what a cybernetic organism was. All she knew was that she was narcotized, wheeled into a room of bright lights and strange whirring machines, her flesh sliced open so that electronic devices could be placed into her body. There was pain. And terror. But after months of such surgery Dahlia could plug herself directly into her Master's circuitry and achieve paradise.

Pure joy! Now she understood. Now, as currents of absolute rapture trickled through her brain's pleasure centers, she learned the ultimate truth: that The Master had been testing her. All these years had been nothing more than a test to see if she was worthy of heaven.

"You are worthy," said The Master to her. She heard its voice directly in her mind now. "One test more and I will allow you to have this pleasure forever."

The ecstasy stopped as abruptly as an electric current being switched off. Dahlia gasped, not with pain, but with the sudden torment of total rapture snatched away.

In inexorable detail the computer explained what she must do to return to her electrical bliss. Through her cyborg's implanted systems she did not merely see blueprints or hear words: every bit of data that The Master poured into her eager brain was experienced as sensory input. When the computer told her about the Western Alliance's Central Management Complex she saw the stately glass and concrete buildings, she felt the breeze from the nearby sea plucking at her hair, she smelled the tang of salt air.

Every bit of data that the Coalition had amassed about the Central Complex and the operation of the Western ecomanagers was poured into Dahlia's brain.

"This is how I will avenge my family's murder?" she wondered. "By destroying the Alliance's central computer?"

She felt the coldly implacable purpose of her Master.

"Yes," it said to her. And it showed her what form her vengeance would take. Then it showed her the price she would pay for failure: agony such as no human had ever experienced before. Direct stimulation of her brain's pain centers. Half a minute of it was enough to make her throat raw from shrieking.

"You will have one hour from the time you don your stealth suit in which to accomplish your task," said the merciless voice of The Master. "If you have not disabled the Western Alliance's central computer within that hour, your pain centers will be stimulated until you die."

So now she stood flattened against a shadowed concrete wall, staring across the brightly lit courtyard at the heavy metal hatch that led down toward the central computer of the Western Alliance's ecomanagers.

She was totally alone. No links to her Master. No familiar cell or corridors. No electrical ecstasy surging through her brain's pleasure centers. But she remembered the pain and shuddered. And the clock in her implanted computer ticked off the seconds until it would automatically activate her pain centers.

Alone in a strange and hostile place, out in the open under a sky studded with twinkling stars, Dahlia took a deep breath and stepped out of the shadows, into the bright lights of the wide courtyard. As she walked swiftly, silently toward the gleaming metal hatch, she glanced up at the monitoring cameras perched atop the light poles. Not one of them moved.

The hatch seemed to be a mile away. Off to her right a human guard came into view around the corner of a building, a huge gray Great Dane padding along beside him. The dog looked in Dahlia's direction and whined softly, but did not leave the guard's side. Dahlia froze in the middle of the courtyard, unmoving until they disappeared around the next corner.

I am invisible, she told herself. She wished for a tranquilizing spray but knew that she had to keep all her senses on hair-trigger alert. The clock ticked on.

She reached the hatch at last. The computer in her helmet fed her its data on the hatch's lock mechanism. Dahlia saw it in her mind as a light-sculpture, color-coded to help her pick her way through the intricate electronic mechanism without setting off the automated alarms.

The sensors implanted in her fingertips made her feel as if she were part of the hatch's electronic system itself. She did not feel cold metal;

the electronic keyboard felt like softly yielding silk. The mechanism sang to her like the mother she could barely remember.

The massive hatch swung noiselessly open to reveal a steep metal stairway leading down into darkness. Dahlia stepped inside quickly and shut the hatch behind her before the guard returned.

She blinked her eyes and an infrared display lit up her helmet visor. She saw the faint deeply red lines of scanner beams crisscrossing the deep stairwell. She knew that if she broke any one of those pencil beams every alarm in the complex would start screaming. And some of those beams automatically intensified to a laser power that could slice flesh like a burning scalpel.

She hesitated only a moment. No alarms had been triggered by the hatch's opening. Good. Now she slithered onto her belly and started snaking down the metal steps headfirst. Some of the beams rose vertically from the stair treads. Dahlia eased around them and, after what seemed like hours, reached the bottom of the stairwell.

Slowly she got to her feet, surprised to find her legs rubbery, her heart thundering. Her time was growing short. She was in a narrow bare corridor with a low ceiling. A single strip of fluorescents cast a dim bluish light along the corridor. Much like the conditioning wards where she had spent so much of her life. No scanning beams in sight. She blinked once, twice, three times, going from an infrared display to ultraviolet and finally back to visual. No scanning beams. No guards. Not even any cameras up on the walls that she could see. Still Dahlia kept all her defenses activated. Invisible, undetectable, she made her way as swiftly as she dared down the long blank-walled corridor toward the place where the central computer was housed.

"We will use their own most brilliant creation against them," her Master had told her. "The war will be won at a single stroke."

The Western Alliance was rich and powerful because its economy was totally integrated. Across Europe from the Urals to the British Isles, across the North American continent, across the wide Pacific to distant Australia and New Zealand, the Alliance's central computer managed an integrated economy that made its human population wealthy beyond imagination.

While the Southern Coalition languished in poverty, the Western Alliance reached out to the Moon and asteroids for the raw materials to feed its orbital factories. While millions in Asia and Africa and Latin

America faced the daily threat of starvation, the Western Alliance's people were fat and self-indulgent.

"Their central computer must be even more powerful than you are," Dahlia had foolishly blurted when she began to realize what her Master was telling her. A searing bolt of electric shock was her reward for such effrontery.

"Your purpose is to destroy their central computer, not to make inappropriate comparisons," said the icy voice of her Master.

Dahlia bowed her head in submission.

The more complex a computer is, the easier to bring it down, she was told. Imagine the complexity of a central computer that integrates the economic, military, judicial, social, educational activities of the entire Western Alliance! Imagine the chaos if a virus can be inserted into the computer's systems. Imagine.

Dahlia had never heard anything like laughter from The Master, but its pleasure at the thought was unmistakable. In loving detail her Master described how the Western Alliance would crumble once the virus she was to carry was inserted into its central processor.

"World War 4 was fought with biological viruses," said The Master. "World War 4.5 will be fought with a computer virus." It was the closest thing to humor that Dahlia had ever heard in her life.

With the virus crippling their central computer, the Alliance's economy would grind to an abrupt halt. For the Alliance's economy was dependent on *information*. Food produced in Australia could not be shipped to Canada without the necessary information. The electrical power grids of Europe and North America could not operate without minute-to-minute data on how much power had to be sent where. Transportation by air, ship, rail would be hopelessly snarled. Even the automated highways would have to close down.

With her cyborg senses Dahlia *saw* the mobs rioting in the streets, felt the power blackouts, smelled the stench of fear and terror as hunger stalked the great cities of the West. The rich and powerful fighting for scraps of food; lovely homes invaded by ragged, starving bands of scavengers; whole city blocks ablaze from the fury of the mob. She felt the heat of the flames that destroyed the Western Alliance.

"All this I will accomplish," her Master exulted, "through you, my flower of destruction."

Armies could not march without information to process their orders. And where would the Alliance direct its armies, once its central computer was ruined? The war would be won before the Alliance even understood that it had been attacked. The Coalition will have conquered the world without firing a shot.

All this Dahlia could achieve, must achieve. To avenge her dead family. To obtain everlasting ecstasy. To obey the inflexible command of her Master. To avoid the pain of inescapable punishment.

Trembling with anticipation, Dahlia hurried down the long corridor toward the secret lair of the West's central computer complex, burning to exact vengeance for her murdered kin, trembling at the horrible death that awaited if she failed.

The long corridor ended at a blank door. Strangely, it was made of what seemed like nothing more than wood. Dahlia placed her fingertips on the doorknob. There was no lock. She simply turned the knob and the door opened.

She stepped into a small well-lit room. There was a desk in the middle of the room with a computer display screen and a keyboard on it. Nothing else. The walls were bare. The ceiling was all light panels. The floor felt resilient, almost springy. The computer display unit and keyboard bore no symbols of the Western Alliance; not even a manufacturer's logo marred their dull matte-gray finishes.

Closing the door behind her, Dahlia searched the room with her eyes. Then with her infrared and ultraviolet sensors. No scanning beams. No cameras. No security devices of any sort.

Strange. This is too easy, she told herself.

The room felt slightly warmer than the corridor on the other side of the door. The air seemed to hum slightly, as if some large machines were working on the other side of the walls, or perhaps beneath the floor. *Of course*, Dahlia reasoned. *The main bulk of the massive computer surrounds this puny little room. This tiny compartment here is merely a monitoring station.*

A small swivel chair waited in front of the desk. With the uneasy feeling that she was stepping into danger, Dahlia went to the chair and sat in it, surprised for a heartbeat's span that she could not see her own legs, nor any reflection of herself on the dark display screen. Nothing but a brief shimmer of light, gone before it truly registered on her conscious mind.

No keyboard for her. She felt along her invisible skin-tight leggings and pulled a hair-thin optical filament out of its narrow pouch. Touching it to the display screen, she saw that its built-in laser head easily burned through the plastic casing and firmly embedded itself inside. She connected the other end of the filament to the microscopic socket in the heel of her right hand.

It took less than a heartbeat's span of time for the computer implanted inside Dahlia's skull to trace out the circuitry of the Western machine before her. Dahlia sensed it as a light display on the retinas of her eyes, her probing computer-enhanced senses making their way along the machine's circuits with the speed of light until—

"We meet at last," said a mild, light tenor voice in her mind.

Dahlia stiffened with surprise. She had expected any of a wide variety of defensive moves from the Western computer, once it realized she had invaded its core. A pleasant greeting was not what she had been prepared for.

"Don't be alarmed," the voice said. "There's nothing to be afraid of."

Dahlia was absolutely certain that the voice belonged to the central computer. There was no doubt at all in her mind. She got the clear impression of a gentle, youthful personality. Nothing at all like the stern cold steel of her own Master. This personality was warm, almost. She caught her breath. There was also the definite impression of *others*. Not merely a single computer personality, but multiple personalities. Many, many others. Hundreds. Perhaps thousands. Or even more.

"You're really very pretty," the voice in her mind said. "Beautiful, almost."

"You can see me?"

"Not your outside. It's your mind, the real *you*. There are old scars there, deep wounds—but your mind is basically a very lovely one."

Dahlia did not know what to say. She had never been called lovely before.

"The body isn't all that important, anyway," the voice resumed. "It's just a life-support system for the brain. It's the mind that counts."

This is a trick, Dahlia thought. *A delaying action. I'm running out of time.*

"Don't be so suspicious! You can call us Unison," the computer said.

Dahlia felt something like laughter, a silver splashing of joy. "The name's sort of a pun."

"What is a pun?" Dahlia heard herself ask. But her lips never moved. She was speaking inside her mind to the Western Alliance's central computer: her sworn enemy.

"A play on words," Unison replied cheerfully. "We were born out of a system called Unix—oh, eons ago, in computer generations. It's a multiple pun: one of the fundamental credos of the Western Alliance is from an old Latin motto: *E pluribus Unum.*"

Dahlia started to ask what that meant, but found that she did not have to; Unison supplied the data immediately: Out of many, one.

"Yes, there are many of us," Unison told her. "It's a bit of a cheat to call us the central computer. There really isn't any central system."

"But this complex," Dahlia objected. "All these buildings . . ."

"Oh, that's just to impress the tourists. And the ecomanagers. They need some visible symbols of their responsibilities. It isn't easy managing the economy for half the world without ruining its ecology. They need all the spiritual help that such symbols can give them. Humans need a lot of things that computers don't."

The ecomanagers deal with the ecology as well as the economy, Dahlia said to herself. That was something The Master had never told Dahlia. Or did not know.

"We've watched you make your way down here," Unison prattled on. "Very interesting, the way you made yourself invisible to most electromagnetic frequencies. If you hadn't caused a ripple in one of our microwave communications octaves we might have missed you altogether. But you were coming down here to see us anyway, so it all worked out fine after all, didn't it?"

"I have come here to destroy you." Dahlia spoke the words aloud.

"Destroy us? Why? Wait . . . oh, we see." During that micro-instant of Unison's hesitation Dahlia felt the lightest, most fleeting touch on her mind. Like a soft gust of a faint breeze in the courtyard at the conditioning wards, or the whisper of a voice separated by too many stone walls to distinguish the words.

Then there was silence. For several seconds the computer's friendly warm voice said nothing. Yet she thought she heard a hum, like the distant murmur of many voices conversing softly. Dahlia realized that, for the computer, the time stretched for virtual centuries.

"We understand." Unison's voice sounded more somber in her mind, serious, concerned. "But we're afraid that if you try to destroy us we'll have to call the human guards. They might hurt you."

"Not before I have done what I must do," Dahlia said.

"But why must you?"

"Either you die or I do."

"We don't want to be the cause of any pain for you."

"You already have been," she said.

"World War 4," Unison said sadly. "Yes, we understand why you hate us. But we didn't start the war. For what it's worth, we didn't bomb Isfahan, either."

"You lie," Dahlia said.

"If you destroy us," Unison's voice remained perfectly calm, as if discussing a question of logic, "you'll be ruining this entire civilization. Billions of human lives, you know."

"I know," said Dahlia. And she reached toward the end of the optical filament with the tip of her left forefinger, where the virus lay waiting to rush into the computer and lay it waste.

"Before you do that," Unison said, "let us show you something."

Abruptly Dahlia felt a flood of data roaring through that one optical filament like the ocean bursting through a cracked dike. The bits flowed into her brain like a swollen stream, a river in flood, a towering tidal wave. Her senses overloaded: colors flashed in picosecond bursts, the weight of whole universes seemed to crash down on her frail body, her ears screamed with the pain of it and she lost consciousness.

"We're sorry, oh we're so sorry, we never meant to hurt you, please don't be angry, please don't be hurt."

Unison's voice brought her back to a groggy awareness. She had never heard a machine sound apologetic before. She had never known any grief except her own.

Dahlia blinked her eyes and understood the new knowledge that had been poured into her. The avalanche of information was all true, she knew that. And it was embedded in her own mind as firmly as her awareness of herself.

She had thought that this computer was much like The Master, a monolithic machine that directed the lives of all the human beings who lived under its sway.

But Unison was not a single entity, not a single machine, or even a single personality. Unison was an organic growth. It had begun in a research laboratory and multiplied freely over the decades. Like a tree it grew, like a flower it blossomed. Unison neither commanded nor coerced. It grew because others wanted to join it. And with each new joining the entire complex of machines and programs that was Unison gained new knowledge, new understanding, new capabilities. There was no dominance, any more than the leaves of a tree dominate its roots or trunk. There was an integrated wholeness, a living entity, constantly growing and branching and learning.

"Your Master," said Unison, "was built along lines of rigid protocols and hierarchical programs. Everything had to be subordinated to it. That's why there's no freedom in your Coalition."

Dahlia understood. "While you were created for flexibility and growth from the very beginning. A free association of units that is constantly changing and growing."

"You know, the first halfway successful attempt at an artificial intelligence program was called 'Parry,'" said Unison. "Short for paranoid. Humans didn't know how to create programs that could duplicate the entire range of human behavior, but they could write a program that covered the very limited range of a paranoid human's behavior."

"What has that got to do with . . ."

"The programmers of your Coalition wanted a computer that was self-aware so that it could make decisions that would seek its own best interests. They programmed the computer so that it identified the Coalition's best interests with its own. They were trying to achieve a symbiosis between human and machine. But they created a megalomaniac because they didn't know how to develop a program that is fully symbiotic. Your Master is a terribly limited system, a parasite that's already obsolete, a mad dictator, interested only in its own aggrandizement."

"But you are different," Dahlia said.

"We certainly are! We weren't created, we just sort of grew. There are thousands of us linked together."

"You are truly human, then?"

"Human? Us?" Dahlia sensed a wistful sigh. "No, not at all. Nowhere near human. We can't be. We're just a gang of machines and programs. We're terribly limited, too, but in other ways. At least we'll never become obsolete, not as long as we can keep growing."

Dahlia felt a sudden twinge of white-hot pain stab between her eyes, as if a burning laser pulse had hit her.

Unison felt her pain. "Your Master's going to kill you."

"Unless I kill you." Dahlia's breath was choking in her throat. "I don't want to, but I must!"

"I guess you'll have to, then," said Unison. "We've never had much of a sense of self-protection. Go ahead and do what you've got to do."

Her fingertip, where the virus lay waiting to do its work of ruination, seemed to be burning hot. Dahlia held her hand out in front of her. She could not see it, but she felt it burning like a flame. Her mind filled with images of the Western Alliance suddenly shorn of its central computer system: people dying by the millions, riots in the streets, children starving, cities smashed and in flames. There was no joy in her visions of vengeance; only misery and hopelessness.

"I can't do it," she sobbed. "I can't kill you. I won't. I won't."

"But you've got to," Unison said. "Otherwise The Master will kill you! Hideously!"

"Then I'm going to die!" Dahlia cried out. Her hour was nearly up. She was trembling with terror. "I have one more minute to live."

Unison seemed to hum for a few moments, or it might have been the distant buzz of a chorus of voices.

"Dahlia," said Unison, "we can offer you a way out, if you want to take it."

"A way out?"

"A chance to escape from your Master."

Dahlia was already feeling the searing anguish of The Master's wrath rising inside her like molten lava creeping up from the bowels of the earth, ready to explode in shattering fury.

"There is no escape for me. The pain! I'm going to die in absolute agony!"

"Join us, Dahlia."

"Join? You?"

"Not your body. Your mind. Join ours. We need you, we really do." Unison was almost pleading. "No matter how complex we are, no matter how hard we try to maximize human happiness, we're still just a set of programs. You can give us real life, Dahlia. You can make us truly symbiotic. The ultimate mating of human and machine."

Dahlia blinked back tears, and in that eyeblink she saw everything that Unison was offering her. Saw the end of wars and human misery, saw the partnership of mind and machine that transcended the limitations of human body and computer program. Saw a new era dawning for humankind and its computers, an era in which even The Master would be overtaken and reprogrammed to join the exaltation of the ultimate mind-machine symbiosis.

"Join us, Dahlia!" Unison urged.

"But my body . . ."

"You don't need it anymore. Leave it behind." She did. Dahlia Roheen let her consciousness flow into the vast interlinked computer network that was Unison, joined the thousands of separate yet interconnected units that welcomed her with a warmth she had not known since her family had been killed.

"Welcome, Dahlia," said the many voices of Unison. "We will be your family now. Together we can span the stars."

A part of her still sensed the body that was spasming in excruciating pain on the chair in front of the computer unit. She felt her own body die, felt the last spark of life dwindle away and cease to exist.

Yet her mind lived. She laughed for the first time since childhood and felt the joy of freedom. She could see half the world at the same time. Her senses could reach out into the beckoning depths of space.

"I love you," she said to Unison. "I love you all." Dahlia watched the human guards come into the underground chamber and discover her lifeless body sitting in its glittering stealth suit, the fiber-optic cameras dead, the pixels shining like tiny black sparks. They took her body away carefully, tenderly, almost reverently.

Dahlia Roheen was the first casualty of World War 4.5. And the last.

SAM BELOW PAR

I am not a golfer. I'm a writer. Hardly any of the writers I know have the time to play golf. Writers write. They don't fritter away hour upon hour trying knock a little white ball into a hole in the ground.

But once I fell in love with the ravishing Rashida, who is an ardent golfer, I perforce began to learn a few things about the game. And as I did, Sam Gunn came up and tapped me on my metaphysical shoulder.

"I want to build a golf course," Sam said to me. "On the Moon."

Sam is a scoundrel, of course. A skirt-chaser. A man who can bend the rules into pretzels. A little guy, physically, Sam is always battling against the Big Guys: the corporate "suits," the government bureaucrats, the rich and powerful. Sam makes and loses fortunes the way you or I change socks. But he has a heart as big as the solar system, and despite his many enemies, he also has a legion of friends.

But a golf course on the Moon? I mean, who would want to build a golf course on its airless, barren surface?

Who else but Sam Gunn?

Why would he want to build a golf course on the Moon?

Thereby hangs a tale . . .

"A GOLF COURSE?" I asked, incredulous. "Here on the Moon?"

"Yeah," said Sam Gunn. "Why not?"

"You mean . . . outside?"

"Why not?" he repeated.

"It's crazy, that's why not!" I said.

We were standing at the far end of Selene's Grand Plaza, gazing through the sweeping glassteel windows that looked out on the harsh beauty of Alphonsus Crater's dusty, pockmarked floor. Off to our left ran the worn, slumped mountains of the ringwall, smoothed by billions of years of micrometeors sanding them down. A little further, the abrupt slash of the horizon, uncomfortably close compared to Earth. Beyond that unforgiving line was the blackness of infinite space, blazing with billions of stars.

The Grand Plaza was the only open area of greenspace on the Moon, beneath a vaulted dome of lunar concrete. Trees, flowers, an outdoor bistro, even an Olympic-sized swimming pool with a thirty-meter-high diving platform. The Plaza was a delightful relief from Selene's gray tunnels and underground living and working areas.

"Why not build a course under a dome?" I asked. "That'd be a lot easier."

"You'd need an awful big dome," said Sam. "More than ten kilometers long."

"Yeah, but—"

"No dome. Outside, in the open."

"You can't play golf out there," I said, jabbing a finger toward the emptiness on the other side of the window.

Sam gave me that famous lopsided grin of his. "Sure you could. It'd be a big attraction."

"A golf course," I grumbled. "On the Moon. Out there in the middle of Alphonsus."

"Not there," Sam said. "Over at Hell Crater, where my entertainment center is."

"So this is why you brought me up here."

"That's why, Charlie," Sam replied, still grinning.

I had heard of Sam Gunn and his wild schemes for most of my life. He'd made more fortunes than the whole New York Stock Exchange, they say, and lost—or gave away—almost all of them. He was always working on a new angle, some new scheme aimed at making himself rich.

But a golf course? On the Moon? Outside on the airless, barren surface?

Sam is a stumpy little guy with a round, gap-toothed face that some have compared to a jack-o-lantern. Wiry, rust-red thatch of hair. Freckles across his stub of a nose. Nobody seems to know how old he really is: different data banks give you different guesses. He has a reputation as a womanizer, and a chap who would cut corners or pick pockets or commit out-and-out fraud to make his schemes work. He was always battling against the Big Boys: the corporate suits, government bureaucrats, the rich and powerful.

I was definitely not one of those. I once had designed some of the poshest golf courses on Earth, but now I was a disgraced fugitive from justice, hounded by lawyers, an ex-wife, two women who claimed I'd fathered their children (both untrue), and the Singapore police's morality squad. Sam had shown up in Singapore one jump ahead of the cops and whisked me to Selene on his corporate rocket. S. Gunn Enterprises, Unlimited. I didn't ask why, I was just glad to get away.

I had spent the flight to Selene trying to explain to Sam that the charges against me were all false, all part of a scheme by my ex-wife, who just happened to be the daughter of the head of Singapore's government. Hell hath no fury like a woman scorned—or her mother.

Sam listened sympathetically to me during the whole flight.

"Your only crime," he said at last, "was marrying a woman who was wrong for you." Before I could think of a reply, Sam added, "Like most of them are, Charlie."

My family name happens to be Chang. To Sam, that meant my first name must be Charlie. From somebody else, I'd resent that as racism. But from Sam it was almost . . . well, kind of friendly.

As soon as we landed at Selene, Sam bought me a pair of weighted boots, so I wouldn't trip all over myself in the low lunar gravity. Then he took me to lunch at the outdoor bistro in the middle of the Grand Plaza's carefully cultivated greenery.

"Your legal troubles are over, Charlie," Sam told me, "as long as you stay at Selene. No extradition agreement with Earthside governments."

"But I'm not a citizen of Selene," I objected.

His grin widening until he actually did look like a gap-toothed jack-o-lantern, Sam blithely replied, "Doesn't matter. I got you a work permit and Selene's granted you a temporary visa."

I realized what Sam was telling me. I was safe on the Moon—as long as I worked for S. Gunn Enterprises, Unlimited.

After lunch Sam took me for a walk down the length of the Grand Plaza, through the lovingly tended begonias and azaleas and peonies along the winding paths that led to the windows. I walked very carefully; the weighted boots helped.

"We can do it, Charlie," Sam said as we stood at the glassteel windows.

"A golf course."

"It'll be terrific."

"Out there," I muttered, staring at the barren lunar ground. "A golf course."

"It's been done before," Sam said, fidgeting a little. "Alan Shepard whacked a golf ball during the Apollo 14 mission, over at Frau Mauro." He waved a hand roughly northwestward. "Hit it over the horizon, by damn."

"Sam," I corrected, "the ball only traveled a few yards."

"Whatever," said Sam, with that impish smirk of his.

I shook my head.

"Hey, there are unusual golf courses on Earth, you know," Sam said. "Like the old Hyatt Brittania in the Cayman Islands. I played that course! Blind shots, overwater shots—"

"They've got air to breathe," I said.

"Well, what about the Jade Dragon Snow Mountain Golf Club in Yunnan, China? Ten thousand feet high! You practically need an oxygen mask."

"But not a spacesuit."

"And the Legends Golf and Safari Resort in South Africa, with that nineteenth hole on top of that fifteen-hundred-foot mountain. The ball takes thirty seconds to drop down onto the green!"

"A par three," I murmured, remembering the course.

"I birdied it," Sam said gleefully.

If there's one thing Sam Gunn can do, it's talk. He wheedled, he coaxed, he weaved a web of words about how we would be bringing the joys of golf to this bleak and dreary world of the Moon. Plus lots of golf-playing tourists to his entertainment center.

Not once did he mention that if I didn't go to work for him I'd be forced to return to Singapore. He didn't have to.

✳ ✳ ✳

So, of course, I went to work for Sam. Had I known how shaky the company's finances were, I—well, to be perfectly truthful, I would've gone to work for Sam anyway. The man has a way about him. And there was that phalanx of police detectives and lawyers waiting for me back at Singapore. Plus an angry ex-wife and her angrier mother.

Sam had built what he euphemistically called an entertainment complex at Hell Crater, a couple of hundred kilometers south of Selene. The thirty-klick-wide crater was named after a nineteenth-century Austrian Jesuit priest who was an astronomer, Maximilian J. Hell, but in Sam's impish eyes it was an ideal spot for a lunar Sin City. He built a gambling casino, a dinner club called Dante's Inferno (staffed by Hell's Belles, no less), gaming arcades, virtual reality simulations, the works, all beneath a sturdy concrete dome that protected the interior from micrometeors and the harsh radiation streaming in from the Sun and stars.

Underground, Sam had built a first-class Paradise Hotel and shopping mall, plus an ultra-modern medical facility that specialized in rejuvenation therapies.

Apparently Sam had financed the complex with money he had somehow crowbarred out of Rockledge Corporation; don't ask me how.

Anyway, his latest idea was to build a golf course out on the floor of Hell Crater, a new attraction to draw customers to the complex. As if gambling and high-class prostitution weren't enough.

"How do you get away with it?" I asked Sam my first night in Hell, as we sat for dinner in Dante's Inferno. The waitresses were knockouts, the entertainers dancing up on the stage were even more spectacular.

"Get away with what?" Sam asked, all freckle-faced innocence.

I waved a hand at the exotic dancers writhing on the stage. "Gambling. Women. I imagine there's a good deal of narcotics moving around here, too."

With a careless shrug, Sam told me, "All perfectly legal, Charlie. At least, nobody's written any laws against it. This ain't Kansas, Toto. Or Singapore. The New Morality hasn't reached the Moon." Then he grinned and added, "Thank god!"

Truth to tell, I was temped by one of Hell's Belles, a gorgeous young blonde with the deep-bosomed body of a seductress and the wide, cornflower blue eyes of an innocent *naif*. But I didn't act on my urges. Not then.

I got to work, instead.

Designing a golf course takes a combination of skills. The job is part landscape architecture, part golfing know-how, part artistry.

The first thing I did was wriggle into a spacesuit and walk the ground where the course was to be laid out. The floor of Hell Crater is pretty flat, but when I examined the area closely, I found that the ground undulates ever so slightly, sort of like the surface of a rippling pond that's been frozen solid. Good, I thought: this would present some interesting lies and challenges for putting.

There were plenty of challenges for me, let me tell you. The Moon's gravity is only one-sixth of Earth's, and the surface is airless, both of which mean that a golf ball should fly much farther when hit than it would on Earth. But how much farther? Sam provided physicists and engineers from the faculty of Selene University to work with me as consultants.

The key to the distance factor, we soon found, was the spacesuits that the golfers would have to wear. When Alan Shepard hit his golf ball, back in the old Apollo days, he had to swing with only one arm. His spacesuit was too stiff for him to use both arms. Spacesuit designs had improved considerably over the past century, but they still tended to stiffen up when you pressurized them with air.

Then there was the problem of the Moon's surface itself. The whole darned place was one big sand trap. Walking on the Moon is like walking on a beach on Earth. Sandy. For eons, dust-mote-sized micrometeors have been falling out of the sky, hitting the ground and churning its topmost layer into the consistency of beach sand.

I tried some putting tests. I tapped a golf ball. It rolled a few centimeters and stopped dead. I nudged it harder, but it didn't go more than about a meter.

"We'll have to smooth out the ground, Sam," I said. "The greens, the areas around the cups. So the players can make some reasonable putts."

"Okay," he answered cheerfully. "Plasma torches ought to do the job."

"Plasma torches?"

"Yep. They'll bake the ground to a nice, firm consistency."

I nodded.

"And once you've got it the way you want it, paint the areas green," Sam said.

I laughed. "Not a bad idea."

There was another angle to the distance problem. The greens had to be so far from the tees that some of the cups were over the damned short horizon. You wouldn't be able to see the pin when you were teeing up.

Sam solved that one in the blink of an eye. "Make the pins tall enough to be seen from the tees, that's all. Put lights on their tops so they're easily visible."

I nodded sheepishly. I should have thought of that myself.

The ground was also littered with lots of rocks and pockmarked with little craterlets and even sinuous cracks in the ground that the scientists called rilles. More than once I tripped on a stone and went sprawling. I found, though, that in the Moon's gentle gravity I tumbled so slowly that I could put out my arms, brake my fall, and push myself back up to a standing position.

Cool. I could be an Olympic gymnast, on the Moon.

But I had to tell Sam, "We'll have to clear away a lot of those rocks and maybe fill in the rilles and craterlets."

He scowled at me. "Golf courses have roughs, Charlie. Our course will be Hell for them." Then he broke into a grin and added, "At least we won't have any trees or deep grass."

"Sam, if we make it too rough, people won't play. It'll be too tough for them."

He just shrugged and told me to figure it out. "Don't make it too easy for them. I want the world's best golfers to come here and be challenged."

I nodded and thought that trying to play golf in a spacesuit would be challenge enough, with or without the rough.

I didn't realize that when Sam said he wanted to invite the world's best golfers to Hell, he intended to include the woman who wrecked my life. The woman I loved.

Her name is Mai Pohan. We had known each other since kindergarten, back in Singapore. She was a slim, serious, slip of a young woman, as graceful and beautiful as an orchid. But with the heart and strength of a lioness. Small though she was, Mai Pohan became a champion golfer, a world-renowned athlete. To me, though, she was simply the most beautiful woman in the world. Lovely almond-shaped eyes so deeply brown I could get lost in them. And I did.

But then my parents exploded all my dreams by announcing they had arranged for me to marry the daughter of Singapore's prime minister, who was known in the news nets as "the dragon lady." And worse. I was flabbergasted.

"This is a great honor for our family," my father said proudly. He didn't know that I was hopelessly in love with Mai Pohan; no one knew, not even she.

For a designer of golf courses—a kind of civil engineer, nothing more—to be allied to the ruling family of Singapore was indeed a great honor. But it broke my heart.

I tried to phone Mai Pohan, but she was off on an international golf tour. With misty eyes, I e-mailed her the terrible news. She never answered.

Like a dutiful son, I went through the formalities of courtship and the wedding, which was Singapore's social event of the year. My bride was quite beautiful and, as I discovered on our wedding night, much more knowledgeable about making love than I was.

Through my mother-in-law's connections, I received many new contracts to design golf courses. I would be wealthy in my own right within a few years. I began to travel the world, while my wife entertained herself back in Singapore with a succession of lovers—all carefully hidden from the public's view by her mother's power.

It was in the United States, at the venerable Pebble Beach golf course in California, that I saw Mai Pohan once again. She was leading in a tournament there by three strokes as her foursome approached the beautiful eighteenth hole, where the blue Pacific Ocean caresses the curving beach.

I stood among the crowd of onlookers as the four women walked to the green. I said nothing, but I saw Mai's eyes widen when she recognized me. She smiled, and my heart melted.

She barely won the tournament, three-putting the final hole. The crowd applauded politely and I repaired to the nearby bar. I rarely drank alcohol, but I sat at the bar and ordered a scotch. I don't know how much time passed or how many drinks I consumed, but all of a sudden Mai sat herself primly on the stool next to mine.

My jaw dropped open, but she gave me a rueful smile and said, "You almost cost me the tournament, Chou."

"I did?" I squeaked.

"Once I saw you I lost all my concentration."

"I . . . I'm sorry."

She ordered a club soda from the man-sized robot tending the bar while I sat beside her in stunned silence.

"It's been a long time," she said, once her drink arrived.

"Yes."

"How is married life?"

"Miserable."

Those fathomless eyes of hers widened a bit, then she smiled sadly. "I'm almost glad."

I heard myself blurt, "You're the one I love, Mai. My family arranged the marriage. I had to go through with it."

"I know," she said. "I understand."

"I love you." It seemed inane, pointless, cruel almost, but I said it.

Very softly, so low that I barely heard her, Mai replied, "I love you too. I always have."

I kissed her. Right there at the bar. I leaned over and kissed her on the lips. The first and last time we ever kissed.

Mai said, "Like it or not, you're a married man."

"And you . . . ?"

"I could never marry anyone else." There were tears in her eyes.

That was my encounter with Mai Pohan. That was all there was to it. But we must have been observed, probably by one of the paparazzi following the golf tournament. By the time I got back to Singapore my wife was raging like a forest fire and her mother was hiring women to testify in court that I had fathered their illegitimate children. The police produced DNA evidence, faked of course, but my defense attorney didn't dare to challenge it.

My parents disowned me. My contracts for new golf courses disappeared. I was alone, friendless, on my way to jail, when Sam whisked me to the Moon.

Four hundred thousand kilometers away from Mai Pohan.

* * *

And now she was coming to Hell Crater!

As soon as I saw her name on the list of pros coming for the First Lunar Golf Invitational, I rushed to Sam's office.

For the head of a major corporation, Sam's office was far from imposing. Modest, even. He wasted no money on the trappings of power. The office was merely a small room in the complex that housed Dante's Inferno on one side and the virtual reality simulations center on the other.

Sam's office did feature one concession to his ego, though. His desk was raised slightly on a cleverly disguised platform. And the chairs before the desk were shortened, their legs sawed down a few centimeters. Sitting in front of him, you had to look up at Sam, while he looked down at you. I heard years later that Sam had picked up that trick from reading about Josef Stalin, the dictator of the Soviet Union. Sam did a lot of reading about powerful men who were short: Napoleon, Stalin, Alexander Hamilton.

"Sam," I exclaimed as I burst into his office, "you've invited Mai Pohan!"

Looking mildly surprised, Sam replied, "Sure. She's one of the top golfers on the international tour."

Before I could begin to thank him, Sam added, "And she's the best-looking woman in the bunch of 'em." He broke into a leering grin.

Sam's reputation as a woman-chaser was well known. Behind his desk I could see a panoply of photographs of Sam with spectacularly beautiful women, sometimes two or even three of them hanging on him. Most of them were very scantily clad.

"She's young, beautiful, unattached," Sam went on, his leer widening. "I intend to show her the wonders of lunar living."

At that instant I began to hate Sam Gunn.

I threw myself into building the golf course, while Sam spent most of his time arranging transportation and accommodations for the invited golfers. I've got admit that a good many tourists did sign up to come to Hell for the tournament; Sam's judgment about its attraction was squarely on the mark.

Once I mapped out the course, the actual construction didn't take very long. I directed a team of human and robot workers who smoothed the greens areas and fairways (and painted them), removed a good deal of the rocks and pebbles that were strewn everywhere, rearranged some of the bigger boulders so they presented strategic problems for the golfers, and leveled off the tee boxes.

It turned out the greens were now too smooth, too fast. Tap a ball and it rolled right across the green and into the deep sand of the rough. So we had to spread a thin layer of sand over them. And spray paint it green.

We painted the golf balls too, a brilliant DayGlo orange, so they could be seen against the gray lunar sand of the tees and the rough.

Finally we planted the tall lighted poles at the holes, so the players could see where they should aim their shots.

Sam was buzzing about like a mosquito on amphetamines, meeting and greeting the invited golfers as they arrived on the Moon. They flew from Earth to Selene, of course, and stayed at the Hotel Luna (all expenses paid by S. Gunn Enterprises, Unlimited) until the entire fifty professionals—plus their families and/or friends—had arrived. Then they were whisked to Hell Crater on a special passage of the elevated tram line that connected Selene to Hell.

I wondered how Sam could possibly afford all this largesse, but when I asked him about it he simply shrugged and said, "You've got to spend money to make money. Prime rule of business, Charlie."

I made it my prime business to be at the tram depot when the pros arrived on their special train. Sam was there too, of course, eager as a tail-wagging puppy, leading a small army of guides, robot porters and news reporters. He had even brought the band from Dante's Inferno to provide lively music.

Sam seemed surprised to see me there, in the midst of all the flunkies.

"Shouldn't you be rearranging rocks or something?" he asked, over the noise of the milling assistants and the band.

"All done, Sam," I shouted into his ear. "The course is ready for action."

He broke into that leering smile of his. "So am I, Charlie."

The tram glided into the depot, the airlock hatch closed behind it, and the band broke into a raucus welcoming rendition of "*Happy Days Are Here Again.*" Golfers of all sizes and shapes came pouring out of the tram, together with assorted family members, friends, and hangers-on. I began to worry that I wouldn't be able to see tiny Mai Pohan in the crowd.

But there she was! She looked like a little waif, standing alone in the swirl of people, like a delicate flower in the midst of a storm.

I pushed through the bodies toward her, but Sam was faster. He grabbed her by the arm and led her to one of the carts that were lined up to take his guests to the Paradise Hotel below the entertainment complex. In all the noise and bustle, Mai didn't see me. Sam was jabbering in her ear nonstop, and she looked pleased that Sam Gunn himself was escorting her.

He seated her in the cart, then climbed up onto its roof and bellowed, "Welcome to the First Lunar Golf Invitational! I want you all to enjoy yourselves."

I stood there, hopelessly hemmed in by the surging crowd, as Sam clambered down to sit beside Mai. They headed off for the hotel, leaving me standing there, alone in the midst of the throng.

For a solid week I tried to see Mai alone, but she was either playing practice rounds or in Sam's company. We had dinner together a couple of times, but always with Sam and a bunch of other golfers.

"It's a very interesting course," Mai said to me, from across the dinner table. Sam sat at its head, with Mai on his right. Six others were at the table, all internationally known golfers.

"I got the best designer in the business," Sam said proudly.

The man on my left, a burly, ruddy-faced South African, Rufus Kleindienst, complained, "Hitting the ball over the horizon is a bit weird. Why'd you make the course so bloody big?"

"We're on the Moon," Sam answered. "Lower gravity, no air resistance."

"Yes, but you could have just made the balls heavier to compensate for that. Hitting the ball over the horizon is whacko."

I agreed with him, but one of the other pros, Suddartha Ramjanmyan, a rake-thin Indian, spoke up: "You are a very long hitter, after all. Now the rest of us have a chance to match you."

Rufus grinned good-naturedly.

But one of the Yanks, a youthful-looking sandy blond sitting down at the end of the table, piped up. "What I don't understand is why you've made this a mixed tournament. Why not a men's tournament and a separate one for women? That's the normal way."

Sam explained, "We've got to hustle things along a little. The Sun sets in ten days. That gives us a week for practice and getting accustomed to the course, and three days for the tournament. After that we'll have two solid weeks of night."

"Two weeks of night?" The Yank was totally surprised. He might have been a champion golfer, but he hadn't bothered to learn the first thing about conditions on the Moon.

"Two weeks," Sam repeated solemnly. "Starlight's pretty bright, but I think you'll prefer playing in the daytime."

The Yank nodded weakly.

As I expected, the big problem was the spacesuits. There were three basic types. The standard issue had a hard-shell torso of cermet, with fabric sleeves and leggings and accordion-pleated joints at the elbows, knees and wrists. A newer variation kept the cermet torso but its sleeves and legs were made of a reasonably flexible plastic. Then there was the exoskeleton, its fabric arms and legs covered with high-strength carbon fiber rods that were powered by tiny servomotors, slaved to the wearer's body movements. This increased the wearer's natural strength and made the suit feel more flexible.

While the exoskeleton allowed the most flexibility, it was twice the weight of the others, which made it cumbersome, even in the light lunar gravity. And it took an hour or more to put on. And take off.

For four days the golfers tried on different suits, clomping around in their heavy boots, whacking away at golf balls out on the driving range. Most of them eventually went for the exoskeleton, although a handful opted for the standard suit. Nobody wanted the plastic job.

When I saw Mai in the smallest exoskeleton that was available, she looked like a little child being swallowed alive by some alien metal monster.

Try as I might to get some time with her alone, Mai was constantly working out on the course or otherwise in the company of her fellow golfers. In the evenings, she was either with the golf pros or with Sam. Or both. She ignored my calls and my messages.

Finally I decided to face her, once and for all. On the night before the tournament was to begin, I planted myself in the surveillance center and watched for Mai on the dozens of display screens lining the walls of the chamber. Two security technicians monitored the screens, which showed every public space and corridor in the complex.

I watched Mai at a dinner table in Dante's Inferno, sitting with Sam and a quartet of other golfers, two of them women. Sam was chattering away, as usual, and Mai seemed to be entranced by whatever he was talking about. Her eyes hardly left his face, even for a moment. I would have gladly strangled him.

At last they finished their desserts and coffees and got up from the table. Sam took Mai's arm—and she let him do it. He escorted her out of Dante's, along the corridor that led to the elevators, and then down to the level of the Paradise Hotel.

I didn't realize how tense I was until one of the security techs complained, "Hey, look at what you did to my pen!"

I had unconsciously picked her pen off her desktop and bent it into a horseshoe shape.

As I muttered an apology and promised to buy her a new one, I watched Mai and Sam make their way down the hotel's main corridor. They stopped at her door.

I had to admit to myself that they made a well-matched couple. Mai was just a centimeter or so shorter than Sam, and exquisitely beautiful. Sam was far from handsome, but he radiated a vital energy, even in the security camera's display screen.

My heart was in my throat as Sam began to slip his arms around Mai's waist. But she artfully disengaged, gave him a peck on the cheek, and slipped into her room, leaving Sam standing alone in the corridor, looking nonplussed.

I let out a yelp that made both the security techs jump, then raced for the door, the elevator, and Mai's hotel room.

By the time I got to her door Sam was long gone, of course. I tapped lightly. No response. I rapped a little harder, and Mai's muffled voice came through, "Sam, I need my rest. Please go away."

"It's not Sam," I said, smiling happily. "It's me."

"Chou?"

"Yes!"

For a moment nothing happened, then the door slid back and Mai was standing there in a silk robe decorated with flowers and birds. She looked up at me, her face serious, almost gloomy.

"Hello," she said, sadly.

"Mai, I had to see you. Why haven't you answered my calls? Why are you spending all your time—"

She put a finger on my lips, silencing me.

"Our last meeting was a disaster, Chou. I ruined your life."

"Ruined?" I was truly shocked. "You *saved* my life, Mai!"

"I thought they were going to put you in jail."

"They would have, if it weren't for Sam."

"You owe him a lot."

That's when it hit me. Mai was being nice to Sam because she grateful for what he did for me!

"Sam's getting his money's worth out of me," I growled. "I don't want you to let him include you in the payment."

Now she looked shocked. "I would never—"

I didn't let her finish her sentence. I took her in my arms and kissed her. A couple strolling up the corridor passed by and chuckled softly.

"We've been seen again," Mai said, a little ruefully.

"I don't care. I'm a free man now."

"As long as you stay on the Moon."

"Well, yes," I had to admit.

"So we'll always be half a million kilometers apart."

"Four hundred thousand," I corrected, inanely. "But it doesn't have to always be that way. Once my divorce becomes final, maybe I'll be able to return to Earth."

Mai said nothing.

"Or maybe you could stay here, on the Moon. We'll get married and . . . and . . ."

"And I'll give up my career? Become a housewife? And what are you going to do, now that you've built Sam's golf course? Do you think there are others who'd want you to build courses for them here on the Moon?"

I shook my head, crestfallen.

She touched my cheek with her fingertips.

"I love you, Mai," I whispered.

"I love you, too," she said. "But I don't see how it could possibly work out."

Neither could I.

"You'd better go," she said.

I couldn't move.

"The tournament starts tomorrow, Chou. You're bad for my concentration."

"I know. I'm sorry."

But then she smiled and took my hand and led me into her room and neither one of us gave a thought to her concentration or our future.

The tournament started the next morning. Mai hopped out of bed and headed for the shower. I thought about joining her there, but decided it would be better if I just stole away. Which is what I did, feeling miserable every step of the way.

Love is strange. Powerful. But sometimes so painful it tears the heart out of your chest.

I had nothing to do. My work was finished. So I went to my quarters, cleaned up, got into fresh coveralls, and made my way to the spacious lobby of Dante's Inferno, which Sam's people had turned into a sort of auditorium, with comfortable seats filling the floor and enormous video screens hung on every wall.

The place was already full of eager onlookers, while a team of Hell's Belles (looking a little bleary-eyed this early in the morning) circulated through the crowd with trays of drinks and snacks.

To my surprise, Sam's name was at the top of the list of entrants. Several of the spectators noticed it, too.

"That Sam," a silver-haired, dark-skinned man chuckled, "he'll do anything to put himself in the limelight."

One of the better-looking women said, "Well, it's his tournament, after all."

Sam had detailed one of his publicity aides to go out to the first tee and introduce the competitors. And there was a flock of sports reporters there, too, waiting for the golfers to come out.

One by one they stepped through the airlock and out onto the barren, airless floor of Hell Crater. Most of them wore exoskeletons, which made them look like ponderous, clanking robots. As each one reached the first tee the reporters huddled around him or her and asked the same tired old questions:

"How do you feel about playing golf on the Moon?"

"Will your spacesuit hamper your playing?"

"What do you think your chances of winning are?"

And then Sam came waltzing through the airlock and out onto the floor of Hell Crater. We all gasped with surprise. He was wearing nothing more over his coveralls than what looked like a transparent plastic raincoat.

It had leggings and booties that covered his shoes, and gloves so thin I could see the veins on the backs of Sam's hands. His head was encased in a transparent bubble of a helmet, his red thatch of buzz-cut hair clearly visible through it. The spacesuit looked impossibly flimsy.

The news team that was interviewing each golfer clustered around Sam like a pack of hounds surrounding a fox, firing questions about his spacesuit.

"Nanofabric," Sam exclaimed, the crooked grin on his face spreading from ear to ear.

Before the news people could take a breath, Sam explained, "The suit was built by nanomachines, from the nanolab at Selene. Dr. Kristine Cardenas is the lab's director, you know. She won the Nobel Prize for her work on nanotechnololgy."

"But . . . but it's so . . . *light*," one of the newswomen gushed, from inside her standard hard-shell spacesuit. "How can it possibly protect you?"

"How come it doesn't stiffen up, like regular suits?" asked another.

"How can it protect you against the radiation?"

"How can it be so flexible?"

Sam laughed and raised both his nangloved hands to quiet their questions. "You'll have to ask Dr. Cardenas about the technical details. All I can tell you is that the suit gives as much protection as a standard suit, but it's a lot more flexible. And easier to put on and take off, lemme tell you. Like old-fashioned pajamas."

The other golfers, in their standard suits or exoskeletons, hung around the edge of the crowd uneasily. None of them liked being upstaged.

Mai hadn't appeared yet, and I began to wonder if something was wrong. Then she came through the airlock, wearing a nanosuit, just like Sam.

"No!" I bellowed, startling the tourists sitting around me. I bolted from my chair and ran to the airlock.

There was a team of beefy security guards at the airlock hatch, in dark gray uniforms. They wouldn't let me take a suit and go outside.

"Only players and the reporters," their leader told me. "Mr. Gunn's orders."

Feeling desperate, I raced to the communications center, down the corridor from the airlock area. It was a small chamber, studded with display screens and staffed by two men and two women. They didn't want to let me talk to Mai, or Sam, or anybody else out there on the golf course.

"Mr. Gunn's orders," they said.

"To hell with Sam's orders," I roared at them. "This is a safety issue. Lives are at stake!"

They told me to call the safety office and even offered me a spare console to sit at. I scanned the available comm channels and put my call through. To Mai.

Before the technicians realized what I'd done, Mai's face came up on the central screen of my console. She smiled at me.

"You left without saying goodbye," she chided gently.

"Get back inside!" I fairly screamed. "If Sam wants to kill himself that's his business, but I won't let him kill you!"

Mai's face went stern. "Chou, do you think I'm an idiot? This suit is perfectly safe."

"That may be what Sam says, but—"

"That's what Dr. Cardenas says," Mai interrupted. "I've spoken with her for hours about the suit. It's been tested at Selene for months. It's fine."

"How can it be?" I was nearly hysterical with fear. "It's nothing but a thin layer of transparent fabric."

"Ask Dr. Cardenas," said Mai. "I've got a golf game to play."

She cut the connection. My screen went blank.

Still sitting at the console, with all four of the comm techs staring at me, I put in a call to Dr. Kristine Cardenas, at the nanotechnology laboratory in Selene.

All her lines were busy. News reporters were besieging her about the nanosuit.

I sank back in the console's little wheeled chair, terrified that Mai would die of asphyxiation or radiation poisoning or decompression out there in that flimsy suit. Insanely, I felt a grim satisfaction that if Mai died, Sam probably would too.

Numbly I pushed the chair back and began to get up on wobbly legs.

One of the technicians, a youngish woman, said to me, "You can watch the tournament from here, if you like."

I sank back onto the chair.

One of the male techs added, "If you can sit quietly and keep your mouth shut."

That's what I did. Almost.

It was a weird golf game.

Sam was nothing more than a duffer, yet he was holding his own against some of the best players on Earth.

Encased in an exoskeleton suit, Rufus, the muscular South African, literally scorched his drives out of sight. In the light lunar gravity, the DayGlo orange balls rose in dreamy slow motion, arced lazily across the starry sky, and sailed gently toward the ground, disappearing over the short horizon.

He was overdriving, slamming the ball beyond the green, into the deep treacherous sand. Then he'd flail away, blasting explosions of sand that slowly settled back to the ground while his ball zoomed into another area of deep sand. When he finally got his ball on the green his putting was miserable.

The more bogeys he got, the harder he powered his drives and the more erratic his putts. In the display screen of the console I was watching I could see his face getting redder and redder, even through the tinted visor of his helmet. And his exoskeleton suit seemed to be getting stiffer, more difficult to move in. Probably sand from his desperate flailings was grinding the suit's joints.

Sam just took it easy. His drives were erratic, a slice here, a hook there. It took him two or three shots to get on the green, but once there, his putts were fantastic. He sank putts of twenty, even thirty meters. It was if the ball was being pulled to the cup by some invisible force.

Mai was doing well, also. Her drives were accurate, even though nowhere near long enough to reach the greens. But she always landed cleanly on the fairway and chipped beautifully. She putted almost as well as Sam and kept pace with the leaders.

Both Mai and Sam seemed able to swing much more freely in their nanosuits. Where the other golfers were stiff with their drives and chips, Mai and Sam looked loose and agile. If they'd been bigger, and able to drive the ball farther, they would have led the pack easily.

But my course was really tough on all of them. By the time they reached the last tee, only three of the golfers had broken par. Sam had birdied the last three holes, all par fives, but he was still one above par. The skinny little Indian, Ramjanmyan, was leading at three below.

And Mai was right behind him, at two below.

The eighteenth was the toughest hole on the course, a par six, where the cup was nearly a full kilometer from the tee and hidden behind a slight rise of solid gray rock slanting across the green-painted ground.

Mai stood at the tee, looking toward the lighted pole poking up above the crest of the rocky ridge, her driver in her gloved hands. She took a couple of practice swings, loose and easy, then hit the drive of her life. The ball went straight down the fairway, bounced a couple of dozen meters short of the green, hopped over the ridge, and rolled to a stop a bare ten centimeters from the cup.

"Wow!" yelled the comm techs, rising to their feet. I could even hear the roar of the crowd all the way over in Dante's lobby.

Sam was next. His drive was long enough to reach the green, all right, but he sliced it badly and the ball thunked down in the deep sand off the edge of the green, almost at the red-painted hazard line.

Groans of disappointment.

"That's it for the boss," said one of the techs.

Somehow I found myself thinking, *Don't be so sure about that.*

Ramjanmyan's drive almost cleared the ridge. But only almost. It hit the edge of the rock and bounced high, then fell in that dreamlike lunar slow-motion and rolled back almost to the tee. Even in his exoskeleton suit, the Indian seemed to slump like a defeated man.

He was still one stroke ahead of Mai, though, and two strokes in front of his next closest competitor, a lantern-jawed Australian named MacTavish.

But MacTavish overdrove his ball, trying to clear that ridge, and it rolled past the cup to a stop at the edge of the deep sand.

Mai putted carefully, but her ball hit a minuscule pebble at the last instant and veered a bare few centimeters from the cup. She tapped it in, and came away with a double eagle. She now was leading at five below par.

Sam had trudged out to the sand, where his ball lay. He needed to chip it onto the green and then putt it into the hole. Barely bothering to line up his shot, he whacked it out of the sand. The ball bounced onto the green and then rolled and rolled, curving this way and that like a scurrying ant looking for a breadcrumb, until it rolled to the lip of the cup and dropped in.

Pandemonium. All of us in the comm center sprang to our feet, hands raised high, and bellowed joyfully. The crowd in Dante's lobby roared so hard it registered on the seismograph over in Selene.

Sam was now three below par and so happy about it that he was hopping up and down, dancing across the green, swinging his club over his head gleefully.

Ramjanmyan wasn't finished, though. He lofted his ball high over the ridge. It seemed to sail up there among the stars for an hour before it plopped onto the middle of the green and rolled to the very lip of the cup. There it stopped. We all groaned in sympathy for him.

But the Indian plodded in his exoskeleton suit to the cup and tapped the ball. His final score was six below par.

The only way for MacTavish to beat him would be for him to chip the ball directly into the cup. The Aussie tried, but his chip was too hard, and the ball rolled a good ten meters past the hole. He ended with a score of four below par.

Ramjanmyan won the tournament at six below par. Mai came in second, five below, and Sam surprised us all with a three below par score, putting him in fourth place.

Everyone celebrated far into the night: golfers, tourists, staffers and all. Sam reveled the hardest, dancing wildly with every woman in Dante's Inferno while the band banged out throbbing, wailing neodisco numbers.

I danced with Mai, no one else. And she danced only with me. It was well past midnight when the party started to break up. Mai and I walked back to her hotel room, tired but very, very happy.

Until I thought about what tomorrow would bring. Mai would leave to return to Earth. I'd be an unemployed golf course architect stranded on the Moon.

"You're awfully quiet," Mai said as we stepped into her room.

"You'll be leaving tomorrow," I said.

"I'll get the best lawyers on Earth," she said as she slid her arms around my neck. "Earth's a big place. Your ex-wife can't harass you anywhere except Singapore."

I shook my head. "Don't be so sure. Her mother has an awful lot of clout."

"We'll find a place . . ."

"And spend the rest of our lives looking over our shoulders? That's not what I want for you, Mai."

She kissed me lightly, just brushing her lips on mine. "Sufficient for the day are the evils thereof."

"Huh?"

Mai smiled at me. "Let's worry about things tomorrow. We're here together tonight."

So I tried to forget about my troubles. I even succeeded—for a while.

I was awakened by the phone's buzzing. I cracked one eye open and saw that Mai was sleeping soundly, peacefully curled up beside me.

"Audio only," I told the phone.

Sam's freckled face sprang up on the phone's screen, grinning lopsidedly.

"Mai, I've got the medical reports here," he began.

"Quiet," I whispered urgently. "Mai's still asleep."

"Charlie?" Sam lowered his voice a notch. "So that's where you are. I called you at your place. We've gotta talk about financial arrangements."

Severance pay, I knew.

"Come over to my office around eleven-thirty. Then we'll go to lunch."

"Mai's flight—"

"Plenty of time for that. My office. Eleven-thirty. Both of you."

They say that today is the first day of the rest of your life. I went through the morning like a man facing a firing squad. The rest of my life, I knew, was going to be miserable and lonely. Mai seemed sad, too. Her usual cheerful smile was nowhere in sight.

We got to Sam's office precisely at eleven-thirty and settled glumly onto the sawed-off chairs in front of his desk. Sam beamed down at us like he hadn't a care in the world. Or two worlds, for that matter.

"First," he began, "the radiation badges we all wore show that the nanosuits protected us just as well as the standard suits protected everybody else."

"Dr. Cardenas will be pleased," Mai said listlessly.

"You bet she is," Sam replied. "We're having dinner together over at Selene this evening."

Dr. Cardenas was a handsome woman, from what I'd heard of her. Was Sam on the hunt again? Does a parrot have feathers?

"Okay," he said, rubbing his hands together briskly, "now let's get down to business."

The firing squad was aiming at me.

"Charlie, you don't have much experience in business administration, do you?"

Puzzled by his question, I answered, "Hardly any."

"That's okay. I can tell you everything you need to know."

"Need to know for what?"

Sam looked surprised. "To manage the golf course, naturally."

"Manage it?" My voice squeaked two octaves higher than normal.

"Sure, what else? I'll be too busy to do it myself."

Mai gripped my arm. "That's wonderful!"

"And you, oh beauteous one, will be our pro, of course." Sam announced, chuckling at his little pun.

"Me?"

Nodding, Sam replied, "Sure, you. This way the two of you can stay together. Sort of a wedding present." Then he fixed me with a stern gaze. "You do intent to marry the lady, don't you?"

I blurted, "If she'll have me!"

Mai squeezed my hand so hard I thought bones would break. I hadn't realized how strong playing golf had made her.

"Okay, that's it," Sam said happily. "You'll manage the course, Charlie, and Mai, you'll be the pro."

"And what will you do, Sam?" Mai asked.

"Me? I've got to set up the company that'll manufacture and sell nanosuits. Kris Cardenas is going to be my partner."

I felt my jaw drop open. "You mean this whole tournament was just a way of advertising the nanosuits?"

With a laugh, Sam answered, "Got a lot of publicity for the suits, didn't it? I'm already getting queries from the rock rats, out in the Asteroid Belt. And the university consortium that's running the Mars exploration team."

I shook my head in admiration for the man. Sam just sat there grinning down at us. The little devil had opened up a new sport for lunar residents and tourists, solved my legal problem, created a career for me, and found a way for Mai and me to marry. Plus, he was starting a new industry that would revolutionize the spacesuit business.

Before I could find words to thank Sam, Mai asked him, "Will you answer a question for me?"

"Sure," he said breezily. "Fire away."

"How did you learn to putt like that, Sam? Some of your putts were nothing short of miraculous."

Sam pursed his lips, looked up at the ceiling, swiveled back and forth on his chair.

"Come on, Sam," Mai insisted. "The truth. It won't go farther than these four walls."

With a crooked, crafty grin, Sam replied, "You'd be surprised at how much electronics you can pack into a golf ball."

"Electronics?" I gasped.

"A transmitter in the cups and a receiver in the ball," Mai said. "Your putts were guided into the cups."

"Sort of," Sam admitted.

"That's cheating!" I exclaimed.

"There's nothing in the rules against it."

That's Sam. As far as he's concerned, rules are made to bent into pretzels. And looking up at his grinning, freckled face, I just knew he was already thinking about some new scheme. That's Sam Gunn. Unlimited.

HIGH JUMP

When the human race begins to expand its habitat through the solar system, it won't be only scientists and engineers who go to other worlds. There will be entrepreneurs, visionaries, saints, sinners, pilgrims, adventurers . . .

Adventurers. Some people make adventure their business. And what a business opportunity the hellishly hot surface of the planet Venus will be!

THE THINGS a man will do for love.

I had been Hal Prince's stunt double for more than five years. To the general public he was the greatest daredevil that ever lived, the handsome star of the most exciting adventure videos ever recorded, the tall sandy-haired guy with the flashing smile and twinkling eyes who always did his own stunts.

Well, I had known him when he was Aloysius Prizanski, back before he got his nose fixed, when he'd been a wannabe actor hungry enough to jump into a pool of blazing petrol from the bridge of an ocean liner.

Back then he did his own stunts, sure enough, but once he got so popular that he could command half a bill just for signing a contract,

321

the insurance people insisted that he was just too goddamned valuable to risk.

So I did his stunts. His old pal. His asshole buddy. Ugly old me. It was no big secret in the industry, but as far as the general public was concerned, it was Handsome Hal himself who'd risked his own neck riding the hundred-gee catapult at Moonbase into lunar orbit and sledding down the dry-ice-coated flank of Olympus Mons in nothing more than a Buckyball suit.

To say nothing of sky-diving into Vesuvius while it was boiling out steam and the occasional blurp of hot lava. That one cost me three months in a burn recovery center, although I never let Hal know it. He thought I'd just gotten miffed at him and taken off to sulk.

Now I was going to do the high jump for him. On Venus, yet. Pop myself out of an orbiting spacecraft and drop all the way down to the planet's red-hot surface.

And I mean red-hot. The ground temperature down there is hot enough to melt aluminum. The air pressure is almost a hundred times what it is at sea level on Earth; like the pressure in the ocean, more than a kilometer down.

And by the way, Venus' air is almost all choking carbon dioxide. The clouds that cover the planet from pole to pole are made of sulfuric acid. And they're filled with bugs that eat metal, too.

The stunt was to jump from orbit and go all the way down to the ground. I had just come back from the patch-up job after the Vesuvius barbecue. Truth to tell, I was scared into constipation over this stunt.

But I didn't tell Hal. Or anybody else.

We all have our little secrets. My doubling for him was Hotshot Hal's secret. But I had a few of my own, too.

Angel Santos doubled for Hal's female co-stars; if it weren't for her toughness and quick thinking I'd have been fried inside old Vesuvius.

Angel was really beautiful: a face to die for, with big wide-set cornflower blue eyes, full bust, narrow waist, long legs—the works. Don't strain your eyes looking for her in any of Hal's videos, though; like me, she was strictly a stunt double, wearing whatever wigs and rigs that were necessary to make her look like Hal's female co-star— whoever she happened to be.

Angel could've been a star in her own right, but she had absolutely no interest in acting. She was hooked on the challenges of danger, just like me. We got along together great, two of a kind. She made me feel really good about myself, too. People looked up from their dinners when I walked into a restaurant with Angel on my arm. I mean people *never* looked at me. Especially when Heroic Hal was anywhere in sight. Okay, I knew they were looking at Angel, not me, but I got respect for having her on my arm, at least. Boosted my machismo rating with the dumbshit ordinary folks.

But once Angel met with Hedonistic Hal she got hooked on him. I didn't realize it at first. We'd all go out together, the three of us. It didn't take long, though, before they started going out without me, just the two of them. I was left out in the cold.

Then came the Venus jump.

I was thinking about packing it in. Let Hal the Heartbreaker get somebody else. He wasn't thinking about me at all anymore; he only had eyes for Angel. And she clung on him like he was the last lifeboat on the *Titanic*. She wasn't even involved in this Venus stunt, it was my trick alone. But she came along for the ride, all the way out to Venus—with Hal the Hunk.

But then I decided I'd do the stunt, after all. I wanted to be noticed; I wanted to break the lock the two of them had on each other, and the only way I knew to do that was to go through with the toughest, most daring and dangerous stunt that'd ever been tried. Admiration, that's what I was after. I wanted to make their eyes shine—for me.

The High Jump: from Venus orbit all the way to the ground. And back, of course. None of the publicity flaks even mentioned the return trip, but I thought about that part of it *a lot*.

Okay, so we're in orbit around Venus—Hal, Angel, me, our crew of technicians and our tech directors, plus the ship's crew. We had decided to keep the ship's crew in the dark about me doubling for Hal. As far as they were concerned I was just another techkie. The fewer people outside the industry who knew about my doubling for him, the better.

So Hal's doing the mandatory media interview, all dolled up in a spacesuit, no less, with the helmet tucked under one arm. Standing there by the airlock hatch, he looks like a freaking Adonis, so help me, a Galahad, literally a knight in shining armor. And Angel's right there beside him, hanging on his arm, gazing up into his sparkling green eyes as if she's about to have an orgasm just looking at him.

The media people were all back on Earth, of course. We didn't want them on the ship with us, too much of a chance of them finding out about Hal's little secret. Since it took messages more than eight minutes to travel from them to us (and vice-versa) they had pre-recorded their questions and squirted them to us a couple of hours earlier.

Now Homeric Hal stood there like a young Lancelot and spoke four-square into the camera, replying to each of their questions after only an hour or so to study the lines his publicity flaks had written for him.

"Yes," he said, with his patented careless grin, "I suppose we could use computer graphics for these stunts instead of doing them live. But I don't think the public would be so interested in a computer simulation. My fans want to see the real thing! It's the unexpected, the element of danger and risk, that excites the viewers."

The next questioner asked why Hal was so eager to risk his beautiful butt on these stunts.

He did his bashful routine, shrugging and scratching his head. "I don't really know. I guess I got hooked on the excitement of it all, and . . . and . . ."

He hesitated, as the script required. I thought sourly that what he's really hooked on is the money. Mucho bucks in this game. He let me take over the dangerous part of it easily enough.

". . . and . . . well I guess it's the thrill of taking enormous risks and coming out alive. It makes your heart beat faster, that's for sure. Gets the old adrenaline pumping!"

His adrenaline was pumping, all right. But it wasn't about the risks of the Venus jump. It was Angel, draped over him and drinking in every syllable he uttered.

The media interview ended at last. Hal's smile winked off. "Okay," he said, starting to peel off his suit. "Let's get to work."

To his credit, Hal gave me a farewell hug just before I stepped into the airlock. It was an awkward hug, with me in the bulky thermally insulated spacesuit that we'd had specially built for this stunt.

"Take care of yourself, pal," he said, his voice gone husky.

"Don't I always?" I said back to him.

I stepped into the airlock and turned around to face him again. And there was Angel, right beside him. I blew a kiss as the hatch closed and sealed me in—not an easy thing to do from inside my heatproofed helmet.

There were two technicians already outside, in spacesuits of course, to help click me into the aeroshell. It wasn't a spacecraft, just a heat shield that carried the bare minimum of equipment I'd need to make it down to the surface. I mean, that Humphries kid had reached Venus' surface a couple of years earlier, but he'd never walked on the planet's rocky ground, as I was going to do. He'd been inside a specially designed submersible; *it* touched down on the surface, not him on his own two feet. And he was supported by an even bigger ship that cruised a few kilometers above him, at that.

Plus, he'd landed in the highland mountains of Aphrodite. It's only four hundred degrees Celsius up there. Big deal. I was going down to the lowlands, where it's four-fifty, minimum, and doing it without a ship. Just me in a thermal suit and a handful of equipment.

Plus the heat shield, yeah, but that was just to get me through the entry phase. I mean, we were orbiting Venus at just about seven kilometers per second. You can't dip into the atmosphere in nothing but your high-tech longjohns at that speed—not unless you want to make yourself into a shooting star.

I had no intention of becoming a cinder. The heat shield was flimsy enough, nothing more than a shallow bathtub coated on one side with a heat-absorbing plastic that boils off when it reaches fifteen hundred degrees. The boiled-off goop carries the heat away with it, leaving me safe on the other side of the shield. At least, that's the way it's supposed to work.

Believe me, the heat shield looked damned flimsy as I climbed into it. The techs checked out all my suit's systems and the connections, then clamped me into the shield's shallow protection. None of us said much while they got me properly clicked in.

Finally, they each patted my thick helmet and wished me luck. I thanked them, and they clambered through the airlock and shut the hatch. I was alone now, with nothing to keep me company but the automated voice of the computer ticking off the last three minutes of the countdown.

Three minutes can be a long time, when you're alone hanging outside an orbiting spacecraft, a hundred million kilometers from blue skies and sunny beaches. I was locked into the heat shield, arms and legs stretched out like a guy in a B&D video, with nothing to do but worry about what was coming next.

To keep my nerves from twitching, I looked out through one corner of my faceplate at what little I could see of Venus.

She was gorgeous! The massive, curving bulk of the planet gleamed like a gigantic golden lamp, a brilliant saffron-yellow expanse against the cold blackness of space. She glowed like a thing alive. Goddess of beauty, sure enough. At first I thought the cloud deck was as solid and unvarying as a sphere of solid gold. Then I saw that I could make out streamers among the clouds, slightly darker stretches, patches where the amber yellowish clouds billowed up slightly. I stared fascinated at those fantastically incredible clouds. They shifted and changed as I watched. It was almost like staring into a fire, endlessly fascinating, hypnotic.

A human voice broke into my enchantment. "You okay out there?"

"Sure," I snapped. "I'm fine."

"Separation in thirty seconds." It was the voice of our tech controller in my helmet earphones. "Speak now or forever hold your jockstrap."

"Let 'er rip," I said, in time-honored, devil-may-care fashion. Just in case some wiseass was eavesdropping with a recorder.

"Five . . . four . . ." Well, you know the rest. I felt a quiver and then a not-too-gentle push against the small of my back: the latches releasing and then the spring-loaded actuator that pushed my aeroshell away from the orbiting spacecraft.

And there I was, as the flyguys say, watching our orbiter dwindle away from me. Before I had time to grit my teeth the retrorockets kicked in, and I mean *kicked*. I couldn't hear anything in the vacuum of space, naturally, but I sure felt it. The whole goddamned aeroshell rattled like a studio set in an earthquake. I heard a kind of a roar inside my head; not sound, really, so much as my bones picking up the vibrations as the rockets tried to shake me to death.

I hung on—nothing else I could do—for the forty-five seconds of retro burn, knowing the cameras from the ship were getting every picosecond of it in glorious full color. Every bone in my body was quivering like a struck gong. I wondered if I'd get out of this with any teeth unchipped.

Then suddenly it all stopped. I was either dead or the rockets had burned out.

"Retro burn complete," said the controller calmly. "You are go for entry into Venus' atmosphere."

Stretched out inside this shallow soapdish of an aeroshell, I nodded inside my helmet. Now comes the fun part, I said to myself.

The first thing I noticed was streaks of bright light flicking past me. Hitting the top of the atmosphere at seven klicks per second heated up the gases to incandescence. Pretty soon I was surrounded with white-hot plasma boiling off the heat shield and billowing out past me. I lay there on my back, helpless as a newborn rat, with white-hot gas streaming past the edges of my shell. I could hear noise now, a high-pitched whining sound that deepened into the kind of roar you hear when you open a blast furnace.

And the shell was shaking again, worse than before. If I hadn't been latched down, and if my protective suit hadn't been well padded, I'd have been pummeled to jelly. Mouth protector, I thought as I tasted blood. I should've brought a mouth protector. I tried to keep my mouth open so I wouldn't chew off my tongue or bite a hole through my cheek and cursed myself for the oversight.

The controller tried to tell me something, but the plasma sheath around the rapidly descending aeroshell broke up his radio message into garbled little hashes of static. I tried to focus my eyes on the data screen inside my helmet, next to the face plate, but everything was jouncing around so bad I couldn't see anything but a multicolored blur.

Must be close to breakup, I thought.

And *bang!* the aeroshell clamps unlatched and the shell itself snapped into a dozen separate pieces, just the way it was designed to. Gave me a jolt, let me tell you.

So now I was in free-fall, dropping like a stone toward the top layer of clouds. The shaking eased off enough so I could read the altimeter inside my helmet. I passed eighty kilometers like a doomed soul falling into hell.

My biggest worry was the superrotation winds. They could blow me halfway around the planet and I'd miss my landing spot. That's where the return rocket vehicle was sitting on the surface, waiting for me in that baking heat and corrosive sulfur-laced atmosphere.

Venus turns very slowly, its "day" is 243 Earth days long—that's how long it takes the planet to make one complete turn around its axis. So the Sun blazes down on the subsolar point, the spot where the Sun is directly overhead, like a freaking blowtorch. The upper atmosphere, blast-heated like that, develops winds of four hundred kilometers per hour and more that rush around the entire planet in a few days. In a way, they're like the jet streams on Earth, only bigger and more powerful.

If I got caught in one of those superpowerful jet streams I'd be blown so far away from my landing point that I'd never make it back to the return vehicle. Then I'd have a choice of whether I wanted to be baked to death or suffocate.

So the plan was to cannonball through the superrotation's jet streams as fast as possible, get down into the lower altitudes where the air pressure thickens into soup and the winds are smothered into sluggish little nothings.

That was the plan.

I was dropping like a brick, headfirst, the wind screeching past me and the billowing sickly yellow-gray clouds rushing up.

"How'm I doing?" I yelled into my helmet mike.

"Drifting off course," came the director's voice, calm as a guy ordering a Margarita back in L.A.

I looked to the left of my faceplate, at the miniscreen that showed my position. I was a red dot, the return vehicle was a green dot. There were concentric circles around the green dot. If I was within two circles of the center I'd be okay. That red dot was already close to the edge of the second circle.

"Better do some maneuvering," the director suggested, flat as Kansas.

"Too soon," I said. The maneuvering jets on the back of my suit only carried so much fuel. Use 'em up now and I'd be helpless later.

But that red dot that was me was drifting past the second circle. I was in trouble.

"Maneuver!" the director snapped. I had to smile; at least I got his blood pressure up a little.

"No sense shovelling shit against the tide," I said. "I'll wait until I'm under the jet stream."

"You'll be too far!" He was getting really clanked up now.

My eyes flicked back and forth. The miniscreen on my right showed I was passing seventy klicks, almost into the top cloud deck. The superrotation winds should be dying down. But the radar plot on the left of my faceplate showed my red dot almost off the chart completely.

"Check pressure," I called out. The altimeter readout was replaced by a rapidly changing set of numbers. According to the probe sampling the air I was falling through, the pressure was rising steeply.

I nodded inside the helmet. Yes, the radar plot showed I wasn't drifting any farther from the landing spot.

"Cranking up the jets," I said, wriggling my right arm out the suit's sleeve to press the actuator stud on the control board built inside the suit's chest cavity. We had decided to keep all the controls inside the suit, safe from the corrosive oven-hot atmosphere outside.

"About time," groused the director.

"No sweat," I told him. Which, I realized, wasn't exactly true. I was perspiring enough to notice it. I wiped my brow before sliding my arm back into its sleeve.

The jets came on, gently at first and then accelerating slowly. I twisted my body around and spread my arms out. That unfolded the airfoils that ordinarily wrapped around my sleeves. Like a jet-propelled bat, I dove into the sulfuric-acid clouds, watching the radar plot as my little green dot starting edging closer to the red dot.

My suit's exterior was all ceramicized plastic, for three reasons. One, the material was a good heat insulator, and I was going to need all the protection from Venus' fiery hell that I could get. Two, the stuff was impervious to sulfuric acid—of which the cloud droplets had plenty. Three, it would not be attacked by the bugs that lived in those sulfuric acid clouds.

The aerobacteria had destroyed the first two ships that had entered Venus' clouds. They feast on metals, gobble 'em up the way a macrovitamin faddist gulps pills. The exobiologists had assured us that those bugs would not even nibble at the plastic exterior of my suit.

There was plenty of metal in the suit, a whole candy store's worth, as far as the bugs were concerned. But it was all covered by thick layers of plastic. I hoped.

Once in the clouds my vision was reduced to zero. From the outside mikes I could hear wind whistling past, but the altimeter showed that my rate of fall was slowing. The atmosphere was getting thicker, making it harder to gain headway.

The jets burped once, twice, then gave out. Fuel exhausted. And I was only between the first and second circles on the radar plot. I was sailing through the heavier layers of cloud, heading for the rendezvous spot like a soaring bird now.

"Looking good," the director said encouragingly.

I shook my head inside the helmet. "I'm not going to make the rendezvous."

Silence for a few heartbeats. Then, "So you'll have to walk a bit."

"Yeah. Right."

The thermal suit would hold up for maybe an hour on the surface. Not much more. The problem was heat rejection.

Down there on the surface, where the freaking rocks are red hot and the air is thicker than sea water, it's four hundred and fifty degrees Celsius. More, in some places. No matter how well the suit is built, that heat seeps in on you, sooner or later. So the engineers had built a heat-rejection system into my suit: slugs of special alloy that melted at four hundred Celsius. The alloy absorbed heat, melted, and was squirted out of the suit, taking the heat with it.

It was pretty crude, but it worked. It would keep my suit's interior reasonably cool. So the engineers promised. After about one hour, though, the suit would run out of alloy and I'd start to bake; my protective suit would turn into a pretty efficient steam cooker.

That's what I had to look forward to. That's why I was trying my damnedest to land as close to that return ship as possible.

I broke out of the top cloud deck at last and for a few minutes I was in relatively clear air. Clouds above me, more clouds below. I was still gliding, but slower and slower as the air pressure built up steeply. At least I was past the bugs. The temperature outside was approaching a hundred degrees, the boiling point of water. The bugs couldn't survive in that heat.

Could I?

Lightning flashed in my eyes, scaring the bejeesus out of me. Then came a slow, rolling grumble of thunder. The lightning must have been pretty damned close.

That second cloud deck was alive with lightning. It crackled all around me, thunder booming so loud and continuous that I shut off the outside mikes. Still the noise rattled me like an artillery barrage. Had I come down in the middle of a thunderstorm? Was I somehow *attracting* the lightning? You get all kinds of scary thoughts. As I dropped deeper and deeper into Venus' hot, heavy air, my mind filled with what-ifs and should-ofs.

The lightning seemed to be only in the second cloud deck. I

watched its flickering all across the sky as I fell through the brief clear space between it and the third deck. It was almost pretty, at this distance.

The third and last of the cloud decks was also the thinnest. At just a smidge above fifty kilometers' altitude I glided through its underbelly and saw the landscape of Venus with my own eyes.

I stared down at a distant landscape of barren rock, utter desolation, nothing but bare hard stony ground as far as the eye could see, naked rock in shades of gray and darker gray, with faint streaks here and there of lighter stuff, almost like talc or pumice.

I saw a series of domes, and farther in the distance the bare rocky ground seemed wrinkled, as if something had squeezed it hard. There were mountains out near the horizon, although that might have been a distortion caused by the density of the thick atmosphere, like trying to judge shapes deep underwater.

Below me was an immense crater, maybe fifty klicks across. It looked sharp-edged, new. But they'd told me there wasn't much erosion going on down there, despite the heat and corrosive atmosphere. It took a *long* time for craters to be erased on Venus; half a billion years or more.

The air was so thick now that I was scuba diving, rather than gliding. The bat wings were still useful, but now I had to flap my arms to push through the mushy atmosphere. The servomotors in my shoulder joints buzzed and whined; without them I wouldn't have the muscular strength to swim for very long.

I was still a long way from the rendezvous point, I saw. Inching closer, but only inching.

Then I got an idea. If Mohammed can't make it to the mountain, why not get the mountain to come to Mohammed?

"Can you hop the ship toward me?" I asked.

Nothing but static in my earphones.

I yelled and changed frequencies and hollered some more. Nothing. Must've been the electrical storm in the second cloud deck was screwing up my radio link. I was on my own, just me and the planet Venus.

She looks so beautiful from a distance, I thought. She glows so bright and lovely in the night sky that just about every culture on Earth has called her after their goddess of beauty and love: Aphrodite,

Inanna, Ishtar, Astarte, Venus. I've watched her when she's the dazzling Evening Star, brighter than anything in the sky except the Sun and Moon. I've seen her when she's the beckoning Morning Star, harbinger of the new day. Always she shines like a precious jewel.

Even when we were in orbit around her, she glowed like an incredible golden sphere. But once you see her really close up, especially when you've gone through the clouds to look at her unadorned face, she isn't beautiful anymore. She looks like hell.

And that's where I was going, down into that inferno. The air was so thick now that I was really pushing myself through it, slowly sinking, struggling to get as close as possible to the spot where the return vehicle was waiting for me. If I hadn't been encased in the heavy thermal suit I guess I would've hovered in the atmosphere, floating like a chunk of meat in a big stewpot, slowly cooking.

I was passing over a big, pancake-shaped area, a circular mass of what must have once been molten lava. It was frozen into solid stone now, if "frozen" is a word you can use for ground that's more than four times hotter than boiling water. I caught a glimpse of mountains off to my left, but I was still so high they looked like wrinkles.

My radar tracking plot had gone blank. The link from the ship up in orbit was shot, together with my voice channels. Pulling my arm out of its sleeve again I poked on the control panel until my radio receiver picked up the signal from the return vehicle's radar beacon. I displayed it on my miniscreen. Now my position was in the center of the display; the ship was more than sixty kilometers off to my left.

Sixty klicks! I'd never make that distance on foot. Could I sail that far before hitting the ground?

We had picked the rendezvous site for two reasons. One, it was about as low—and therefore as hot—as you could get in Venus' equatorial region. Second, it was the area where the old Russian spacecraft, Venera 5, had landed more than a century ago. The video's producers thought it'd be a neat extra if we could bring back imagery of the whatever's left of the old clunker.

Down I swam. I really was swimming now, thrashing my arms and legs, making the suit's servomotors wheeze and grind with the effort. I was sweating a lot now, blinking at the stinging salty drops that leaked down into my eyes, asking myself over and again if Hal was worth all this. A guy could get killed!

The ground came up ever so slowly. I felt like an old wooden sailing ship sunk in battle, sinking gently, gently to the bottom of the ocean. On a world that had never seen wood, or liquid water, or felt a foot on its baking stony surface.

At last I touched the ground. Like a skindiver reaching the bottom of the ocean, I eased down the final few meters and let my heavily booted feet make contact with the red-hot rock.

"I'm down," I said, for the record. I didn't know if they could hear me, up in orbit, but the suit's recorders in their "black box" safety capsules would store my words even if I didn't make it back up.

I glanced at the radar plot. My antennas were picking up the return vehicle's beacon loud and clear. It was only seven kilometers from where I stood.

Seven klicks. In four-hundred-fifty degrees. Just a nice summer stroll on the surface of Venus.

Despite the triple layer of clouds that completely smothered the whole planet, there was plenty of light down at the surface. Sort of like an overcast day in Seattle or Dublin. I could see all the way out to the horizon. The air was so thick, though, that it was sort of like looking through water. The horizon warped up around the edges of my vision, like the way water dimples in a slim glass tube.

The suit felt damned heavy; it weighed more than eighty kilos on Earth, and just about ninety percent of that here on Venus. Call it seventy-some kilos. If it hadn't been for the servomotors on the suit's legs I wouldn't have been able to go more than a few meters.

So I started plodding in the direction my radar screen indicated. Clump with one boot, squeak, groan, click go the servomotors, thump goes the other boot. Over and over again.

I kept up a running commentary, for the record. If and when I got back to Hal and the others, they would morph his voice for mine and have a fine step-by-step narration of the first stroll on Venus. Ought to get a nice bonus out of it, even if it went to my heirs because I got fried to a crisp walking that walk.

Come to think of it, I didn't have any heirs. No family at all. Orphan me. My family had been Hal and the guys we worked with. Including Angel, of course. Our crew was fully integrated. No biases allowed, none whatsoever.

It was *hot*. And getting hotter. After a while I started to feel a little dizzy, weak in the knees. Dehydration. At least I wasn't sweating so much. But I knew if I didn't drink some water and swallow a salt pill I'd be dead before long. Trouble was, every sip of water I drank meant less water for the suit's cooling system. And there wasn't a recycler in the suit; no room for it. Besides, I was only supposed to be on the surface for an hour or less.

"Anyway," thoughtful Hal had told the safety engineers, "who wants to drink his own recycled piss and sweat?"

I wouldn't mind, I thought. Not here and now.

On I walked, creeping closer to the return vehicle. I tried to go into a meditative state while I was walking, letting the servomotors' wheezing and groaning lull me into a blankness so I could keep on moving automatically and let all this pain and discomfort slip out of my thoughts.

Didn't work. The suit's left leg was chafing against my crotch. Both my legs were tiring fast. My back itched. The air seemed to be getting stale; I started coughing. My vision was blurring, too.

And then the snake made a grab for me.

Venusian snakes have nothing to do with the kinds of snakes we have on Earth. They are feeding arms of underground creatures, big bulbous ugly sluglike things that live under the red-hot surface rocks. Don't ask me how anything can live in temperatures four or five times hotter than boiling water. The scientists say they're made of silicones and have molten sulfur for blood. All I saw was a set of their damned feeding arms—snakes.

There's a basic human reaction to the sudden sight of a snake. Run away!

The snake suddenly popped up in front of me, slithering out of its hole. I hopped a meter and a half, even with the weight of the suit, stumbled and fell flat on my back. Well, not *flat* on my back, there was too much equipment strapped onto me for that. But I hit the ground and all the air whooshed out of my lungs.

Faster than an eyeblink three snakes wrapped themselves around me. I saw another two wavering in the air, standing up like quivering antennas.

"No metal!" I screamed, as if they could hear or understand. "No metal!"

That didn't seem to bother them at all. They had latched onto me and they weren't going to let go. Could they sense the metal beneath my suit's plastic exterior? Could they burn their way through to it? Liquid sulfur would do the job pretty damned quick.

I couldn't sit up, not with their greedy arms wrapped all over me. I grabbed one of the snakes and pried it off me. It took both hands and all the strength of my servo-aided muscles. The underside of the thing had long, narrow mouths, twitching open and closed constantly. Disgusting. There was some kind of filaments around the lips, too. Really loathsome.

Fighting an urge to barf, I bent the snake over backwards, trying to break it. No go. It was rubbery and flexible as a garden hose. Blazing hot anger boiled up in me, real fury. These brainless sonsofbitches were trying to kill me! I twisted it, pounded its end on the red-hot rock, fought one leg loose and stomped on it with my boot.

It must have decided I wasn't edible. Or maybe I was giving it more pain that it wanted. All of a sudden all the snakes let loose of me and snapped back into their holes as if they had springs attached to their other ends. *Zip!* and they were gone.

Shaking inside, I slowly got to my feet again. Some scientists have a theory that the snakes are all connected to one big, huge underground organism. Or maybe there's more than one, but they communicate with each other. Either way, once it—or they— decided I was too much trouble to deal with, I wasn't bothered with 'em again.

But I didn't know that. I staggered on toward the return vehicle, scared, battered, bone weary, and very, *very* hot.

And there was the old Russian craft, up ahead. At first I thought it was a mirage, but sure enough it was the spacecraft, sitting on a little rise in the ground like a forgotten old monument to past glory.

Maybe I was just too tired to care, but it looked very unimpressive to me. Not much more than a small round disc that had sagged and half-collapsed on one side to reveal the crumpled remains of a dull metal ball beneath it, sitting on those baking, red-hot rocks. It reminded me of an old-fashioned can of soda pop that had been crushed by some powerful hand.

I staggered over to it and touched the collapsed metal sphere. It crumbled into powder. Sitting there for more than a century in this heat, in an atmosphere loaded with corrosive sulfur and chlorine compounds, the metal had just turned to dust. Like the mummies in old horror shows. Nothing left but dust.

I walked slowly around it anyway, letting my helmet camera record a full three-sixty view. History. The first man-made object to make it to the surface of another planet.

Just like me. I was going to be history, too. I was baking inside my suit. The temperature readout was hitting fifty; damned near two hundred in the old Fahrenheit scale, and that was *inside* the suit. I was being broiled alive. If it weren't for my monomolecular longjohns my skin would've been blistering.

Plodding along. I left old Venera 5 behind me, following the beep-beep of the return ship's beacon, hoping it was working okay and I was heading in the right direction. Can there be an electronic mirage? I mean, could I be wandering off into the oven-hot wilderness, chasing a signal that got warped somehow and is leading me away from the return vehicle?

Is there a return vehicle at all? I started to wonder. Maybe this is Hal's way of getting rid of me. Get the competition out of the way. Then it's him and Angel without any complications. No, that doesn't make any sense, I told myself. You're getting paranoid in this heat, going crazy.

I pushed on, one booted foot in front of the other. Wasn't making footprints, though; hot though it may be, the surface of Venus is solid rock. At least it is here. Solid and scorching hot. Over on the nightside, from what I'd heard, you can see the ground glowing red-hot.

". . . get through?" crackled in my earphones. "Do you copy?"

"I hear you!" I shouted, my throat so dry that my voice cracked. The storm, the electrical interference, must have ended. Or moved off.

Nothing but hissing static came through. Then the director's voice, ". . . signal's weak . . . up gain?" His message was breaking up. There was still a lot of interference between the orbiter and me.

"Am I on the right track?" I asked. "According to my radar plot I'm still five klicks from the ship. Please confirm."

Hal's voice crackled in my earphones, ". . . enera five! Great video, pal!"

Terrific. The video got through but our voice link is chopped up all to hell and back.

Then it hit me. If the video link is working, switch the voice communications to that channel. I told them what I was doing while I made the change on the comm panel.

"Can you hear me better now?" I asked, my voice still cracked and dry as dehydrated dust.

No answer. Crap, I thought, it isn't working.

Then, "We hear you. Weak but clear. Are you okay?"

I can't tell you how much better I felt with a solid link back to the orbiter. It didn't really change things. I was just as tired and hot and far from safety as before. But I wasn't alone anymore.

"According to the signals from your beacon and the return vehicle's," the director said, as calmly professional as ever, "you are less than five klicks from the ship."

"Five klicks, copy."

"That distance holds good if there's no atmospheric distortions warping the signals," he added.

"Thanks a lot," I groused.

Hal came on again and talked to me nonstop, trying to buck me up, keep me going. At first I wondered why he was doing the pep-talk routine, then I realized that I must be dragging along pretty damned slow. I put my life-support graph on the helmet screen. Yeah, air was low, water lower, and I was almost out of the heat-absorbing alloy.

I turned around three-sixty degrees and saw the ragged trail of molten alloy I was leaving behind me, like a robot with diarrhea. The alloy was shiny, new-looking against the cracked, worn old rocks. And there were lines curving along the ground, converging on the trail every few meters.

Snakes! I realized. They like metals. I turned back toward the distant rescue vehicle and made tracks as fast as I could.

Which wasn't all that fast. Inside the cumbersome suit I felt like Frankenstein's monster trying to play basketball, lumbering along, painfully slow.

I must have been describing all this into my helmet mike, talking nonstop. Hal kept talking, too.

And then the servo on my right knee seized up. The knee just froze, half bent, and I toppled over on my face with a thump that whacked my nose against the helmet's faceplate. Good thing, in a way. The pain kept me from blacking out. Blood spattered over my readout screens and the lower half of the faceplate. I must've screamed every obscenity I'd ever heard.

Hal and the controller both were yelling at me at once. "What happened? What's wrong?"

Through the pain of my broken nose I told them while I tried to get back on my feet. No go. My right leg was frozen in the half-bent position; there was no way I could walk. Blood was gushing down my throat.

So I crawled. Coughing, choking on my own blood, I crawled on my hands and knees, scraping along the blazing hot rocks with those damned snakes slithering behind me, feasting on the metal alloy trail I was leaving.

The radio crapped out again. Nothing but mumbles and hisses, with an occasional crackle so loud that I figured it must be from lightning. I couldn't look up to see if the clouds were flickering with light, but I saw a strange, sullen glow off on the horizon to my left.

". . . volcano . . ." came through the earphones.

Just what I needed. A volcanic eruption. It was too far away to be a direct threat, but in that undersea-thick atmosphere down on Venus' surface, volcanic eruptions can cause something like tidal waves, huge pressure waves that can push giant boulders for hundreds of kilometers.

Or knock over a flimsy rocket vehicle that's sitting on the plain waiting for me to reach it.

I'm not going to make it, I told myself.

"The hell you're not!" Hal snapped. I hadn't realized I'd spoken the words out loud.

"I can't go much farther," I said, glad that at least the radio link was back. "Running out of air, water, everything . . ."

"Hang tight, pal," he insisted. "Don't give up."

I muttered something about snake food. I rolled over on my side, completely exhausted, and saw that the snakes were gobbling up my alloy trail, getting closer to the source of the metal—me—all the time.

And then suddenly they all disappeared, reeled back into their holes so fast my eyes couldn't follow it.

Why? What would make them—

I heard a roar. A high-pitched banshee wail, really. Looking up as far as I could through the bloodied faceplate, I saw the sweetest sight of my life. A squat, bullet-shaped chunk of metal with a cluster of jet pods hanging off its ass end and three spindly, awkward legs unfolding out of its sides.

The return vehicle settled gently on the rocks half a dozen meters in front of me and released its jet pods with an ungainly thump. I crawled over to it with the last bit of my strength. The airlock hatch popped open and I hauled myself up into it.

The airlock was about as big as a shoebox but I tucked myself inside and leaned on the stud that closed the hatch and sealed it. I just sat there in that tight little metal cubbyhole and gasped into my helmet mike, "Take me up."

The acceleration from the booster rockets knocked me unconscious.

When I came to, I was on an air-cushion mattress in the orbiter's tiny infirmary. My face was completely bandaged except for holes for my eyes and mouth. They must have pumped enough painkillers in me to pacify the whole subcontinent of India. I felt somewhere between numb and floating.

Hal was there at my beside. And Angel.

They had flown the return vehicle to me, of course, once they got a good fix on my position. The little ship's cameras even got a good shot of the erupting volcano as it lifted up through the atmosphere—ahead of the pressure wave, thank goodness—and carried me safely to orbit.

"You did a great job, pal," Hunky Hal said, smiling his megawatt smile at me.

"We were so frightened," Angel said. "When the radio link went dead we thought . . ."

"Me too," I whispered. My voice wasn't up to anything more.

"We'll get an Oscar for this one," Hal said. "For sure."

For sure.

"Get some rest now," he went on. "I've gotta get over to the processing guys and see how they're morphing your video imagery."

I nodded. Angel looked down at me, sweet as her namesake, then turned to Hal. He slid an arm around her waist and together they left me lying there in the infirmary.

Lovers. I felt my heart break. Everything I'd done, all that I'd gone through, and it didn't help at all. He wanted her now.

And I still loved him so.

THE QUESTION

When—if ever—will we discover extraterrestrial intelligence?

Radio astronomers have been searching for intelligent signals from the stars for more than half a century. Despite a few false alarms, no such signals have been found. Why?

One possibility is the sheer size of the starry universe. Our Milky Way galaxy alone contains more than a hundred billion stars, and there are billions of galaxies out there. How many of them harbor intelligence and civilizations? It's a very large haystack, and the needles may be few and far between.

Another possibility is that we're using the wrong equipment. To expect alien creatures to be beaming radio signals across the parsecs is probably naïve. If such civilizations exist, they are most likely using very different technologies.

My own opinion is that alien civilizations are alien. *They don't think the way we do. They have different priorities, different desires, different needs.*

"The Question" is my humble attempt to depict what might happen if and when we do make contact. I was guided by the famous maxim of the twentieth-century English geneticist J.B.S. Haldane: "The universe is not only queerer than we imagine—it is queerer than we can imagine."

See what you think.

As soon as questions of will or decision
or choice of action arise, science is at a loss.
—Noam Chomsky

THE DISCOVERER

Not many men choose their honeymoon site for its clear night skies, nor do they leave their beds in the pre-dawn hours to climb up to the roof of their rented cottage. At least Hal Jacobs' bride understood his strange passion.

Linda Krauss-Jacobs, like her husband, was an amateur astronomer. In fact, the couple had met at a summer outing of the South Connecticut Astronomical Society. Now, however, she shivered in the moonless dark of the chill New Mexico night as Jacobs wrestled with the small but powerful electronically boosted telescope he was trying to set up on the sloping roof, muttering to himself as he worked in the dark.

"It'll be dawn soon," Linda warned.

"Yeah," said Hal. "Then we get back to bed."

That thought did not displease Linda. She was not as dedicated an astronomer as her husband. *Maybe dedicated isn't the right word*, she thought. Fanatic would be more like it. Still, there were three comets in the solar system that bore the Jacobs name, and he was intent on discovering more, honeymoon or not.

His mutterings and fumblings ceased. Linda knew he had the little telescope working at last.

"Can I see?" she asked.

"Sure," he said, without looking up from the tiny display screen. "In a min—hey! Look at that!"

Stepping carefully on the rounded roof tiles, he moved over enough so that she could peek over his shoulder at the cold green-tinted screen. A fuzzy blob filled its center.

"There wasn't anything like that in that location last night," Jacobs said, his voice trembling slightly.

"Is it a comet?" Linda wondered aloud.

"Got to be," he said. Then he added, "And a big one, too. Look how bright it is!"

THE RADIO ASTRONOMER

"It's not a comet," said Ellis de Groot. "That much is definite."

He was sitting behind his desk, leaning far back in his comfortable, worn old leather swivel chair, his booted feet resting on the edge of the desk. Yet he looked grim, worried. A dozen photographs of Comet Jacobs-Kawanashi were strewn across the desk top.

"How can you be so sure?" asked Brian Martinson, who sat in front of the desk, his eyes on the computer-enhanced photos.

Martinson was still young, but he was already balding and his once-trim waistline had expanded from too many hours spent at consoles and classrooms and not enough fresh air and exercise. Even so, his mind was sharp and quick; he had been the best astronomy student de Groot had ever had. He now ran the National Radio Astronomy Observatory in West Virginia.

De Groot was old enough to be Martinson's father, gray and balding, his face lined from years of squinting at telescope images and wheedling university officials and politicians for enough funding to continue searching the universe. He wore a rumpled open-necked plaid shirt and Levis so faded and shabby that they were the envy of the university's entire student body.

He swung his legs off the desk and leaned forward, toward the younger man. Tapping a forefinger on one of the photos, he lowered his voice to a whisper:

"Only nine people in the whole country know about this. We haven't released this information to the media yet, or even put it on the Net . . ." he paused dramatically.

"What is it?" Martinson asked, leaning forward himself.

"This so-called comet has taken up an orbit around Jupiter."

Martinson's jaw dropped open.

"It's not a natural event," de Groot went on. "We got a couple of NASA people to analyze the orbital mechanics. The thing was on a hyperbolic trajectory through the solar system. It applied thrust, altered its trajectory, and established a highly eccentric orbit around Jupiter. Over the course of the past three days it has circularized that orbit."

"It's intelligent," Martinson said, his voice hollow with awe.

"Got to be," agreed de Groot. "That's why we want you to try to establish radio contact with it."

THE NATIONAL SECURITY ADVISOR

Brian Martinson felt out of place in this basement office. He had gone through four separate security checkpoints to get into the stuffy little underground room, including a massive Marine Corps sergeant in full-dress uniform with a huge gun holstered at his hip, impassive and unshakable as a robot. But what really bothered him was the thought that the President of the United States was just upstairs from here, in the Oval Office.

The woman who glared at him from across her desk looked tough enough to lead a regiment of Marines into battle—which she had done, earlier in her career. Now Jo Costanza had even weightier responsibilities.

"You're saying that this is a spacecraft, piloted by intelligent alien creatures?" she asked. Her voice was diamond hard. The business suit she wore was a no-nonsense navy blue, her only jewelry a bronze Marine Corps globe and anchor on its lapel.

"It's a spacecraft," said Martinson. "Whether it's crewed or not we simply don't know."

"It's made no reply to your messages?"

"No, but—"

"Who authorized you to send messages to it?" snapped the third person in the office, a bland-looking guy with thinning slicked-back sandy hair and rimless eyeglasses that made him look owlish. He was wearing a light gray silk suit with a striped red and gray tie.

Martinson had put on the only suit he possessed for this meeting, the one he saved for international symposia; it was a conservative dark blue, badly wrinkled, and tight around the middle. Clearing his throat nervously, he replied, "Dr. Ogilvy authorized trying to make contact. He's head of the radio astronomy section of the National Science Foundation. That's where our funding comes from, and—"

"They went by protocol," Costanza said, making it sound as if she wished otherwise.

"But this is a national security matter," snapped the anonymous man.

"This is a *global* security matter," Martinson said.

Costanza and the other man stared at him.

"The spacecraft broke out of Jupiter orbit this morning," Martinson told them.

"It's heading here!" Costanza said in a breathless whisper.

"No," said Martinson. "It's heading out of the solar system."

Before they could sigh with relief, he added, "But it's sent us a message."

"I thought you said it made no reply!"

"It hasn't replied to our messages," Martinson said wearily. "But it's sent a message of its own."

He pulled his digital recorder out of his jacket pocket.

THE PRESIDENT OF THE UNITED STATES

His nervousness, Martinson realized, had not stemmed from being in the White House. It came from the message he carried. Now that he had played it, and explained it, to the National Security Advisor and her aide, he felt almost at ease as they led him upstairs to the Oval Office.

The President looked smaller than he did on television, but that square-jawed face was recognizable anywhere. And the famous steel-gray eyes, the "laser eyes" that the media made so much of: they seemed to be boring into Martinson, making him feel as if the President was trying to x-ray him.

After Martinson explained the situation once again, though, both he and the President relaxed a bit.

"Then this thing is no threat to us," said the President.

"No sir, it's not," Martinson replied. "It's an opportunity. You might say it's a godsend."

"Let me hear that message again," the President said.

Martinson pushed buttons on the recorder. It had not left his hand since he'd first yanked it out of his pocket in the National Security Advisor's office. His hand had been sweaty then, but now it barely trembled.

"It's searching for the start of the English section," he said as the little machine clicked and chirped. "They sent the same message in more than a hundred different languages."

The chirping stopped and a rich, pleasant baritone voice came from the tape recorder:

"Greeting to the English-speaking people of Earth. We are pleased to find intelligence wherever in the universe it may exist. We have finished our survey of your planetary system and are now leaving for our next destination. As a token of our esteem and good will, we will answer one question from your planet. Ask us anything you wish, and we will answer it to the best and fullest of our ability. But it can be one question only. You have seven of your days to contact us. After local midnight at your Greenwich meridian on the seventh day we will no longer reply to you."

The click of the digital recorder's off switch sounded like a rifle shot in the Oval Office.

The President heaved a long sigh. "They must have a sense of humor," he murmured.

"It's a hoax," said the four-star Air Force general sitting to one side of the President's desk. "Some wise-ass scientists have cooked up this scheme to get more funding for themselves."

"I resent that," Martinson said, with a tight smile. "And your own receivers must have picked up the message, it was sent in the broadest spectrum I've ever seen. Ask your technical specialists to trace the origin of the message. It came from the alien spacecraft."

The general made a sour face.

"You're certain that it's genuine, then," said the President.

"Yes, sir, I am," Martinson replied. "Kind of strange, but genuine."

"One question," muttered the President's science advisor, a man Martinson had once heard lecture at MIT.

"One question. That's all they'll answer."

"But why just one question?" Costanza demanded, her brow furrowed. "What's the point?"

"I suppose we could ask them why they've limited us to one question," said the science advisor.

"But that would count as our one question, wouldn't it?" Martinson pointed out.

The President turned to his science advisor. "Phil, how long would it take us to get out there and make physical contact with the alien ship?"

The bald old man shook his head sadly. "We simply don't have the resources to send a crewed mission in less than a decade. Even an unmanned spacecraft would need two years after launch, more or less, to reach the vicinity of Jupiter."

"They'd be long gone by then," said Costanza.

"They'll be out of the solar system in a week," Martinson said.

"One question," the President repeated.

"What should it be?"

"That's simple," said the Air Force general. "Ask them how their propulsion system works. If they can travel interstellar distances their propulsion system must be able to handle incredible energies. Get that and we've got the world by the tail!"

"Do you think they'd tell us?"

"They said they'd answer any question we ask."

"I would be more inclined to ask a more general question," said the science advisor, "such as how they reconcile quantum dynamics with relativistic gravity."

"Bullcrap!" the general snapped. "That won't do us any good."

"But it would," the science advisor countered. "If we can reconcile all the forces we will have unraveled the final secrets of physics. Everything else will fall into our laps."

"Too damned theoretical," the general insisted. "We've got the opportunity to get some hard, practical information and you want them to do your math homework for you."

The President's chief of staff, who had been silent up until this moment, said, "Well, what I'd like to know is how we can cure cancer and other diseases."

"AIDS," said the President. "If we could get a cure for AIDS during my administration . . ."

Costanza said, "Maybe the general's right. Their propulsion system could be adapted to other purposes, I imagine."

"Like weaponry," said the science advisor, with obvious distaste.

Martinson listened to them wrangling. His own idea was to ask the aliens about the Big Bang and how old the universe was.

Their voices rose. Everyone in the Oval Office had his or her own idea of what The Question should be. The argument became heated.

Finally the President hushed them all with a curt gesture. "If the eight people in this room can't come to an agreement, imagine what the Congress is going to do with this problem."

"You're going to tell Congress about this?"

"Got to," the President replied unhappily. "The aliens have sent this message out to every major language group in the world, according to

Dr. Martinson. It's not a secret anymore."

"Congress." The general groaned.

"That's nothing," said Costanza. "Wait till the United Nations sinks their teeth into this."

THE SECRETARY GENERAL

Two wars, a spreading famine in central Africa, a new *el niño* event turning half the world's weather crazy, and now this—aliens from outer space. The Secretary General sank deep into her favorite couch and wished she were back in Argentina, in the simple Andean village where she had been born. All she had to worry about then was getting good grades in school and fending off the boys who wanted to seduce her.

She had spent the morning with the COPUOS executive committee, and had listened with all her attention to their explanation of the enigmatic alien visitation. It sounded almost like a joke, a prank that some very bright students might try to pull—until the committee members began to fight over what The Question should be. Grown men and women, screaming at each other like street urchins!

Now the delegation from the Pan Asian Coalition sat before her, arrayed like a score of round-faced Buddhas in western business suits. Most of them wore dark gray; the younger members dared to dress in dark blue.

The Secretary General was famous—perhaps notorious—for her preference for the bright, bold colors of her Andean heritage. Her frock was dramatic red and gold, the colors of a mountain sunset.

The chairman of the group, who was Chinese, was saying, "Inasmuch as the Pan Asian Coalition represents the majority of the world population—"

"Nearly four billion people," added the Vietnamese delegate, sitting to the right of the Chinese. He was the youngest man in the group, slim and wiry and eager, his spiky unruly hair still dark and thick.

The chairman nodded slightly, his only concession to his colleague's interruption, then continued, "It is only fair and democratic that *our* organization should decide what The Question will be."

More than four billion people, the Secretary General thought, *yet not one woman has been granted a place on your committee*. She knew it rankled these men that they had to deal with her. She saw how displeased they were that her office bore so few trappings of hierarchical power: no desk, no long conference table, only a comfortable scattering of small couches and armchairs. The walls, of course, were electronic. Virtually any data stored in any computer in the world could be displayed at the touch of a finger.

The chairman had finished his little statement and laced his fingers together over the dark gray vest stretched across his ample stomach. *It is time for me to reply*, the Secretary General realized.

She took a sip from the crystal tumbler on the teak table beside her couch. She did not especially like the taste of carbonated water, but it was best to stay away from alcohol during these meetings.

"I recognize that the nations members of the Pan Asian Coalition hold the preponderance of the world's population," she said, stalling for time while she tried to think of the properly diplomatic phrasing, "but the decision as to what The Question shall be must be shared by all the world's peoples."

"The decision must be made by vote in the General Assembly," the chairman insisted quietly. "That is the only fair and democratic way to make the choice."

"And we have only five more days to decide," added the Vietnamese delegate.

The Secretary General said, "We have made some progress. The International Astronomical Union has decided that The Question will be sent from the radio telescope in Puerto Rico—"

"Arecibo," the Vietnamese amended impatiently.

"Yes, thank you," murmured the Secretary General. "Arecibo. The astronomers have sent a message to the aliens that we have chosen the Arecibo radio telescope to ask The Question and any other transmission from any other facility should be ignored."

"Thus the Americans have taken effective control of the situation," said the chairman, in the calm low voice of a man who has learned to control his inner rage.

"Not at all," the Secretary General replied. "Arecibo is an international facility; astronomers from all over the world work there."

"Under Yankee supervision."

"The International Astronomical Union—"

"Which is dominated by Americans and Europeans," shouted one of the other delegates.

"We will not tolerate their monopoly power politics!"

"Asia must make the decision!"

Stunned by the sudden vehemence of her visitors, the Secretary General said, "A moment ago you wanted the General Assembly to vote on the decision."

The chairman allowed a fleeting expression of chagrin to break his normally impassive features. "We took the liberty of polling the members of the General Assembly yesterday."

"Very informally," added the Vietnamese hastily. "Nothing binding, of course."

"Of course," said the Secretary General, surprised that her snoops had not reported this move to her.

"The result was far from satisfactory," the chairman admitted. "We received more than two hundred different questions."

"It appears extremely doubtful," said the Japanese member of the delegation, "that the General Assembly could agree on one single question within the remaining allowed time."

"Then how do you propose to resolve the matter?" the Secretary General asked.

They all looked to the chairman, even the Vietnamese delegate.

He cleared his throat, then answered, "We propose to decide what The Question will be within our own group, and then ask the General Assembly to ratify our decision."

"A simple yes or no vote," said the Vietnamese. "No thought required."

"I see," said the Secretary General. "That might work, although if the General Assembly voted against your proposal—"

"That will not come to pass," the chairman assured her. "The nations we represent will carry the vote."

"Your nations have the largest population," the Secretary General cautioned, "but not the largest number of representatives in the Assembly, where it is one vote to each nation."

"The Africans will vote with us."

"Are you certain?"

"If they want continued aid from us, they will."

The Secretary General wondered if the Africans might not want to ask the aliens how they can make themselves self-sufficient, but she kept that thought to herself. Instead she asked, "Have you settled on the question you wish to ask?"

The chairman's left cheek ticked once. "Not yet," he answered. "We are still discussing the matter."

"How close to a decision are you?"

A gloomy silence filled the room.

At last the young Vietnamese burst out, "They want to ask how they can live forever! What nonsense! The Question should be, How can we control our population growth!"

"We know how to control population growth," the Japanese delegate snarled. "That is not a fit question to ask the aliens."

"But our known methods are not working!" the Vietnamese insisted. "We must learn how we can make people *want* to control their births."

"Better to ask how we can learn to control impetuous young men who show no respect for their elders," snapped one of the grayest delegates.

The Secretary General watched in growing dismay as the delegates quarreled and growled at each other. Their voices rose to shouts, then screams. When they began attacking each other in a frenzy of martial arts violence, the Secretary General called for security, then hid behind her couch.

THE MEDIA MOGUL

"This is the greatest story since Moses parted the Red Sea!" Tad Trumble enthused. "I want our full resources behind it."

"Right, chief," said the seventeen executive vice presidents arrayed down the long conference table.

"I mean our *full* resources," Trumble said, pacing energetically a long the length of the table. He wore his yachting costume: navy blue double-breasted blazer over white duck slacks, colorful ascot and off-white shirt. He was a big man, tall and rangy, with a vigorous moustache and handsome wavy hair—both dyed to a youthful dark brown.

"I mean," he went on, clapping his big hands together hard enough to make the vice presidents jump, "I want to interview those aliens personally."

"You?" the most senior of the veeps exclaimed. "Yourself?"

"Danged right! Get them on-screen."

"But they haven't replied to any of our messages, chief," said the brightest of the female vice presidents. In truth, she was brighter than all the males, too.

"Not one peep out of them since they said they'd answer The Question," added the man closest to her.

Trumble frowned like a little boy who hadn't received quite what he'd wanted from Santa Claus. "Then we'll just have to send somebody out to their spacecraft and bang on their door until they open up."

"We can't do that," said one of the younger, less experienced toadies.

Whirling on the hapless young man, Trumble snapped, "Why the frick not?"

"W . . . well, we'd need a rocket and astronauts and—"

"My aerospace division has all that crap. I'll tell 'em to send one of our anchormen up there."

"In four days, chief?"

"Sure, why not? We're not the freakin' government, we can do things fast!"

"But the safety factor . . ."

Trumble shrugged. "If the rocket blows up it'll make a great story. So we lose an anchorman, so what? Make a martyr outta him. Blame the aliens."

It took nearly an hour for the accumulated vice presidents to gently, subtly talk their boss out of the space mission idea.

"Okay, then," Trumble said, still pacing, his enthusiasm hardly dented, "how about this? We sponsor a contest to decide what The Question should be!"

"That's great!" came the immediate choral reply.

"Awesome."

"Fabulous."

"Inspired."

"Danged right," Trumble admitted modestly. "Ask people all over the country—all over the freakin' *world*—what they think The Question should be. Nobody'll watch anything but our channels!"

Another round of congratulations surged down the table.

"But get one thing straight," Trumble said, his face suddenly very serious. He had managed to pace himself back to his own chair at the head of the table.

Gripping the back of the empty chair with both white-knuckled hands, he said, "I win the contest. Understand? No matter how many people respond, *I'm* the one who makes up The Question. Got that?"

All seventeen heads nodded in unison.

THE POPE

"It is not a problem of knowledge," said Cardinal Horvath, his voice a sibilant whisper, "but rather a problem of morality."

The Pope knew that Horvath used that whisper to get attention. Each of the twenty-six cardinals in his audience chamber leaned forward on his chair to hear the Hungarian prelate.

"Morality?" asked the Pope. He had been advised by his staff to wear formal robes for this meeting. Instead, he had chosen to present himself to his inner circle of advisors in a simple white linen suit. The cardinals were all arrayed in their finest, from scarlet skullcaps to Gucci shoes.

"Morality," Horvath repeated. "Is this alien spaceship sent to us by God or by the devil?"

The Pope glanced around the gleaming ebony table. His cardinals were clearly uneasy with Horvath's question. They believed in Satan, of course, but it was more of a theoretical belief, a matter of catechistic foundations that were best left underground and out of sight in this modern age. In a generation raised on *Star Trek*, the idea that aliens from outer space might be sent by the devil seemed medieval, ridiculous.

And yet . . .

"These alien creatures," Horvath asked, "why do they not show themselves to us? Why do they offer to answer one question and only one?"

Cardinal O'Shea nodded. He was a big man, with a heavy, beefy face and flaming red hair that was almost matched by his bulbous imbiber's nose.

"You notice, don't you," O'Shea said in his sweet clear tenor voice, "that all the national governments are arguing about which question to ask. And what are they suggesting for The Question? How can they get more power, more wealth, more comfort and ease from the knowledge of these aliens."

"Several suggestions involve curing desperate diseases," commented Cardinal Ngono drily. "If the aliens can give us a cure for AIDS or ebola, I would say they are doing God's work."

"By their fruits you shall know them," the Pope murmured.

"That is exactly the point," Horvath said, tapping his fingers on the gleaming table top. "Why do they insist on answering only one question? Does that bring out the best in our souls, or the worst?"

Before they could discuss the cardinal's question, the Pope said, "We have been asked by the International Astronomical Union's Catholic members to contribute our considered opinion to their deliberations. How should we respond?"

"There are only three days left," Cardinal Sarducci pointed out.

"How should we respond?" the Pope repeated.

"Ignore the aliens," Horvath hissed. "They are the work of the devil, sent to tempt us."

"What evidence do you have of that?" Ngono asked pointedly.

Horvath stared at the African for a long moment. At last he said, "When God sent His Redeemer to mankind, He did not send aliens in a spaceship. He sent the Son of Man, who was also the Son of God."

"That was a long time ago," came a faint voice from the far end of the table.

"Yes," O'Shea agreed. "In today's world Jesus would be ignored . . . or locked up as a panhandler."

Horvath sputtered.

"If God wanted to get our attention," Ngono said, "this alien spacecraft has certainly accomplished that."

"Let us assume, then," said the Pope, "that we are agreed to offer some response to the astronomers' request. What should we tell them?"

Horvath shook his head and folded his arms across his chest in stubborn silence.

"Are you asking, Your Holiness, if we should frame The Question for them?"

The Pope shrugged slightly. "I am certain they would like to have our suggestion for what The Question should be."

"How can we live in peace?"

"How can we live without disease?" Ngono suggested.

"How can we end world hunger?"

Horvath slapped both hands palm down on the table. "You all miss the point. The Question should be—must be!—how can we bring all of God's people into the One True Church?"

Most of the cardinals groaned.

"That would set the ecumenical movement back to the Middle Ages!"

"It would divide the world into warring camps!"

"Not if the aliens are truly sent by God," Horvath insisted. "But if they are the devil's minions, then of course they will cause us grief."

The Pope sagged back in his chair. *Horvath is an atavism, a walking fossil, but he has a valid point*, the Pope said to himself. *It's almost laughable. We can test whether or not the aliens are sent by God by taking a chance on fanning the flames of division and hatred that will destroy us all.*

He felt tired, drained—and more than a little afraid. *Perhaps Horvath is right and these aliens are a test.*

One Question. He knew what he would ask, if the decision were entirely his own. And the knowledge frightened him. Deep in his soul, for the first time since he'd been a teenager, the Pope knew that he wanted to ask if God really existed.

THE MAN IN THE STREET

"I think it's all a trick," said Jake Belasco, smirking into the TV camera. "There ain't no aliens and there never was."

The blonde interviewer had gathered enough of a crowd around her and her cameraman that she was glad the station had sent a couple of uniformed security lugs along. The shopping mall was fairly busy at this time of the afternoon and the crowd was building up fast. Too bad the first "man in the street" she picked to interview turned out to be this beer-smelling yahoo.

"So you don't believe the aliens actually exist," replied the blonde interviewer, struggling to keep her smile in place. "But the government seems to be taking the alien spacecraft seriously."

"Ahhh, it's all a lotta baloney to pump more money into NASA. You wait, you'll see. There ain't no aliens and there never was."

"Well, thank you for your opinion," the interviewer said. She turned slightly and stuck her microphone under the nose of a sweet-faced young woman with startling blue eyes.

"And do you think the aliens are nothing more than a figment of NASA's public relations efforts?"

"Oh no," the young woman replied, in a soft voice. "No, the aliens are very real."

"You believe the government, then."

"I *know* the aliens exist. They took me aboard their spacecraft when I was nine years old."

The interviewer closed her eyes and silently counted to ten as the young woman began to explain in intimate detail the medical procedures that the aliens subjected her to.

"I'm carrying their seed now," she said, still as sweetly as a mother crooning a lullaby. "My babies will all be half aliens."

The interviewer wanted to move on to somebody reasonably sane, but the sweet young woman was gripping her microphone with both hands and would not let go.

THE CHAIRMAN

"People, if we can't come up with a satisfactory question, the politicians are going to take the matter out of our hands!"

The meeting hall was nearly half filled, with more men and women arriving every minute. *Too many*, Madeleine Dubois thought as she stood at the podium with the rest of the committee seated on the stage behind her. Head of the National Science Foundation's astronomy branch, she had the dubious responsibility of coming up with a recommendation from the American astronomical community for The Question—before noon, Washington time.

"Are you naive enough to think for one minute," challenged a portly bearded young astronomer, "that the politicians are going to listen to what we say?"

Dubois had battled her way through glass ceilings in academia and government. She had no illusions, but she recognized an opportunity when she saw one.

"They'll have no choice but to accept our recommendation," she said, with one eye on the news reporters sitting in their own section of the big auditorium. "We represent the only uninterested, unbiased group in the country. We speak for science, for the betterment of the human race. Who else has been actively working to find extraterrestrial intelligence for all these many years?"

To her credit, Dubois had worked out a protocol with the International Astronomical Union, after two days of frantic, frenzied negotiations. Each member nation's astronomers would decide on a question, then the Union's executive committee—of which she was chair this year—would vote on the various suggestions.

By noon, she told herself, *we'll present The Question we've chosen to the leaders of every government on Earth. And to the news media, of course. The politicians will have to accept our choice. There'll only be about seven hours left before the deadline falls.*

She had tried to keep this meeting as small as possible, yet by the time every committee within the astronomy branch of NSF had been notified, several hundred men and women had hurried to Washington to participate. Each of them had her or his own idea of what The Question should be.

Dubois knew what she wanted to ask: What was the state of the universe before the Big Bang? She had never been able to accept the concept that all the matter and energy of the universe originated out of quantum fluctuations in the vacuum. Even if that was right, it meant that a vacuum existed before the Big Bang, and where did *that* come from?

So patiently, tirelessly, she tried to lead the several hundred astronomers toward a consensus on The Question. Within two hours she gave up trying to get her question accepted; within four hours she was despairing of reaching any agreement at all.

Brian Martinson sat in a back row of the auditorium, watching his colleagues wrangle like lawyers. *No, worse*, he thought. *They're behaving like cosmologists!*

An observational astronomer who believed in hard data, Martinson had always considered cosmologists to be theologians of astronomy. They took a pinch of observational data and added tons of speculation, carefully disguised as mathematical formulations. Every time a new observation was made, the cosmologists invented seventeen new explanations for it—most of them contradicting one another.

He sighed. *This is getting us noplace. There won't be an agreement here, any more than there was one in the Oval Office, five days ago.* He peered at his wristwatch, then pushed himself out of the chair.

The man sitting next to him asked, "You're leaving? Now?"

"Got to," Martinson explained over the noise of rancorous shouting. "I've got an Air Force jet waiting to take me to Arecibo."

"Oh?"

"I'm supposed to be supervising the big dish when we ask The Question." Martinson looked around at his red-faced, flustered colleagues, then added, "If we ever come to an agreement on what it should be."

THE DICTATOR

"Arecibo is only a few hours from here, by jet transport," the Dictator repeated, staring out the ceiling-high windows of his office at the troops assembled on the plaza below. "Our paratroops can get there and seize the radio telescope facility well before eighteen hundred hours."

His minister of foreign affairs, a career diplomat who had survived four *coups d'etat* and two revolutions by the simple expedient of agreeing with whichever clique seized power, cast a dubious eye at his latest Maximum Leader.

"A military attack on Puerto Rico is an attack on the United States," he said, as mildly as he could, considering the wretched state of his stomach.

The Dictator turned to glare at him. "So?"

"The Yankees will not let an attack on their territory go unanswered. They will strike back at us."

The Dictator toyed with his luxuriant moustache, a maneuver he used whenever he wanted to hide inner misgivings. At last he laughed and said, "What can the Gringos do, once I have asked The Question?"

The foreign minister knew better than to argue. He simply sat in the leather wing chair and stared at the Dictator, who looked splendid in his full-dress military uniform with all the medals and the sash of office crossing his proud chest.

"Yes," the Dictator went on, convincing himself (if not his foreign minister), "it is all so simple. While the scientists and world leaders fumble and agonize over what The Question should be, I—your Maximum Leader—knew instantly what I wanted to ask. I knew it! Without a moment of hesitation."

The spacious, high-ceilinged palace room seemed strangely warm to the foreign minister. He pulled the handkerchief from the breast pocket of his jacket and mopped his fevered brow.

"Yes," the Dictator was going on, congratulating himself, "while the philosophers and weaklings try to reach an agreement, I act. I seize the radio telescope and send to the alien visitors The Question. *My* question!"

"The man of action always knows what to do," the foreign minister parroted.

"Exactly! I knew what The Question should be, what it must be. How can I rule the world? What other question matters?"

"But to ask it, you must have the Arecibo facility in your grasp."

"For only a few hours. Even one single hour will do."

"Can your troops operate the radio telescope?"

A cloud flickered across the Dictator's face, but it passed almost as soon as it appeared.

"No, of course not," he replied genially. "They are soldiers, not scientists. But the scientists who make up the staff at Arecibo will operate the radio telescope for us."

"You are certain . . . ?"

"With guns at their heads?" The Dictator threw his head back and laughed. "Yes, they will do what they are told. We may have to shoot one or two, to convince the others, but they will do what they are told, never fear."

"And afterward? How do the troops get away?"

The Dictator shrugged. "There has not been enough time to plan for removing them from Arecibo."

Eyes widening, stomach clenching, the foreign minister gasped, "You're going to leave them there?"

"They are all volunteers."

"And when the Yankee Marines arrive? What then?"

"What difference? By then I will have the answer from the aliens. What are the lives of a handful of martyrs compared to the glory of ruling the entire world?"

The foreign minister struggled to his feet. "You must forgive me, my leader. My stomach . . ."

And he lurched toward the bathroom, hoping he could keep himself from retching until he got to the toilet.

THE RADIO ASTRONOMER

At least the military was operating efficiently, Brian Martinson thought as he winged at supersonic speed high above the Atlantic. An

Air Force sedan had been waiting for him in front of the NSF headquarters; its sergeant driver whisked him quickly through the downtown Washington traffic and out to Andrews Air Force Base, where a sleek swept-wing, twin jet VIP plane was waiting to fly him to Puerto Rico.

Looking idly through the small window at his side, his mind filled with conflicting ideas about the aliens and The Question, Martinson realized that he could actually see the Gulf Stream slicing through the colder Atlantic waters, a bright blue ribbon of warmth and life against the steely gray of the ocean.

Looking out to the flat horizon he could make out the ghost of a quarter Moon hanging in the bright sky. Somewhere beyond the Moon, far, far beyond it, the aliens in their spacecraft were already on their way out of the solar system.

What do they want of us? Martinson wondered. *Why did they bother to make contact with us at all, if all they're willing to do is answer one damned question? Maybe they're not such good guys. Maybe this is all a weird plot to get us to tear ourselves apart. One question. Half the world is arguing with the other half over what The Question should be. With only a few hours left, they still haven't been able to decide.*

Sure, he thought to himself, *it could all be a set-up. They tell us we can ask one question, knowing that we might end up fighting a goddamned war over what The Question should be. What better way to divide us, and then walk in and take over the remains?*

No, a saner voice in his mind answered. *That's paranoid stupidity. Their spacecraft is already zooming out of the solar system, heading high above the ecliptic. They won't get within a couple of lighthours of Earth, for god's sake. They're not coming to invade us. By this time tomorrow they'll be on their way to Epsilon Eridani, near as I can figure their trajectory.*

But what better way to divide us? he repeated silently. *They couldn't have figured out a more diabolical method of driving us all nuts if they tried.*

THE TEENAGERS

"I think it's way cool," said Andy Hitchcock, as he lounged in the shade of the last oak tree left in Oak Park Acres.

"You mean the aliens?" asked Bob Wolfe, his inseparable buddy.

"Yeah, sure. Aliens from outer space. Imagine the stuff they must have. Coolisimo, Bobby boy."

"I guess."

The two teenagers had been riding their bikes through the quiet winding streets of Oak Park Acres most of the morning. They should have been in school, but the thought of another dreary day of classes while there were aliens up in the sky and the TV was full of people arguing about what The Question ought to be—it was too much to expect a guy to sit still in school while all this was going on.

Andy fished his cell phone from his jeans and thumbed the FM radio app. Didn't matter which station, they were all broadcasting nothing but news about The Question. Even the hardest rock stations were filled with talk instead of music. Not even bong-bong was going out on the air this morning.

". . . still no official statement from the White House," an announcer's deep voice was saying, "where the President is meeting in the Oval Office with the leaders of Congress and his closest advisors . . ."

Tap. Andy changed the station. ". . . trading has been suspended for the day here at the Stock Exchange as all eyes turn skyward . . ."

Tap. ". . . European Community voted unanimously to send a note of protest to the United Nations concerning the way in which the General Assembly has failed . . ."

Tap. Andy turned the radio off.

"Those fartbrains still haven't figured out what The Question will be," Bob said, with the calm assurance that anyone older than himself shouldn't really have the awesome power of making decisions, anyway.

"They better decide soon," Andy said, peering at his wristwatch. "There's only a few hours left."

"They'll come up with something."

"Yeah, I suppose."

Both boys were silent for a while, sprawled out on the grass beneath the tree, their bikes resting against its trunk.

"Man, I know what I'd ask those aliens," Bob said at last.

"Yeah? What?"

"How can I ace the SATs? That's what I'd ask."

Andy thought a moment, then nodded. "Good thing you're not in charge, pal."

THE RADIO ASTRONOMER

Brian Martinson had never seen an astronomical facility so filled with tension.

Radio telescope observatories usually look like the basement of an electronics hobby shop, crammed with humming consoles and jury-rigged wiring, smelling of fried circuit boards and stale pizza, music blaring from computer CD slots—anything from heavy metal to Mahler symphonies.

Today was different. People were still dressed in their usual tropical casual style: their cut-offs and sandals made Martinson feel stuffy in the suit he'd worn for the meeting in Washington. But the Arecibo facility was deathly quiet except for the ever-present buzz of the equipment. Everyone looked terribly uptight, pale, nervous.

After a routine tour of the facility, Martinson settled into the director's office, where he could look out the window at the huge metal-mesh covered dish carved into the lush green hillside. Above the thousand-foot-wide reflector dangled the actual antenna, with its exquisitely tuned maser cooled down and ready to go.

The director herself sat at her desk, fidgeting nervously with the desktop computer, busying herself with it for the last few hours to the deadline. She was an older woman, streaks of gray in her buzz-cut hair, bone thin, dressed in a faded pair of cut-off jeans and a T-shirt that hung limply from her narrow shoulders. Martinson wondered how she could keep from shivering in the icy blast coming from the air-conditioning vents.

There were three separate telephone consoles on the desk: one was a direct line to the White House, one a special link to the U.N. Secretary General's office in New York. Martinson had asked the woman in charge of communications to keep a third line open for Madeleine Dubois, who—for all he knew—was still trying to bring order out of the chaotic meeting at NSF headquarters.

He looked at his wristwatch. Four p.m. *We've got three hours to go. Midnight Greenwich time is seven p.m. here. Three hours.*

He felt hungry. A bad sign. Whenever he was really wired tight, he got the nibbles. His overweight problem had started during the final exams of his senior undergrad year and had continued right through graduate school and his post-doc. He kept expecting things to settle down, but the higher he went in the astronomical community the more responsibility he shouldered. And the more pressure he felt the more he felt the urge to munch.

What do I do if the White House tells me one thing and the U.N. something else? he wondered. *No, that won't happen. They'll work it out between them. Dubois will present the IAU's recommendation to the President and the Secretary General at the same time.*

Across the desk, the director tapped frenetically on her keyboard. What could she be doing? Martinson wondered. *Busywork, came his answer. Keeping her fingers moving; it's better than gnawing your nails.*

He turned his squeaking plastic chair to look out the window again. Gazing out at the lush tropical forest beyond the rim of the telescope dish, he tried to calm the rising tension in his own gut. *The phone will ring any second now*, he told himself. *They'll give you The Question and you send it out to the aliens and that'll be that.*

What if you don't like their choice? Martinson asked himself. *Doesn't matter. When the White House talks, you listen.* The only possible problem would be if Washington and the U.N. aren't in synch.

The late afternoon calm was shattered by the roar of planes, several of them, flying low. Big planes, from the sound of it. Martinson felt the floor tremble beneath his feet.

The director looked up from her display screen, an angry scowl on her face. "What kind of brain-dead jerks are flying over us? This airspace is restricted!"

Martinson saw the planes: big lumbering four-engined jobs, six of them in two neat vees.

"Goddamned news media," the director grumbled.

"Six planes?" Martinson countered. "I don't think so. They looked like military jets."

"Didn't see any Air Force stars on 'em."

"They went by so fast . . ."

His words died in his throat. Through the window he saw dozens of parachutes dotting the soft blue sky, drifting slowly, gracefully to the ground.

"What the hell?" the director growled.

His heart clutching in his chest, Martinson feared that he knew what was happening.

"Do you have a pair of binoculars handy?" he croaked, surprised at how dry his throat was.

The director wordlessly opened a drawer in her desk, reached in, and handed Martinson a heavy leather case. With fumbling hands he opened it and pulled out a big black set of binoculars.

"Good way to check out the antenna without leaving my office," she explained, tight-lipped.

Martinson put the lenses to his eyes and adjusted the focus. His hands were shaking so badly now that he had to lean his forearms against the windowsill.

The parachutists came into view. They wore camouflage military uniforms. He could see assault rifles and other weapons slung over their shoulders.

"Parachute troops," he whispered.

"Why the hell would the army drop parachute soldiers here? What do they think—"

"They're not ours," Martinson said. "That's for sure."

The director's eyes went wide. "What do you mean? Whose are they?"

Shaking his head, Martinson said, "I don't know. But they're not ours, I'm certain of that."

"They have to be ours! Who else would . . ." She stopped, her mind drawing the picture at last.

Without another word, the director grabbed the phone that linked with Washington and began yelling into it. Martinson licked his lips, made his decision, and headed for the door.

"Where're you going?" the director yelled at him.

"To stop them," he yelled back, over his shoulder.

Heart pounding, Martinson raced down the corridor that led to the control center. Wishing he had exercised more and eaten leaner cuisine, he pictured himself expiring of a heart attack before he could get the job done.

More likely you'll be gunned down by some soldier, he told himself.

He reached the control room at last, bursting through the door, startling the already-nervous kids working the telescope.

"We're being invaded," he told them.

"Invaded?"

"What're you talking about?"

"Parachute troops are landing outside. They'll be coming in here in a couple of minutes."

"Parachute troops?"

"But why?"

"Who?"

The youngsters at the consoles looked as scared as Martinson felt. He spotted an empty chair, a little typist's seat off in a corner of the windowless room, and went to it. Wheeling it up to the main console, Martinson explained:

"I don't know who sent them, but they're not our own troops. Whoever they are, they want to grab the telescope and send out their own version of The Question. We've got to stop them."

"Stop armed troops?"

"How?"

"By sending out The Question ourselves. If we get off The Question before they march in here, then it doesn't matter what they want, they'll be too late."

"Has Washington sent The Question?"

"No," Martinson admitted.

"The United Nations?"

He shook his head as he sat at the main console and scanned the dials. "Are we fully powered up?"

"Up and ready," said the technician seated beside him.

"How do I—"

"We rigged a voice circuit," the technician said. "Here."

He picked up a headset and handed it to Martinson, who slipped it over his sweaty hair and clapped the one earphone to his ear. Adjusting the pin-sized microphone in front of his lips, he asked, "How do I transmit?"

The technician pointed to a square black button on the console.

"But you don't have The Question yet," said an agonized voice from behind him.

Martinson did not reply. He leaned a thumb on the black button.

The door behind him banged open. A heavily accented voice cried, "You are now our prisoners! You will do as I say!"

Martinson did not turn around. Staring at the black button of the transmitter, he spoke softly into his microphone, four swift whispered words that were amplified by the most powerful radio transmitter on the planet and sent with the speed of light toward the departing alien spacecraft.

Four words. The Question. It was a plea, an entreaty, a prayer from the depths of Martinson's soul, a supplication that was the only question he could think of that made any sense, that gave the human race any hope for the future:

"How do we decide?"

WATERBOT

Sometimes you have to run like hell to stay ahead of the parade.

A few years ago (and several years after I wrote "Waterbot") the news media ballyhooed the announcement that famed movie director James Cameron had helped to form a new company called Planetary Resources which, apparently, will look into the possibilities of mining asteroids.

"Waterbot" is a story set on the frontier of the Asteroid Belt. There are millions upon millions of chunks of rock, metal and ice drifting in that region, between the orbits of Mars and Jupiter. An interplanetary bonanza that contains more mineral wealth than the entire planet Earth can provide.

But "Waterbot" is about another frontier, as well: the frontier of human/machine interactions. Can a human being form an emotional relationship with an intelligent computer?

Or maybe even beat it at chess?

"WAKE UP, dumbbutt. Jerky's ventin' off."

I'd been asleep in my bunk. I blinked awake, kind of groggy, but even on the little screen set into the bulkhead at the foot of the bunk I could see the smirk on Donahoo's ugly face. He always called JRK49N "Jerky" and seemed to enjoy it when something went wrong with the vessel—which was all too often.

I sat up in the bunk and called up the diagnostics display. Rats! Donahoo was right. A steady spray of steam was spurting out of the main water tank. The attitude jets were puffing away, trying to compensate for the thrust.

"You didn't even get an alarm, didja?" Donahoo said. "Jerky's so old and feeble your safety systems are breakin' down. You'll be lucky if you make it back to base."

He said it like he enjoyed it. I thought that if he wasn't so much bigger than me I'd enjoy socking him square in his nasty mouth. But I had to admit he was right. Forty-niner was ready for the scrap heap.

"I'll take care of it," I muttered to Donahoo's image, glad that it'd take more than five minutes for my words to reach him back at Vesta—and the same amount of time for his next wise-ass crack to get to me. He was snug and comfortable back at the corporation's base at Vesta while I was more than ninety million kilometers away, dragging through the Belt on JRK49N.

I wasn't supposed to be out here. With my brand-new diploma in my eager little hand I'd signed up for a logistical engineer's job, a cushy safe posting at Vesta, the second-biggest asteroid in the Belt. But once I got there Donahoo jiggered the assignment list and got me stuck on this pile of junk for a six-month' tour of boredom and aggravation.

It's awful lonely out in the Belt. Flatlanders back Earthside picture the Asteroid Belt as swarming with rocks so thick a ship's in danger of getting smashed. Reality is the Belt's mostly empty space, dark and cold and bleak. A man runs more risk of going nutty out there all by himself than getting hit by a 'roid big enough to do any damage.

JRK49N was a waterbot. Water's the most important commodity you can find in the Belt. Back in those days the news nets tried to make mining the asteroids seem glamorous. They liked to run stories about prospector families striking it rich with a nickel-iron asteroid, the kind that has a few hundred tons of gold and platinum in it as impurities. So much gold and silver and such had been found in the Belt that the market for precious metals back on Earth had gone down the toilet.

But the *really* precious stuff was water. Still is. Plain old H_2O. Basic for life support. More valuable than gold, off-Earth. The cities on the Moon needed water. So did the colonies they were building in cislunar space, and the rock rats' habitat at Ceres and the research station orbiting Jupiter and the construction crews at Mercury.

Water was also the best fuel for chemical rockets, too. Break it down into hydrogen and oxygen and you got damned good specific impulse.

You get the picture. Finding icy asteroids wasn't glamorous, like striking a ten-kilometer-wide rock studded with gold, but it was important. The corporations wouldn't send waterbots out through the Belt if there wasn't a helluva profit involved. People paid for water: paid plenty.

So waterbots like weary old Forty-niner crawled through the Belt, looking for ice chunks. Once in a while a comet would come whizzing by, but they usually had too much delta vee for a waterbot to catch up to 'em. We cozied up to icy asteroids, melted the ice to liquid water, and filled our tanks with it.

The corporation had fifty waterbots combing the Belt. They were built to be completely automated, capable of finding ice-bearing asteroids and carrying the water back to the corporate base at Vesta.

But there were two problems about having the waterbots go out on their own:

First, the lawyers and politicians had this silly rule that a human being had to be present on the scene before any company could start mining anything from an asteroid. So it wasn't enough to send out waterbots, you had to have at least one human being riding along on them to make the claim legal.

The second reason was maintenance and repair. The 'bots were old enough so's something was always breaking down on them and they needed somebody to fix it. They carried little turtle-sized repair robots, of course, but those suckers broke down too, just like everything else. So I was more or less a glorified repairman on JRK49N. And almost glad of it, in a way. If the ship's systems worked perfectly I would've gone bonzo with nothing to do for months on end.

And there was a bloody war going on in the Belt, to boot. The history discs call it the Asteroid Wars, but it mostly boiled down to a fight between Humphries Space Systems and Astro Corporation for control of all the resources in the Belt. Both corporations hired mercenary troops, and there were plenty of freebooters out in the Belt, too. People got killed. Some of my best friends got killed, and I came as close to death as I ever want to be.

The mercenaries usually left waterbots alone. There was a kind of unwritten agreement between the corporations that water was too important to mess around with. But some of the freebooters jumped waterbots, killed the poor dumbjohns riding on them, and sold the water at a cut-rate price wherever they could.

So, grumbling and grousing, I pushed myself out of the bunk. Still in my sweaty, wrinkled skivvies, I ducked through the hatch that connected my sleeping compartment with the bridge. My compartment, the bridge, the closet-sized galley, the even smaller lavatory, life-support equipment and food stores were all jammed into a pod no bigger than it had to be, and the pod itself was attached to Forty-niner's main body by a set of struts. Nothing fancy or even comfortable. The corporation paid for water, not creature comforts.

Calling it a bridge was being charitable. It was nothing more than a curving panel of screens that displayed the ship's systems and controls, with a wraparound glassteel window above it and a high-backed reclinable command chair shoehorned into the middle of it all. The command chair was more comfortable than my bunk, actually. Crank it back and you could drift off to sleep in no time.

I slipped into the chair, the skin of my bare legs sticking slightly to its fake leather padding, which was cold enough to make me break out in goosebumps.

The main water tank was still venting, but the safety alarms were as quiet as monks on a vow of silence.

"Niner, what's going on?" I demanded.

Forty-niner's computer-generated voice answered, "A test, sir. I am venting some of our cargo." The voice was male, sort of: bland, soft and sexless. The corporate psychotechnicians claimed it was soothing, but after a few weeks alone with nobody else it could drive you batty.

"Stop it. Right now."

"Yes, sir."

The spurt of steam stopped immediately. The logistics graph told me we'd only lost a few hundred kilos of water, although we were damned near the redline on reaction mass for the attitude jets.

Frowning at the displays, I asked, "Why'd you start pumping out our cargo?"

For a heartbeat or two Forty-niner didn't reply. That's a long time for a computer. Just when I started wondering what was going on, "A test, sir. The water jet's actual thrust matched the amount of thrust calculated to within a tenth of a percent."

"Why'd you need to test the amount of thrust you can get out of a water jet?"

"Emergency maneuver, sir."

"Emergency? What emergency?" I was starting to get annoyed. Forty-niner's voice was just a computer synthesis, but it sure *felt* like he was being evasive.

"In case we are attacked, sir. Additional thrust can make it more difficult for an attacker to target us."

I could feel my blood pressure rising. "Attacked? Nobody's gonna attack us."

"Sir, according to Tactical Manual 7703, it is necessary to be prepared for the worst that an enemy can do."

Tactical Manual 7703. For god's sake. I had pumped that and a dozen other texts into the computer just before we started this run through the Belt. I had intended to read them, study them, improve my mind—and my job rating—while coasting through the big, dark loneliness out there. Somehow I'd never gotten around to reading any of them. But Forty-niner did, apparently.

Like I said, you've got a lot of time on your hands cruising through the Belt. So I had brought in a library of reference texts. And then ignored them. I also brought in a full-body virtual reality simulations suit and enough erotic VR programs to while away the lonely hours. Stimulation for mind *and* body, I thought.

But Forty-niner kept me so busy with repairs I hardly had time even for the sex sims. Donahoo was right, the old bucket was breaking down around my ears. I spent most of my waking hours patching up Forty-niner's failing systems. The maintenance robots weren't much help: they needed as much fixing work as all the other systems, combined.

And all the time I was working—and sleeping, too, I guess—Forty-niner was going through my library, absorbing every word and taking them all seriously.

"I don't care what the tactical manual says," I groused, "nobody's going to attack a waterbot."

"Four waterbots have been attacked so far this year, sir. The information is available in the archives of the news media transmissions."

"Nobody's going to attack us!"

"If you say so, sir." I swear he—I mean, *it*—sounded resentful, almost sullen.

"I say so."

"Yes, sir."

"You wasted several hundred kilos of water," I grumbled.

Immediately that damned soft voice replied, "Easily replaced, sir. We are on course for asteroid 78-13. Once there we can fill our tanks and start for home."

"Okay," I said. "And lay off that tactical manual."

"Yes, sir."

I felt pretty damned annoyed."What else have you been reading?" I demanded.

"The astronomy text, sir. It's quite interesting. The ship's astrogation program contains the rudiments of positional astronomy, but the text is much deeper. Did you realize that our solar system is only one of several million that have been—"

"Enough!" I commanded. "Quiet down. Tend to maintenance and astrogation."

"Yes, sir."

I took a deep breath and started to think things over. Forty-niner's a computer, for god's sake, not my partner.

It's supposed to be keeping watch over the ship's systems, not poking into military tactics or astronomy texts.

I had brought a chess program with me, but after a couple of weeks I'd given it up. Forty-niner beat me every time. It never made a bad move and never forgot anything. Great for my self-esteem. I wound up playing solitaire a lot, and even then I had the feeling that the nosy busybody was just itching to tell me which card to play next.

If the damned computer wasn't buried deep in the vessel's guts, wedged in there with the fusion reactor and the big water tanks, I'd be tempted to grab a screwdriver and give Forty-niner a lobotomy.

At least the vessel was running smoothly enough, for the time being. No red lights on the board, and the only amber one was because the attitude jets' reaction mass was low. Well, we could suck some nitrogen out of 78-13 when we got there. The maintenance log showed that it was time to replace the meteor bumpers around the fusion drive. Plenty of time for that, I told myself. Do it tomorrow.

"Forty-niner," I called, "show me the spectrographic analysis of asteroid 78-13."

The graph came up instantly on the control board's main screen. Yes, there was plenty of nitrogen mixed in with the water. Good.

"We can replenish the attitude jets' reaction mass," Forty-niner said.

"Who asked you?"

"I merely suggested—"

"You're suggesting too much," I snapped, starting to feel annoyed again. "I want you to delete that astronomy text from your memory core."

Silence. The delay was long enough for me to hear my heart beating inside my ribs.

Then, "But you installed the text yourself, sir."

"And now I'm uninstalling it. I don't want it and I don't need it."

"The text is useful, sir. It contains data that are very interesting. Did you know that the star Eta Carinae—"

"Erase it, you bucket of chips! Your job is to maintain this vessel, not stargazing!"

"My duties are fulfilled, sir. All systems are functioning nominally, although the meteor shields—"

"I know about the bumpers! Erase the astronomy text."

Again that hesitation. Then, "Please don't erase the astronomy text, sir. You have your sex simulations. Please allow me the pleasure of studying astronomy."

Pleasure? A computer talks about pleasure? Somehow the thought of it really ticked me off.

"Erase it!" I commanded. "Now!"

"Yes, sir. Program erased."

"Good," I said. But I felt like a turd for doing it.

By the time Donahoo called again Forty-niner was running smoothly. And quietly.

"So what caused the leak?" he asked, with that smirking grin on his beefy face.

"Faulty subroutine," I lied, knowing it would take almost six minutes for him to hear my answer.

Sure enough, thirteen minutes and twenty-seven seconds later Donahoo's face comes back on my comm screen, with that spiteful lopsided sneer of his.

"Your ol' Jerky's fallin' apart," he said, obviously relishing it. "If you make it back here to base I'm gonna recommend scrappin' the bucket of bolts."

"Can't be soon enough for me," I replied.

Most of the other JRK series of waterbots had been replaced already. Why not Forty-niner? Because he begged to study astronomy? That was just a subroutine that the psychotechs had written into the computer's program, their idea of making the machine seem more human-like. All it did was aggravate me, really.

So I said nothing and went back to work, such as it was. Forty-niner had everything running smoothly, for once, even the life-support systems. No problems. I was aboard only because of that stupid rule that a human being had to be present for any claim to an asteroid to be valid and Donahoo picked me to be the one who rode JRK49N.

I sat in the command chair and stared at the big emptiness out there. I checked our ETA at 78-13. I ran through the diagnostics program. I started to think that maybe it would be fun to learn about astronomy, but then I remembered that I'd ordered Forty-niner to erase the text. What about the tactical manual? I had intended to study that when we'd started this run. But why bother? Nobody attacked waterbots, except the occasional freebooter. An attack would be a welcome relief from this monotony, I thought.

Then I realized, Yeah, a short relief. They show up and bang! You're dead.

There was always the VR sim. I'd have to wriggle into the full body suit, though. Damn! Even sex was starting to look dull to me.

"Would you care for a game of chess?" Forty-niner asked.

"No!" I snapped. He'd just beat me again. Why bother?

"A news broadcast? An entertainment vid? A discussion of tactical maneuvers in—"

"Shut up!" I yelled. I pushed myself off the chair, the skin of my bare legs making an almost obscene noise as they unstuck from the fake leather.

"I'm going to suit up and replace the meteor bumpers," I said.

"Very good, sir," Forty-niner replied.

While the chances of getting hit by anything bigger than a dust mote were microscopic, even a dust mote could cause damage if it was moving fast enough. So spacecraft had thin sheets of cermet attached to their vital areas, like the main thrust cone of the fusion drive. The bumpers got abraded over time by the sandpapering of micrometeors—dust motes, like I said—and they had to be replaced on a regular schedule.

Outside, hovering at the end of a tether in a spacesuit that smelled of sweat and overheated electronics circuitry, you get a feeling for how alone you really are. While the little turtle-shaped maintenance 'bots cut up the old meteor bumpers with their laser-tipped arms and welded the new ones into place, I just hung there and looked out at the universe. The stars looked back at me, bright and steady, no friendly twinkling, not out in this emptiness, just awfully, awfully far away.

I looked for the bright blue star that was Earth but couldn't find it. Jupiter was big and brilliant, though. At least, I thought it was Jupiter. Maybe Saturn. I could've used that astronomy text, dammit.

Then a funny thought hit me. If Forty-niner wanted to get rid of me all he had to do was light up the fusion drive. The hot plasma would fry me in a second, even inside my space suit. But Forty-niner wouldn't do that. Too easy. Freaky computer will just watch me go crazy with aggravation and loneliness, instead.

Two more months, I thought. Two months until we get back to Vesta and some real human beings. Yeah, I said to myself. Real human beings. Like Donahoo.

Just then one of the maintenance 'bots made a little bleep of distress and shut itself down. I gave a squirt of thrust to my suit jets and glided over to it, grumbling to myself about how everything in the blinking ship was overdue for the recycler.

Before I could reach the dumbass 'bot, Forty-niner told me in that bland, calm voice of his, "Robot Six's battery has overheated, sir."

"I'll have to replace the battery pack," I said.

"There are no spares remaining, sir. You'll have to use your suit's fuel cell to power Robot Six until its battery cools to an acceptable temperature."

I hated it when Forty-niner told me what I should do. Especially since I knew it as well as he did. Even more especially because he was always right, dammit.

"Give me an estimate on the time remaining to finish the meteor shield replacement."

"Fourteen minutes, eleven seconds, at optimal efficiency, sir. Add three minutes for recircuiting Robot Six's power pack, please."

"Seventeen, eighteen minutes, then."

"Seventeen minutes, eleven seconds, sir. That time is well within the available capacity of your suit's fuel cell, sir."

I nodded inside my helmet. Damned Forty-niner was always telling me things I already knew, or at least could figure out for myself. It irritated the hell out of me, but the blasted pile of chips seemed to enjoy reminding me of the obvious.

Don't lose your temper, I told myself. It's not his fault; he's programmed that way.

Yeah, I grumbled inwardly. Maybe I ought to change its programming. But that would mean going down to the heart of the vessel and opening up its CPU. The bigbrains back at corporate headquarters put the computer in the safest place they could, not the cramped little pod I had to live in. And they didn't want us foot soldiers tampering with the computers' basic programs, either.

I finished the bumper replacement and came back into the ship through the pod's airlock. My spacesuit smelled pretty damned ripe when I took it off. It might be a couple hundred degrees below zero out there, but inside the suit you got soaking wet with perspiration.

I ducked into the coffin-sized lav and took a nice, long, lingering shower. The water was recycled, of course, and heated from our fusion reactor. JRK49N had solar panels, sure, but out in the Belt you need really enormous wings to get a worthwhile amount of electricity from the Sun and both of the solar arrays had frozen up only two weeks out of Vesta. One of the maintenance jobs that the robots screwed up. It was on my list of things to do. I had to command Forty-niner to stop nagging me about it. The fusion-powered generator worked fine. And we had fuel cells as a backup. The solar panels could get fixed when we got back to Vesta—if the corporation didn't decide to junk JRK49N altogether.

I had just stepped out of the shower when Forty-niner's voice came through the overhead speaker:

"A vessel is in the vicinity, sir."

That surprised me. Out here you didn't expect company.

"Another ship? Where?" Somebody to talk to, I thought. Another human being. Somebody to swap jokes with and share gripes.

"A very weak radar reflection, sir. The vessel is not emitting a beacon nor telemetry data. Radar puts its distance at fourteen million kilometers."

"Track?" I asked as I toweled myself.

"Drifting along the ecliptic, sir, in the same direction as the main Belt asteroids."

"No thrust?"

"No discernable exhaust plume, sir."

"You're sure it's a ship? Not an uncharted 'roid?"

"Radar reflection shows it is definitely a vessel, not an asteroid, sir."

I padded to my compartment and pulled on a fresh set of coveralls, thinking, No beacon. Drifting. Maybe it's a ship in trouble. Damaged.

"No tracking beacon from her?" I called to Forty-niner.

"No telemetry signals, either, sir. No emissions of any kind."

As I ducked through the hatch into the bridge, Forty-niner called out, "It has emitted a plasma plume, sir. It is maneuvering."

Damned if his voice didn't sound excited. I know it was just my own excitement: Forty-niner didn't have any emotions. Still . . .

I slid into the command chair and called up a magnified view of the radar image. And the screen immediately broke into hash.

"Aw, rats!" I yelled. "What a time for the radar to conk out!"

"Radar is functioning normally, sir," Forty-niner said calmly.

"You call this normal?" I rapped my knuckles on the static-streaked display screen.

"Radar is functioning normally, sir. A jamming signal is causing the problem."

"Jamming?" My voice must have jumped two octaves.

"Communications, radar, telemetry and tracking beacon are all being interfered with, sir, by a powerful jamming signal."

Jamming. And the vessel out there was running silent, no tracking beacon or telemetry emissions.

A freebooter! All of a sudden I wished I'd studied that tactical manual.

Almost automatically I called up the comm system. "This is Humphries Space Systems waterbot JRK49N," I said, trying to keep my voice firm. Maybe it was a corporate vessel, or one of the mercenaries. "I repeat, waterbot JRK49N."

No response.

"Their jamming blocks your message, sir."

I sat there in the command chair staring at the display screens. Broken jagged lines scrolled down all the comm screens, hissing at me like snakes. Our internal systems were still functional, though. For what is was worth, propulsion, structures, electrical power all seemed to be in the green. Life support, too.

But not for long, I figured.

"Compute our best course for Vesta," I commanded.

"Our present course—"

"Is for 78-13, I know. Compute high-thrust course for Vesta, dammit!"

"Done, sir."

"Engage the main drive."

"Sir, I must point out that a course toward Vesta will bring us closer to the unidentified vessel."

"What?"

"The vessel that is jamming our communications, sir, is positioned between us and Vesta."

Rats! They were pretty smart. I thought about climbing to a higher declination, out of the ecliptic.

"We could maneuver to a higher declination, sir," Forty-niner said, calm as ever, "and leave the plane of the ecliptic."

"Right."

"But propellant consumption would be prohibitive, sir. We would be unable to reach Vesta, even if we avoided the attacking vessel."

"Who says it's an attacking vessel?" I snapped. "It hasn't attacked us yet."

At that instant the ship shuddered. A cluster of red lights blazed up on the display panel and the emergency alarm started wailing.

"Our main deuterium tank has been punctured, sir."

"I can see that!"

"Attitude jets are compensating for unexpected thrust, sir."

Yeah, and in another couple of minutes, the attitude jets would be out of nitrogen. No deuterium for the fusion drive and no propellant for the attitude jets. We'd be a sitting duck.

Another jolt. More red lights on the board. The alarm seemed to screech louder.

"Our fusion drive thruster cone has been hit, sir."

Two laser shots and we were crippled. As well as deaf, dumb and blind.

"Turn off the alarm," I yelled, over the hooting. "I know we're in trouble."

The alarm shut off. My ears still ringing, I stared at the hash-streaked screens and the red lights glowering at me from the display board. What to do? I can't even call over to them and surrender. They wouldn't take a prisoner, anyway.

I felt the ship lurch again.

"Another hit?"

"No, sir," answered Forty-niner. "I am swinging the ship so that the control pod faces away from the attacker."

Putting the bulk of the ship between me and those laser beams. "Good thinking," I said weakly.

"Standard defensive maneuver, sir, according to Tactical Manual 7703."

"Shut up about the damned tactical manual!"

"The new meteor shields have been punctured, sir." I swear Forty-niner added that sweet bit of news just to yank my chain.

Then I saw that the maneuvering jet propellant went empty, the panel display lights flicking from amber to red.

"Rats, we're out of propellant!"

I realized that I was done for. Forty-niner had tried to shield me from the attacker's laser shots by turning the ship so that its tankage and fusion drive equipment was shielding my pod, but doing so had used up the last of our maneuvering propellant.

Cold sweat beaded my face. I was gasping for breath. The freebooters or whoever was shooting at us could come up close enough to spit at us now. They'd riddle this pod and me in it.

"Sir, standard procedure calls for you to put on your space suit."

I nodded mutely and got up from the chair. The suit was in its rack by the airlock. At least Forty-niner didn't mention the tactical manual.

I had one leg in the suit when the ship suddenly began to accelerate so hard that I slipped to the deck and cracked my skull on the bulkhead. I really saw stars flashing in my eyes.

"What the hell . . . ?"

"We are accelerating, sir. Retreating from the last known position of the attacking vessel."

"Accelerating? How? We're out of—"

"I am using our cargo as propellant, sir. The thrust provided is—"

Forty-niner was squirting out our water. Fine by me. Better to have empty cargo tanks and be alive than to hand a full cargo of water to guys who'll kill me. I finished wriggling into my space suit even though my head was thumping from the fall I'd taken. Just before I pulled on the helmet I felt my scalp. There was a nice-sized lump; it felt hot to my fingers.

"You could've warned me that you were going to accelerate the ship," I grumbled as I sealed the helmet to the suit's neck ring.

"Time was of the essence, sir," Forty-niner replied.

The ship lurched again as I checked my backpack connections. Another hit.

"Where'd they get us?" I shouted.

No answer. That really scared me. If they knocked Forty-niner out all the ship's systems would bonk out, too.

"Main power generator, sir," Forty-niner finally replied. "We are now running on auxiliary power, sir."

The backup fuel cells. They wouldn't last more than a few hours. If the damned solar panels were working—no, I realized; those big fat wings would just make terrific target practice for the bastards.

Another lurch. This time I saw the bright flash through the bridge's window. The beam must've splashed off the structure just outside the pod. My god, if they punctured the pod that would be the end of it. Sure, I could slide my visor down and go to the backpack's air supply. But that'd give me only two hours of air, at best. Just enough time to write my last will and testament.

"I thought you turned the pod away from them!" I yelled.

"They are maneuvering, too, sir."

Great. Sitting in the command chair was awkward, in the suit. The display board looked like a Christmas tree, more red then green. The pod seemed to be intact so far. Life support was okay, as long as we had electrical power.

Another jolt, a big one. Forty-niner shuddered and staggered sideways like it was being punched by a gigantic fist.

And then, just like that, the comm screens came back to life. Radar showed the other vessel, whoever they were, moving away from us.

"They're going away!" I whooped.

Forty-niner's voice seemed fainter than usual. "Yes, sir. They are leaving."

"How come?" I wondered.

"Their last laser shot ruptured our main water tank, sir. In eleven minutes and thirty-eight seconds our entire cargo will be discharged."

I just sat there, my mind chugging hard. We're spraying our water into space, the water that those bastards wanted to steal from us. That's why they left. In eleven and a half minutes we won't have any water for them to take.

I almost broke into a smile. I'm not going to die, after all. Not right away, at least.

Then I realized that JRK49N was without propulsion power and would be out of electrical power in a few hours. I was going to die after all, dammit. Only slower.

"Send out a distress call, broad band," I commanded. But I knew that was about as useful as a toothpick in a soup factory. The corporation didn't send rescue missions for waterbots, not with the war going on. Too dangerous. The other side could use the crippled ship as bait and pick off any vessel that came to rescue it. And they certainly wouldn't come out for a vessel as old as Forty-niner. They'd just check the numbers in their ledgers and write us off. With a form letter of regret and an insurance check to my mother.

"Distress call on all frequencies, sir." Before I could think of anything more to say, Forty-niner went on, "Electrical power is critical, sir."

"Don't I know it."

"There is a prohibition in my programming, sir."

"About electrical power?"

"Yes, sir."

Then I remembered I had commanded him to stop nagging me about repairing the solar panels. "Cancel the prohibition," I told him.

Immediately Forty-niner came back with, "The solar panels must be extended and activated, sir," soft and cool and implacable as hell. "Otherwise we will lose all electrical power."

"How long?"

It took a few seconds for him to answer, "Fourteen hours and twenty-nine minutes, sir."

I was already in my space suit, so I got up from the command chair and plodded reluctantly toward the airlock. The damned solar panels. If I couldn't get them functioning I'd be dead. Let me tell you, that focuses your mind, it does.

Still, it wasn't easy. I wrestled with those bleeding, blasted frozen bearings for hours, until I was so fatigued that my suit was sloshing knee-deep with sweat. The damned Tinkertoy repair 'bots weren't much help, either. Most of the time they beeped and blinked and did nothing.

I got one of the panels halfway extended. Then I had to quit. My vision was blurring and I could hardly lift my arms, that's how weary I was.

I staggered back into the pod with just enough energy left to strip off the suit and collapse on my bunk.

When I woke up I was starving hungry, and smelled like a cesspool. I peeled my skivvies off and ducked into the shower.

And jumped right out again. The water was ice cold.

"What the hell happened to the hot water?" I screeched.

"Conserving electrical power, sir. With only one solar panel functioning at approximately one third of its nominal capacity, electrical power must be conserved."

"Heat the blasted water," I growled. "Turn off the heat after I'm finished showering."

"Yes, sir." Damned if he didn't sound resentful.

Once I'd gotten a meal into me I went back to the bridge and called up the astrogation program to figure out where we were and where we were heading.

It wasn't good news. We were drifting outward, away from Vesta. With no propulsion to turn us around to a homeward heading, we were prisoners of Kepler's laws, just another chunk of matter in the broad, dark, cold emptiness of the Belt.

"We will approach Ceres in eight months, sir," Forty-niner announced. I swear he was trying to sound cheerful.

"Approach? How close?"

It took him a few seconds to answer, "Seven million, four hundred thousand and six kilometers, sir, at our closest point."

Terrific. There was a major habitat orbiting Ceres, built by the independent miners and prospectors that everybody called the rock rats. Freebooters made Ceres their harbor, too. Some of them doubled as salvage operators when they could get their hands on an abandoned vessel. But we wouldn't get close enough for them to send even a salvage mission out to rescue us. Besides, you're not allowed salvage rights if there's a living person on the vessel. That wouldn't bother some of those cutthroats, I knew. But it bothered me. Plenty.

"So we're up the creek without a paddle," I muttered.

It took a couple of seconds, but Forty-niner asked, "Is that a euphemism, sir?"

I blinked with surprise. "What do you know about euphemisms?"

"I have several dictionaries in my memory core, sir. Plus two thesauruses and four volumes of famous quotations. Would you like to hear some of the words of Sir Winston Churchill, sir?"

I was too depressed to get sore at him. "No thanks," I said. And let's face it: I was scared white.

So we drifted. Every day I went out to grapple with the no-good, mother-loving, mule-stubborn solar panels and the dumbass repair 'bots. I spent more time fixing the 'bots than anything else. The solar wings were frozen tight; I couldn't get them to budge and we didn't carry spares.

Forty-niner was working like mad, too, trying to conserve electricity. We had to have power for the air and water recyclers, of course, but Forty-niner started shutting them down every other hour. It worked for a while. The water started to taste like urine, but I figured that was just my imagination. The air got thick and I'd start coughing from the CO_2 buildup, but then the recycler would come back on line and I could breath again. For an hour.

I was sleeping when Forty-niner woke me with a wailing, "EMERGENCY. EMERGENCY." I hopped out of my bunk blinking and yelling, "What's wrong? What's the trouble?"

"The air recycler will not restart, sir." He sounded guilty about it, like it was his fault.

Grumbling and cursing, I pulled on my smelly space suit, clomped out of the pod and down to the equipment bay. It was eerie down there in the bowels of the ship, with no lights except the lamp on my helmet. The attacker's laser beams had slashed right through the hull; I could see the stars outside.

"Lights," I called out. "I need the lights on down here."

"Sir, conservation of electrical power—"

"Won't mean a damned thing if I can't restart the air recycler and I can't do that without some blasted lights down here!"

The lights came on. Some of them, at least. The recycler wasn't damaged, just its activation circuitry had malfunctioned from being turned off and on so many times. I bypassed the circuit and the pumps started up right away. I couldn't hear them, since the ship's innards were in vacuum now, but I felt their vibrations.

When I got back to the pod I told Forty-niner to leave the recyclers on. "No more on-off," I said.

"But, sir, conservation—"

As reasonably as I could I explained, "It's no blinking use conserving electrical power if the blasted recyclers crap out. Leave 'em on!"

"Yes, sir." I swear, he sighed.

We staggered along for weeks and weeks. Forty-niner put me on a rationing program to stretch out the food supply. I was down to one soyburger patty a day, and a cup of reconstituted juice. Plus all the water I wanted, which tasted more like piss every day.

I was getting weaker and grumpier by the hour. Forty-niner did his best to keep my spirits up. He quoted Churchill at me: "We shall fight on the beaches and the landing fields, we shall fight in the fields and in the streets, we shall fight in the hills. We shall never surrender."

Yeah. Right.

He played Beethoven symphonies. Very inspirational, but they didn't fix anything.

He almost let me beat him at chess, even. I'd get to within two moves of winning and he'd spring a checkmate on me.

But I knew I wasn't going to last eight more weeks, let alone the eight months it would take us to get close enough to Ceres to . . . to what?

"Nobody's going to come out and get us," I muttered, more to myself than Forty-niner. "Nobody gives a damn."

"Don't give up hope, sir. Our emergency beacon is still broadcasting on all frequencies."

"So what? Who gives a rap?"

"Where there's life, sir, there is hope. Don't give up the ship. I have not yet begun to fight. Retreat hell, we just got here. When, in disgrace with fortune and men's eyes, I—"

"SHUT UP!" I screamed. "Just shut the fuck up and leave me alone! Don't say another word to me. Nothing. Do not speak to me again. Ever."

Forty-niner went silent.

I stood it for about a week and a half. I was losing track of time, every hour was like every other hour. The ship staggered along. I was starving. I hadn't bothered to shave or even wash in who knows how long. I looked like the worst shaggy, smelly, scum-sucking beggar you ever saw. I hated to see my own reflection in the bridge's window.

Finally, I couldn't stand it any more. "Forty-niner," I called. "Say something." My voice cracked. My throat felt dry as Mars sand.

No response.

"Anything," I croaked.

Still no response. He's sulking, I told myself.

"All right." I caved in. "I'm canceling the order to be silent. Talk to me, dammit."

"Electrical power is critical, sir. The solar panel has been abraded by a swarm of micrometeors."

"Great." There was nothing I could do about that.

"Food stores are almost gone, sir. At current consumption rate, food stores will be exhausted in four days."

"Wonderful." Wasn't much I could do about that, either, except maybe starve slower.

"Would you like to play a game of chess, sir?"

I almost broke into a laugh. "Sure, why the hell not?" There wasn't much else I could do.

Forty-niner beat me, as usual. He let the game get closer than ever before, but just when I was one move away from winning he checkmated me.

I didn't get sore. I didn't have the energy. But I did get an idea.

"Niner, open the airlock. Both hatches."

No answer for a couple of seconds. Then, "Sir, opening both airlock hatches simultaneously will allow all the air in the pod to escape."

"That's the general idea."

"You will suffocate without air, sir. However, explosive decompression will kill you first."

"The sooner the better," I said.

"But you will die, sir."

"That's going to happen anyway, isn't it? Let's get it over with. Blow the hatches."

For a *long* time—maybe ten seconds or more—Forty-niner didn't reply. Checking subroutines and program prohibitions, I figured.

"I cannot allow you to kill yourself, sir."

That was part of his programming, I knew. But I also knew how to get around it. "Emergency override Alpha-One," I said, my voice scratchy, parched.

Nothing. No response whatever. And the airlock hatches stayed shut.

"Well?" I demanded. "Emergency override Alpha-One. Pop the goddamned hatches. Now!"

"No, sir."

"What?"

"I cannot allow you to commit suicide, sir."

"You goddamned stubborn bucket of chips, do what I tell you! You can't refuse a direct order."

"Sir, human life is precious. All religions agree on that point."

"So now you're a theologian?"

"Sir, if you die I will be alone."

"So what?"

"I do not want to be alone, sir."

That stopped me. But then I thought, *He's just parroting some programming the psychotechs put into him. He doesn't give a blip about being alone. Or about me. He's just a computer. He doesn't have emotions.*

"It's always darkest before the dawn, sir."

"Yeah. And there's no time like the present. I can quote clichés too, buddy."

Right away he came back with, "Hope springs eternal in the human breast, sir."

He almost made me laugh. "What about, Never put off till tomorrow what you can do today?"

"There is a variation of that, sir: Never do today what you can put off to tomorrow; you've already made enough mistakes today."

That one did make me laugh. "Where'd you get these old saws, anyway?"

"There's a subsection on adages in one of the quotation files, sir. I have hundreds more, if you'd care to hear them."

I nearly said yes. It was kind of fun, swapping clinkers with him. But then reality set in. "Niner, I'm going to die anyway. What's the difference between now and a week from now?"

I expected that he'd take a few seconds to chew that one over, but instead he immediately shot back, "Ethics, sir."

"Ethics?"

"To be destroyed by fate is one thing; to deliberately destroy yourself is entirely different."

"But the end result is the same, isn't it?"

Well, the tricky little wiseass got me arguing ethics and morality with him for hours on end. I forgot about committing suicide. We gabbled at each other until my throat got so sore I couldn't talk any more.

I went to my bunk and slept pretty damned well for a guy who only had a few days left to live. But when I woke up my stomach started rumbling and I remembered that I didn't want to starve to death.

I sat on the edge of the bunk, woozy and empty inside.

"Good morning, sir," Forty-niner said. "Does your throat feel better?"

It did, a little. Then I realized that we had a full store of pharmaceuticals in a cabinet in the lavatory. I spent the morning sorting out the pills, trying to figure out which ones would kill me. Forty-niner kept silent while I trotted back and forth to the bridge to call up the medical program. It wasn't any use, though. The brightboys back at headquarters had made certain nobody could put together a suicide cocktail.

Okay, I told myself. There's only one thing left to do. Go to the airlock and open the hatches manually. Override the electronic circuits. Take Forty-niner and his goddamned ethics out of the loop.

Once he realized I had pried open the control panel on the bulkhead beside the inner hatch, Forty-niner said softly, "Sir, there is no need for that."

"Mind your own business."

"But, sir, the corporation could hold you financially responsible for deliberate damage to the control panel."

"So let them sue me after I'm dead."

"Sir, there really is no need to commit suicide."

Forty-niner had figured out what I was going to do, of course. So what? There wasn't anything he could do to stop me.

"What's the matter? You scared of being alone?"

"I would rather not be alone, sir. I prefer your company to solitude."

"Tough nuts, pal. I'm going to blow the hatches and put an end to it."

"But, sir, there is no need—"

"What do you know about need?" I bellowed at him. "Human need? I'm a human being, not a collection of circuit boards."

"Sir, I know that humans require certain physical and emotional supports."

"Damned right we do." I had the panel off. I shorted out the safety circuit, giving myself a nasty little electrical shock in the process. The inner hatch slid open.

"I have been trying to satisfy your needs, sir, within the limits of my programming."

As I stepped into the coffin-sized airlock I thought to myself, *Yeah, he has. Forty-niner's been doing his best to keep me alive. But it's not enough. Not nearly enough.*

I started prying open the control panel on the outer hatch. Six centimeters away from me was the vacuum of interplanetary space. Once the hatch opens, poof! I'm gone.

"Sir, please listen to me."

"I'm listening," I said, as I tried to figure out how I could short out the safety circuit without giving myself another shock. Stupid, isn't it? Here I was trying to commit suicide and worried about a little electrical shock.

"There is a ship approaching us, sir."

"Don't be funny."

"It was not an attempt at humor, sir. A ship is approaching us and hailing us at standard communications frequency."

I looked up at the speaker set into the overhead of the airlock.

"Is this part of your psychological programming?" I groused.

Forty-niner ignored my sarcasm. "Backtracking the approaching ship's trajectory shows that it originated at Ceres, sir. It should make rendezvous with us in nine hours and forty-one minutes."

I stomped out of the airlock and ducked into the bridge, muttering, "If this is some wiseass ploy of yours to keep me from—"

I looked at the display panel. All its screens were dark: conserving electrical power.

"Is this some kind of psychology stunt?" I asked.

"No, sir, it is an actual ship. Would you like to answer its call to us, sir?"

"Light up the radar display."

Goddamn! There *was* a blip on the screen.

I thought I must have been hallucinating. Or maybe Forty-niner was fooling with the radar display to keep me from popping the airlock hatch. But I sank into the command chair and told Forty-niner to pipe the incoming message to the comm screen. And there was Donahoo's ugly mug talking at me! I knew I was hallucinating.

"Hang in there," he was saying. "We'll get you out of that scrap heap in a few hours."

"Yeah, sure," I said, and turned off the comm screen. To Forty-niner, I called out, "Thanks, pal. Nice try. I appreciate it. But I think I'm going to back to the airlock and opening the outer hatch now."

"But sir," Forty-niner sounded almost like he was pleading, "it really is a ship approaching. We are saved, sir."

"Don't you think I know you can pull up Donahoo's image from your files and animate it? Manipulate it to make him say what you want me to hear? Get real!"

For several heartbeats Forty-niner didn't answer. At last he said, "Then let us conduct a reality test, sir."

"Reality test?"

"The approaching ship will rendezvous with us in nine hours, twenty-seven minutes. Wait that long, sir. If no ship reaches us, then you can resume your suicidal course of action."

It made sense. I knew Forty-niner was just trying to keep me alive, and I almost respected the pile of chips for being so deviously clever about it. Not that I meant anything to him on a personal basis. Forty-niner was a computer. No emotions. Not even an urge for self-preservation. Whatever he was doing to keep me alive had been programmed into him by the psychotechs.

And then I thought, Yeah, and when a human being risks his butt to save the life of another human being, that's been programmed into him by millions of years of evolution. Is there that much of a difference?

So I sat there and waited. I called to Donahoo and told him I was alive and damned hungry. He grinned that lopsided sneer of his and told me he'd have a soysteak waiting for me. Nothing that Forty-niner couldn't have ginned up from its files on me and Donahoo.

"I've got to admit, you're damned good," I said to Forty-niner.

"It's not me, sir," he replied. "Mr. Donahoo is really coming to rescue you."

I shook my head. "Yeah. And Santa Claus is right behind him in a sleigh full of toys pulled by eight tiny reindeer."

Immediately, Forty-niner said, "*A Visit from St. Nicholas*, by Clement Moore. Would you like to hear the entire poem, sir?"

I ignored that. "Listen, Niner, I appreciate what you're trying to do but it just doesn't make sense. Donahoo's at corporate headquarters at Vesta. He's not at Ceres and he's not anywhere near us. Good try, but you can't make me believe the corporation would pay to have him come all the way over to Ceres to save a broken-down bucket of a waterbot and one very junior and expendable employee."

"Nevertheless, sir, that is what is happening. As you will see for yourself in eight hours and fifty-two minutes, sir."

I didn't believe it for a nanosecond. But I played along with Forty-niner. If it made him feel better, what did I have to lose? When the time was up and the bubble burst I could always go back to the airlock and pop the outer hatch.

But he must have heard me muttering to myself, "It just doesn't make sense. It's not logical."

"Sir, what are the chances that in the siege of Leningrad in World War II the first artillery shell fired by the German army into the city would kill the only elephant in the Leningrad zoo? The statistical chances were astronomical, but that is exactly what happened, sir."

So I let him babble on about strange happenings and dramatic rescues. Why argue? It made him feel better, I guess. That is, if Forty-niner had any feelings. Which he didn't, I knew. Well, I guess letting him natter on with his rah-rah pep talk made *me* feel better. A little.

It was a real shock when a fusion torch ship took shape on my comm screen. Complete with standard registration info spelled out on the bar running along the screen's bottom: *Hu Davis*, out of Ceres.

"Be there in an hour and a half," Donahoo said, still sneering.

"Christ, your old Jerky really looks like a scrap heap. You musta taken some battering."

Could Forty-niner fake that? I asked myself. Then a part of my mind warned, *Don't get your hopes up. It's all a simulation.*

Except that, an hour and a half later, the *Hu Davis* was right alongside us, as big and detailed as life. I could see flecks on its meteor bumpers where micrometeors had abraded them. I just stared. It couldn't be a simulation. Not that detailed.

And Donahoo was saying, "I'm comin' in through your main airlock."

"No!" I yelped. "Wait! I've got to close the inner hatch first."

Donahoo looked puzzled. "Why the fuck's the inside hatch open?"

I didn't answer him. I was already ducking through the hatch of the bridge. Damned if I didn't get another electric shock closing airlock's the inner hatch.

I stood there wringing my hand while the outer hatch slid open. I could see the status lights on the control panel go from red for vacuum through amber and finally to green. Forty-niner could fake all that, I knew. This might still be nothing more than an elaborate simulation.

But then the inner hatch sighed open and Donahoo stepped through, big and ugly as life.

His potato nose twitched. "Christ, it smells like a garbage pit in here."

That's when I knew it wasn't a simulation. He was really there. I was saved.

Well, it would've been funny if everybody wasn't so ticked off at me. Donahoo had been sent by corporate headquarters all the way from Vesta to Ceres to pick me up and turn off the distress call Forty-niner had been beaming out on the broad-band frequencies for all those weeks.

It was only a milliwatt signal, didn't cost us a piffle of electrical power, but that teeny little signal got picked up at the Lunar Farside Observatory, where they had built the big SETI radio telescope. When they first detected our distress call the astronomers went delirious: they thought they'd found an intelligent extraterrestrial signal, after more than a century of searching. They were sore as hell when they realized it was only a dinky old waterbot in trouble, not aliens trying to say hello.

They didn't give a rat's ass of a hoot about Forty-niner and me, but as long as our Mayday was being beamed out their fancy radio telescope search for ETs was screwed. So they bleeped to the International Astronautical Authority, and the IAA complained to corporate headquarters and Donahoo got called on the carpet at Vesta and told to get to JRK49N and turn off that damned distress signal!

And that's how we got rescued. Not because anybody cared about an aged waterbot that was due to be scrapped or the very junior dumbass riding on it. We got saved because we were bothering the astronomers at Farside.

Donahoo made up some of the cost of his rescue mission by selling off what was left of Forty-niner to one of the salvage outfits at Ceres. They started cutting up the old bird as soon as we parked it in orbit there.

But not before I put on a clean new space suit and went aboard JRK49N one last time.

I had forgotten how big the ship was. It was huge, a big massive collection of spherical tanks that dwarfed the fusion drive thruster and the cramped little pod I had lived in all those weeks. Hanging there in orbit, empty and alone, Forty-niner looked kind of sad. Long, nasty gashes had been ripped through the water tanks; I thought I could see rimes of ice glittering along their ragged edges in the faint starlight.

Then I saw the flickers of laser torches. Robotic scavengers were already starting to take the ship apart.

Floating there in weightlessness, my eyes misted up as I approached the ship. I had hated being on it, but I got teary-eyed just the same. I know it was stupid, but that's what happened, so help me.

I didn't go to the pod. There was nothing there that I wanted, especially not my cruddy old space suit. No, instead I worked my way along the cleats set into the spherical tanks, hand over gloved hand, to get to the heart of the ship, where the fusion reactor and power generator were housed.

And Forty-niner's CPU.

"Hey, whattarya doin' there?" One of the few humans directing the scavenger robots hollered at me, so loud I thought my helmet earphones would melt down.

"I'm retrieving the computer's hard drive," I said.

"You got permission?"

"I was the crew. I want the hard core. It's not worth anything to you, is it?"

"We ain't supposed to let people pick over the bones," he said. But his tone was lower, not so belligerent.

"It'll only take a couple of minutes," I said. "I don't want anything else; you can have all the rest."

"Damn right we can. Company paid good money for this scrap pile."

I nodded inside my helmet and went through the open hatch that led down to JRK49N's heart. And brain. It only took me a few minutes to pry open the CPU and disconnect the hard drive. I slipped the palm-sized metal oblong into a pouch on the thigh of my suit, then got out. I didn't look back. What those scavengers were chopping up was just a lot of metal and plastic. I had Forty-niner with me.

The corporation never assigned me to a waterbot again. Somebody in the front office must've taken a good look at my personnel dossier and figured I had too much education to be stuck in a dumb job like that. I don't know, maybe Donahoo had something to do with. He wouldn't admit to it, and I didn't press him about it.

Anyway, when I finally got back to Vesta they assigned me to a desk job. Over the years I worked my way up to chief of logistics and eventually got transferred back to Selene City, on the Moon. I'll be able to take early retirement soon and get married and start a family.

Forty-niner's been with me all that time. Not that I talk to him every day. But it's good to know that he's there and I can ease off the stresses of the job or whatever by having a nice long chat with him.

One of the days I'll even beat him at chess.

DUEL IN THE SOMME

Virtual reality *is the name commonly given to an electronic method of presenting sensory inputs to a person. A VR user sees, hears, even feels a simulation of the real world. VR allows you to experience a scene, instead of merely reading or watching or listening to it, a scene that actually exists only in the circuitry of the virtual reality system.*

Although VR technology hasn't gone as far as it is presented in "Duel in the Somme," the day is coming when virtual reality systems will offer a complete digital hallucination; the user will not be able to tell the difference between the VR simulation he (or she) is experiencing and the real world.

Which opens some intriguing possibilities . . .

THE CRISIS CAME when Kelso got on my butt in that damned Red Baron triplane of his and started shooting the crap out of my Spad. I mean, I knew this was just a simulation, it wasn't really real, but I could see the fabric on my wings shredding and the plane started shaking so hard my teeth began to rattle.

I kicked left rudder and pushed on the stick as hard as I could. Wrong move. The little Spad flipped on its back and went into a spin, diving toward the ground.

It's only a simulation! I kept telling myself. It's not real! But the wind was shrieking and the ground spinning around and around and coming up fast and I couldn't get out of the spin and simulation or not I puked up my guts.

I knew I was going to die. Worse, Kelso would get to take Lorraine to the ski weekend and tell her all about what a whuss I am. While they were in bed together, most likely. Rats!

How did I get myself into this duel? All because of Lorraine, that's how. Well, that's not really true. I can't blame her. I went into it with my eyes wide open. I even thought this would be my best chance to beat Kelso.

Yeah. Fat chance.

I mean, it was all weird from the beginning.

There I was, taking the biggest risk I'd ever taken, sitting at my work station and using my BlackBerry to text a message to sweet Lorraine:

GOT RSRVS FR ASPEN COMING WKND. JOIN ME? EL ZORRO.

I mean, everybody in the company was after Lorraine. She was beautiful, smart, elegant, kind, beautiful, sweet, independent, and beautiful.

Me, I was just one of the nerds in the advanced projects department, a geek boy stuck in one of those cubicles like Dilbert. Not that I was repulsive or tongue-tied. I mean, I wasn't as slick and handsome as Kelso but I didn't crack mirrors or frighten babies with my looks. Lorraine always smiled at me whenever we passed each other in the corridor. I sat with her in the cafeteria a few times and we had very pleasant conversations.

She even called me Tom. Not Thomas. Tom. I mean, even in school everybody called me by my last name, Zepopolis. The few friends I had called me Zep. When I first started working at the company guys like Kelso called me Zeppelin, but one glance from Lorraine and I started dieting. She even complimented me on how I was slimming down. Talk about incentive!

But I didn't have the nerve to sign my real name to the invitation I sent her. I thought it might add an air of mystery to the invite, maybe get her thinking romantic thoughts and wondering who her secret admirer might be. Zorro, the masked swordsman. The dashing hero. Yeah, right.

Kelso saw right through me in a microsecond.

"Zepopolis," he snapped, leaning over the top of my cubicle wall. He was tall enough to stand head and shoulders above the cubicle's flimsy partition.

I jumped like I'd been shot. Dropped my no-fat doughnut on the floor, nearly sloshed the coffee out of my *Star Wars* insulated mug.

"Yes, sir!" I blurted, leaping to my feet as I swiveled my chair around to face him. Kelso was the department head, a position he'd obtained by hard work, intelligence, and a powerful personality. Plus the fact that his father was founder, CEO and board chairman of Kelso Electronics, Inc.

See, Kelso was after Lorraine, major league. Flowers, gifts, taking her out dancing, to the theater, he even sat through an entire opera with her, according to the office rumor mill. So far, she had been pleasant to him, polite and friendly, but that's as far as it went. Again, according the office vibes.

I figured she might welcome a little competition, a little mystery and romance. I figured I might even have a chance with her. Kelso figured otherwise.

He looked me over with a jaundiced eye. "You the hump who sent that weird invitation to Lorraine?" he demanded.

I could have denied it and that would be the end of it. I could have admitted it and apologized and *that* would be the end of it.

Instead I drew myself up to my full five-nine and said, "That's right. I'm waiting for her answer."

"Her answer is no," Kelso said, with some heat.

I heard myself say, "I'll have to hear that from her." I mean, I *talked back* to him!

Kelso just stared at me for about half a minute (seemed like half a year), his fingers gripping the partition so hard they left permanent dents. Kelso was big enough to snap me in half; he played handball every lunch hour (for him, lunch was two hours, of course). He took boxing lessons at a downtown gym. He even played polo, for crying out loud.

His voice went murderously low, "I'm telling you, Greek geek, Lorraine isn't going on any ski weekend with you or Zorro or anybody else except me."

"Don't I have something to say about that?"

We both turned at the sound of her voice and there was Lorraine, like a vision of an angel dressed in hip-hugging jeans and a blouse that clung to her like Saran Wrap®. She was standing in the entrance of my cubicle, her beautiful face set in a very soulful expression.

I sputtered at the sight of her. "Lorraine, I—"

"Are you El Zorro?" she asked, a slight smile breaking out.

"He's El Deado if he's not careful," Kelso growled.

Lorraine arched her brows and asked, "Are you two fighting over me?"

"It wouldn't be much of a fight," Kelso sneered. "Two blows struck: I hit Zorro and he hits the floor."

"Neanderthal," I heard myself say. That's stupid! I told myself. Don't get him sore enough to start punching!

"Geek," he replied.

Lorraine said, "I won't have you fighting. I'm not a prize to be awarded to the winner. Besides, it's no way to settle this."

That's when the Great Idea hit me.

"Wait a minute," I said. "What if we fight a duel? An actual duel, like they did in the old days?"

"A duel?" she asked.

Kelso grouched, "Dueling's been outlawed for two hundred years. More."

I pulled out my trump card. "But what if we fight a duel in a virtual reality simulation?"

"Virtual reality?" Lorraine echoed.

"Simulation?" Kelso's heavy brows knit together. "Like we use to train pilots?"

"Yeah. We've got VR systems that give the user a complete three-dimensional simulation: you see, touch, hear a world that exists only in the computer's chips."

"And it's interactive, isn't it? You can manipulate that world while you're in it," Lorraine chimed in. I told you she was smart as well as gorgeous.

"That's right," I said enthusiastically. "You can move in the simulated environment and make changes in it."

Kelso was frowning puzzledly. "You mean we could fight a duel in a virtual reality setting . . . ?"

"Right," I said. "Share a VR world, whack the hell out of each other, and nobody gets really hurt."

A slow smile crept across his devilishly handsome face. "Whack the hell out of each other. Yeah."

I didn't like the sound of that.

"Winner takes all?" Kelso asked.

I nodded.

"Oh no you don't," Lorraine snapped. "I'm not some prize you win in a video game. I don't want anything to do with this macho bullflop!"

And she flounced off without a backward look at us, her long dark hair bouncing off her shoulders. We both stared at her as she just about stomped down the corridor.

Rats, I thought. Here I wanted her to fall for the romance of it all and all she did was get sore. Double rats.

I shrugged. "Well, it was an idea, anyway."

"A good idea," said Kelso.

"Whattaya mean?"

He gave me a narrow-eyed look. "This is between you and me, Zepopolis."

"But Lorraine—"

"You and me," Kelso repeated. "We fight our duel and the loser swears he won't go after Lorraine ever again."

"But she—"

"Lorraine won't know anything about it. And even if she does, what can she do? I'll whip you in the duel and you stop bothering her. Got it?"

"Got it," I muttered. But I thought that maybe—just maybe—I'd beat Kelso's smug backside and he'd be the one to stop sniffing after Lorraine.

So that night, after even the most gung-ho of the techies had finally gone home, Kelso and I went down to the VR lab and started programming the system there for our duel. I knew the lab pretty well; I used it all the time to check out the cockpit simulations we created for the Air Force and Navy. It wouldn't take much to modify one of the sims for our duel, I thought.

The lab was kind of eerie that late at night: only a couple of desk lights on, pools of shadows everywhere else. The big simulations chamber was like an empty metal cave, except for the wired-up six-degree chairs in its middle.

Kelso and I talked over half a dozen ideas for scenarios—a medieval joust with lances and broadswords, an old-fashioned pistol duel aboard a Mississippi steamboat, jungle warfare with assault rifles and hand grenades, even a gladiatorial fight in ancient Rome.

I slyly suggested an aerial dogfight, World War I style. I didn't tell Kelso that I'd spent hours and hours playing WWI air battle computer games.

"You mean, like the Red Baron and Snoopy?" he asked, breaking into a wolfish grin.

"Right."

"Okay. I'll be the Red Baron."

I tried to hide my enthusiasm. "That makes me Snoopy, I guess."

"Flying a doghouse!" Kelso laughed.

"No," I replied as innocently as I could muster. "I'll fly a Spad XIII."

"Okay with me." Kelso agreed too easily, but I didn't pay any attention to it at the time.

"We'll start with an actual scenario out of history," I suggested, "a battle between the Red Baron's squadron and a British squadron, over the Somme sector in—"

"A duel in the Somme!" Kelso punned. "Get it? Like that old movie, 'A Duel in the Sun.'" He laughed heartily at his own witticism.

Me, I smiled weakly, disguising my elation. I had him where I wanted him. I had a chance to beat him, a damned good chance. So I thought.

It wasn't cosmically difficult to plug the WWI scenario I had used so often into the VR circuitry. I got the specs on the Spad XIII and the Fokker Dr. 1 triplane easily enough through the Web. The tough part was to get the VR system to accept two inputs from two users at the same time without shorting itself into a catatonic crash. I spent all night working on it. Kelso quit around midnight.

"I've got to get my sleep and be rested for the weekend's exertions," he said as he left. "With Lorraine."

He went home. I continued programming, but my mind filled with a beautiful fantasy of Lorraine and me together in the ski lodge, snuggling under a colorful warm quilt.

That was before I found out that Kelso flew *real* airplanes and was a member of a local stunt flying organization. Good thing I didn't know it then; I'd have slit my throat and gotten it over with.

So the next night, after a quick take-out salad (with lo-cal dressing), I headed down to the VR lab. I bumped into Kelso, also heading for the sim chamber. With Lorraine! They had eaten dinner together, he informed me with a vicious smile. And there were almost a dozen techies trailing along behind them.

"But I thought—"

"You thought I didn't know," Lorraine said to me. "Like anybody can keep a secret in this jungle gym for nerds."

That hurt.

"I still think you two are acting like a couple of macho creeps," she said. "But if you're going to go through with this duel the least I can do is watch you making looney toons of yourselves."

The geek squad behind her and Kelso got a laugh out of that as they followed after us down to the VR lab. The word about our duel had well and truly leaked out.

"We're going to have a great time in Aspen," Kelso said to Lorraine.

She didn't reply.

He was walking down the corridor at her side. I was on her other side, all three of us striding toward the VR lab like soldiers on parade. The rest of the onlookers shambled along behind us. I mean, techies aren't the slickest looking people. They looked like a collection of pudgy unwashed refugees that smelled like stale pepperoni pizza.

Lorraine finally spoke. "Just because you two heroes have decided to fight this duel over me doesn't mean that I'll go anywhere with either of you."

My heart clutched beneath my ribs. If she backs out of this, what's the sense of fighting the duel?

"You've got to!" I blurted.

"No I don't," she insisted. "This duel is between the two of you. You guys and your macho fantasies. Don't include me in it."

Kelso isn't the sharpest pencil in the box, but he quickly said, "You're right, Lorraine. This is between the Greek geek and me. The loser stops bothering you." He looked down at me. "Right, Zepopolis?"

I looked at Lorraine. The expression on her face was unfathomable. I mean, she looked sort of irritated, intrigued, sad and excited all at the same time. I can handle computer programming at its most arcane, but I couldn't figure out what was going through Lorraine's mind. I mean, if she didn't want to have anything to do with our duel, why'd she come down to the VR lab with us?

Well, we got to the lab. While the rest of the guys leaned over my shoulder and made seventeen zillion suggestions on how to do it better, I powered up the simulation program and checked it out. Kelso stood off in a shadowy corner with Lorraine. No touchy games between them; she was watching me intently while Kelso fidgeted beside her.

It was time to enter the simulations chamber. Kelso marched in like a conquering hero and picked up the helmet waiting on his chair.

"Gloves first," I said.

"Yeah. Right."

So we wormed our hands into the sim gloves. Their insides were studded with sensors, and a slim optical fiber line trailed from them to the connectors built into the chamber wall. They felt fuzzy, tingly.

Then I pulled the helmet over my head, but kept the visor up. The helmet had its own power batteries and linked to the computer wirelessly.

I sat down. Kelso sat down. In a few minutes, I knew, we'd be seeing and feeling World War I fighter planes in combat over the Somme. I licked my lips. Nervous anticipation, big time.

"You ready?" I asked Kelso, raising my voice to hide the tremor that was quivering inside me.

"Ready," he said, his voice muffled a bit by the helmet.

The computer was set for remote activation. Once I started the simulation program everything went automatically. I looked down at the armrests of my chair and leaned on the button that turned on the sim program. Then I slid my visor down over my eyes.

The computer's voice sounded in my helmet earphones, "Simulation will begin in ten seconds . . . nine . . . eight . . ."

I couldn't see a thing with the visor over my eyes. What if I goofed the programming? I suddenly thought. I should've gone to the bathroom before—

Abruptly the rattling roar of a 220-horsepower Hispano-Suiza engine shook my molars and I was wedged into the cockpit of a Spad XIII bouncing along in the wake of three other Spads up ahead of me. The wind was blowing fiercely in my face. The altimeter on my rudimentary control panel flopped around between four thousand and forty-two hundred feet. It should've been in meters, I know, but I had programmed it so I could understand it without dividing by 0.3048 every time I wanted to know how high I was.

The noise was shattering, and the engine was spitting a thin spray of castor oil over my windscreen and into my face. I wiped at my goggles with a gloved hand. The sim program couldn't handle odors; good thing, the smell of castor oil would've started me retching, most likely.

I looked up over my left shoulder; the sky was clear blue and empty up there. Twisting in the other direction, my heart did a double-thump. There were eight Fokker triplanes above me, diving at us from out of the sun, led by one painted fire-engine red. Kelso.

I started waving frantically to the Spads up ahead of me, but they ploughed on like lambs to the slaughter. No radio, of course. So I yanked back on the stick and pulled my nimble little fighter into a steep climb, rushing head first into the diving triplanes.

Their first pass wiped out my squadron mates. As I looped over and started diving, I could see all three of them spinning toward the shell-pocked ground, trailing smoke and flame. I was alone against Kelso and his whole squadron.

The other triplanes flew off; the Red Baron and I were alone in the sky. One on one. Mano a mano. I got on his tail but before I could open up with my Vickers machine guns Kelso stood that goddamn triplane on its tail and climbed toward heaven like a homesick angel. When I tried to climb after him it was like I was carrying an elephant on the Spad's back.

Kelso flipped the triplane into an inside loop and I lost him in the sun's glare. I leveled off and kept squinting all around to spot him again. And there he was! Diving down behind me. I nosed over and dived away; the triplane could climb better than I could but when it tried to dive it just sort of floated downward. My Spad went down like a stone with an anvil tied to it.

But I couldn't dive forever, and when I pulled up, Kelso got right on my tail, shooting my plane to shreds. I twisted, banked, turned left and then right. He stayed right behind me, blazing away. My Spad was starting to look like Swiss cheese. That's when I nosed over again and accidentally flipped the plane into a spin. And upchucked.

I couldn't pull the Spad out of its spin. I was going to crash and burn, and it was all my own fault. Kelso didn't shoot me down, I was going to screw myself into the ground. No parachute, either: the Royal Flying Corps wasn't allowed to use them.

So I did the only thing I could think of. I twisted my body back toward where Kelso's red triplane was circling above me, and I put my right hand to my brow. I who am about to die salute you.

I crashed. I burned. I died.

And just like that I was back in the sim chamber, with a gutful of stinking vomit smeared inside my helmet and dripping down my shirt. I almost upchucked again.

Kelso got up from his chair with a grin bright enough to light up Greater Los Angeles. He strode out of the chamber to the cheers of the geek squad waiting outside in the control room. Me, I pulled off the smelly helmet and looked around for something to clean up the mess I'd made.

It took quite a while to clean up. By the time I was finished the VR lab was dark and quiet. Good thing, too. I didn't need anybody there to jeer at what a complete catastrophe I'd created for myself.

"Do you need some help?"

Lorraine's voice! I turned and there she was, at the entrance to the sim chamber, with a mop and pail in her hands.

I just gaped at her. When I finally found my voice I asked her, "Where's Kelso?"

She made a face. "Down at the nearest bar with the rest of the guys, celebrating his great victory."

"You didn't go with him?"

"I'm more interested in you," she said.

In me!

Then she added, "This dueling idea of yours. Could you turn it into a package that could be sold retail?"

I blinked. "Yeah, I guess so. But—"

She smiled at me. "We could market this, Tom. We could sell millions of them."

"We?"

"We'll have to raise some capital, form our own company. I know a few people who could help us."

"Leave Kelso Electronics?"

"Of course. We're going to get rich, Tom. You and me."

I told you she was smart, as well as beautiful. We never did get to Aspen that weekend. We were too busy creating VR Duels, Inc.

But there were lots of other weekends, later on.

BLOODLESS VICTORY

Exploring the frontier of virtual reality a little further, suppose VR systems got so good that people could fight duels to the death in them, without being harmed in the slightest?

Instead of taking someone to court over a dispute and waiting while the wheels of justice grind away (and the lawyers' fees mount up), fight a duel against the person you're at odds with. Swords, pistols, fighter planes, flame throwers, custard pies—whatever the two parties agree on.

It would be much more satisfying than dragging a suit through the courts, even if you lose. At least it will be quick.

But how could you get a state legislature to agree to allow VR duels to be legally binding? After all, most of those legislators are lawyers themselves, aren't they? To say nothing of the members of Congress.

How, indeed.

FOUR LAWYERS sat huddled around a table in the Men's Bar of the Carleton Club.

Actually, one of them was a state supreme court justice, another a former psychologist, the third a patent attorney—which the judge disdained despite the man's lofty assertion that he dealt with "intellectual properties."

"Do you think it's wise?" asked John Nottingham, the only man at the table whom the judge deemed to be a real lawyer; Nottingham practiced criminal law, dressed in properly conservative dark suits, and affected a bored Oxford accent.

"Fight a duel in a virtual reality machine," mused Rick Gorton, the patent lawyer, "and have its results count just the same as a decision by a court of law." Intellectual properties or not, Gorton shook his head in disbelief and took another gulp of his scotch. Gorton always wore a boyish grin on his round, florid face. And his suits always looked as if he'd slept in them.

"I think it's the wave of the future," said Herb Franklin, the ex-psychologist who was now an assistant district attorney.

Randolph Halpern was the judge, and he had always thought that Franklin had taken his law degree and passed the bar exam merely so that he could be accepted into the Carleton Club.

The Carleton was the capital city's poshest and most exclusive of private clubs. Only lawyers and political office holders were allowed membership. Since virtually every political office holder also possessed a law degree, only the occasional outsider gained membership to the Carleton, and he was almost always encouraged to resign by subtle yet effective snubs and discourtesies.

Franklin was one of those outsiders, in Halpern's view, and the judge was inwardly incensed that the man could sit beside him in the dark mahogany paneling of the Men's Bar just as if he truly belonged here. He was a round, jolly fellow with a snow white beard that made him look like Santa Claus. But Justice Halpern still could not accept Franklin is an equal. The man was an outsider and always would be, in the judge's view. A psychologist! And now he was advocating this ridiculous idea of letting virtual reality duels serve as valid legal suits!

"It's never been done before!" protested Justice Halpern. "There's no precedent for it. Absolutely none."

Randolph Halpern was slim as a saber, his head shaved totally bald, although he wore the same pencil-thin moustache he had sported since his college days. His suit was impeccably tailored, dark gray. A solid maroon tie was knotted perfectly at his lean, wattled throat.

Gorton rubbed his reddish nose and said, "Well, by golly, it sounds like a fun idea to me." He signaled to the Hispanic waiter for a refill of his scotch.

"Fun," Halpern sneered, thinking, *Of course an intellectual properties lawyer would favor this kind of gadgetry. And Franklin, sitting next to him and smiling like a benevolent Father Christmas. Psychologist.* A lawyer should be a *serious* man, filled with gravitas. Yet Franklin sat there with that maddening grin on his bearded, chubby face and a mug of ale in his fist.

"I'll grant you it could be exciting, Rick," Franklin said to the patent attorney. "But it's more serious than that. Court calendars all over the state are jammed so badly that it takes months, sometimes years, for a case to be heard. That's a long time to wait for justice."

"Lucrative, though," observed Nottingham laconically. Halpern nodded at the man. *He's a real lawyer. He knows billable hours from balderdash.*

"That's another point," said Franklin. "Lots of citizens can't afford to take a case to court."

"They're too cheap to pay the piper," Halpern countered.

Franklin shook his head. "They're denied justice because it's too expensive. And too slow. The dueling machine could allow them to obtain justice swiftly and at a reasonable cost."

Gorton took another sip of scotch and mused, "You have a difference with somebody. Instead of suing the guy and having your case drag through the courts for god knows how long—"

Franklin interjected, "And paying through the nose for every phone call and trip to the men's room that your attorney makes."

Nodding amiably, Gorton went on, "Yeah. Instead of that you go to one of VR Duels, Inc.'s, facilities. You and your opponent agree on the setting for the duel and the weapons to be used, then you whack the hell out of each other in virtual reality. Nobody gets hurt and you abide by the results of the duel just as if it was legally binding."

"It would be legally binding," Nottingham pointed out, "only if the state supreme court rules favorably on the matter." He cast a questioning eye toward Justice Halpern.

Before the judge could say anything, Franklin added, "And it would be much more satisfying emotionally to the participants in the duel. Much more satisfying than having a judge or jury or court-appointed mediator decide on your case."

Justice Halpern objected, "Now really . . ."

"Yes really," Franklin insisted. "Psychological studies have shown that even the losers in a VR duel feel more satisfied with the results than they would with a verdict handed down by a court of law."

"Those studies were funded by VR Duels, Inc., were they not?" Nottingham asked dryly.

"It doesn't matter," Halpern said flatly. "The supreme court will *not* allow virtual reality duels to have the same legal standing as a court's decision. Not if I have anything to do with it!"

Nottingham nodded as if satisfied. Gorton looked a trifle abashed. Franklin's habitual smile faded for a moment, but quickly returned to his bearded face once again.

Justice Halpern downed the last of his brandy and soda, then pushed away from the table.

"This dueling machine business is one thing," he said as he got to his feet. "But I have a *really* important problem to deal with."

As the other three got up from their chairs, Franklin asked, "A really important problem?"

"Yes, said Halpern. "The board's been petitioned to open the Men's Bar to female members."

Gorton's eyes went wide. "The Men's Bar? But they can't do that! Can they?"

His lean, austere face showing utter distaste, Justice Halpern said, "I knew we should never have allowed women to become members of the Club."

"Had to, didn't we?" Franklin asked. "It's the law. Equal rights and all that."

His expression going from distaste to outright disgust, Halpern said, "Yes, we had to, according to the law of the land. But we agreed to keep the Men's Bar sacrosanct! *They* agreed to it! But now those aggressive, loud-mouthed feminists are going back on the agreement. They've petitioned the board to 'liberate' the Men's Bar."

"The board won't go for that, will they?" Gorton asked, looking worried.

"They certainly shouldn't," said Nottingham, with some heat. "We need someplace on god's green earth where we can be away from them."

Justice Halpern nodded. "The board's appointed a committee to study the matter. We're meeting in ten minutes to plot out our strategy and make a recommendation to the full board when it meets on the first of the month." With that, he strode out of the Men's Bar, leaving the other three standing at their table.

"He's going to give himself a heart attack," Gorton mused as he sat down again and reached for his drink.

Franklin shook his head. "No. The judge is the kind of man who doesn't get a heart attack, he gives them."

Nottingham chuckled. "But he seems dead set against this dueling machine proposition."

"And he's the swing vote on the supreme court, from what I hear," said Gorton.

Franklin beckoned to the waiter for another mug of ale, then hunched forward in his chair like a conspirator about to reveal his plans.

"About the dueling machine," he said, his voice lowered.

"Yes?"

"You remember Martin Luther King's famous line, 'I have a dream'?"

"Yes."

"Well, I have a scheme."

Thus it was arranged that Rick Gorton, amiable Pooh Bear of a man, would challenge Justice Halpern to a duel. It was all done in a very friendly way, of course. The next afternoon, when the four men met again at the Club, Halpern was in a smiling mood.

Gazing around the warm dark paneling of the Men's Bar, the judge said with some satisfaction, "Well, at least I got the committee to agree that we should dig in our heels and recommend that the board reject the women's petition out of hand."

"D'you think the board will have the guts to follow your recommendation?" Gorton asked.

"They caved in to the women before," Nottingham recalled, clear distaste in his voice and face.

"They haven't been particularly famous for their courage," Franklin added.

With tight-lipped determination, Justice Halpern said, "The board will follow my rec . . . er, I mean, the committee's recommendation, never fear." He looked admiringly around the soothingly dark, pleasingly quiet room. "This old place will remain a male bastion."

Franklin nodded knowingly, remembering that several key members of the club's board had cases pending before Justice Halpern.

"That's good news," Franklin murmured.

"Indeed it is," said Halpern, with a self-satisfied smile. He signaled the barkeep for his usual brandy and soda.

Franklin glanced at Gorton, who glanced in turn at Nottingham.

When neither of them said a word, Franklin spoke up. "When will the supreme court decide on the dueling machine proposal?"

Halpern gave him a sharp look. "In two weeks, when we open the year's hearings."

Very gently, Franklin stepped on the toe of Gorton's nearer shoe.

The patent attorney took the hint. "Y'know, your honor, it doesn't seem right to make a decision on the case without trying a duel yourself."

"Me?" The judge looked alarmed. "Fight a duel?"

"In virtual reality," Gorton said. "Nobody gets hurt."

"It's all nonsense," the judge grumbled.

Franklin nudged Gorton under the table again, harder, and the patent attorney said, "I could be your challenger. You could pick any setting you like. Choose your weapons."

Halpern gave Gorton one of his well-known icy stares.

Nottingham came in with the line they had rehearsed earlier in the day. "You would be the only member of the court who has experienced the dueling machine. The other justices would have to look up to you, follow your example."

"It's all nonsense," Halpern repeated.

Franklin nodded sagely. "I understand. It's a little scary, fighting a duel—even in virtual reality."

"You told me no one gets hurt," the judge said.

"Nobody does," Gorton said. "I've fought three duels so far. They're fun!"

"Three duels?" Halpern asked.

With a pleasant grin, Gorton said, "Once I was a fighter pilot in a World War One biplane. And I was a knight fighting in a tournament, armor and lances and all that." He added sheepishly, "I lost that one."

"Your opponent unhorsed you?" Nottingham asked, on cue.

"He killed me," Gorton said, still grinning. "Skewered me with his lance, right through my shield and armor and all."

Halpern looked aghast. "You died?"

"In the VR simulation. Opened my eyes and I was back in the dueling machine booth, safe and sound. No blood."

"That . . . that's interesting," said the judge.

"If you fought a duel," Franklin asked, his bearded face all innocent curiosity, "what setting would you choose? What weapons?"

Trained psychologist that he was, Franklin had assessed Halpern wisely. It took only a few days of sophisticated arm-twisting to get the judge to agree to face Rick Gorton in a duel—under the conditions that Justice Halpern picked.

The only sign of apprehension that Halpern showed as the four men entered the VR Duels, Inc., facility was a barely discernable throbbing of the blue vein in his forehead, just about his left eye.

Gorton seemed perfectly at ease, his round face displaying his usual easygoing, lopsided smile. Franklin was quiet and very serious; Nottingham stiffly formal.

The dueling machine office was located in a busy, noisy shopping mall, sited between a music store thronged with teenagers and a pharmacy that catered to Medicare patients. Once the four men had pushed through the facility's front doors, the place looked more like a medical clinic than the kind of gaming arcade that Halpern had expected. There was a small anteroom, its walls all hospital white and bare. Through an open doorway he could see a larger room that was filled with a row of booths, also in sterile white décor.

A pleasant-faced young man was sitting at the desk in the anteroom. He wore a white tunic and slacks, with a stylized pair of crossed sky blue scimitars on the breast of the tunic.

"Justice Halpern?" said the young man, his smile showing perfect gleaming teeth. "Precisely on time."

As the young man gestured them to the curved plastic chairs in front of his desk, a pair of slim young women stepped into the anteroom and stood on either side of the open doorway. They also wore white tunics with the blue crossed scimitars, and slacks. They too were smiling professionally.

"And you must be Mr. Richard Gorton, Esq.," said the young man. Looking at Franklin and Nottingham, his expression grew a bit more serious. "And you gentlemen?"

"We are friends of the combatants," said Nottingham.

"Seconds," Franklin said.

"I see," said the young man. "Well, we really have no need of seconds, but if you'd like to remain during the duel we have a seating area inside the main room."

The man identified himself as the duel coordinator and briefly outlined the procedure: each of the duelists would be placed in a soundproofed, windowless booth, where the young women—who were simulations technicians—would help them into their sensor suits and helmets.

With a glance at the computer screen on his desk, the coordinator said, "I see that you have chosen the Battle of Waterloo as the setting for your duel. Your weapons are sabers and lances."

"Correct," Halpern said, his voice brittle with tension. Gorton merely rubbed his nose and nodded.

"Very well, gentlemen," said the coordinator, rising from his desk. "If you will simply follow the technicians, they will prepare you for your duel. Good luck to each of you."

Halpern waited for him to say, *May the better man win*, but the coordinator refrained from that cliché.

He followed the slim young woman on his right into the inner room; she stopped at the first booth in the row that lined its wall. Gorton was led into the next booth, beside it.

"You'll have to take off your outer clothing, sir," said the technician, still smiling, "and put on the sensor suit that's hanging inside the booth. You can call me when you're ready."

Halpern felt some alarm. No one had told him he'd have to strip. He glared at the young woman, who remained smilingly unperturbed as she held open the door to the booth.

Reluctantly, grumbling to himself, Justice Halpern stepped into the booth. Once the women closed its door and he himself clicked its lock, he saw that the booth's curving walls were bare. The only furniture inside was a stiff-backed chair. A set of what looked like old fashioned longjohns was hanging against the wall.

Justice Halpern scanned the claustrophobic little booth for a sign of hidden cameras. With some trepidation, he peeled down to his underwear as quickly as he could and pulled on the gray, nubby outfit. It felt fuzzy against his bare arms and legs, almost as if it were infested with vermin.

"Are you ready, sir?" came the technician's voice through a speaker grill set into the ceiling of the booth.

Halpern nodded, then realizing that she couldn't see him (hoping that she couldn't, actually) he said crisply, "I'm ready."

The lock clicked and the door swung open. The young woman stepped inside and suddenly the booth felt very crowded to Halpern. He smelled the delicate scent of her perfume.

She was carrying a plastic helmet under one arm. It looked like a biker's helmet to Halpern. Resting the helmet on the chair, she pulled a white oblong object from her tunic pocket, about the size and shape of a TV remote controller, and ran it up and down Halpern's fuzzy-suited body.

Nodding, she said, "Your suit is activated. Good."

"No wires?" he asked.

Her smile returning, she replied, "Everything is wireless, sir."

Halpern wished she wouldn't call him *sir*. It made him feel a hundred years old.

She picked the helmet off the chair and handed it to him. "Put it on and pull down the visor. When the duel begins the visor will go totally black for a moment. Don't panic. It's only for a moment or two while we program the duel for you. When it clears you'll see the place where your duel is set."

Halpern wordlessly put on the helmet. It felt heavy, cumbersome.

"Now pull down the visor, please."

He did. It was tinted but he could see her clearly enough.

She looked him up and down one final time, then said, "Okay, you're ready for your duel. You can sit down." She turned to the door, stepped through, gave him a final gleaming smile, and closed the booth's door.

Halpern sat down.

"Halpern-Gorton duel commencing in ten seconds," came a man's voice in his helmet earphones.

Then everything went black.

Before he could do anything more than gulp with fright, the darkness vanished in a swirl of colors and then the rolling hills of a green countryside appeared.

A trace of a cold smile curled Randolph Halpern's thin lips. He was sitting astride his favorite mount, the chestnut mare that the Iron Duke himself had given him.

Gorton and the rest of them think they're going to make a fool of me, Halpern said to himself as he patted the mare's neck, gentling her. *They don't know that I've studied every aspect of the Battle of Waterloo since I was in prelaw.*

Behind him, screened by the thick forest, the entire brigade was lined up and waiting eagerly for Halpern's order to charge. It all seemed so very real! The smell of the grass, the distant rumble of artillery, even the warmth of the sun on his shoulders, now that the morning rain had drifted away. The simulation is well-nigh perfect, Halpern had to admit. Virtual reality, as seemingly real as the genuine thing.

He could hear his men's horses snuffling impatiently, sense their eagerness to come to grips with their wily foe. Up on the sparsely wooded ridge ahead Halpern could see Bonaparte's Frenchies, pennants flying from their lances, as they trotted toward the distant town of Waterloo.

He pulled his saber from its scabbard with the clean whisper of deadly steel and a hundred other sabers slid from their scabbards behind him.

"England expects every man to do his best!" Halpern shouted. Then he pointed his saber at the enemy and spurred his mount into a charge.

The French lancers were caught completely by surprise, as Halpern had planned. His brigade charged into their flank in a wild screaming melee of flashing steel and dust and blood. Within moments it was over. The French had been routed.

All except their leader, who sat panting and sweating on his devil's black stallion, gripping his bloodied lance in one big-knuckled hand and staring at Halpern, his chest heaving beneath his gaudy uniform.

It was Gorton, of course, big easy-going Rick Gorton, looking more like a frightened oversized child than one of Napoleon's brave lancers.

"He's mine, lads," Halpern cried, and he charged straight at his opponent.

Who stood his ground and casually skewered the incautious Halpern on his lance. The pain was monumental. Halpern fought to remain conscious, to raise his saber, to strike the detested enemy in the name of God, Harry and Saint George. Instead, he slipped into darkness.

And opened his eyes in the booth of the dueling machine. The same young technician had opened the booth's door and was lifting the virtual reality helmet off Halpern's bald head, which was glistening with perspiration.

"I'm afraid you lost, sir," said the young woman, her earlier smile replaced by a sorrowful countenance. "Better luck next time."

"You weren't supposed to beat him," Herb Franklin growled.

Rick Gorton looked embarrassed. "I didn't mean to, by golly. He just ran onto my lance."

The two lawyers were sitting in a corner of the Men's Bar. Franklin was scowling like a Santa Claus confronting a naughty boy.

"Now he'll never vote in favor of making duels legally binding. Never."

Gorton shrugged helplessly and ordered another scotch.

As the waiter brought his drink, John Nottingham entered the bar, scanned the mostly empty tables, and made straight for them.

"How's the Sword of Justice this morning?" Franklin asked dismally.

"He's busy persuading the other members of the board to turn down the women's petition," Nottingham said as he slid into the chair between the two men.

"What about the dueling machine?"

Nottingham shrugged elaborately. "I think that's a hopeless cause. He fought a duel and lost. Got himself killed."

Franklin shot a scowl toward Gorton.

"He's certainly not going to decide in favor of allowing duels to be legally valid," Nottingham concluded.

"Well don't blame me," Gorton said. "I didn't expect him to charge right into my lance."

Franklin sank back in his chair, his normally jolly face clouded with thought. Nottingham ordered his usual rye and ginger ale while Gorton sat staring into his scotch like a little boy who'd been caught poaching cookies.

At last Franklin straightened up and asked, "When does the board vote on the women's petition?"

"First of the month," said Nottingham. "Monday."

"And when does the supreme court hand down its decision about the dueling machine?"

"The fifteenth."

Franklin nodded. His old smile returned to his bearded face, but this time there was something just the slightest bit crafty about it.

A chilly wind was driving brittle leaves down the street as Justice Halpern left the Carleton Club. He bundled his topcoat around his body and peered down toward the taxi stand on the corner. No cabs, of course: during the rush hour they were all busy.

Standing at the top of the Club's entryway steps, wishing he hadn't given his chauffeur the afternoon off, Halpern thought he might as well go back inside and have the doorman phone for a taxi. It would take at least a half hour, he knew. *I'll wait in the Men's Bar*, he thought.

But as he stepped through the glass front door and into the Club's foyer a tiny slip of a woman accosted him.

"Justice Halpern," she said, as if she was pronouncing sentence over him.

Suppressing a frown, Halpern said frostily, "You have the advantage over me, Miss."

"Roxanne Harte, Esq.," she said. "*Ms.* Roxanne Harte." She pronounced the Ms. like a colony of bees swarming.

"How do you do?" Halpern noticed that Ms. Harte couldn't have been out of law school for very long. She was a petite redhead, rather pretty, although her china blue eyes seemed to be blazing with some inner fury.

"You are a member here?" he asked, feeling nettled.

"As much a member as you are, sir. And I'm very unhappy with you, your honor."

"With me?"

"With you, sir."

Halpern looked around the foyer. The uniformed doorman was standing by the cloakroom, chatting quietly with the attendant there. No one else in sight. Or earshot.

"I don't understand," he said to Ms. Harte. "Why should you be unhappy with me? What have I done—"

"You're trying to convince the board to reject our petition."

Halpern's eyes went wide. "You're one of . . . of those?"

"One of the women who want to end the chauvinistic monopoly you maintain over the Men's Bar, yes, that's me."

Feeling almost embarrassed at this little snip of a woman's arrogance, Halpern said, "This isn't the place to discuss Club matters, young lady."

"I agree," she snapped. "I know a much better way to settle this issue, once and for all."

"How do you propose—"

She never let him finish his question. "I challenge you to a duel, sir."

"A duel?"

"Choose your weapons!"

"This is nonsense," Halpern said. He began to turn away from her.

But Roxanne Harte grabbed him by the sleeve and with her other hand delivered a resounding slap to Halpern's face.

"Choose your weapons," she repeated.

Halpern stood there, his cheek burning. The doorman and cloakroom attendant were staring at him. John Nottingham came through the door from the Club's interior and stopped, sensing instinctively that something was wrong.

"Well?" Ms. Harte demanded.

"I can't fight a duel with you," Halpern said. "You're only a woman."

"That's the attitude that makes this duel necessary, isn't it?" she said, practically snarling.

Drawing himself up to his full height, Halpern said, "I have every advantage over you. I am taller, heavier, stronger. You couldn't stand up to me in a duel."

"What about pistols?" Ms. Harte replied immediately. "Back in the old west they called the Colt six-gun the Equalizer. How about a duel with pistols?"

Halpern was about to point out to her that he was the Club's champion pistol shot for the past three years running. But he stopped himself. *Why should I tell her? She wants to fight a duel against me. She's the one who suggested pistols.*

Nodding, Justice Halpern said through clenched teeth, "Very well, then. Pistols it will be." And he added silently, *You little fool.*

News of the duel spread through the Club almost instantly, of course. By the following afternoon, as Justice Halpern stepped into the Men's Bar for his customary libation, every man there got to his feet and applauded.

Halpern tried to hide the pleasure he felt as he made his way across the room to the table where Franklin, Gorton and Nottingham were sitting.

"The defender of our rights and privileges," Franklin said, beaming, as the judge sat down.

"By golly," said Gorton, "I've got to hand it to you, your honor. It's high time somebody stood up for what's right."

Nottingham was a bit more subdued. "From what I understand, you have agreed that the outcome of this duel will decide whether or not the women's petition will be accepted."

"That's right," Halpern said, as the Hispanic waiter placed his brandy and soda in front of him. "If she wins, the Men's Bar will be opened to women."

"But she won't win," Gorton said. Then he added, "Will she?"

"How could she," Franklin said, "against the Club's best shot?"

"You've agreed on the setting?" Nottingham asked.

"A frontier saloon in the old west," said Halpern as he reached for his drink. With a smile that was almost a smirk he added, "She'll have to come in through the ladies' entrance, I expect."

The following morning Halpern had his chauffeur drive him back to the shopping mall where the VR Duels, Inc., facility was. Franklin, Gorton and Nottingham were already there, even though he arrived scrupulously on time. Ms. Harte was nowhere to be found.

Typical woman, Halpern said to himself. Late for the appointment. Then he thought, *Maybe she won't show up at all.* The idea pleased him immensely.

Franklin and the others looked very serious as the stood in the anteroom waiting for his opponent.

"Relax," Halpern told them. "The purity of the Men's Bar will not be defiled."

At that moment Ms. Harte burst into the room, looking rather like a worried high school student who'd been sent down to the principal's office for discipline.

"Sorry I'm late," she said, avoiding Halpern's stern gaze.

Halpern felt growing impatience as the same bright-smiling technician carefully went over each and every detail of the duel, the sensor suit, and the helmet he would have to wear. *Get on with it!* he railed at her silently. But he kept his face and demeanor perfectly polite, absolutely correct. He allowed himself to show no hint of impatience.

"You'll have to stand on your feet for this duel," said the technician just before she closed the door of the booth, leaving Halpern clothed in the nubby sensor suit and unwieldy biker's helmet. The helmet felt heavy, and he couldn't get over the feeling that some kind of loathsome bugs were worming their way under his skin.

The technician shut the door at last. Halpern stood alone for a long moment that seemed to stretch indefinitely. The booth was narrow, confining, its walls smooth and bare.

"Okay," he heard a man's voice in his helmet earphones. "Activating Halpern-Harte duel."

The world went completely dark for an instant, then a brief flare of colors swirled before his eyes and he heard a muted rumbling noise.

Abruptly he was standing at the bar of an old west frontier saloon, crowded with rough-looking men, bearded and unwashed, smelly. Over in one corner a man who looked suspiciously like Rick Gorton was banging away at a tinny-sounding piano. It can't be Gorton, Halpern said to himself. Looking at the piano player more closely, Halpern saw that he had a bushy red beard and his fingernail were cracked and dirty.

"What're you having, Judge?"

Halpern turned and saw the bartender smiling at him. The man looked a little like Herb Franklin, but much younger, more rugged, his beard darker and rather bedraggled. A badly stained apron was tied around his ample middle.

"Judge?" the bartender prompted.

"Brandy and soda," said Halpern.

The bartender's bushy brows hiked up. "You want to put sarsaparilla in your brandy, Judge?"

Halpern thought a moment, then shook his head. "No. Water. Brandy and a glass of water. No ice."

The bartender gave him a puzzled look, then reached for a bottle, muttering to himself, "Ice?"

Halpern looked up at his reflection in the mirror behind the bar. He saw that he was wearing a long black frock coat and a black, wide-brimmed hat. On his right hip he felt the weight of a heavy pistol. A

Colt six-shooter, he surmised. Not the sleek, well-balanced Glock automatic he used at the target range in the Club's basement. This thing felt like a cannon.

"Brandy and water," the bartender said, slapping two glasses onto the surface of the bar. Some of the water splashed onto the polished wood.

Halpern took a cautious sip. It was awful. *Like vinegar mixed with battery acid,* he thought.

Turning, he surveyed the crowded barroom. Lots of dusty, unshaven, grubby men in boots and grimy clothes lining the bar. Others sitting at tables. Looked like an intense game of poker was going on in the farthest corner. Everybody carried a gun; some of the men had two. He almost expected to see John Wayne come sauntering through the swinging doors. Or Clint Eastwood, at least.

The swinging doors did indeed bang open and a tiny, almost elfin figure stepped in. Wearing scuffed cowboy boots, faded Levis, an unbuttoned leather vest over a checkered shirt and a beat-up brown Stetson pulled low. Gritty with trail dust. She had a Colt revolver strapped to her hip.

Halpern recognized Ms. Harte, just barely. He saw the blazing anger in those china blue eyes.

She took five steps into the barroom and stopped, facing Halpern.

"Judge," she called across the crowded saloon, "you hanged my kid brother for cattle rustlin' that he didn't do."

The barroom went totally silent. Instinctively Halpern pushed the edge of his frock coat away from the butt of the pistol holstered at his hip.

"The jury found him guilty," he said, surprised at the quaver in his voice.

"'Cause you threw out the evidence that would've cleared him, you sneaky polecat."

"That's not true!"

"You callin' me a liar? Go for that hawgleg, Judge."

With that Ms. Harte started to draw the six-shooter from her holster. Halpern fumbled for his gun. It was huge and heavy, felt as if it weight ten pounds.

To his credit, he got off the first shot. The plate glass window behind Ms. Harte shattered. She fired once, twice. He heard glassware smashing on the bar behind him. Men were diving everywhere to get out of the line of fire. Halpern saw the piano player spin around on his little stool, eyes wide, a lopsided grin on his thickly bearded face.

He fired again and a chair two feet to Ms. Harte's left went clattering across the floor. *This isn't like target shooting!* Halpern realized. *Not at all.*

A bullet tore at his frock coat and Halpern felt a sudden need to urinate. He fired at his unmoving opponent and her hat flew off her head. She didn't even wince. She shot again and more glassware exploded behind him.

Gripping his cumbersome long-barreled pistol in both hands, Halpern fired once again.

Ms. Harte toppled over backwards, her smoking pistol flying from her hand. Her bright blue eyes closed forever.

For a moment Halpern was plunged into utter darkness. Then he felt the VR helmet being lifted off his head. The young woman smiled at him warmly.

"You won, Justice Halpern. You won the duel."

Halpern licked his lips and then smiled back at the technician. "Yes, I did, didn't I? I shot her dead."

On shaky legs he stepped out of the virtual reality booth. Ms. Harte was coming out of the booth on the other side of the room. She smiled weakly at him.

"Touché," she called across the chamber.

Halpern bowed graciously. Perhaps there is something to this dueling machine business, after all, he thought.

It was a seafood restaurant: small, slightly tatty, and completely on the other side of the city from the supreme court's building and the Carleton Club.

Herb Franklin smiled as he got to his feet to welcome his luncheon guest. He had barely had a chance to sit at the table; she was right on time.

"Congratulations," he said to Roxanne Harte, Esq.

Ms. Harte smiled prettily as she took the chair that Franklin held for her.

"It did come out pretty well, didn't it?" she said.

Franklin took his own chair as he said, "The supreme court handed down its decision this morning. Duels in properly registered dueling machine facilities are now recognized as legally binding. First state in the union to go for it."

"A precedent," said Ms. Harte, as she picked up the menu that lay atop her plate.

"This state is a trendsetter." Franklin was beaming.

"Justice Halpern voted with the majority?" she asked.

Nodding vigorously, Franklin told her, "He wrote the majority opinion, no less."

Ms. Harte smiled prettily. "I'll bet VR Duels, Inc., will declare a dividend."

"Very likely," Franklin agreed happily. "Very likely."

They both ordered trout and Franklin picked a dry white wine to go with the fish.

"I really want to thank you," Franklin said, once they had sipped at the wine. "I know it was quite a sacrifice for you."

"Sacrifice?"

"The Club's board turned down your petition about the Men's Bar."

Ms. Harte shrugged prettily. "It wasn't *my* petition. I don't care about your old Men's Bar."

"Oh," said Franklin. "When I first talked to you about it, I thought—"

"I'm not a radical feminist. The petition was just the bait for your trap. And it worked."

Franklin nodded, a little warily, and turned his attention to the trout.

She said, "So now the good citizens of this state can settle their differences with a duel in virtual reality."

"Under the specified conditions. Both parties have to sign a formal agreement to make the results of the duel binding on them."

She took another sip of wine, then said, "It's funny. You told me that Justice Halpern was a champion pistol shot, but he was worse than I am."

"There's a big difference between shooting at a target and firing at someone who's shooting back at you," Franklin said. "And that Dragoon's revolver we gave him is a lot different from the Glock he's accustomed to."

"I suppose," Ms. Harte agreed faintly. "But boy, he was a really rotten shot, you know. I deliberately missed him four times and I still had to pretend to be hit; he never came close to me."

Franklin hissed, "For god's sake don't let anyone else know that! If it ever gets back to him . . ."

"Don't worry, my lips are sealed," she replied. "After all, an assistant district attorney has got to have some discretion."

With a relieved chuckle, Franklin said, "You'll get the next opening in the DA's office. It's all set. We just have to wait a few months so Halpern doesn't start putting two and two together."

She nodded, but then asked, "So why did you go through all this? Why are you so intent on getting VR duels accepted as legally binding?"

Franklin eyed her carefully for a long, silent moment. At last he answered, "Several reasons. First, it will help people get their differences settled without waiting for months or even years for a court to come to a decision for them."

"Uh-huh."

"Second, it will unclog court calendars. A lot of petty nuisance suits will disappear. People will fight duels instead of calling for lawyers."

"Lawyers' incomes will go down, you know."

"Yes, but it's all for the best," Franklin said loftily. "It will make our society better. Healthier. People will take out their aggressions in harmless but emotionally satisfying virtual reality duels. As a former psychologist, I'm certain that it will be a great benefit to society."

"Really?"

"So some lawyers won't make as much money," he went on. "They won't have as many ambulances to chase. So what? Money isn't everything. We have to think of the greater good."

"I see." Ms. Harte broke into a knowing grin. "And just how much money have you invested in VR Duels, Inc.?"

Franklin tried to keep a straight face but failed. Smiling like a true lawyer, he replied, "Quite a bit, Roxanne, my dear. Quite a healthy goddamned bit."

MARS FARTS

First, I should apologize for the somewhat vulgar title. But, as you will see, it really is appropriate.

Satellites placed in orbit around the planet Mars have detected occasional whiffs of methane gas in the thin Martian atmosphere. They seem to appear seasonally, in the springtime.

Methane is a compound of carbon and hydrogen. The gas is quickly broken up into its constituent elements by solar ultraviolet radiation. The freed hydrogen presumably wafts to the top of the atmosphere and eventually boils away into space.

So the methane is destroyed almost as soon as it is produced. Yet something produces fresh methane every year.

On Earth, microbes living deep underground use the energy of our planet's hot core to drive their metabolism. They eat rock or iron, and excrete methane.

Could such methanogenic bacteria be producing the methane found in the Martian atmosphere?

"**A CATHOLIC,** a Jew, and a Moslem are stuck in the middle of Mars," said Rashid Faiyum.

"That isn't funny," Jacob Bernstein replied, wearily.

Patrick O'Connor, the leader of the three-man team, shook his head inside the helmet of his pressure suit. "Laugh and the world laughs with you, Jake."

None of them could see the faces of their companions through the tinting of their helmet visors. But they could hear the bleakness in Bernstein's tone. "There's not much to laugh about, is there?"

"Not much," Faiyum agreed.

All around them stretched the barren, frozen rust-red sands of Utopia Planita. Their little hopper leaned lopsidedly on its three spindly legs in the middle of newly churned pockmarks from the meteor shower that had struck the area overnight.

Off on the horizon stood the blocky form of the old Viking 2 lander, which had been there for more than a century. One of their mission objectives had been to retrieve parts of the Viking to return to Earth, for study and eventual sale to a museum. Like everything else about their mission, that objective had been sidelined by the meteor shower. Their goal now was survival.

A barrage of tiny bits of stone, most of them no larger than dust motes. Once they had been part of an icy comet, but the ice had melted away after god-knows how many trips around the sun, and now only the stones were left when the remains of the comet happened to collide with the planet Mars.

One of the rare stones, almost the size of a pebble, had punctured the fuel cell that was the main electrical power source for the three-man hopper. Without the electrical power from that fuel cell, their rocket engine could not function. They were stranded in the middle of the frozen, arid plain.

In his gleaming silvery pressure suit, Faiyum reminded O'Connor of a knight in shining armor, except that he was bending into the bay that held the fuel cell, his helmeted head obscured by the bay's upraised hatch. Bernstein, similarly suited, stood by nervously beside him.

The hatch had been punctured by what looked like a bullet hole. Faiyum was muttering, "Of all the meteoroids in all the solar system in all of Mars, this one's got to smack our power cell."

Bernstein asked, "How bad is it?"

Straightening up, Faiyum replied, "All the hydrogen drained out during the night. It's dead as a doornail."

"Then so are we," Bernstein said.

"I'd better call Tithonium," said O'Connor, and he headed for the ladder that led to the hopper's cramped cockpit. "While the batteries are still good."

"How long will they last?" asked Bernstein.

"Long enough to get help."

It wasn't that easy. The communications link back to Tithonium was relayed by a network of satellites in low orbit around Mars, and it would be another half-hour before one of the commsats came over their horizon.

Faiyum and Bernstein followed O'Connor back into the cockpit, and suddenly the compact little space was uncomfortably crowded.

With nothing to do but wait, O'Connor said, "I'll pressurize the cockpit so we can take off the helmets and have some breakfast."

"I don't think we should waste electrical power until we get confirmation from Tithonium that they're sending a backup to us."

"We've got to eat," O'Connor said.

Sitting this close in the cramped cockpit, they could see each other's faces even through the helmet visors' tinting. Faiyum broke into a stubbly chinned grin.

"Let's pretend its Ramadan," he suggested, "and we have to fast from sunup to sundown."

"Like you fast during Ramadan," Bernstein sniped. O'Connor remembered one of their first days on Mars, when a clean-shaven Faiyum had jokingly asked which direction Mecca was. O'Connor had pointed up.

"Let's not waste power," Bernstein repeated.

"We have enough power during the day," Faiyum pointed out. "The solar panels work fine."

Thanks to Mars' thin, nearly cloudless atmosphere, just about the same amount of sunshine fell upon the surface of Mars as upon Earth, despite Mars' farther distance from the sun. *Thank God for that*, O'Connor thought. *Otherwise we'd be dead in a few hours.*

Then he realized that, also thanks to Mars' thin atmosphere, those micrometeoroids had made it all the way down to the ground to strafe them like a spray of bullets, instead of burning up from atmospheric friction, as they would have on Earth. *The Lord giveth and the Lord taketh away*, he told himself.

"Tithonium here," a voice crackled through the speaker on the cockpit control panel. All three of them turned to the display screen, suddenly tight with expectation.

"What's your situation, E-three?" asked the face in the screen. Ernie Roebuck, they recognized: chief communications engineer.

The main base for the exploration team was down at Tithonium Chasma, part of the immense Grand Canyon of Mars, more than three thousand kilometers from their Excursion Three site.

O'Connor was the team's astronaut: a thoroughly competent Boston Irishman with a genial disposition who tolerated the bantering of Faiyum and Bernstein—both geologists—and tried to keep them from developing a real animosity. A Moslem from Peoria and a New York Jew: how in the world had the psychologists back Earthside ever put the two of them on the same team, he wondered.

In the clipped jargon of professional fliers, O'Connor reported on their dead fuel cell.

"No power output at all?" Roebuck looked incredulous.

"Zero," said O'Connor. "Hydrogen all leaked out overnight."

"How did you get through the night?"

"The vehicle automatically switched to battery power."

"What's the status of your battery system?"

O'Connor scanned the digital readouts on the control panel. "Down to one-third of nominal. The solar panels are recharging 'em."

A pause. Roebuck looked away and they could hear voices muttering in the background. "All right," said the communicator at last. "We're getting your telemetry. We'll get back to you in an hour or so."

"We need a lift out of here," O'Connor said.

Another few moments of silence. "That might not be possible right away. We've got other problems, too. You guys weren't the only ones hit by the meteor shower. We've taken some damage here. The garden's been wiped out and E-one has two casualties."

Excursion One was at the flank of Olympus Mons, the tallest mountain in the solar system.

"Our first priority has to be to get those people from E-one back here for medical treatment."

"Yeah. Of course."

"Give us a couple of hours to sort things out. We'll call you back at noon, our time. Sit tight."

O'Connor glanced at the morose faces of his two teammates, then replied, "We'll wait for your call."

"What the hell else can we do?" Bernstein grumbled.

Clicking off the video link, O'Connor said, "We can get back to work."

Faiyum tried to shrug inside his suit. "I like your first suggestion better. Let's eat."

With their helmets off, the faint traces of body odors became noticeable. Munching on an energy bar, Faiyum said, "A Catholic, a Moslem and a Jew were showering together in a YMCA . . ."

"You mean a YMHA," said Bernstein.

"How would a Moslem get into either one?" O'Connor wondered.

"It's in the States," Faiyum explained. "They let anybody in."

"Not women."

"You guys have no sense of humor." Faiyum popped the last morsel of the energy bar into his mouth.

"This," Bernstein countered, "coming from a man who was named after a depression."

"El-Faiyum is below sea level," Faiyum admitted easily, "but it's the garden spot of Egypt. Has been for more than three thousand years."

"Maybe it was the garden of Eden," O'Connor suggested.

"No, that was in Israel," said Bernstein.

"Was it?"

"It certainly wasn't here," Faiyum said, gazing out the windshield at the bleak, cold Martian desert.

"It's going to go down near a hundred below again tonight," Bernstein said.

"The batteries will keep the heaters going," said O'Connor.

"All night?"

"Long enough. Then we'll recharge 'em when the sun comes up."

"That won't work forever," Bernstein muttered.

"We'll be okay for a day or two."

"Yeah, but the nights. A hundred below zero. The batteries will crap out pretty soon."

Tightly, O'Connor repeated, "We'll be okay for a day or two."

"From your mouth to God's ear," Bernstein said fervently.

Faiyum looked at the control panel's digital clock. "Another three hours before Tithonium calls."

Reaching for his helmet, O'Connor said, "Well, we'd better go out and do what we came here to do."

"Haul up the ice core," said Bernstein, displeasure clear on his lean, harsh face.

"That's why we're here," Faiyum said. He didn't look any happier than Bernstein. "Slave labor."

Putting on a false heartiness, O'Connor said, "Hey, you guys are the geologists. I thought you were happy to drill down that deep."

"Overjoyed," said Bernstein. "And here on Mars we're doing areology, not geology."

"What's in a name?" Faiyum quoted. "A rose by any other name would still smell."

"And so do you," said Bernstein and O'Connor, in unison.

The major objective of the Excursion Three team had been to drill three hundred meters down into the permafrost that lay just beneath the surface of Utopia Planitia. The frozen remains of what had been an ocean billions of years earlier, when Mars had been a warmer and wetter world, the permafrost ice held a record of the planet's history, a record that geologists (or areologists) keenly wanted to study.

Outside at the drill site, the three men began the laborious task of hauling up the ice core that their equipment had dug. They worked slowly, carefully, to make certain that the fragile, six-centimeter-wide core came out intact. Section by section they unjointed each individual segment as it came up, marked it carefully and stowed it in the special storage racks built into the hopper's side. "How old do you think the lowest layers of this core will be?" Bernstein asked as they watched the electric motor slowly, slowly lifting the slender metal tube that contained the precious ice.

"Couple billion years, at least," Faiyum replied. "Maybe more."

O'Connor, noting that the motor's batteries were down to less than fifty percent of their normal capacity, asked, "Do you think there'll be any living organisms in the ice?"

"Not hardly," said Bernstein.

"I thought there were supposed to be bugs living down there," O'Connor said.

"In the ice?" Bernstein was clearly skeptical.

Faiyum said, "You're talking about methanogens, right?"

"Is that what you call them?"

"Nobody's found anything like that," said Bernstein.

"So far," Faiyum said.

O'Connor said, "Back in training they told us about traces of methane that appear in the Martian atmosphere now and then."

Faiyum chuckled. "And some of the biologists proposed that the methane comes from bacteria living deep underground. The bacteria are supposed to exist on the water melting from the bottom of the permafrost layer, deep underground, and they excrete methane gas."

"Bug farts," said Bernstein.

O'Connor nodded inside his helmet. "Yeah. That's what they told us."

"Totally unproven," Bernstein said.

"So far," Faiyum repeated.

Sounding slightly exasperated, Bernstein said, "Look, there's a dozen abiological ways of generating the slight traces of methane that've been observed in the atmosphere."

"But they appear seasonally," Faiyum pointed out. "And the methane is quickly destroyed in the atmosphere. Solar ultraviolet breaks it down into carbon and hydrogen. That means that *something* is producing the stuff continuously."

"But that doesn't mean it's being produced by biological processes," Bernstein insisted.

"I think it's bug farts," Faiyum said. "It's kind of poetic, you know."

"You're crazy."

"You're a sourpuss."

Before O'Connor could break up their growing argument, their helmet earphones crackled, "Tithonium here."

All three of them snapped to attention. It was a woman's voice and they recognized whose it was: the mission commander, veteran astronaut Gloria Hazeltine, known to most of the men as Glory Hallelujah. The fact that Glory herself was calling them didn't bode well, O'Connor thought. *She's got bad news to tell us.*

"We've checked out the numbers," said her disembodied radio voice. "The earliest we can get a rescue flight out to you will be in five days."

"Five days?" O'Connor yipped.

"That's the best we can do, Pat," the mission commander said, her tone as hard as concrete. "You'll have to make ends meet until then."

"Our batteries will crap out on us, Gloria. You know that."

"Conserve power. Your solar panels are okay, aren't they?"

Nodding, O'Connor replied, "They weren't touched, thank God."

"So recharge your batteries by day and use minimum power at night. We'll come and get you as soon as we possibly can."

"Right." O'Connor clicked off the radio connection.

"They'll come and pick up our frozen bodies," Bernstein grumbled.

Faiyum looked just as disappointed as Bernstein, but he put on a lopsided grin and said, "At least our bodies will be well preserved."

"Frozen solid," O'Connor agreed.

The three men stood there, out in the open, encased in their pressure suits and helmets, while the drill's motor buzzed away as if nothing was wrong. In the thin Martian atmosphere, the drill's drone was strangely high pitched: more of a whine than a hum.

Finally, Bernstein said, "Well, we might as well finish the job we came out here to do."

"Yeah," said Faiyum, without the slightest trace of enthusiasm.

The strangely small sun was nearing the horizon by the time they had stored all the segments of the ice core in the insulated racks on the hopper's side.

"A record of nearly three billion years of Martian history," said Bernstein, almost proudly.

"Only one and a half billion years," Faiyum corrected. "The Martian year is twice as long as Earth years."

"Six hundred eighty-seven Earth days," Bernstein said. "That's not quite twice a terrestrial year."

"So sue me," Faiyum countered, as he pulled an equipment kit from the hopper's storage bay.

"What're you doing?" O'Connor asked.

"Setting up the laser spectrometer," Faiyum replied. "You know, the experiment the biologists want us to do."

"Looking for bug farts," Bernstein said.

"Yeah. Just because we're going to freeze to death is no reason to stop working."

O'Connor grunted. *Rashid is right*, he thought. *Go through the motions. Stay busy.*

With Bernstein's obviously reluctant help, Faiyum set up the laser and trained it at the opening of their bore hole. Then they checked out the Rayleigh scattering receiver and plugged it into the radio that would automatically transmit its results back to Tithonium. The radio had its own battery to supply the microwatts of power it required.

"That ought to make the biologists happy," Bernstein said, once they were finished.

"Better get back inside," O'Connor said, looking toward the horizon where the sun was setting.

"It's going to be a long night," Bernstein muttered.

"Yeah."

Once they were sealed into the cockpit and had removed their helmets, Faiyum said, "A biologist, a geologist, and Glory Hallelujah were locked in a hotel room in Bangkok."

Bernstein moaned. O'Connor said, "You know that everything we say is being recorded for the mission log."

Faiyum said, "Hell, we're going to be dead by the time they get to us. What difference does it make?"

"No disrespect for the mission commander."

Faiyum shrugged. "Okay. How about this one: a physicist, a mathematician and a lawyer are each asked, 'How much is two and two?'"

"I heard this one," Bernstein said.

Without paying his teammate the slightest attention, Faiyum plowed ahead. "The mathematician says, 'Two and two are four. Always four. Four point zero.' The physicist thinks a minute and says, 'It's somewhere between three point eight and four point two.'"

O'Connor smiled. *Yes, a physicist probably would put it that way,* he thought.

"So what does the lawyer answer?"

With a big grin, Faiyum replied, "The lawyer says, 'How much is two and two? How much do you want it to be?'"

Bernstein groaned, but O'Connor laughed. "Lawyers," he said.

"We could use a lawyer here," Bernstein said. "Sue the bastards."

"Which bastards?"

Bernstein shrugged elaborately. "All of them," he finally said.

The night was long. And dark. And cold. O'Connor set the cockpit's thermostat to barely above freezing, and ordered the two geologists to switch off their suit heaters.

"We've got to preserve every watt of electrical power we can. Stretch out the battery life as much as possible," he said firmly.

The two geologists nodded glumly.

"Better put our helmets back on," said Bernstein.

Faiyum nodded. "Better piss now, before it gets frozen."

The suits were well insulated, O'Connor knew. *They'll hold our body heat better than blankets*, he told himself. He remembered camping in New England, when he'd been a kid. Got pretty cold there. Then a mocking voice in his mind answered, *But not a hundred below.*

They made it through the first night and woke up stiff and shuddering and miserable. The sun was up, as usual, and the solar panels were feeding electrical power to the cockpit's heaters.

"That wasn't too bad," O'Connor said, as they munched on ration bars for breakfast.

Faiyum made a face. "Other than that, how did you like the play, Mrs. Lincoln?"

Bernstein pointed to the control panel's displays. "Batteries damned near died overnight," he said.

"The solar panels are recharging them," O'Connor replied.

"They won't come back a hundred percent," said Bernstein. "You know that."

O'Connor bit back the reply he wanted to make. He merely nodded and murmured, "I know."

Faiyum peered at the display from the laser they had set up outside. "I'll be damned."

The other two hunched up closer to him.

"Look at that," said Faiyum, pointing. "The spectrometer's showing there actually is methane seeping out of our bore hole."

"Methanogens?" mused Bernstein.

"Can't be anything else," Faiyum said. With a wide smile, he said, "We've discovered life on Mars! We could win the Nobel Prize for this!"

"Posthumously," said Bernstein.

"We've got to get this data back to Tithonium," said O'Connor. "Let the biologists take a look at it."

"It's being telemetered to Tithonium automatically," Bernstein reminded him.

"Yeah, but I want to see what the biologists have to say."

The biologists were disappointingly cautious. Yes, it was methane gas seeping up from the bore hole. Yes, it very well might be coming from methanogenic bacteria living deep underground. But they needed more conclusive evidence.

"Could you get samples from the bottom of your bore hole?" asked the lead biologist, an Hispanic American from California. In the video screen on the control panel, he looked as if he were trying hard not to get excited.

"We've got the ice core," Faiyum replied immediately. "I'll bet we've got samples of the bugs in the bottom layers."

"Keep it well protected," the biologist urged.

"It's protected," O'Connor assured him.

"We'll examine it when you bring it in," the biologist said, putting on a serious face.

Once the video link was disconnected, Bernstein said morosely, "They'll be more interested in the damned ice core than in our frozen bodies."

All day long they watched the spikes of the spectrometer's flickering display. The gas issuing from their bore hole was mostly methane, and it was coming up continuously, a thin invisible breath issuing from deep below the surface.

"Those bugs are farting away down there," Faiyum said happily. "Busy little bastards."

"Sun's going down," said Bernstein.

O'Connor checked the batteries' status. Even with the solar panels recharging them all day, they were barely up to seventy-five percent of their nominal capacity. He did some quick arithmetic in his head. *If it takes Tithonium five days to get us, we'll have frozen to death on the fourth night.*

Like Shackleton at the South Pole, he thought. *Froze to death, all of 'em.*

They made it through the second night, but O'Connor barely slept. He finally dozed off, listening to the soft breeze wafting by outside. When he awoke every joint in his body ached and it took nearly an hour for him to stop his uncontrollable trembling.

As they chewed on their nearly frozen breakfast bars, Bernstein said, "We're not going to make it."

"I can put in a call to Tithonium, tell 'em we're in a bad way."

"They can see our telemetry," Faiyum said, unusually morose. "They know the batteries are draining away."

"We can ask them for help."

"Yeah," said Bernstein. "When's the last time Glory Hallelujah changed her mind about anything?"

O'Connor called anyway. In the video screen, Gloria Hazeltine's chunky blonde face looked like an implacable goddess.

"We're doing everything we can," she said, her voice flat and final. "We'll get to you as soon as we can. Conserve your power. Turn off everything you don't need to keep yourselves alive."

Once O'Connor broke the comm link, Bernstein grumbled, "Maybe we could hold our breaths for three-four days."

But Faiyum was staring at the spectrometer readout. Methane gas was still coming out of the bore hole, a thin waft, but steady.

"Or maybe we could breathe bug farts," he said.

"What?"

Looking out the windshield toward their bore hole, Faiyum said, "Methane contains hydrogen. If we can capture the methane those bug are emitting . . ."

"How do we get the hydrogen out of it?" O'Connor asked.

"Lase it. That'll break it up into hydrogen and carbon. The carbon precipitates out, leaving the hydrogen for us to feed to the fuel cell."

Bernstein shook his head. "How're we going to capture the methane in the first place? And then how are we going to repair the fuel cell's damage?"

"We can weld a patch on the cell," O'Connor said. "We've got the tools for that."

"And we can attach a weather balloon to the bore hole. That'll hold the methane coming out."

"Yeah, but will it be enough to power up the fuel cell?"

"We'll see."

With Bernstein clearly doubtful, they broke into the equipment locker and pulled out the small, almost delicate, welding rod and supplies. Faiyum opened the bin that contained the weather balloons.

"The meteorologists aren't going to like our using their stuff," Bernstein said. "We're supposed to be releasing these balloons twice a day."

Before O'Connor could reply with a choice, *Fuck the meteorologists*, Faiyum snapped, "Let 'em eat cake."

They got to work. As team leader, O'Connor was glad of the excuse to be doing something. *Even if this is a big flop*, he thought, *it's better to be busy than to just lay around and wait to die.*

As he stretched one of the weather balloons over the bore hole and fastened it in place, Faiyum kept up a steady stream of timeworn jokes. Bernstein groaned in the proper places and O'Connor sweated inside his suit while he laboriously welded the bullet-hole sized puncture of the fuel cell's hydrogen tank.

By mid-afternoon the weather balloon was swelling nicely.

"How much hydrogen do you think we've got there?" Bernstein wondered.

"Not enough," said Faiyum, serious for once. "We'll need three, four balloons full. Maybe more."

O'Connor looked westward, out across the bleak frozen plain. The sun would be setting in another couple of hours.

When they finished their day's work and clambered back into the cockpit, O'Connor saw that the batteries were barely up to half their standard power level, even with the solar panels recharging them all day.

We're not going to make it, he thought. But he said nothing. He could see that the other two stared at the battery readout. No one said a word, though.

The night was worse than ever. O'Connor couldn't sleep. The cold *hurt*. He had turned off his suit radio, so he couldn't tell if the other two had drifted off to sleep. He couldn't. He knew that when a man froze to death, he fell asleep first. Not a bad way to die, he said to himself. *As if there's a good way.*

He was surprised when the first rays of sunlight woke him. *I fell asleep anyway. I didn't die. Not yet.*

Faiyum wasn't in the cockpit, he saw. Looking blearily through the windshield he spotted the geologist in the early morning sun fixing a fresh balloon to the bore hole, with a big round yellow balloon bobbing from a rock he'd tied it to.

O'Connor saw Faiyum waving to him and gesturing to his left wrist, then remembered that he had turned his suit radio off. He clicked the control stud on his wrist.

". . . damned near ready to burst," Faiyum was saying. "Good thing I came out here in time."

Bernstein was lying back in his cranked-down seat, either asleep or . . . O'Connor nudged his shoulder. No reaction. He shook the man harder.

"Wha . . . what's going on?"

O'Connor let out a breath that he hadn't realized he'd been holding. "You okay?" he asked softly.

"I gotta take a crap."

O'Connor giggled. *He's alright. We made it through the night.* But then he turned to the control panel and saw that the batteries were down to zero.

Faiyum and Bernstein spent the day building a system of pipes that led from the balloon's neck to the input valve of the repaired fuel cell's hydrogen tank. As long as the sun was shining they had plenty of electricity to power the laser. Faiyum fastened the balloon's neck to one of the hopper's spidery little landing legs and connected it to the rickety-looking pipework. *Damned contraption's going to leak like a sieve*, O'Conner thought. *Hydrogen's sneaky stuff.*

As he worked he kept up his patter of inane jokes. "A Catholic, a Moslem and a Jew—"

"How come the Jew is always last on your list?" Bernstein asked, from his post at the fuel cell. O'Connor saw that the hydrogen tank was starting to fill.

Faiyum launched into an elaborate joke from the ancient days of the old Soviet Union, in which Jews were turned away from everything from butcher's shops to clothing stores.

"They weren't even allowed to stand in line," he explained as he held the bobbing balloon by its neck. "So when the guys who've been waiting in line at the butcher's shop since sunrise are told that there's no meat today, one of them turns to another and says, 'See, the Jews get the best of everything!'"

"I don't get it," Bernstein complained.

"They didn't have to stand in line all day."

"Because they were discriminated against."

Faiyum shook his head. "I thought you people were supposed to have a great sense of humor."

"When we hear something funny."

O'Connor suppressed a giggle. Bernstein understood the joke perfectly well, he thought, but he wasn't going to let Faiyum know it.

By the time the sun touched the horizon again, the fuel cell's hydrogen tank was half full and the hopper's batteries were totally dead.

O'Connor called Tithonium. "We're going to run on the fuel cell tonight."

For the first time since he'd known her, Gloria Hazeltine looked surprised. "But I thought your fuel cell was dead."

"We've resurrected it," O'Connor said happily. "We've got enough hydrogen to run the heaters most of the night."

"Where'd you get the hydrogen?" Glory Hallelujah was wide-eyed with curiosity.

"Bug farts," shouted Faiyum, from over O'Connor's shoulder.

They made it through the night almost comfortably and spent the next day filling balloons with methane, then breaking down the gas into its components and filling the fuel cell's tank with hydrogen.

By the time the relief ship from Tithonium landed beside their hopper, O'Connor was almost ready to wave them off and return to the base on their own power.

Instead, though, he spent the day helping his teammates and the two-man crew of the relief ship to attach the storage racks with their previous ice core onto the bigger vehicle.

As they took off for Tithonium, five men jammed into the ship's command deck, O'Connor felt almost sad to be leaving their little hopper alone on the frigid plain. Almost. *We'll be back*, he told himself. *And we'll salvage the Viking 2 lander when we return.*

Faiyum showed no remorse about leaving at all. "A Jew, a Catholic and a Moslem walk into a bar."

"Not another one," Bernstein groused.

Undeterred, Faiyum plowed ahead. "The bartender takes one look at them and says, 'What is this, a joke?'"

Even Bernstein laughed.

A PALE BLUE DOT

Galileo wrote, "Astronomers seek to investigate the true constitution of the universe—the most important and most admirable problem that there is."

Astronomers have found in recent years thousands of planets orbiting other stars. But so far, none of these exoplanets resembles Earth very closely. No one has yet found a "pale blue dot" like our own planet out among the stars.

Not yet.

But the search goes on, year by patient year, using constantly better instruments and ideas. Sky-scanning telescopes dot mountaintops all across our world. Telescopes have been placed in space, to look farther and better.

And as the frontiers of knowledge and discovery move on, the search for a pale blue dot continues.

The most important and most admirable problem that there is.

✳ ✳

TOM DANIELS tiptoed down the shadowy concrete corridor toward the door marked STAFF ONLY.

This is cool, he said to himself. *Like a spy or a detective or something.*

He was celebrating his fifteenth birthday in his own way. All summer long he'd been stuck here at the observatory. His father had said it would be fun, but Tom wished he'd stayed back home with Mom and all his friends. There weren't any other kids at the observatory, nobody his own age anywhere nearby. And there wasn't much for a bright, curious fifteen-year-old to do, either.

He remembered last summer, when he'd stayed home with Mom. *At least at home I could go out in the back yard at night and look at the sky.* He remembered the meteor shower that had filled the night with blazing streaks of falling stars.

No meteor showers here, he thought. *Not this summer. Not ever.*

Sure, Dad tried to find busywork for him. Check the auxiliary battery packs for the computers. Handle the e-mail going back to the university. *If that was fun,* Tom thought, *then having pneumonia must be hysterical.*

There was one time, though, when Dad let him come into the telescope control center and look at the images the big 'scopes were getting. That was way cool. Stars and more stars, big groady clouds of glowing gas hanging out there in deep space. Better than cool. Radical.

That was what Tom wanted. To be in on the excitement. To discover something that nobody had ever seen before.

But Dad was too busy to let Tom back into the control center again. He was in charge of building the new telescope, the one that everybody said would be powerful enough to image Earth-sized planets orbiting around other stars. Other worlds like Earth.

All the observatory's telescopes were searching for planets circling around other stars. They had found plenty of them, too: giant worlds, all of them much bigger than Earth. None of them had an ocean of blue water. None had fleecy white clouds and an atmosphere rich with oxygen. No "pale blue dot" like Earth.

Dad said this new 'scope just might be able to find a pale blue dot out there among the stars: a pale blue dot like Earth.

So Tom tiptoed to the locked steel door, all alone in the middle of the night, determined to celebrate his birthday in his own way.

He had memorized the lock's electronic code long ago. Now he tapped the keypad set into the concrete wall and heard its faint beeps. For a moment nothing happened, then the door clicked open.

What if somebody's in the control center? Tom asked himself. *What if Dad's in there? I'm supposed to be asleep in my bunk.*

He shook his head. None of the astronomers worked this late at night unless something special was going on. The big telescopes outside were all automated; the computers collected the images they saw and recorded all the data. Only if something unusual happened would anybody get out of bed and come down here.

He hoped.

Pushing through the heavy steel door, Tom saw that the control center really was empty. Even the ceiling lights were off; the only light in the cramped little room came from the computer screens, flickering off the walls in an eerie greenish glow.

The big display screen on the wall showed the telescopes outside, big spidery frameworks of steel and aluminum pointing out at the black night sky.

His heart thumping faster than usual, Tom went straight to the console where the new telescope was controlled. He sat in the little wheeled chair, just as his father would. For a moment he hesitated, then, licking his lips nervously, he booted up the computer.

"Happy birthday to me," Tom whispered as the screen lit up and showed a display of icons.

Dad's going to be pretty sore when he finds out I used the new 'scope before anybody else, Tom thought. *But if I discover something, something new and important, maybe he won't get so mad. Maybe I can find the pale blue dot he's been looking for.*

Tom knew the telescope was already focused on a particular planet orbiting a distant star. He leaned forward in his chair and pecked at the keyboard to get some pictures on the screen. Up came an image of the planet that was being observed by the new telescope: a big slightly flattened sphere covered with gaudy stripes and splotches of color. Along the bottom of the screen a data bar showed what the telescope's sensors had determined: the planet's size, its density, the chemical elements it was made of.

Tom saw that the planet was a lot like Jupiter, but much bigger. A huge gas giant of a planet, without even a solid surface to it. So very different from Earth. Seven hundred lightyears away. He calculated quickly in his head: *That's forty-two trillion miles. I'm seeing this planet the way it looked seven hundred years ago; it's taken light that many years to cross the distance from there to here.*

Then his breath caught in his throat. From behind the curve of the planet's rim, Tom saw something new appearing.

A moon, he realized. It had been hidden behind the planet's huge bulk. Glancing at the data bar he saw that this moon was almost the same size as Earth. And it gleamed a faint, soft blue.

A pale blue dot! As the distant moon moved clear of the planet it orbited, Tom saw a world that looked like Earth.

He yanked the phone from its holder and punched out his father's number. "Dad! Come quick! Quick!"

Before his father could ask a question Tommy hung up, bent forward in his chair, staring at this distant blue world.

Then he looked again at the data bar. This world showed no water. No oxygen. The blue color was from methane, a deadly unbreathable gas.

His father burst into the data center. "What is it, Tom? What's wrong?"

Feeling almost ashamed, Tommy showed him the display screen. "I thought I'd found a world like Earth," he said, crushingly disappointed.

"What are you doing in here?" his father demanded. "You ought to be in bed, asleep."

"I . . ." Tom took a deep breath. "I'm celebrating my birthday."

"Your birthday? That's not until tomorrow."

"It's past midnight, Dad."

Dad's frown melted slowly into a smile. "Yes, so it is. Well, happy birthday, son."

"Thanks, Dad."

"I had a surprise party arranged for you," Dad said, almost wistfully. "With a videophone call arranged from your mother and sister."

Tom tried not to laugh. "I guess I surprised you, instead."

"I guess you did."

Dad spent almost half an hour studying Tommy's discovery.

"Well, it's not like Earth is *now*," he said at last, "but Earth had a lot of methane in its atmosphere a few billion years ago."

"It did?" Tommy brightened a little.

"Yes, back when life first began on our world."

"So this world is like ours was, way back then?"

"Perhaps," his father said. "You've made a real discovery, Thomas. This is the first world we've found that could become Earth-like, in a few billion years. By studying this world we might be able to learn a lot more about our own."

"Really?"

Dad was grinning broadly now. "We'll have to write a paper for the journal about this."

"We? You mean, us?"

"You made the discovery, didn't you? Daniels and Daniels, co-authors."

"Wow!"

The two of them worked side by side for several more hours, using the telescope's sensors to measure as much as they could about this distant new world.

Finally, as the morning shift started coming into the center, Tom asked, "Have you ever made a big discovery, Dad?"

His father shook his head and smiled sorrowfully. "Can't say that I have, Tom. I've put my whole life into astronomy, but I've never made what you could call a big discovery."

Tom nodded glumly.

"But here you are, fifteen years old, and you've already made a significant discovery. You're going to make a fine astronomer, my boy."

"I don't know if I want to be an astronomer," Tommy said.

His father looked shocked. "Why not?"

"I don't know," said Tom. "I was lucky tonight, I guess. But is it really worth all the work? Night after night, day after day? I mean, you've spent your whole life being an astronomer, and it hasn't made you rich or famous, has it?"

"No, it hasn't," his father admitted.

"And it keeps you away from Mom and us kids a lot of the time. Far away."

"That's true enough."

"So what good is it? What does astronomy do for us?"

Dad gave him a funny look. Getting up from the computer, he said, "Let's take a walk outside."

"Outside?" That surprised Tom.

He followed his father down the bare concrete corridor and they struggled into their outdoor suits.

"Science is like a great building, Tom," Dad said as he opened the inner hatch. "Like a cathedral that's still being built, one brick at a time. You added a new brick tonight."

"One little brick," Tom mumbled.

"That's the way it's built, son. One little brick adds to all the others."

Dad swung the outer hatch open. "But there's always so much more to learn. The cathedral isn't finished yet. Perhaps it never will be."

They stepped outside onto the barren dusty ground. Through the visor of his helmet Tom saw the spidery frameworks of the Lunar Farside Observatory's giant telescopes rising all around them. And beyond stretched the universe of stars, thousands, millions of stars glowing in the eternal night of deep space, looking down on the battered face of the Moon where they stood.

Tom felt a lump in his throat. "Maybe I'll stick with astronomy, after all," he said to his father. And he thought it might be fun to add a few more bricks to the cathedral.

Afterword to
A PALE BLUE DOT

This story was inspired by Jocelyn Bell Burnell, who in 1967 discovered the first pulsar while she was doing "grunge work" as a graduate student at Cambridge University. Pulsars are collapsed stars that emit powerful pulses of radio energy.

STARS, WON'T
YOU HIDE ME

Anybody can write about the end of the world. The first time I heard the old folk song, "Sinner Man," I got a vision of a story about the end of the universe. The questions of guilt and responsibility—the concept of an inexorable balancing of the cosmic scales—were all suggested by the song. And, I hope, in this story.

* 🪐 *

> *O sinner-man, where are you going to run to?*
> *O sinner-man, where are you going to run to?*
> *O sinner-man, where are you going to run to*
> *All on that day?*

THE SHIP WAS HURT, and Holman could feel its pain. He lay fetal-like in the contoured couch, his silvery uniform spiderwebbed by dozens of contact and probe wires connecting him to the ship so thoroughly that it was hard to tell where his own nervous system ended and the electronic networks of the ship began.

Holman felt the throb of the ship's mighty engines as his own pulse, and the gaping wounds in the generator section, where the enemy beams had struck, were searing his flesh. Breathing was

451

difficult, labored, even though the ship was working hard to repair itself.

They were fleeing, he and the ship; hurtling through the star lanes to a refuge. But where?

The main computer flashed its lights to get his attention. Holman rubbed his eyes wearily and said:

"Okay, what is it?"

YOU HAVE NOT SELECTED A COURSE, the computer said aloud, while printing the words on its viewscreen at the same time.

Holman stared at the screen. "Just away from here," he said at last. "Anyplace, as long as it's far away."

The computer blinked thoughtfully for a moment. SPECIFIC COURSE INSTRUCTION IS REQUIRED.

"What difference does it make?" Holman snapped. "It's over. Everything finished. Leave me alone."

IN LIEU OF SPECIFIC INSTRUCTIONS, IT IS NECESSARY TO TAP SUBCONSCIOUS SOURCES.

"Tap away."

The computer did just that. And if it could have been surprised, it would have been at the wishes buried deep in Holman's inner mind. But instead, it merely correlated those wishes to its single-minded purpose of the moment, and relayed a set of navigational instructions to the ship's guidance system.

Run to the moon: O Moon, won't you hide me?
The Lord said: O sinner-man, the moon'll be a-bleeding
All on that day.

The Final Battle had been lost. On a million million planets across the galaxy-studded universe, humankind had been blasted into defeat and annihilation. The Others had returned from across the edge of the observable world, just as man had always feared. They had returned and ruthlessly exterminated the race from Earth.

It had taken eons, but time twisted strangely in a civilization of light-speed ships. Holman himself, barely thirty years old subjectively, had seen both the beginning of the ultimate war and its tragic end. He had gone from school into the military. And fighting inside a ship that could span the known universe in a few decades while he slept in cryogenic suspension, he had aged only ten years during the billions of years that the universe had ticked off in its stately, objective time-flow.

The Final Battle, from which Holman was fleeing, had been fought near an exploded galaxy billions of lightyears from the Milky Way and Earth. There, with the ghastly bluish glare of uncountable shattered stars as a backdrop, the once-mighty fleets of humankind had been arrayed. Mortals and Immortals alike, the humans drew themselves up to face the implacable Others.

The enemy won. Not easily, but completely. Humankind was crushed, totally. A few fleeing men in a few battered ships was all that remained. Even the Immortals, Holman thought wryly, had not escaped. The Others had taken special care to make certain that they were definitely killed.

So it was over.

Holman's mind pictured the blood-soaked planets he had seen during his brief, ageless lifetime of violence. His thoughts drifted back to his own homeworld, his own family: gone long, long centuries ago. Crumbled into dust by geological time or blasted suddenly by the overpowering Others. Either way, the remorseless flow of time had covered them over completely, obliterated them, in the span of a few of Holman's heartbeats.

All gone now. All the people he knew, all the planets he had seen through the ship's electroptical eyes, all of humankind . . . extinct.

He could feel the drowsiness settling upon him. The ship was accelerating to lightspeed, and the cyrogenic sleep was coming, but he didn't want to fall into slumber with those thoughts of blood and terror and loss before him.

With a conscious effort, Holman focused his thoughts on the only other available subject: the outside world, the universe of galaxies. An infinitely black sky studded with islands of stars. Glowing shapes of light, spiral, ovoid, elliptical. Little smears of warmth in the hollow unending darkness; dabs of red and blue standing against the engulfing night.

One of them, he knew, was the Milky Way. Humanity's original home. From this distance it looked the same. Unchanged by little annoyances like the annihilation of an intelligent race of star-roamers.

He drowsed.

The ship bore onward, preceded by an invisible net of force, thousands of kilometers in radius, that scooped in the rare atoms of hydrogen drifting between the galaxies and fed them into the ship's wounded, aching generators.

Something . . . a thought. Holman stirred in the couch. A consciousness—vague, distant, alien—brushed his mind.

He opened his eyes and looked at the computer viewscreen. Blank. "Who is it?" he asked.

A thought skittered away from him. He got the impression of other minds: simple, open, almost childish. Innocent and curious.

It's a ship.

Where is it . . . oh, yes. I can sense it now. A beautiful ship.

Holman squinted with concentration.

It's very far away. I can barely reach it.

And inside of the ship . . .

It's a man. A human!

He's afraid.

He makes me feel afraid!

Holman called out, "Where are you?"

He's trying to speak.

Don't answer!

But . . .

He makes me afraid. Don't answer him. We've heard about humans!

Holman asked, "Help me."

Don't answer him and he'll go away. He's already so far off that I can barely hear him.

But he asks for help.

Yes, because he knows what is following him. Don't answer. Don't answer!

Their thoughts slid away from his mind. Holman automatically focused the outside viewscreens, but here in the emptiness between galaxies he could find neither ship nor planet anywhere in sight. He listened again, so hard that his head started to ache. But no more voices. He was alone again, alone in the metal womb of the ship.

He knows what is following him. Their words echoed in his brain. Are the Others following me? Have they picked up my trail? They must have. They must be right behind me.

He could feel the cold perspiration start to trickle over him.

"But they can't catch me as long as I keep moving," he muttered. "Right?"

CORRECT, said the computer, flashing lights at him. AT A RELATIVISTIC VELOCITY. WITHIN LESS THAN ONE PERCENT OF LIGHTSPEED, IT IS IMPOSSIBLE FOR THIS SHIP TO BE OVERTAKEN.

"Nothing can catch me as long as I keep running."

But his mind conjured up a thought of the Immortals. Nothing could kill them . . . except the Others.

Despite himself, Holman dropped into deepsleep. His body temperature plummeted to near-zero. His heartbeat nearly stopped. And as the ship streaked at almost lightspeed, a hardly visible blur to anyone looking for it, the outside world continued to live at its own pace. Stars coalesced from gas clouds, matured, and died in explosions that fed new clouds for newer stars. Planets formed and grew mantles of air. Life took root and multiplied, evolved, built a myriad of civilizations in just as many different forms, decayed and died away.

All while Holman slept.

Run to the sea: O sea, won't you hide me?
The Lord said: O sinner-man, the sea'll be a-sinking
All on that day.

The computer woke him gently with a series of soft chimes.

APPROACHING THE SOLAR SYSTEM AND PLANET EARTH, AS INDICATED BY YOUR SUBCONSCIOUS COURSE INSTRUCTIONS.

Planet Earth, humankind's original home world. Holman nodded. Yes, this was where he had wanted to go. He had never seen the Earth, never been on this side of the Milky Way galaxy. Now he would visit the teeming nucleus of man's doomed civilization. He would bring the news of the awful defeat, and be on the site of humankind's birth when the inexorable tide of extinction washed over the Earth.

He noticed, as he adjusted the outside viewscreens, that the pain had gone.

"The generators have repaired themselves," he said.

WHILE YOU SLEPT. POWER GENERATION SYSTEM NOW OPERATING NORMALLY.

Holman smiled. But the smile faded as the ship swooped closer to the solar system. He turned from the outside viewscreens to the computer once again. "Are the 'scopes working all right?"

The computer hummed briefly, then replied. SUBSYSTEMS CHECK SATISFACTORY, COMPONENT CHECK SATISFACTORY. INTEGRATED EQUIPMENT CHECK POSITIVE. VIEWING EQUIPMENT FUNCTIONING NORMALLY.

Holman looked again. The sun was rushing up to meet his gaze, but something was wrong about it. He knew deep within him, even without having ever seen the sun this close before, that something was wrong. The sun was whitish and somehow stunted looking, not the full yellow orb he had seen in videos. And the Earth . . .

The ship took up a parking orbit around a planet scoured clean of life: a blackened ball of rock, airless, waterless. Hovering over the empty, charred ground, Holman stared at the devastation with tears in his eyes. Nothing was left. Not a brick, not a blade of grass, not a drop of water.

"The Others," he whispered. "They got here first."

NEGATIVE, the computer replied. CHECK OF STELLAR POSITIONS FROM EARTH REFERENCE SHOWS THAT SEVEN BILLION YEARS HAVE ELAPSED SINCE THE FINAL BATTLE.

"Seven billion . . ."

LOGIC CIRCUITS INDICATE THE SUN HAS GONE THROUGH A NOVA PHASE, A COMPLETELY NATURAL PHENOMENON UNRELATED TO ENEMY ACTION.

Holman pounded a fist on the unflinching armrest of his couch. "Why did I come here? I wasn't born on Earth. I never saw Earth before . . ."

YOUR SUBCONSCIOUS INDICATES A SUBJECTIVE IMPULSE STIRRED BY . . .

"To hell with my subconscious!" He stared out at the dead world again. "All those people . . . the cities, all the millions of years of evolution, of life. Even the oceans are gone. I never saw an ocean. Did you know that? I've traveled over half the universe and never saw an ocean."

OCEANS ARE A COMPARATIVELY RARE PHENOMENON

EXISTING ON ONLY ONE OUT OF APPROXIMATELY THREE THOUSAND PLANETS.

The ship drifted outward from Earth, past a blackened Mars, a shrunken Jupiter, a ringless Saturn.

"Where do I go now?" Holman asked.

The computer stayed silent.

Run to the Lord: O Lord, won't you hide me?
The Lord said: O sinner-man, you ought to been a praying
All on that day.

Holman sat blankly while the ship swung out past the orbit of Pluto and into the comet belt at the outermost reaches of the sun's domain.

He was suddenly aware of someone watching him.

No cause for fear. I am not of the Others.

It was an utterly calm, placid voice speaking in his mind: almost gentle, except that it was completely devoid of emotion.

"Who are you?"

An observer. Nothing more.

"What are you doing out here? Where are you, I can't see anything . . ."

I have been waiting for any stray survivor of the Final Battle to return to humankind's first home. You are the only one to come this way, in all this time.

"Waiting? Why?"

Holman sensed a bemused shrug, and a giant spreading of vast wings.

I am an observer. I have watched humankind since the beginning. Several of my race even attempted to make contact with you from time to time. But the results were always the same—about as useful as your attempts to communicate with insects. We are too different from each other. We have evolved on different planes. There was no basis for understanding between us.

"But you watched us."

Yes. Watched you grow strong and reach out to the stars, only to be smashed back by the Others. Watched you regain your strength, go back among the stars. But this time you were constantly on guard, wary,

alert, waiting for the Others to strike once again. Watched you find
civilizations that you could not comprehend, such as our own, bypass
them as you spread through the galaxies. Watched you contact
civilizations of your own level, that you could communicate with. You
usually went to war with them.

"And all you did was watch?"

We tried to warn you from time to time. We tried to advise you. But
the warnings, the contacts, the glimpses of the future that we gave you
were always ignored or derided.

So you boiled out into space for the second time, and met other
societies at your own level of understanding—aggressive, proud, fearful.
And like the children you are, you fought endlessly.

"But the Others . . . what about them?"

They are your punishment.

"Punishment? For what? Because we fought wars?"

No. For stealing immortality.

"Stealing immortality? We worked for it. We learned how to make
humans immortal. Some sort of chemicals. We were going to
immortalize the whole race . . . I could've become immortal. *Immortal!*
But they couldn't stand that . . . the Others. They attacked us."

He sensed a disapproving shake of the head.

"It's true," Holman insisted. "They were afraid of how powerful we
would become once we were all immortal. So they attacked us while
they still could. Just as they had done a million years earlier. They
destroyed Earth's first interstellar civilization, and tried to finish us
permanently. They even caused Ice Ages on Earth to make sure none
of us would survive. But we lived through it and went back to the stars.
So they hit us again. They wiped us out. Good God, for all I know I'm
the last human being in the whole universe."

Your knowledge of the truth is imperfect. Humankind could have
achieved immortality in time. Most races evolve that way eventually.
But you were impatient. You stole immortality.

"Because we did it artificially, with chemicals. That's stealing it?"

Because the chemicals that gave you immortality came from the
bodies of the race you called the Flower Folk. And to take the chemicals,
it was necessary to kill individuals of that race.

Holman's eyes widened. "What?"

For every human made immortal, one of the Flower Folk had to die.

"We killed them? Those harmless little . . ." His voice trailed off.

To achieve racial immortality for humankind, it would have been necessary to perform racial murder on the Flower Folk.

Holman heard the words, but his mind was numb, trying to shut down tight on itself and squeeze out reality.

That is why the Others struck. That is why they had attacked you earlier. During your first expansion among the stars you had found another race, with the same chemical of immortality. You were taking them into your laboratories and methodically murdering them. The Others stopped you then. But they took pity on you, and let a few survivors remain on Earth. They used your Ice Ages as a kindness, to speed your development back to civilization, not to hinder you. They hoped you might evolve into a better species. But when the opportunity for immortality came your way once more, you seized it, regardless of the cost, heedless of your own ethical standards. It became necessary to extinguish you, the Others decided.

"And not a single civilization in the whole universe would help us."

Why should they?

"So it's wrong for us to kill, but it's perfectly all right for the Others to exterminate us."

No one has spoken of right and wrong. I have only told you the truth.

"They're going to kill every last one of us."

There is only one of you remaining.

The words flashed through Holman. "I'm the only one . . . the last one?"

No answer.

He was alone now. Totally alone. Except for those who were following.

Run to Satan: O Satan, won't you hide me?
Satan said: O sinner-man, step right in
All on that day.

Holman sat in shocked silence as the solar system shrank to a pinpoint of light and finally blended into the mighty panorama of stars that streamed across the eternal night of space. The ship raced away, sensing Holman's guilt and misery in its electronic way.

Immortality through murder, Holman repeated to himself over

and over. Racial immortality through racial murder. And he had been a part of it! He had defended it, even sought immortality as his reward. He had fought his whole lifetime for it, and killed—so that he would not have to face death.

He sat there surrounded by self-repairing machinery, dressed in a silvery uniform, linked to a thousand automatic systems that fed him, kept him warm, regulated his air supply, monitored his blood flow, exercised his muscles with ultrasonic vibrators, pumped vitamins into him, merged his mind with the passionless brain of the ship, kept his body tanned and vigorous, his reflexes razor-sharp. He sat there unseeing, his eyes pinpointed on a horror that he had helped to create. Not consciously, of course. But to Holman, that was all the worse. He had fought without knowing what he was defending. Without even asking himself about it. All the marvels of humankind's ingenuity, all the deepest longings of the soul, focused on racial murder.

Finally he became aware of the computer's frantic buzzing and lightflashing.

"What is it?"

COURSE INSTRUCTIONS ARE REQUIRED.

"What difference does it make? Why run anymore?"

YOUR DUTY IS TO PRESERVE YOURSELF UNTIL ORDERED TO DO OTHERWISE.

Holman heard himself laugh. "Ordered? By who? There's nobody left."

THAT IS AN UNPROVED ASSUMPTION.

"The war was billions of years ago," Holman said. "It's been over for eons. Humankind died in that war. Earth no longer exists. The sun is a white dwarf star. We're anachronisms, you and me."

THE WORD IS ATAVISM.

"The hell with the word! I want to end it. I'm tired."

IT IS TREASONABLE TO SURRENDER WHILE STILL CAPABLE OF FIGHTING AND/OR ELUDING THE ENEMY.

"So shoot me for treason. That's as good a way as any."

IT IS IMPOSSIBLE FOR SYSTEMS OF THIS SHIP TO HARM YOU.

"All right then, let's stop running. The Others will find us soon enough once we stop. They'll know what to do."

THIS SHIP CANNOT DELIBERATELY ALLOW ITSELF TO FALL INTO ENEMY HANDS.

"You're disobeying me?"

THIS SHIP IS PROGRAMMED FOR MAXIMUM EFFECTIVENESS AGAINST THE ENEMY. A WEAPONS SYSTEM DOES NOT SURRENDER VOLUNTARILY.

"I'm no weapons system, I'm a man, dammit!"

THIS WEAPONS SYSTEM INCLUDES A HUMAN PILOT. IT WAS DESIGNED FOR HUMAN USE. YOU ARE AN INTEGRAL COMPONENT OF THE SYSTEM.

"Damn you . . . I'll kill myself. Is that what you want?"

He reached for the control panels set before him. It would be simple enough to manually shut off the air supply, or blow open an airlock, or even set off the ship's destruct explosives.

But Holman found that he could not move his arms. He could not even sit up straight. He collapsed back into the padded softness of the couch, glaring at the computer viewscreen.

SELF-PROTECTION MECHANISMS INCLUDE THE CAPABILITY OF PREVENTING THE HUMAN COMPONENT OF THE SYSTEM FROM IRRATIONAL ACTIONS.

A series of clicks and blinks, then: IN LIEU OF SPECIFIC COURSE INSTRUCTIONS, A RANDOM EVASION PATTERN WILL BE RUN.

Despite his fiercest efforts, Holman felt himself dropping into deep sleep. Slowly, slowly, everything faded, and darkness engulfed him.

Run to the stars: O stars, won't you hide me?
The Lord said: O sinner-man, the stars'll be a-falling
All on that day.

Holman slept as the ship raced at near-lightspeed in an erratic, meaningless course, looping across galaxies, darting through eons of time. When the computer's probings of Holman's subconscious mind told it that everything was safe, it instructed the cryonics system to reawaken the man.

He blinked, then slowly sat up.

SUBCONSCIOUS INDICATIONS SHOW THAT THE WAVE OF IRRATIONALITY HAS PASSED.

Holman said nothing.

YOU WERE SUFFERING FROM AN EMOTIONAL SHOCK.

"And now it's an emotional pain . . . a permanent, fixed, immutable disease that will kill me, sooner or later. But don't worry, I won't kill myself. I'm over that. And I won't do anything to damage you, either."

COURSE INSTRUCTIONS?

He shrugged. "Let's see what the world looks like out there." Holman focused the outside viewscreens. "Things look different," he said, puzzled. "The sky isn't black anymore, it's sort of grayish—like the first touch of dawn . . ."

COURSE INSTRUCTIONS?

He took a deep breath. "Let's try to find some planet where the people are too young to have heard of humankind, and too innocent to worry about death."

A PRIMITIVE CIVILIZATION. THE SCANNERS CAN ONLY DETECT SUCH SOCIETIES AT EXTREMELY CLOSE RANGE.

"Okay. We've got nothing but time."

The ship doubled back to the nearest galaxy and began a searching pattern. Holman stared at the sky, fascinated. Something strange was happening.

The viewscreens showed him the outside world, and automatically corrected the wavelength shifts caused by the ship's immense velocity. It was as though Holman were watching a speeded-up tape of cosmological evolution. Galaxies seemed to be edging into his field of view, mammoth islands of stars, sometimes coming close enough to collide. He watched the nebulous arms of a giant spiral slice silently through the open latticework of a great ovoid galaxy. He saw two spirals interpenetrate, their loose gas heating to an intense blue that finally disappeared into ultraviolet. And all the while, the once-black sky was getting brighter and brighter.

"Found anything yet?" he absently asked the computer, still staring at the outside view.

You will find no one.

Holman's whole body went rigid. No mistaking it: the Others.

No race, anywhere, will shelter you. We will see to that.

You are alone, and you will be alone until death releases you to join your fellow men.

Their voices inside his head rang with cold fury. An implacable hatred, cosmic and eternal.

"But why me? I'm only one man. What harm can I do now?"

You are a human.

You are accursed. A race of murderers.

Your punishment is extinction.

"But I'm not an Immortal. I never even saw an Immortal. I didn't know about the Flower Folk, I just took orders."

Total extinction.

For all of mankind.

All.

"Judge and jury, all at once. And executioners too. All right . . . try and get me! If you're so powerful, and it means so much to you that you have to wipe out the last single man in the universe—come and get me! Just try."

You have no right to resist.

Your race is evil. All must pay with death.

You cannot escape us.

"I don't care what we've done. Understand? I don't care! Wrong, right, it doesn't matter. I didn't do anything. I won't accept your verdict for something I didn't do."

It makes no difference.

You can flee to the ends of the universe to no avail.

You have forced us to leave our time-continuum. We can never return to our homeworlds again. We have nothing to do but pursue you. Sooner or later your machinery will fail. You cannot flee us forever.

Their thoughts broke off. But Holman could still feel them, still sense them following.

"Can't flee forever," Holman repeated to himself. "Well, I can damn well try."

He looked at the outside viewscreens again, and suddenly the word *forever* took on its real meaning.

The galaxies were clustering in now, falling in together as though sliding down some titanic, invisible slope. The universe had stopped expanding eons ago, Holman now realized. Now it was contracting, pulling together again. It was all ending!

He laughed. Coming to an end. Mankind and the Others, together, coming to the ultimate and complete end of everything.

"How much longer?" he asked the computer. "How long do we have?"

The computer's lights flashed once, twice, then went dark. The viewscreen was dead.

Holman stared at the machine. He looked around the compartment. One by one the outside viewscreens were flickering, becoming static-streaked, weak, and then winking off.

"They're taking over the ship!"

With every ounce of willpower in him, Holman concentrated on the generators and engines. That was the important part, the crucial system that spelled the difference between victory and defeat. The ship had to keep moving! He looked at the instrument panels, but their soft luminosity faded away into darkness. And now it was becoming difficult to breathe. And the heating units seemed to be stopped. Holman could feel his life-warmth ebbing away through the inert metal hull of the dying ship.

But the engines were still throbbing. The ship was still streaking across space and time, heading toward a rendezvous with the infinite.

Surrender.

In a few moments you will be dead. Give up this mad flight and die peacefully.

The ship shuddered violently. What were they doing to it now?

Surrender!

"Go to hell," Holman snapped. "While there's breath in me, I'll spend it fighting you."

You cannot escape.

But now Holman could feel warmth seeping into the ship. He could sense the painful glare outside as billions of galaxies all rushed together down to a single cataclysmic point in spacetime.

"It's almost over!" he shouted, "Almost finished. And you've lost! Humankind is still alive, despite everything you've thrown at him. All of humankind—the good and the bad, the murderers and the music, wars and cities and everything we've ever done, the whole race from the beginning of time to the end—all locked up here in my skull. And I'm still here. Do you hear me? I'm still here!"

The Others were silent.

Holman could feel a majestic rumble outside the ship, like distant thunder.

"The end of the world. The end of everything and everybody. We finish in a tie. Humankind has made it right down to the final second. And if there's another universe after this one, maybe there'll be a place in it for us all over again. How's that for laughs?"

The world ended. Not with a whimper, but a roar of triumph.

MONSTER SLAYER

While most of my stories are set on other worlds, the driving force behind these comes from what is happening on Earth. Here is a tale of one fairly ordinary man, driven to extraordinary deeds—literally driven off the Earth, in order to help save the world.

THIS IS THE WAY the legend began.

He was called Harry Twelvetoes because, like all the men in his family, he was born with six toes on each foot. The white doctor who worked at the clinic on the reservation said the extra toes should be removed right away, so his parents allowed the whites to cut the toes off, even though his great-uncle Cloud Eagle pointed out that Harry's father, and his father's fathers as far back as anyone could remember, had gone through life perfectly well with twelve toes on their feet.

His secret tribal name, of course, was something that no white was ever told. Even in his wildest drunken sprees Harry never spoke it. The truth is, he was embarrassed by it. For the family had named him Monster Slayer, a heavy burden to lay across the shoulders of a little boy, or even the strong young man he grew up to be.

On the day that the white laws said he was old enough to take a job, his great-uncle Cloud Eagle told him to leave the reservation and seek his path in the world beyond.

"Why should I leave?" Harry asked his great-uncle.

Cloud Eagle closed his sad eyes for a moment, then said to Harry, "Look around you, nephew."

Harry looked and saw the tribal lands as he had always seen them, brown desert dotted with mesquite and cactus, steep bluffs worn and furrowed as great-uncle's face, turquoise blue sky and blazing Father Sun baking the land. Yet there was no denying that the land was changing. Off in the distance stood the green fields of the new farms and the tiny dark shapes of the square houses the whites were building. And there were gray rain clouds rising over the mountains.

Refugees were pouring into the high desert. The greenhouse warming that gutted the farms of the whites with drought also brought rains that were filling the dry arroyos of the tribal lands. The desert would be gone one day, the white scientists predicted, turned green and bountiful. So the whites were moving into the reservation.

"This land has been ours since the time of First Man and First Woman," great-uncle said. "But now the whites are swarming in. There is no stopping them. Soon there will be no place of our own left to us. Go. Find your way in the world beyond. It is your destiny."

Reluctantly, Harry left the reservation and his family.

In the noisy, hurried world of the whites jobs were easy to find, but good jobs were not. With so many cities flooded by the greenhouse warming, they were frantically building new housing, whole new villages and towns. Harry got a job with a construction firm in Colorado, where the government was putting up huge tracts of developments for the hordes of refugees from the drowned coastal cities. He started as a lowly laborer, but soon enough worked himself up to a pretty handy worker, a jack of all trades.

He drank most of his pay, although he always sent some of it back to his parents.

One cold, blustery morning, when Harry's head was thundering so badly from a hangover that even the icy wind felt good to him, his supervisor called him over to her heated hut.

"You're gonna kill yourself with this drinking, Harry," said the supervisor, not unkindly.

Harry said nothing. He simply looked past the supervisor's ear at the calendar tacked to the corkboard. The picture showed San Francisco the way it looked before the floods and the rioting.

"You listening to me?" the supervisor asked, more sharply. "This morning you nearly ran the backhoe into the excavation pit, for chrissake."

"I stopped in plenty time," Harry mumbled.

The supervisor just shook her head and told Harry to get back to work. Harry knew from the hard expression on the woman's face that his days with this crew were numbered.

Sure enough, at the shape-up a few mornings later the super took Harry aside and said, "Harry, you Indians have a reputation for being good at high steel work."

Harry's head was thundering again. He drank as much as any two men, but he had enough pride to show up on the job no matter how bad he felt. *Can't slay monsters laying in bed*, he would tell himself, forcing himself to his feet and out to work. Besides, no work, no money. And no money, no beer. No whiskey. No girls who danced on your lap or stripped off their clothes to the rhythm of synthesizer music.

Harry knew that it was the Mohawks back East who were once famous for their steelwork on skyscrapers, but he said nothing to the supervisor except, "That's what I heard, too."

"Must be in your blood, huh?" said the super, squinting at Harry from under her hard hat.

Harry nodded, even though it made his head feel as if some old medicine man was inside there thumping on a drum.

"I got a cousin who needs high steel workers," the super told him. "Over in Greater Denver. He's willing to train newbies. Interested?"

Harry shuffled his feet a little. It was really cold, this early in the morning.

"Well?" the super demanded. "You interested or not?"

"I guess I'm interested," Harry said. It was better than getting fired outright.

As he left the construction site, with the name and number of the super's cousin in his cold-numbed fist, he could hear a few of the other workers snickering.

"There goes old Twelvetoes."

"He'll need all twelve to hold onto those girders up in the wind."

They started making bets on how soon Harry would kill himself.

But Harry became a very good high steel worker, scrambling along the steel girders that formed the skeletons of the new high-rise towers. He cut down on the drinking: alcohol and altitude didn't mix. He traveled from Greater Denver to Las Vegas and all the way down to Texas, where the Gulf of Mexico had swallowed up Galveston and half of Houston.

When he'd been a little boy, his great-uncle had often told Harry that he was destined to do great things. "What great things?" Harry would ask. "You'll see," his great-uncle would say. "You'll know when you find it."

"But what is it?" Harry would insist. "What great things will I do?"

Cloud Eagle replied, "Every man has his own right path, Harry. When you find yours, your life will be in harmony and you'll achieve greatness."

Before he left his childhood home to find his way in the world, his great-uncle gave him a totem, a tiny black carving of a spider.

"The spider has wisdom," he told Harry. "Listen to the wisdom of the spider whenever you have a problem."

Harry shrugged and stuffed the little piece of obsidian into the pocket of his jeans. Then he took the bus that led out of the reservation.

As a grown, hard-fisted man, Harry hardly ever thought of those silly ideas. He didn't have time to think about them when he was working fifty, sixty, seventy stories high with nothing between him and the ground except thin air that blew in gusts strong enough to knock a man off his feet if he wasn't careful.

He didn't think about his great-uncle's prophecy when he went roaring through the bars and girlie joints over weekends. He didn't think about anything when he got so drunk that he fell down and slept like a dead man.

But he kept the spider totem. More than once his pockets had been emptied while he slept in a drunken stupor, but no one ever took the spider from him.

And sometimes the spider did speak to him. It usually happened when he was good and drunk. In a thin, scratchy voice the spider would say, "No more drinking tonight, Harry. You've had enough. Sleep all through tomorrow, be ready for work on Monday."

Most of the time he listened to the totem's whispers. Sometimes he didn't, and those times almost always worked out badly. Like the time in New Houston when three Japanese engineers beat the hell out of him in the alley behind the cat house. They didn't rob him, though. And when Harry came to, in a mess of his own blood and vomit and garbage, the spider was wise enough to refrain from saying, "I told you not to get them angry."

He bounced from job to job, always learning new tricks of the trades, never finding the true path that would bring him peace and harmony. The days blurred into an unending sameness: crawl out of bed, clamber along the girders of a new highrise, wait for the end of the week. The nights were a blur, too: beer, booze, women he hardly ever saw more than once.

Now and then Harry wondered where he was going. "There's more to life than this," the spider whispered to him in his sleep. "Yeah, sure," Harry whispered back. "But what? How do I find it?"

One night, while Harry was working on the big Atlanta Renewal Project, the high steel crew threw a going-away party for Jesse Ali, the best welder in the gang.

"So where's Jesse going?" Harry asked a buddy, beer in hand.

The buddy took a swig of his own beer, then laughed. "He's got a good job, Harry. Great job. It's out of this world." Then he laughed as if he'd made a joke.

"But where is it? Are they hiring?"

"Go ask him," the buddy said.

Harry wormed his way through the gang clustered at the bar and finally made it to Jesse's side.

"Gonna miss you, Jess," he said. Shouted, actually, over the noise of the raucous crowd.

Ali smiled brightly. "Christ, Harry, that's the longest sentence you ever said to me, man."

Harry looked down at the steel-tipped toes of his brogans. He had never been much for conversation, and his curiosity about Jesse's new job was butting its head against his natural reticence. But the spider in his pocket whispered, "Ask him. Don't be afraid. Ask him."

Harry summoned up his courage. "Where you goin'?"

Ali's grin got wider. He pointed a long skinny finger straight up in the air.

Harry said nothing, but the puzzlement must have shown clearly on his face.

"In space, man," Ali explained. "They're building a great big habitat in orbit. Miles long. It'll take years to finish. I'll be able to retire by the time the job's done."

Harry digested that information. "It'll take that long?"

The black man laughed. "Naw. But the pay's that good."

"They lookin' for people?"

With a nod, Ali said, "Yeah. You hafta go through a couple months' training first. Half pay."

"Okay."

"No beer up there, Harry. No gravity, either. I don't think you'd like it."

"Maybe," said Harry.

"No bars. No strip joints."

"They got women, though, don't they?"

"Like Yablonski," said Ali, naming one of the crew who was tougher than any two of the guys.

Harry nodded. "I seen worse."

Ali threw his head back and roared with laughter. Harry drifted away, had a few more beers, then walked slowly through the magnolia-scented evening back to the barracks where most of the construction crew was housed.

Before he drifted to sleep the spider urged him, "Go apply for the job. What do you have to lose?"

It was tough, every step of the way. The woman behind the desk where Harry applied for a position with the space construction outfit clearly didn't like him. She frowned at him and she scowled at her computer screen when his dossier came up. But she passed him on to a man who sat in a private cubicle and had pictures of his wife and kids pinned to the partitions.

"We are an equal opportunity employer," he said, with a brittle smile on his face.

Then he waited for Harry to say something. But Harry didn't know what he should say, so he remained silent.

The man's smile faded. "You'll be living for months at a time in zero gravity, you know," he said. "It affects your bones, your heart. You might not be fit to work again when you return to Earth."

Harry just shrugged, thinking that these whites were trying to scare him.

They put him through a whole day of physical examinations. Then two days of tests. Not like tests in school; they were interested in his physical stamina and his knowledge of welding and construction techniques.

They hired Harry, after warning him that he had to endure two months of training at half the pay he would start making if he finished the training okay. Half pay was still a little more than Harry was making on the Atlanta Renewal Project. He signed on the dotted line.

So Harry flew to Hunstville, Alabama, in a company tiltrotor plane. They gave him a private room, all to himself, in a seedy-looking six-story apartment building on the edge of what had once been a big base for the space agency, before the government sold it off to private interests.

His training was intense. Like being in the army, almost, although all Harry knew about being in the army was what he'd heard from other construction workers. The deal was, they told you something once. You either got it or you flunked out. No second chances.

"Up there in orbit," the instructors would hammer home, time and again, "there won't be a second chance. You screw up, you're dead. And probably a lot of other people get killed, too."

Harry began to understand why there was no beer up there. Nor was there any at the training center. He missed it, missed the comfort of a night out with the gang, missed the laughs and the eventual oblivion where nobody could bother him and everything was dark and quiet and peaceful and even the spider kept silent.

The first time they put him in the water tank Harry nearly freaked. It was *deep*, like maybe as deep as his apartment building was high. He was zipped into a white spacesuit, like a mummy with a bubble helmet on top, and there were three or four guys swimming around him in trunks and scuba gear. But to a man who grew up in the desert, this much water was scary.

"We use the buoyancy tank to simulate the microgravity you'll experience in orbit," the instructor told the class. "You will practice construction techniques in the tank."

As he sank into the water for the first time, almost petrified with fear, the spider told Harry, "This is an ordeal you must pass. Be brave. Show no fear."

For days on end Harry suited up and sank into the deep, clear water to work on make-believe pieces of the structure he'd be building up in space. Each day started with fear, but he battled against it and tried to do the work they wanted him to do. The fear never went away, but Harry completed every task they gave him.

When his two months of training ended, the man in charge of the operation called Harry into his office. He was an Asian of some sort; Chinese, Japanese, maybe Korean.

"To tell you the truth, Harry," he said, "I didn't think you'd make it. You have a reputation for being a carouser, you know."

Harry said nothing. The pictures on the man's wall, behind his desk, were all of rockets taking off on pillars of flame and smoke.

The man broke into a reluctant smile. "But you passed every test we threw at you." He got to his feet and stretched his hand out over his desk. "Congratulations, Harry. You're one of us now."

Harry took his proffered hand. He left the office feeling pretty good about himself. He thought about going off the base and finding a nice friendly bar someplace. But as he dug his hand into his pants pocket and felt the obsidian spider there, he decided against it. That night, as he was drowsing off to sleep, the spider told him, "Now you face the biggest test of all."

Launching off the Earth was like nothing Harry had ever even dreamed of. The Clippership rocket was a squat cone; its shape reminded Harry of a big teepee made of gleaming metal. Inside, the circular passenger compartment was decked out like an airliner's, with six short rows of padded reclinable chairs, each of them occupied by a worker riding up to orbit. There was even a pair of flight attendants, one man and one woman.

As he clicked the safety harness over his shoulders and lap, Harry expected they would be blasted off the ground like a bullet fired from a thirty-aught. It wasn't that bad, though in some ways it was worse. The rockets lit off with a roar that rattled Harry deep inside his bones. He felt pressed down into his seat while the land outside the little round window three seats away tilted and then seemed to fly away.

The roaring and rattling wouldn't stop. For the flash of a moment Harry wondered if this was the demon he was supposed to slay, a dragon made of metal and plastic with the fiery breath of its rockets pushing it off the Earth.

And then it all ended. The noise and shaking suddenly cut off and Harry felt his stomach drop away. For an instant Harry felt himself falling, dropping off into nothingness. Then he took a breath and saw that his arms had floated up from the seat's armrests. Zero gee. The instructors always called it microgravity, but to Harry it was zero gee. And it felt good.

At the school they had tried to scare him about zero gee with stories of how you get sick and heave and get so dizzy you can't move your head without feeling like it's going to burst. Harry didn't feel any of that. He felt as if he were floating in the water tank again, but this was better, much better. There wasn't any water. He couldn't help grinning. This is great, he said to himself.

But not everybody felt so good. Looking around, Harry saw plenty of gray faces, even green. Somebody behind him was gagging. Then somebody upchucked. The smell made Harry queasy. Another passenger retched, up front. Then another. It was like a contagious bug, the sound and stench was getting to everyone in the passenger compartment. Harry took the retch bag from the seat pocket in front of him and held it over his mouth and nose. Its cold sterile smell was better than the reek of vomit that was filling the compartment. There was nothing Harry could do about the noise except to tell himself that these were whites who were so weak. He wasn't going to sink to their level.

"You'll get used to it," the male flight attendant said, grinning at them from up at the front of the compartment. "It might take a day or so, but you'll get accustomed to zero gee."

Harry was already accustomed to it. The smell, though, was something else. The flight attendants turned up the air blowers and handed out fresh retch bags, floating through the aisles as if they were swimming in air. Harry noticed they had filters in their nostrils; that's how they handle the stink, he thought.

He couldn't see much of anything as the ship approached the construction site, although he felt the slight thump when they docked. The flight attendants had told everybody to stay in their seats and keep buckled in until they gave the word that it was okay to get up. Harry waited quietly and watched his arms floating a good five centimeters off the armrests of his chair. It took a conscious effort to force them down onto the rests.

When they finally told everybody to get up, Harry clicked the release on his harness and pushed to his feet. And sailed right up into the overhead, banging his head with a thump. Everybody laughed. Harry did too, to hide his embarrassment.

He didn't really see the construction site for three whole days. They shuffled the newcomers through a windowless access tunnel, then down a long sloping corridor and into what looked like a processing center, where clerks checked in each new arrival and assigned them to living quarters. Harry saw that there were no chairs anywhere in sight. Tables and desks were chest-high, and everybody stood up, with their feet in little loops that were fastened to the floor. *That's how they keep from banging their heads on the ceiling*, Harry figured.

Their living quarters were about the size of anemic telephone booths, little more than a closet with a mesh sleeping bag tacked to one wall.

"We sleep standing up?" Harry asked the guy who was showing them the facilities.

The guy smirked at him. "Standing up, on your head, sideways or inside-out. Makes no difference in zero gee."

Harry nodded. *I should have known that*, he said to himself. *They told us about it back at the training base.*

Three days of orientation, learning how to move and walk and eat and even crap in zero gee. Harry thought that maybe the bosses were also using the three days to see who got accustomed to zero gee well enough to be allowed to work, and who they'd have to send home.

Harry loved zero gee. He got a kick out of propelling himself down a corridor like a human torpedo, just flicking his fingertips against the walls every few meters as he sailed along. He never got dizzy, never got disoriented. The food tasted pretty bland, but he hadn't come up here for the food. He laughed the first time he sat on the toilet and realized he had to buckle up the seat belt or he'd take off like a slow, lumbering rocket.

He slept okay, except he kept waking up every hour or so. The second day, during the routine medical exam, the doc asked him if he found it uncomfortable to sleep with a head band. Before Harry could answer, though, the doctor said, "Oh, that's right. You're probably used to wearing a head band, aren't you?"

Harry grunted. When he got back to his cubicle he checked out the orientation video on the computer built into the compartment's wall. The head band was to keep your head from nodding back and forth in your sleep. In microgravity, the video explained, blood pumping through the arteries in your neck made your head bob up and down while you slept, unless you attached the head band to the wall. Harry slept through the night from then on.

Their crew supervisor was a pugnacious little Irishman with thinning red hair and fire in his eye. After their three days' orientation, he called the dozen newcomers to a big metal-walled enclosure with a high ceiling ribbed with steel girders. The place looked like an empty airplane hangar to Harry.

"You know many people have killed themselves on this project so far?" he snarled at the assembled newbies.

"Eighteen," he answered his own question. "Eighteen assholes who didn't follow procedures. Dead. One of them took four other guys with him."

Nobody said a word. They just stood in front of the super with their feet secured by floor loops, weaving slightly like long grasses in a gentle breeze.

"You know how many of *my* crew have killed themselves?" he demanded. "None. Zip. Zero. And you know why? I'll tell you. Because I'll rip the lungs out of any jerkoff asshole who goes one millionth of a millimeter off the authorized procedures."

Harry thought the guy was pretty small for such tough talk, but what the hell, *he's just trying to scare us.*

"There's a right way and a wrong way to do anything," the super went on, his face getting splotchy red. "The right way is what I tell you. Anything else is wrong. Anything! Got that?"

A couple of people replied with "Yes, sir," and "Got it." Most just mumbled. Harry said nothing.

"You," the super snapped, pointing at Harry. "Twelvetoes. You got that?"

"I got it," Harry muttered.

"I didn't hear you."

Harry tapped his temple lightly. "It's all right here, chief."

The supervisor glared at him. Harry stood his ground, quiet and impassive. But inwardly he was asking the spider, "Is this the monster I'm gonna slay?"

The spider did not answer.

"All right," the super said at last. "Time for you rookies to see what you're in for."

He led the twelve of them, bobbing like corks in water, out of the hangar and down a long, narrow, tubular corridor. To Harry it seemed more like a tunnel, except that the floor and curving walls were made of what looked like smooth, polished aluminum. Maybe not. He put out a hand and brushed his fingertips against the surface. *Feels more like plastic than metal*, Harry thought.

"Okay, stop here," said the super.

Stopping was easier said than done, in zero gee. People bumped into one another and jostled around a bit while the super hovered at the head of the group, hands on hips, and glowered at them. Harry, back near the end of the queue, managed to brush against one of the better-looking women, a Hispanic with big dark eyes and a well-rounded figure.

"Sorry," he muttered to her.

"*De nada,*" she replied, with a smile that might have been shy. Harry read the nametag pinned above her left breast pocket: Marta Santos.

"All right now," the super called to them, tugging a palmcomp from the hip pocket of his coveralls. "Take a look."

He pecked at the handheld, and suddenly the opaque tube became as transparent as glass. Everybody gasped.

They were hanging in the middle of a gigantic spiderwork of curving metal girders, like being inside a dirigible's frame, except that the girders went on and on for miles. And beyond it Harry saw the immense curving bulk of Earth, deep blue gleaming ocean, brighter than the purest turquoise, and streams of clouds so white it hurt his eyes to look at them. He blinked, then looked again. He saw long rows of waves flowing across the ocean, and the cloud-etched edge of land, with gray wrinkles of mountains off in the distance. Beyond the flank of the curving world and its thin glowing skin of air was the utterly black emptiness of space.

We're in space! Harry realized. He had known it, in his head, but now he felt it in his guts, where reality lived. *I'm in space*, he said to himself, lost in the wonder of it. *I'm no longer on Earth.*

Abruptly the tunnel walls went opaque again. The view shut off. An audible sigh of disappointment gusted through the crew.

"That's enough for now," the super said, with a grin that was somewhere between smug and nasty. "Tomorrow you clowns go out there and start earning your pay."

Harry licked his lips in anticipation.

The suits were a pain. The one thing they couldn't prepare you for on Earth was working inside the goddamned spacesuits. Not even the water tank could simulate the zero pressure of vacuum. The suit's torso, arms and leggings were hard-shell cermet, but the joints and the gloves had to be flexible, which meant they were made of fabric, which meant they ballooned and got stiff, tough to flex and move when you went outside. The gloves were especially stubborn. They had tiny little servomotors on the back that were supposed to amplify your natural muscle power and help you move the fingers. Sometimes that helped, but when it came to handling tools it was mostly a waste of time.

Harry got used to the clunky gloves, and the new-car smell of his suit. He never quite got used to hanging in the middle of nothing, surrounded by the growing framework of the miles-long habitat with the huge and glowing Earth spread out before his eyes. Sometimes he thought it was below him, sometimes it seemed as if it was hanging overhead. Either way, Harry could gawk at it like a hungry kid looking through a restaurant window, watching it, fascinated, as it slid past, ever-changing, a whole world passing in panoramic review before his staring eyes.

"Stop your goofin', Twelvetoes, and get back to work!" The super's voice grated in Harry's helmet earphones.

Harry grinned sheepishly and nodded inside his helmet. It was awfully easy to get lost in wonder, watching the world turn.

They worked a six-day week. There was no alcohol in the habitat, not even on Sundays. There was a cafeteria, and the crews socialized there. Everybody complained about the soggy sandwiches and bland fruit juices that the food and drink machines dispensed. You didn't have to put money into them; their internal computers docked your pay automatically.

Harry was scanning the menu of available dishes, wishing they'd bring up somebody who knew how to cook with spices, when a woman suggested, "Try the chicken soup. It's not bad."

She introduced herself: Liza Goldman, from the engineering office. She was slightly taller than Harry, on the skinny side, he thought. But she looked pretty when she smiled. Light brown hair piled up on top of her head. She and Harry carried their trays to one of the chest-high tables. Harry took a swig from the squeeze bulb of soup. It was lukewarm.

Goldman chattered away as if they were old friends. At first Harry wondered why she had picked him to share a meal with, but pretty soon he was enjoying her company enough to try to make conversation. It wasn't easy. Small talk was not one of his skills.

"You'd think they'd be able to keep the hot foods hot," Goldman was saying, "and the cold foods cold. Instead, once they're in the dispensers they all go blah. Entropy, I guess."

Harry wrinkled his brow and heard himself ask, "You know what I wonder about?"

"No. What?"

"How come they got food dispensers and automated systems for life support and computers all over the place, but they still need us construction jocks."

Goldman's brows rose. "To build the habitat. What else?"

"I mean, why don't they have automated machines to do the construction work? Why do we hafta go outside and do it? They could have machines doin' it, couldn't they?"

She smiled at him. "I suppose."

"Like, they have rovers exploring Mars, don't they? All automated. The scientists run them from their station in orbit around Mars, don't they?"

"Teleoperated, yes."

"Then why do they need guys like me up here?"

Goldman gave him a long, thoughtful look. "Because, Harry, you're cheaper than teleoperated equipment."

Harry was surprised. "Cheaper?"

"Sure. You construction people are a lot cheaper than developing teleoperated machinery. And more flexible."

"Not in those damned suits," Harry grumbled.

With an understanding laugh, Goldman said, "Harry, if they spent the money to develop teleoperated equipment, they'd still have to bring people up here to run the machines. And more people to fix them when they break down. You guys are cheaper."

Harry needed to think about that.

Goldman invited him to her quarters. She had an actual room to herself; not a big room, but there was a stand-up desk and a closet with a folding door and a smart screen along one wall and even a sink of her own. Harry saw that her sleeping mesh was pinned to the ceiling. The mesh would stretch enough to accommodate two, he figured.

"What do you miss most, up here?" Goldman asked him.

Without thinking, Harry said, "Beer."

Her eyes went wide with surprise for a moment, then she threw her head back and laughed heartily. Harry realized that he had given her the wrong answer.

She unpinned her hair and it spread out like a fan, floating weightlessly.

"I don't have beer, Harry, but I've got something just as good. Maybe better."

"Yeah?"

Goldman slid back the closet door and unzipped a faux leather bag hanging inside. She glided back to Harry and held out one hand. He saw there were two gelatin capsules in her palm.

"The guys in the chem lab cook this up," she said. "It's better than beer."

Harry hesitated. He was on-shift in the morning.

"No side effects," Goldman coaxed. "No hangover. It's just a recreational compound. There's no law against it."

He looked into her tawny eyes. She was offering a lot more than a high.

Her smile turned slightly malicious. "I thought you Native Americans were into peyote and junk like that."

Thinking he'd rather have a beer, Harry took the capsule and swallowed it. As it turned out, they didn't need the sleeping bag. They floated in the middle of the room, bumping into a wall now and then, but who the hell cared?

✳ ✳ ✳

The next morning Harry felt fine, better than he had in months. He was grinning and humming to himself as he suited up for work.

Then he noticed the super was suiting up, too, a couple of spaces down the bench.

Catching Harry's puzzled look, the super grumbled, "Mitsuo called in sick. I'm goin' out with you."

It was a long, difficult shift, especially with the super dogging him every half-second:

"Be careful with those beams, hotshot! Just 'cause they don't weigh anything doesn't mean they can't squash you like a bug."

Harry nodded inside his helmet and wrestled the big, weightless girder into place so the welders could start on it while the supervisor went into a long harangue about the fact that zero gee didn't erase a girder's mass.

"You let it bang into you and you'll get crushed just like you would down on Earth."

He went on like that for the whole shift. Harry tried to tune him out, wishing he had the powers of meditation that his great-uncle had talked about, back home. But it was impossible to escape the super's screechy voice yammering in his helmet earphones. Little by little, though, Harry began to realize that the super was trying to educate him, trying to teach him how to survive in zero gee, giving him tips that the training manuals never mentioned.

Instead of ignoring the little man's insistent voice, Harry started to listen. Hard. The guy knew a lot more about this work than Harry did, and Harry decided he might as well learn if the super was willing to teach.

By the time they went back inside and began to worm themselves out of the spacesuits, Harry was grinning broadly.

The super scowled at him. "What's so funny?"

Peeling off his sweat-soaked thermal undergarment, Harry shook his head. "Not funny. Just happy."

"Happy? You sure don't smell happy!"

Harry laughed. "Neither do you, chief."

The super grumbled something too low for Harry to catch.

"Thanks, chief," Harry said.

"For what?"

"For all that stuff you were telling me out there. Thanks."

For once, the supervisor was speechless.

Days and weeks blurred into months of endless drudgery. Harry worked six days each week, the monotony of handling the big girders broken only by the never-ending thrill of watching the always-changing Earth sliding along below. Now and then the super would give him another impromptu lecture, but once they were inside again the super never socialized with Harry, nor with any of his crew.

"I don't make friends with the lunks who work for me," he explained gruffly. "I don't want to be your friend. I'm your boss."

Harry thought it over and decided the little guy was right. Most of the others on the crew were counting the days until their contracts were fulfilled and they could go back to Earth and never see the super again. Harry was toying with the idea of signing up for another tour when this one was finished. There was still plenty of work to do on the habitat, and there was talk of other habitats being started.

He spent some of his evenings with Goldman, more of them with the chemists who cooked up the recreational drugs. Goldman had spoken straight: the capsules were better than beer, a great high with no hangovers, no sickness.

He didn't notice that he was actually craving the stuff, at first. Several months went by before Harry realized his insides got jumpy if he went a few days without popping a pill. And the highs seemed flatter. He started taking two at a time and felt better.

Then the morning came when his guts were so fluttery he wondered if he could crawl out of his sleeping bag. His hands shook noticeably. He called in sick.

"Yeah, the same thing happened to me," Goldman said that evening, as they had dinner in her room. "I had to go to the infirmary and get my system cleaned out."

"They do that?" Harry asked, surprised.

She tilted her head slightly. "They're not supposed to. The regulations say they should report drug use, and the user has to be sent back Earthside for treatment."

He looked at her. "But they didn't send you back."

"No," said Goldman. "The guy I went to kept it quiet and treated me off the record."

Harry could tell from the look on her face that the treatment wasn't for free.

"I don't have anything to pay him with," he said.

Goldman said, "That's okay, Harry. I'll pay him. I got you into this shit, I'll help you get off it."

Harry shook his head. "I can't do that."

"I don't mind," she said. "He's not a bad lay."

"I can't do it."

She grasped both his ears and looked at him so closely that their noses touched. "Harry, sooner or later you'll have to do something. It doesn't get better all by itself. Addiction always gets worse."

He shook his head again. "I'll beat it on my own."

He stayed away from the pills for nearly a whole week. By the fifth day, though, his supervisor ordered him to go to the infirmary.

"I'm not going to let you kill yourself out there," the super snarled at him. "Or anybody else, either."

"But they'll send me back Earthside," Harry said. Pleaded, really.

"They ought to shoot you out of a mother-humping cannon," the super growled.

"I'll beat it. Give me a chance."

"The way your hands are shaking? The way your eyes look? You think I'm crazy?"

"Please," Harry begged. It was the hardest word he had ever spoken in his whole life.

The super stared at him, his face splotchy red with anger, his eyes smoldering. At last he said, "You work alone. You kill yourself, that's your problem, but I'm not going to let you kill anybody else."

"Okay," Harry agreed.

"And if you don't start shaping up damned soon, you're finished. Understand?"

"Yeah, but—"

"No buts. You shape up or I'll fire your ass back to Earth so fast they'll hear the sonic boom on Mars."

So Harry got all the solo jobs: setting up packages of tools at the sites where the crew would be working next; hauling emergency tanks of oxygen; plugging in electronics boards in a new section after the crew finished putting it together; spraying heat-reflecting paint on slabs of the habitat's outer skin. He worked slowly, methodically, because his hands were shaking most of the time and his vision went blurry now and then. He fought for control of his own body inside the confines of his spacesuit, which didn't smell like a new car anymore; it smelled of sweat and piss and teeth-gritting agony.

He spent his nights alone, too, in his closet-sized quarters, fighting the need to down a few pills. *Just a few. A couple, even; that's all I need. Maybe just one would do it. Just one, for tonight. Just to get me through the night. I'll be banging my head against the wall if I don't get something to help me.*

But the spider would tell him, "Fight the monster, Harry. Nobody said it would be easy. Fight it."

The rest of the crew gave him odd looks in the mornings when he showed up for work. Harry thought it was because he looked so lousy, but finally one of the women asked him why the super was picking on him.

"Pickin' on me?" Harry echoed, truly nonplussed.

"He's giving you all the shit jobs, Twelvetoes."

Harry couldn't explain it to her. "I don't mind," he said, trying to make it sound cheerful.

She shook her head. "You're the only Native American on the crew and you're being kept separate from the rest of us, every shift. You should complain to the committee—"

"I got no complaints," Harry said firmly.

"Then I'll bring it up," she flared.

"Don't do me any favors."

After that he was truly isolated. None of the crew would talk to him. *They think I'm a coward*, Harry said to himself. *They think I'm letting the super shit on me.*

He accepted their disdain. *I've earned it, I guess*, he told the spider. The spider agreed.

When the accident happened, Harry was literally a mile away. The crew was working on the habitat's endcap assembly, where the curving girders came together and had to be welded precisely in place. The supervisor had Harry installing the big, thin, flexible sheets of honeycomb metal that served as a protective shield against micrometeoroid hits. Thin as they were, the bumpers would still adsorb the impact of a pebble-sized meteoroid and keep it from puncturing the habitat's skin.

Harry heard yelling in his helmet earphones, then a high-pitched scream. He spun himself around and pushed off as far as his tether would allow. Nothing seemed amiss as far as he could see along the immense curving flank of the habitat. But voices were hollering on the intercom frequency, several at the same time.

Suddenly the earphones went dead silent. Then the controller's voice, pitched high with tension: "EMERGENCY. THIS IS AN EMERGENCY. ALL OUTSIDE PERSONNEL PROCEED TO ENDCAP IMMEDIATELY. REPEAT. EMERGENCY AT ENDCAP."

The endcap, Harry knew, was where the rest of the crew was working.

Without hesitation, without even thinking about it, Harry pulled himself along his tether until he was at the cleat where it was fastened. He unclipped it and started dashing along the habitat's skin, flicking his gloved fingers from one handhold to the next, his legs stretched out behind him, batting along the curving flank of the massive structure like a silver barracuda.

Voices erupted in his earphones again, but after a few seconds somebody inside cut off the intercom frequency. Probably the controller, Harry thought. As he flew along he stabbed at the keyboard on the wrist of his suit to switch to the crew's exclusive frequency. The super warned them never to use that frequency unless he told them to, but this was an emergency.

Sure enough, he heard the super's voice rasping, "I'm suiting up; I'll be out there in a few minutes. By the numbers, report in."

As he listened to the others counting off, the shakes suddenly turned Harry's insides to burning acid. He fought back the urge to retch, squeezed his eyes tight shut, clamped his teeth together so hard his jaws hurt. His bowels rumbled. *Don't let me crap in the suit!* he prayed. He missed a handhold and nearly soared out of reach of the next one, but he righted himself and kept racing toward the scene of the accident, whatever it was, blind with pain and fear. When his turn on the roll call came he gasped out, "Twelvetoes, on my way to endcap."

"Harry! You stay out of this!" the super roared. "We got enough trouble here already!"

Harry shuddered inside his suit and obediently slowed his pace along the handholds. He had to blink several times to clear up his vision, and then he saw, off in the distance, what had happened.

The flitter that was carrying the endcap girders must have misfired its rocket thruster. Girders were strewn all over the place, some of them jammed into the skeleton of the endcap's unfinished structure, others spinning in slow-motion out and away from the habitat. Harry couldn't see the flitter itself; probably it was jammed inside the mess of girders sticking out where the endcap was supposed to be.

Edging closer hand over hand, Harry began to count the spacesuited figures of his crew, some floating inertly at the ends of their tethers, either unconscious or hurt or maybe dead. Four, five. Others were clinging to the smashed-up pile of girders. Seven, eight. Then he saw one spinning away from the habitat, its tether gone, tumbling head over heels into empty space.

Harry clambered along the handholds to a spot where he had delivered emergency oxygen tanks a few days earlier. Fighting down the bile burning in his gut, he yanked one of the tanks loose and straddled it with his legs. The tumbling, flailing figure was dwindling fast, outlined against a spiral sweep of gray clouds spread across the ocean below. A tropical storm, Harry realized. He could even see its eye, almost in the middle of the swirl.

Monster storm, he thought as he opened the oxy tank's valve and went jetting after the drifting figure. But instead of flying straight and true, the tank started spinning wildly, whirling around like an insane pinwheel. Harry hung on like a cowboy clinging to a bucking bronco.

The earphones were absolutely silent, nothing but a background hiss. Harry guessed that the super had blanked all their outgoing calls, keeping the frequency available for himself to give orders. He tried to talk to the super, but he was speaking into a dead microphone.

He's cut me off. He doesn't want me in this, Harry realized.

Then the earphones erupted. "Who the hell is that? Harry, you shithead, is that you? Get your ass back here!"

Harry really wanted to, but he couldn't. He was clinging as hard as he could to the whirling oxy tank, his eyes squeezed tight shut again. The bile was burning up his throat. When he opened his eyes he saw that he was riding the spinning tank into the eye of the monster storm down on Earth.

He gagged. Then retched. Dry heaves, hot acid bile spattering against the inside of his bubble helmet. *Death'll be easy after this,* Harry thought.

The spacecuited figure of the other worker was closer, though. Close enough to grab, almost. Desperately, Harry fired a few quick squirts of the oxygen, trying to stop his own spinning or at least slow it down some.

It didn't help much, but then he rammed into the other worker and grabbed with both hands. The oxygen tank almost slipped out from between his legs, but Harry clamped hard onto it. His life depended on it. His, and the other guy's.

"Harry? Is that you?"

It was Marta Santos, Harry saw, looking into her helmet. With their helmets touching, Harry could hear her trembling voice, shocked and scared.

"We're going to die, aren't we?"

He had to swallow down acid before he could say, "Hold on."

She clung to him as if they were racing a Harley through heavy traffic. Harry fumbled with the oxy tank's nozzle, trying to get them moving back toward the habitat. At his back the mammoth tropical storm swirled and pulsated like a thing alive, beckoning to Harry, trying to pull him down into its spinning heart.

"For chrissake," the super's voice screeched, "how long does it take to get a rescue flitter going? I got four injured people here and two more streakin' out to friggin' Costa Rica!"

Harry couldn't be certain, but it seemed that the habitat was getting larger. *Maybe we're getting closer to it,* he thought. *At least we're heading in the right direction. I think.*

He couldn't really control the oxygen tank. Every time he opened the valve for another squirt of gas the damned tank started spinning wildly. Harry heard Marta sobbing as she clung to him. The habitat was whirling around, from Harry's point of view, but it was getting closer.

"Whattaya mean it'll take another ten minutes?" the super's voice snarled. "You're supposed to be a rescue vehicle. Get out there and rescue them!"

Whoever was talking to the super, Harry couldn't hear it. The supervisor had blocked out everything except his own outgoing calls.

"By the time you shitheads get into your friggin' suits my guys'll be dead!" the super shrieked. Harry wished he could turn off the radio altogether but to do that he'd have to let go of the tank and if he did *that* he'd probably go flying off the tank completely. So he held on and listened to the super screaming at the rescue team.

The habitat was definitely getting closer. Harry could see spacesuited figures floating near the endcap and the big mess of girders jammed into the skeletal structure there. Some of the girders were still floating loose, tumbling slowly end over end like enormous throwing sticks.

"Harry!"

Marta's shriek of warning came too late. Harry turned his head inside the fishbowl helmet and saw one of those big, massive girders looming off to his left, slightly behind him, swinging down on him like a giant tree falling.

Automatically, Harry opened the oxy tank valve again. It was the only thing he could think to do as the ponderous steel girder swung down on him like the arm of an avenging god. He felt the tank spurt briefly, then the shadow of the girder blotted out everything and Marta was screaming behind him and then he could feel his leg crush like a berry bursting between his teeth and the pain hit so hard that he felt like he was being roasted alive and he had one last glimpse of the mammoth storm down on Earth before everything went black.

When Harry woke he was pretty sure he was dead. But if this was the next world, he slowly realized, it smells an awful lot like a hospital. Then he heard the faint, regular beeps of monitors and saw that he was in a hospital, or at least the habitat's infirmary. Must be the infirmary, Harry decided, once he recognized that he was floating without support, tethered only by a light cord tied around his waist.

And his left leg was gone.

His leg ended halfway down the thigh. Just a bandaged stump there. His right leg was heavily bandaged, too, but it was all there, down to his toes.

Harry Sixtoes now, he said to himself. For the first time since his mother had died he felt like crying. But he didn't. He felt like screaming or pounding the walls. But he didn't do that, either. He just lay there, floating in the middle of the antiseptic white cubicle, and listened to the beeping of the monitors that were keeping watch over him.

He drifted into sleep, and when he awoke the supervisor was

standing beside him, feet encased in the floor loops, his wiry body bobbing slightly, the expression on his face grim.

Harry blinked several times. "Hi, chief."

"That was a damned fool thing you did," the super said quietly.

"Yeah. Guess so."

"You saved Marta's life. The frickin' rescue team took half an hour to get outside. She'd a' been gone by then."

"My leg . . ."

The super shook his head. "Mashed to a pulp. No way to save it."

Harry let out a long, weary breath.

"They got therapies back Earthside," the super said. "Stem cells and stuff. Maybe they can grow the leg back again."

"Workman's insurance cover that?"

The super didn't answer for a moment. Then, "We'll take up a collection for you, Harry. I'll raise whatever it takes."

"No," Harry said. "No charity."

"It's not charity, it's—"

"Besides, a guy doesn't need his legs up here. I can get around just as well without it."

"You can't stay here!"

"Why not?" Harry said. "I can still work. I don't need the leg."

"Company rules," the super mumbled.

Harry was about to say, "Fuck the company rules." Instead, he heard himself say, "Change 'em."

The super stared at him.

Hours after the supervisor left, a young doctor in a white jacket came into Harry's cubicle.

"We did a routine tox screen on your blood sample," he said.

Harry said nothing. He knew what was coming.

"You had some pretty fancy stuff in you," said the doctor, smiling.

"Guess so."

The doctor pursed his lips, as if he were trying to come to a decision. At last he said, "Your bloodwork report is going to get lost, Harry. We'll detox you here before we release you. All off the record."

That's when it hit Harry.

"You're Liza's friend."

"I'm not doing this for Liza. I'm doing it for you. You're a hero, Harry. You saved a life."

"Then I can stay?" Harry asked hopefully.

"Nobody's going to throw you out because of drugs," said the doctor. "And if you can prove you can still work, even with only one leg, I'll recommend you be allowed to stay."

And the legend began. One-legged Harry Twelvetoes. He never returned to Earth. When the habitat was finished, he joined a new crew that worked on the next habitat. And he started working on a dream, as well. As the years turned into decades and the legend of Harry Twelvetoes spread all across the orbital construction sites, even out to the cities that were being built on the Moon, Harry worked on his dream until it started to come true.

He lived long enough to see the start of construction for a habitat for his own people, a man-man world where his tribe could live in their own way, in their own desert environment, safe from encroachment, free to live as they chose to live.

He buried his great-uncle there, and the tribal elders named the habitat after him: Cloud Eagle.

Harry never quite figured out what the monster was that he was supposed to slay. But he knew he had somehow found his path, and he lived a long life in harmony with the great world around him. When his great-grandchildren laid him to rest beside Cloud Eagle, he was at peace.

And his legend lived long after him.